Sarah's Promise

Country Road Chronicles

Rorey's Secret
Rachel's Prayer
Sarah's Promise

Related books by Leisha Kelly

Julia's Hope
Emma's Gift
Katie's Dream

Sarah's Promise

A Novel

Leisha Kelly

Revell
a division of Baker Publishing Group
Grand Rapids, Michigan

© 2008 by Leisha Kelly

Published by Revell
a division of Baker Publishing Group
P.O. Box 6287, Grand Rapids, MI 49516-6287
www.revellbooks.com

Printed in the United States of America

Library of Congress Cataloging-in-Publication Data
Kelly, Leisha.
    Sarah's promise : a novel / Leisha Kelly.
        p.   cm. — (Country road chronicles ; bk. 3)
    ISBN 978-0-8007-5987-2 (pbk.)
    1. World War, 1939–1945—United States—Fiction. 2. Domestic
fiction. I. Title.
PS3611.E45S27 2008
813'.6—dc22   2008014933

1

Sarah

January 3, 1946

From a kitchen window I watched Frank load a box of tools into his truck. His breath hung in the air like a cloud as the early morning sun glinted against one of the truck windows. His limp seemed more pronounced than usual as he turned around to the workshop for a load of something else, but maybe I was just noticing it more. I let the curtain drop back to its place and went on measuring flour for pancakes, but I couldn't turn my mind from Frank so easily.

   He was planning to drive his truck all the way to Camp Point, Illinois, to help his oldest brother's family move to Jacksonville. Sam and Thelma would be taking their six kids home from our house on the train, but Frank was going to drive more than 200 miles alone over roads he'd never seen before. In the winter. And he was happy about the adventure, I could tell.

Sam was putting on his coat to go see if Frank could use a hand. I tried to keep my attention on the pancakes, knowing that Sam and Thelma's children, along with everybody else, would be bustling around ready to eat before long. But I forgot how much flour I'd already put in the bowl and had to guess, and then after Sam went outside I dropped an egg on the floor. Thelma was busy with the baby, Mom was getting little Pearl dressed, and Katie was folding the last of Thelma's laundry yet to be packed. Thank goodness none of them were close enough to notice what a hard time I was having.

Everybody else seemed confident that Frank would be fine. I was too, or at least I tried to be. I'd always been confident in him. He could do almost anything he set his mind to. But he'd never set his mind on something like this before. And he couldn't read the road signs. What if the weather got bad and he lost his way? I tried not to think like that, but even though I'd heard him before sunup reciting his route for my father, the butterflies still raced around inside me.

"Stop and ask somebody if you need help with directions," Dad had told him. And I wondered how my sensible father could be so relaxed about this. Or Mom. Why were they treating such a trip like little more than a jaunt into Belle Rive?

With her new Christmas rag doll in her arms, three-year-old Pearl came running into the kitchen singing "Jingle Bells."

"Ssh," I told her. "Not everybody's awake yet."

"Your daddy sleepin'?"

"No. He's out milking, and your daddy's gone outside too. But your Uncle Bert and all your brothers and sisters are still asleep, except baby Sammy."

"Where Unca Harry?"

"Gone with Kirk last night to see to things on their own farm, remember?"

I didn't know why I was talking to her like she was old enough to know. She didn't even understand that I wouldn't really be related to her until the wedding in June. We were all one family as far as any of Sam's kids were concerned. The youngest of Frank's brothers and sisters were practically the same way. They didn't remember a time when Worthams and Hammonds weren't doing things together. Instead of neighboring farms, this place was like one big farm to them, with two houses set almost a mile apart and a stretch of timber in between.

Mom came into the kitchen, followed by Thelma holding the baby.

"I'm glad for that new job Sam found," my mother was telling Thelma. "It'll be so much easier for you to be right in Jacksonville, close to Albert's school."

Thelma sat in the nearest chair and stretched the baby out on his belly across her lap. "Oh, I know. I might a' been pitiful nervous otherwise, but we'll only be 'bout a mile and a half from the deaf school now. I wish to goodness you could see the place! It's so big I worry he'll be scared, but the teacher we talked to says he oughta fit right in. She thinks they can teach him to talk an' read lips an' get along jus' fine."

Mom poured Thelma a cup of coffee, then took a look in the top of the coffeepot and set our second pot on the stove right away. I should have thought of that. With so many here, we'd need both pots for sure. Especially when Kirk and Harry came from the other farm.

"I expect Albert will enjoy the opportunity to learn," Mom was saying. "And you're bound to find it quite a blessing when he can tell you what's going on in that bright mind of his."

Stirring the batter, I glanced out the window again. Frank and Sam were loading a cedar chest into the back of Frank's truck. It was one of the nicest Frank had ever

7

made, and he'd told me he was going to put a toddler chair, a wall plaque, and an eagle carving inside it to take with him—all samples of his woodwork.

And that meant his long drive was not the only problem. Just as bad was the notion that he might choose to stay so far away. He'd told me there was a good chance he could get the job in Camp Point that Sam was leaving behind. Thelma's uncle wanted someone to run his store for him, and Sam had put in a good word for Frank.

I'd been as glad as anybody to see Sam and his family for the Christmas holidays, but it was tough not being angry with him now for coming down here with his bright ideas and turning Frank's whole thinking around like this. We were going to be married. Frank had been looking at houses close to Dearing or Mcleansboro, thinking to move his shop to town and make a life around here where we grew up. But now? More than two hundred miles away?

Frank's youngest sister, Emmie, interrupted my thoughts by bursting into the kitchen like she always did, eager to lend a hand.

"You need me to go out and get the eggs?"

I turned away from the window again. "I did that, but thanks."

"Anything else I can do to help?" She was looking at me instead of Mom, her usually bright eyes shadowed somehow. She hadn't been happy four years ago when her oldest brother moved his family so far away. And she didn't look very happy with the thought of Frank going now.

"I've got pancakes ready to cook," I said. "You can fix eggs if anybody wants any."

"Georgie will when he's up," Thelma told us. "Scrambled. Just like every morning."

"We should pack some of the Christmas cookies," Mom suddenly said. "I'm sure the children would enjoy a treat on the train. And Frank could use a taste of home along the way too."

Her simple suggestion made me feel like crying. I poured batter on the hot griddle with my back to everybody else. Mom took the cookie jar out of the cupboard and got a couple of sacks out of a drawer. My hand was suddenly shaking. I hoped she couldn't tell. I hadn't told anybody how I felt about Frank going away. Not Mom or even Frank. What could I say, when he seemed so completely happy and sure of himself? Would he think I was just being a big baby and trying to baby him?

Lord, help me understand why he would want to do this. Help me not to worry so. And, oh, God, keep him safe.

"You're being mighty brave about everything, Sarah," Thelma said then. "I'm not sure what I'd a' thought if Sam had took off like this when *we* were engaged."

I couldn't answer. I didn't want to take the chance of betraying my shaky feelings. How could she tell me that and not speak to her husband against Frank driving so far to help them? She ought to know that Frank wasn't like Sam. Frank wasn't like anybody. He was amazingly smart, enough to make me shake my head and wonder sometimes. But I couldn't manage to shove from my mind the problems he'd always had with reading. So the map Sam had so carefully marked for him would be almost useless. Didn't any of them stop and think what kind of trouble that could be?

"We sure are glad for the help," Thelma went on. "And Uncle Milty's looking forward to talking things over with Frank. He don't wanna have to close down and have the store sitting there empty."

I grabbed for a spatula, wondering why Thelma's "Uncle Milty" couldn't find somebody closer to buy his business. Or just run it himself.

Albert wandered into the room, holding the sturdy

little truck Frank had made him for Christmas. Quiet as always, he sat in a chair beside his mother and looked around at all of us. I knew Sam and Thelma were making the right decision, getting him into the School for the Deaf as young as they could, and moving to be close to him there. But why did they have to draw Frank up that way? I tried turning a pancake, and it flopped on the edge of the griddle and made a mess.

"Sarah," Mom said gently. "I can do that if there's something you need to see to."

I couldn't look at her because I was afraid I might cry. She must've understood, at least a little. "I think I'll go outside a minute."

"That's fine, honey," Mom said in the same soft voice. "Bundle up."

I set the batter bowl and spatula down and went for my coat on the hook by the back door. I was wishing Sam would come back in so Frank and I could be alone when suddenly the door opened and there he was.

"Franky says he's almost done," Sam told us. "Said I might as well come an' have my coffee."

I darted out the door before I got my coat buttoned. Dad would be back from the barn before long. Kirk and Harry would show up soon too. Probably in time for breakfast. And Frank was surely getting hungry. But I wanted another chance to talk to him. Just for a minute. While we could.

He turned his head when I stepped out to the porch. He'd been part of our lives since we came to Illinois when I was about six, and even more a part of us after his mother died. It had been that way with all of the Hammonds, but Frank especially. He was so familiar, and I liked it that way. I liked seeing him almost daily, knowing that he'd be working in the woodshop or in the field, alongside my dad often enough. How could he stand rushing off into the unfamiliar this way? *I could* hardly stand it, I knew that for sure. This place wouldn't be the same while he was gone.

Frank set a bag of something in the truck and smiled big in my direction. His smooth dark hair rustled a little in the cold breeze and his eyes shone. "Almost wish I could take you along," he called.

I couldn't answer him. I felt as if there was a huge hole in me already. And I wished he'd take somebody with him. Anybody. But he'd even said he liked the idea of going alone.

Maybe he knew how I was feeling about it. He didn't wait for me to cross the frosty yard to him. He met me by the porch steps faster than I expected. I'd wanted to talk, but now I didn't know what to say. And he pulled me into his strong arms and kissed my forehead.

"You're not gonna worry too much, are you, Sarah Jean? I've drove a long way before."

"Not this long! Only to Carbondale to make deliveries. And Dad was with you the first time. You were back the same day. It wasn't the same at all. It wasn't even winter!"

"I'll have tools for the truck and plenty to keep me warm an' fed," he assured me. "Two spare tires, plus chains an' shovels an' sand. An' I ain't no kid. I'll be fine."

His silvery eyes were so earnest that I couldn't argue. I knew this was important to him in ways I didn't understand. He felt he needed this, but I didn't know why. I buried my face in the coolness of his coat.

"I'll miss you," he said softly. "But I sure wish you wouldn't worry."

"Do you really think—" I struggled with the words. "Are you really sure you can find the place all right?"

"Of course I can find it. Sam gives good directions." I saw the tiny spark of sadness in him. He wanted me to believe in him, to be as confident as he was. "I'm looking forward to this. Don't you know I can manage all right?"

I couldn't say another word about it. There was no way I could have told him no. But I couldn't quite bear to encourage him either.

"I hope you understand," he went on. "Sam needs the help. An' about that store, I just thought it'd be worth it to us, you know, to find out more. Don't be upset with me."

"Do you really think you might like the place?"

"I don't know." He lifted my face a little so he could look in my eyes. "I just need to go find out. But if you hate the thought of bein' that far away, I can come back after Sam's settled in his new house. I can leave the whole idea alone."

I could see his eyes pleading with me for a chance to follow his heart in this unhindered. I could read his hope so plain that it scared me all the more. He *wanted* to like that store up there. He was hoping it would all work out. But why?

"Oh, Franky." I sighed, calling him the name everybody else used but I hardly ever said. "Don't you like Dearing or Mcleansboro anymore? This is home."

He nodded. "Always will be. I know. But home's where you make it too. And I want us to have something that's our own."

"We will! We do."

"The trip'll go fine. Just let me look at the place. Please? Don't be scared. I won't do nothin' till I talk to you first. I promise."

Frank hardly ever asked for anything. He rarely did anything at all for himself. I couldn't refuse him. I couldn't dampen the spark in those eyes any further with my fears.

"All right," I managed to say, my heart doing flip-flops I hoped he couldn't feel.

12

"I love you," he whispered.

I heard a car, and we both turned our heads. Harry and Kirk were driving up the lane in the old car they'd bought together from Mr. Post. Kirk liked horses better, just like their father had, but he'd come back from the service knowing the practicality of having a vehicle too. He was the one running the Hammond farm since he'd gotten home. Both of the Hammond parents were dead, and Frank had kept the farm going and most of the family together while Kirk was gone away in the war. They'd lost a brother in the fighting, and another brother, Willy, was still in the service.

For a while I'd been sure that Kirk would need Frank to stay on the farm with him, or at least close by. But the two younger brothers, Harry and Bert, were mostly grown now and good farm help. And it seemed that Frank was itching to get out on his own.

I sighed, thinking about WH Hardwoods, the woodworking business Frank had shared with my father since we were children. Frank's talent with wood had shown itself young, and he'd made some money with it. He and my father had grown to be close friends besides business partners. Why wasn't that good enough? Especially since Dad had gotten too busy with our farm and his work at Charlie Hunter's service station in town to keep up WH anymore. It was all Frank's now. If he went away, it would just shut down. Dad didn't seem to mind, but to me it was like part of our lives dying away. How could I know what to expect next?

Harry and Kirk parked close beside the truck, and Frank took my hand and gave it a little squeeze.

"'Bout ready to go?" Kirk asked first thing.

"I better," Frank told him. "Earlier start, the sooner I get there."

"Think you'll beat the train?"

"Not much chance a' that."

"Remember to hole up if the weather turns bad."

I tensed, thinking of how Mr. Hammond, their father, had died one wintry night when the truck he'd been driving had run off the road and overturned. But that situation was nothing at all like this one. And Frank was nothing like his father, except for the tiniest bit of family resemblance.

"I've been knowing for a long time what to do with a storm," Frank assured his older brother. "Besides, the forecast's all right. Don't be worryin' Sarah with talk like that."

Kirk looked at me and gave Frank a playful nudge. "Don't be missin' this knucklehead too awful bad," Kirk told me. "He'll be back."

There was nothing especially bad in the way he said that. Surely he was only meaning to set my mind to ease, but I could see something strange working in Frank's eyes. The words troubled him far more than I could have expected, but Kirk didn't seem to notice and Frank didn't say anything in reply.

"Got anything else to load?" Harry asked.

"Nope." Frank looked toward the house. "Just got my good-byes to be sayin'."

"You'll sit down and have breakfast, won't you?" I asked quickly. "There's pancakes ready by now."

"Better to leave on a full stomach," Kirk agreed. "Take a bite with you too."

Again, Frank didn't answer. He started for the house, and I realized he wasn't wearing his hat, scarf, or gloves. I hated to say anything about it. Frank got to thinking deep sometimes and forgot things like that, but he was almost twenty-three and he hated anybody treating him like a kid. Maybe I could just make sure he had them in the truck, and a blanket too, without making a fuss.

Dad came from the barn with the milk pail, and Frank was quick to take it out of his hand, even though with his limp it looked like he'd have more trouble with it than the rest of us. But Dad let him have it, even patting him on the back. My dad loved Frank. He believed in him. And he wasn't scared by any of this going on. I took a deep breath and glanced over in time to see Kirk shake his head a little at Harry. I didn't know why.

Mom poured us coffee as soon as we stepped in. She had a sack of cookies packed for Frank, plus some sandwiches and three or four hard-boiled eggs. I should have known she'd be thinking like me. "I folded a blanket for you to take," she told him. "Just a winter precaution. Where are your gloves and hat?"

"On my front seat," Frank answered her, picking up little Pearl from the chair where she stood reaching for him. He gave her a spin and then set her down again. Right away, Albert started tapping at the chair beside him. He didn't do that with anybody but Frank, and Frank was always good to sit beside him when the tapping started. This time Albert set his wooden truck on Frank's knee and gave one of the wheels a roll.

"You ready for pancakes?" Emmie asked.

"I better eat and go," Frank answered her. "Give my buddy here some at the same time."

"Me too!" Pearl whined. "Me too!"

I wasn't sure if she was demanding pancakes or if she wanted to make it clear that she was Frank's "buddy" just as much as Albert was. Maybe both. She climbed up on Frank's lap and reached for a fork.

"You need your own chair, sweetie," Thelma told her youngest daughter. "How's a man gonna eat with you on his lap?"

"I can manage," Frank offered graciously. "She's all right."

Frank really loved his nieces and nephews. But I knew he liked some time alone too. I wondered if he'd get a moment's peace once he got up there staying with Sam's family. Maybe he'd like all the attention. But maybe he'd get to missing his quiet woodshop on this usually quiet farm and try coming back all the sooner.

Emmie gave Frank, Albert, and Pearl each a plate of pancakes. Frank poured the warm maple syrup for all three of them, but it hardly took him any time to finish his.

"Want more?" Emmie asked immediately.

He shook his head and downed his coffee. "Got to get goin'."

I stood looking at him with my heart thundering inside, and he turned to me with a smile. "Come 'ere, Sarah Jean."

He looked so absolutely handsome. My heart hurt with the thought of missing him already. I wanted so badly to be alone with him again, just for a minute before he left, but I didn't think we'd find a place away from everybody else now. Even Mom and Dad's room had kids sleeping in it. And Georgie and Bert were upstairs. But Frank took my hand and pulled me toward the cellar steps.

"I wouldn't mind takin' along a jar a' those bread and butter pickles you put up last summer, if it's all right with you."

"Sure," I told him, feeling shaky again. "I'll go down and get it."

"I'll help you."

He followed me down the stairs, not caring what anybody thought, and took me into his arms as soon as we were at the bottom. "To everythin' there is a season," he quoted. "A time to every purpose under heaven. We got another season almost on us. Do you know what I mean?"

"I'm not sure. Do you mean beginning a life together?"

"Seems like we've always been together. I mean a life on our own."

16

I looked down for a minute and leaned into his shoulder. I knew how he felt about this and what he was talking about. Moving. "But I kind of like being in the middle of things with everybody here."

"I do too, sometimes. But movin' away from the farms—from your folks and all my fam'ly—would make things all the more ours."

"Yes." I struggled with my answer. "But we were talking about someplace just up the road, close enough to visit two or three times a week. Emmie'll be awfully hurt if she doesn't get to see us more than once or twice a year the way it's been with Sam."

He pulled away just enough to get a good look at me, and his eyes were shining with determination. "I'm not sayin' nothing for sure 'bout movin' up that way. But if it was to work out, I wouldn't mind if Emmie came for a while. She could even stay with us and finish school up there if she wanted to."

"But I thought you wanted a place away from family."

"She's my kid sister. That's different."

I wasn't sure how. I probably should have asked. But he reached to a shelf for the jar of pickles and then leaned suddenly and kissed me.

"A time to plant, an' a time to pluck up what's planted."

I knew he was still quoting the Bible, and I knew he meant something specific about it too, about us being plucked up from our childhood home and being planted in a new life as man and wife. But I was still scared for him about this drive, and I didn't say anything at all about his Scripture.

He had a sudden question. "Do you remember the poem Mattie Mueller recited that same year you and Rorey and Kate sang together for the school program?"

I shook my head, stunned at his recollection. "She

did a poem every year, Frank, but I don't remember any of them."

"The one her grandma wrote about trees in the forest. Sometimes I feel like that sapling growin' in the shade, you know what I mean? I need to get off by myself—out away from the other trees—to be what I'm supposed to be, do you understand?"

"I guess so," I told him, but I wasn't really sure that I did, and he let it drop.

"Everything'll be all right, Sarah, you'll see. I'll call your dad at the Marathon station tomorrow and tell you all about the trip. Sam says I'll be able to use the telephone at the store up there."

I wished we had a telephone at home already. But that wouldn't happen till summer. Maybe Dad would let me ride to town with him tomorrow, so I could be there for Frank's call. I already knew I'd be awfully anxious to hear his voice.

"You want to take some blackberry jam?" I asked, mainly to have something positive to say.

"If you wanna send a jar, I wouldn't turn it down, but your mother's already made me sandwiches. So I might be sharin' the jam with Sam's bunch once I get there."

"I'd best send two jars then," I told him, reaching for the shelf.

He took one of the jars for me. "Will you write?"

The question got me shaky inside all over again. It was bad enough that he would make this crazy trip, but he must be planning to stay awhile. He was all prepared for it, with woodworking tools and not just his truck tools packed in beside the cedar chest and his old suitcase full of clothes. Of course, moving Sam and Thelma and their houseful of things would take days. Sam had to continue working and they'd only have Frank's truck, so they wouldn't be able to move everything all at once. Sam'd already told me I ought to expect Frank to be gone at least two weeks. But since their new house needed some work, I figured he'd be happy if he could keep Frank around longer than that.

"I'll write," I promised, picturing Thelma reading the letters to Frank in the evenings, and maybe helping him to write me back. Two weeks. Maybe more. Maybe lots more. Once he got Sam's family moved to Jacksonville, Frank might even fall in love with Camp Point and want to stay there forever. When I only wanted us to be home.

I could feel the tears welling inside me just thinking like that, but it was ridiculous and I wasn't about to give them vent. If I turned all this around in my mind, I knew it wasn't near enough to be crying about. Frank was sensible. And not facing any known dangers. Plenty of people dealt with far worse things. Frank's sister Rorey had been separated from her fiancé by thousands of miles during the war, and then he got killed and never made it home. This wouldn't be half so terrible as that. And it wasn't quite so bold as my own brother, Robert, either, who was preaching half a world away even though he still needed crutches sometimes when his war injury got to bothering him. We often got letters from him and his wife, and they were truly happy.

The whole world had changed as we grew up, and some of the changes I didn't like. Things had been good when we were little, with ten Hammond kids and two Worthams, plus Katie from my dad's family, always around. I liked a crowd. So did Mom, I was pretty sure. The farther away we all got, the lonelier we were likely to be.

Poor Mom and Dad. Katie's beau, a soldier friend of Kirk's, lived all the way up in Wisconsin. If things kept on like they were going, would we ever get together the same anymore? Already this past Christmas, Robert and Rachel hadn't come home. Neither had Frank's brother Willy, nor his sister Rorey.

"Trust me," Frank whispered, taking the other jar out of my hands even though he was already holding the pickles and the first jar of jam. "I'm just gonna look around up there. And help Sam."

I nodded.

"I really got to get goin', Sarah Jean," he said with a sigh. "But I hate to be leaving you upset."

"I'm okay," I told him as convincingly as I could. "I'll just miss you while you're gone."

"I'll miss you too. But it's only for a little while."

We kissed again, and the jars jiggled together between us. I claimed one back, just to be sure it didn't get dropped. *Lord, guide him every mile*, I prayed. *Touch his wonderful memory to keep track of every place he's supposed to go through. Bless him. Go with him.*

"I better take along that scarf you made me," he said then.

I smiled a little. "Did you leave it in the workshop?"

"Prob'ly. It kinda got in the way when I was sandin' last night."

We went up the stairs together, and I packed the jam and pickles into the food basket with the rest of the things Mom had gotten ready. Frank started hugging everybody. Sam asked him to name off all the towns he'd be going through again, and Frank rolled his eyes in impatience.

"Don't be turnin' off no place without stoppin' to ask somebody where you are," Kirk told him, and Frank didn't reply to that at all.

"Drive careful," Katie added, and I felt the tears trying to come at me again, but I wouldn't let them have their way.

"Stop when you need a break," Mom said. "Stay warm."

Dad didn't say anything at all, just walked out to the truck with Frank and gave him a hug. Most of the rest of

20

us went out to see him off too. Frank set Mom's basket on the seat, hugged me one last time, and climbed in the truck. Both of us nearly forgot that silly scarf.

"Oh! Wait!" I called out and ran for the woodshop. It was on the hook just inside the door where I thought it would be. Last year's birthday present from me to Frank. But that thought jarred me as I ran with the scarf back to the truck. His birthday was only about two weeks away. We might not be together on that day for the first time since his mother died when he was eight and I was only six.

With a sniff I ran to the open driver door of the truck and tossed the scarf around his neck. He smiled his gorgeous smile and pulled me close for one last kiss, in front of everybody.

"Drive careful," I told him weakly, echoing Katie's words and wondering if his truck had ever been half so far. He'd bought it after the war from Willis McNutt, and he'd been very proud to get it.

As he pulled away down the lane, I stood and watched with crazy worries circling around my head begging for notice. What if he missed a turn and didn't even realize it? Or what if he had trouble with the truck that he couldn't fix? He was so good with engines, I wasn't sure what that could be, but the thought struck at me nonetheless. What if it got awfully cold, or even blizzard-like while he was driving? What if he got lost somewhere halfway?

Of course, he had Sam's road map with him, clearly marked with route and destination. He'd memorized the names of the towns. If he had trouble, all he had to do was ask somebody. But I was still nervous about it. What must it be like to find the wording on road maps and signs practically incomprehensible? There was something extra odd about Frank that he hadn't been able to master reading and writing despite his years of trying. He knew Scripture right and left. And he could quote just

21

about anything else he'd ever heard too. It didn't make much sense. I wasn't sure I'd ever understand.

But I knew I should quit being fearful. Frank had a head on his shoulders. He was wise about so many things. And he knew what to do in cold weather. Lord knows he'd encountered enough of it on the farm. It wouldn't do any good for me to keep on fretting about him like he was a child. My father seemed sure that Frank would be fine. He acted like this was just the thing to do, that it all made sense somehow.

I tried, but I didn't know how to stop the worry. Already this morning I'd been imagining that Frank's constant limp might be worse than usual. Was he already tired from the packing? Would the long trip wear on him too? And then how would he feel after days of moving furniture and dealing with Sam's boisterous kids, all of whom loved climbing on him?

It didn't seem fair that Sam would be riding in a train car while Frank drove all that way alone. But for Sam to leave Thelma alone on the train with six children or to expect her to squeeze them all into Frank's truck for so many miles was just unworkable. Why couldn't I let all this go from my mind? Frank had helped people move before—not so far away, of course. But he'd put in many a day of hard work, not only moving furniture, but haying, harvesting, and all number of other things. He was strong and he always managed fine despite the limp he'd had since a bad broken leg when he was nine. He never let it slow him down.

Most everybody else was turning to go back in where it was warm. Soon Sam and his family'd have to bundle up for the ride to the train station. I would've preferred that Frank take the train with them if he felt he had to go. Surely Sam could have found somebody up there that would let them borrow or barter the use of a truck. But Frank had wanted his truck with him.

Mom let me stand in the driveway for a minute in silence, but then she put her arm around my shoulders. "It might be a little hard on all of us," she said softly, "to let Franky become his own man."

I turned and stared at her. "He's been his own man for a long time."

She smiled. "You'll understand what I mean. Eventually." She started back for the house.

"Mom!"

She stopped and took my hand. "I know you love him, honey. But he's got needs different from yours. All you have to do is respect him in it, and everything will work out fine."

My heart was suddenly thundering. "Did he talk to you about something special?"

"No. But I've been seeing something working in him for quite a while now."

What in the world could she mean? Now I was flustered wondering about that. What was working in him? Why hadn't I seen it?

I knew about his willingness to help people that needed it, especially family. There was nothing new about that. So it must be about the job opportunity. Was something driving him away from here? Wasn't he his own man already? My head hurt just thinking about it, but there was no way I could sort it all out now.

2

Frank

More than an hour into the trip I made my first stop, at Ashley, for gasoline. The sky had been clear, but now I was seeing the start of wintry-white clouds off to the west.

Felt strange to be away from home. I'd hardly been anywhere, especially not alone. God's providence had planted me next to the farm where Sarah grew up, and through good times and hard times the Worthams had been shelter to my brothers and sisters and me. But God wasn't calling me to stay under that same shelter all the time even though it might be easy to do. There was more. There had to be.

I checked the tie-downs on the canvas tarp covering the back of my truck. If it started snowin', I didn't want damage to the cedar chest and other things I was bringing along. I paid for my gas and took off for the highway again. The sky was cloudy overhead by the time I come to Nashville, Illinois, where I turned on the road going north. I knew from the look of the clouds that there was a storm threatening. Hopefully it would hold off till I got to Sam's house and not snow back home at all, or Sarah would worry worse than she already was.

I was hungry by the time I got to Carlyle. A little road ran off from the main road toward a lake, and it seemed like the perfect place to stop despite the cold. I couldn't drive close to the water, but I parked where I could see it. The whole lake was mostly froze and kept going far enough to make your eyes feel like they'd had exercise. That was the kind of water I liked. Big enough to make you think about the bigness of the earth and how vast God must be to make stuff like this.

"Lord God, you put things together pretty when you made this world," I said into the wind. "A man can see that, even in winter. I want you to know I'm thankful for this trip. Use it some way. An' use me."

I almost forgot I'd come to eat. Mrs. Wortham's food basket was waiting, but just as I was about to reach for it, a redbird come flying out from the bare trees to one side of the truck. A cardinal. Male. All alone, just like me.

"What are you doin' out here?" I asked him. "You got a girl waitin' someplace while you're off gallivantin' the countryside?"

The bird chirped and flew off. I helped myself to the sandwiches and three of Mrs. Wortham's cookies. But when the wind picked up I decided I'd better move along.

It started to snow, gentle at first, as I was headed back to the main road. Past Donnellson it picked up and started getting slick. I stopped and put on the tire chains. The next town on my memorized route would be Hillsboro, but I wasn't sure exactly how far I had to go to get there. So I coaxed the truck along slow for a while, not wanting to just sit by the roadside and wait.

That was the only time I considered that driving so far alone might not a' been the best idea, but the notion didn't stick in me long. Would've been ignorant to stay home just because it might snow, or some other such worry. I pulled into the next café I saw for a cup of coffee and a chance to warm up awhile.

The place smelled like bacon even though it was the middle of the day. With checkered tablecloths and a radio playing "Don't Fence Me In," the café seemed ready for a crowd, but it was almost empty. The waitress reminded me a little of Sarah Jean, with her long brown hair pulled back. She brought me my coffee and sat at the end of a long counter. There wasn't but one other customer in the place, an elderly fellow bent over a newspaper. What might today's paper be saying? More about the reconstruction in Europe? Or the Communist threat, or studies of the new drug called penicillin?

Sometimes it annoyed me awful that I couldn't read about such things for myself. And with that trouble plus my limp and folks otherwise thinkin' me peculiar, nobody seemed to believe I could manage on my own. Everybody expected me to settle as close as I could to Mr. Wortham and work with him like I'd been doin' since I was a kid, so I wouldn't fall flat on my face someplace else.

I downed my coffee in a hurry, trying to clear my head a' thoughts like that. The radio started playing "Accentuate the Positive," and I decided to move on. No use waiting on the weather. The snow wasn't deep yet, and roads were passable, even with the drifts. Gettin' to the next town'd be relief because I'd have more than half the trip behind me.

I went through Pawnee and straight north. Not another soul was on that road. Barren snow-covered fields run along both sides of the road, and in some places it was hard to tell where road stopped and field started.

Six miles like that, and I seen a dark shape off in the ditch. A four-door coupe up against the fence line. I slowed down, knowing the road must be slick. The car'd hit a fence post. A big fellow was in the driver seat. I couldn't see nobody else, and I hoped the man wasn't hurt 'cause I didn't know where nothin' was up here to get help. Maybe all he'd need was a ride to the next town. I pulled up close and stopped. And then I heard crying. A child. And someone else was moving now in the front seat, their head bowed and bloody. This wasn't gonna be so simple as I'd hoped. *Lord, have mercy.*

3

Sarah

Our house seemed strangely empty now. Mom and Katie and I were cleaning up after Sam's wild and messy bunch. Dad had taken them to the train on his way to work, and I tried not to let it bother me that the sky had gradually filled with clouds. About mid-morning, we heard a ruckus. Something had our chickens frantic. Mom and I grabbed our coats and ran outside to see what the matter was, expecting to scare off a fox. But it was no fox this time. Something big had bent down part of the fence and broken one of the chicken-house windows. One hen was gone and one was wounded.

Whatever it was left a flurry of feathers and a mottle of blood behind. Strange for something to be out hunting in the broad daylight like this. I propped the fence as best I could without Dad there to fix it, and fetched a board to nail over the window. Katie came from the house to find out what was keeping us and see if she could help.

"We'll have to be watchful for the chickens after dark," Mom said. "Whatever did this is liable to come back."

"What do you think it was?" Katie asked.

"Stray dog. Too big to get through the chickens' door. It was desperate to try breaking through the window. If you see it, keep your distance, all right?"

Mom was calm when she said it, but we took her seriously. We were used to foxes coming around so that wasn't much cause for alarm. But this dog was a lot bigger than a fox. We found evidence of that before we went inside. One huge paw print in what was left of last week's snow. I set my gloved hand down beside the track, and my hand was only a little bigger. That was one big dog.

Dad was supposed to be back by supper, and Mom said we should wait on evening chores until he got home. I usually pitched in, or even did the evening chores myself on days Dad was working in town. Kate'd help too, when she wasn't working at the five-and-dime. But it'd be dark by chore time, and Mom didn't seem to want us out after dark. We didn't argue. We just went back inside to our work, and the house seemed even more empty than it had before.

Once we'd gotten things out of disarray and Mom had settled by the fire in the sitting room with the mending, Katie went back out to check the mail. She always did in the middle of the day when she was home. Her boyfriend wrote a lot of letters, and she was often rewarded for the jaunt down the lane and back.

I had just finished mopping the kitchen floor and she'd taken the bucket outside with her to dump for me. In a little while, I was measuring flour for muffins, but she still wasn't back. She wouldn't have to wait down by the road for the mailman. He'd have gone by a long time ago. So what could be keeping her?

I looked out the window by the cupboard but didn't see anything. So I was on my way to check the window closest to the door when I thought I heard her voice.

"Sarah—"

I yanked open the door and looked out. She was by the well, but she wasn't alone. The biggest, blackest dog I'd ever seen stood between her and the house with its head lowered and its neck hairs standing up all scruffy. It looked almost like a black bear, and it wasn't one mite friendly. I knew without even seeing from the front that he was baring his teeth at her, and that got my blood racing. I stepped out into the frosty air, and Katie saw me.

"Sarah—"

"Back up slow to the barn," I told her. "I'll run him off."

She took a step back, but the dog matched with a step in her direction. I yelled, but it ignored me. I tried throwing a stick at it and yelling some more, but I missed, and it ignored me again. So I ran to get the hunting rifle my brother Robert had left for us. I didn't know what else to do. Surely one shot into the air would be enough to startle this creature and make it turn tail and run.

It didn't take me long to grab and load that rifle. Katie hadn't made it to the barn yet. She didn't dare move fast because the dog was keeping pace with her, and a sudden move might've set him off to jumping at her. I could hear him growling, low and fearsome. She was pale. Scared. What in the world was the matter with this dog that he'd act like this? He ought to be friendly finding a person outside like this. Or nervous enough to run off if he wasn't used to people.

I stepped out to the porch and fired a shot into the air. The big dog turned his head and looked at me with its fierce eyes. It did look like a bear standing there. A big, black, shaggy bear. But even a bear ought to run off. This dog didn't. It just turned its head back to Katie and growled again.

I went closer and fired another shot. Something was wrong with this dog. This time when it turned and looked at me, it looked a little longer. Katie took the chance to run for the barn door. It lunged at her, but she got the door shut between them just in time. So the dog turned on me.

Lord, help. Its shining eyes showed a fury I didn't think I'd ever seen in anything and I hoped to never see again. That dog was mad. It came running at me, and I fumbled with Robert's rifle. I'd never been really good with it. I could hear Mom behind me now on the porch, but I knew there was nothing she could do in time. I fired. But the fool beast didn't fall. Shaking, scared, trying to back up, I fired again, aiming right between those devil eyes, and finally it stopped in its tracks, teetered a little, and fell. I was so shook that I fell too.

Mom came running up. Kate peeked out of the barn and then came out toward us. That big black furry shape lay in a heap less than two yards from me. I heaved a giant breath, trying to slow my racing heart. *Oh, Lord, thank you. I could have been bit. Me or Katie, either one could have been mauled by that mad thing. Thank you, thank you for your help.*

My hands were still shaking. Mom tried to help me up, concern and relief mingled together in her expression. A single white snowflake flittered down between us as she took my hand. And then more snowflakes. Bushels. Like my firing at the sky had opened up holes for them to pour through.

With my nerves still a-jitter, I assured Mom I was fine. I gave Katie a big hug, and we all went back toward the house as the snowflakes dusted that big black body with white. It was freezing cold out, even worse than it had been when Frank left, and I realized for the first time that I hadn't taken time to grab my coat.

"I'd best separate the wounded hen and do away with it," Mom said somberly. "I don't know if sickness can spread to chickens, but we don't want to take the chance.

We'll have to dispose of that big carcass too, but I suppose that can wait till your father gets home."

Frank should be here, I couldn't help thinking. If he were, he'd have been the one to shoot that dog. He could kill the chicken for Mom, fix the chicken house window, and dispose of the carcass too. He could look at me with his casual grin and serious eyes and tell me that this was no big deal, and then maybe quote a Scripture or two.

Suddenly I burst into tears. It was absolute foolishness, I knew that plain enough, but I couldn't seem to stop.

"Sarah, are you all right?" Mom asked, taking the rifle to hold for me.

"Yes," I tried my best to answer her. "Just . . . just shaken a little, I guess."

I couldn't tell her any more. The snow pouring down made me think of Frank, miles and miles away on the open road. Was it snowing where he was too? It wasn't supposed to snow today. It was supposed to be clear, that was what the radio forecast had said. But the weatherman was just plain wrong. Dad was in town, and Frank was way off who knows where by now. All alone.

"How about some tea?" Mom asked me. "Let's get you inside where it's warm."

I nodded my head, but I couldn't turn my mind from Frank. Maybe I was making mountains out of molehills right then because I was still a bundle of nerves over that dog, but I felt scared for him. He should be here with us where he belonged, working in the woodshop, or doing any of so many other things he was always applying his hands to around the farm. He could sure help us right now, and then come inside and sit in front of the fireplace with his leg propped up, sipping a cup of coffee to get warm again.

He shouldn't have gone. Surely there were plenty of strong young men in Camp Point that Sam and Thelma could have gotten to help them move. This happening today, with that mad dog, that was plenty of evidence, more than I'd ever need, that he ought to be home. With Dad working so much and Robert overseas, we needed him. We'd always needed him. Right here.

※

I tried to put all that from my mind without much success. And we were done with tea and back to our work before Katie remembered the mail. She'd had it tucked in her coat pocket. Just one letter. For me. I slid my batch of cinnamon muffins into the oven, wiped my hands, and sat on a kitchen chair, ready to give the letter my attention. The envelope was handwritten, with no return address. Postmarked right in Dearing, the nearest town. I wasn't sure what to expect. Certainly not what I found. A neatly printed flyer, advertising a winter carnival and dance sponsored by the Lion's Auxiliary Club. And at the bottom, the only personal message on the page:

"Won't you join me for a fun evening? I can pick you up or meet you in town. Thinking of you, Donald Mueller."

Incensed, I crumpled the page and threw it into the kindling box. Donald Mueller, who knew I was engaged! How dare he invite me to a dance? Had someone told him Frank was going away?

I threw the envelope into the kindling box along with the flyer and then started setting the table.

"Advertisement?" Katie asked.

I nodded, unwilling to disclose the reality of the matter. Donald was stupid. Why would he try inviting me to a dance? The idea was crazy. He'd probably omitted his return address because I'd have thrown the letter away unopened if I'd seen his name. How could he possibly think that getting me to open the envelope would make any difference?

Mom came back to the kitchen and stirred the pot of beans she'd left on to simmer. We'd have bean soup tonight, which always hit the spot for me when it was cold. I didn't tell her about the letter, and I was glad Katie didn't say anything more. I guess it was just too embarrassing to mention that I'd been asked out on a date. We were planning a wedding, for goodness sake. I prayed Donald would have the good sense to never try such a stunt again.

"Everything all right, Sarah?" Mom asked cheerfully as she started peeling an onion to go in the beans.

"Yes," I answered quietly, trying to think of another chore to keep me distracted.

"Don't worry about Franky, honey," Mom said suddenly. "He'll manage fine."

I knew the words were meant as comfort, but they seemed like nothing but a jabbing reminder. How would *I* manage for two weeks without Frank here? What if he decided to stay even longer?

Mom was chopping onion, quickly and rhythmically. She didn't seem bothered by the snow, or the big dog I'd shot, or Frank's absence. Sometimes I wished I could be more like her. Peaceful about everything. At least, that's the way she appeared.

The snow hadn't gotten worse, but it still bothered me. For Dad's sake, with his drive home from town, but mostly for Frank. *I know he's going to be all right, Lord. I know it. He's in your hands.*

I tried to sew, but it was hard to concentrate, so I prayed in my head for Frank and for our future together. Just as I thought I'd put other things out of my mind, thoughts of Donald's invitation broke in again.

How dare he! Hopefully if I gave him no reply he'd get the message that he was barking up the wrong tree. I wouldn't even consider going to that winter carnival, but I didn't want to have to answer his letter to say so. I didn't want to deal with him in any way at all.

34

Mom was almost done cutting the onion when we heard a dog barking in the south field. It didn't sound like the Hammonds' dog, and we didn't usually hear any others out here. Feeling peculiar, I moved to the window and looked out, but that horrible black beast was still right where we'd left it. Dead and almost invisible now under a blanket of snow.

I was very glad when Dad pulled in. He hadn't wanted to get stuck in town if the roads drifted shut, so he'd called Buck Norton to fill in for him at the service station and came home early.

"It might not be snowing north of here," he tried to assure me.

But I didn't feel any better about things. If it kept up, Dad wouldn't be able to get to work tomorrow, and we'd miss our prearranged telephone call from Frank.

Dad closed the big dog's carcass in a barn stall because the wind was too strong to do any burning and the ground was too frozen solid to dig. He said he'd take care of it in tomorrow's light. When we told him the story, he hugged us all, relieved that everything had come out all right. And he said he was proud of me, taking care of things like that.

I don't know why, but his words almost made me want to cry again. I was getting frustrated with myself. Things didn't bother me so much most of the time. It was the situation with Frank that had started it all. Life would change immensely if he took a job somewhere else. Did he want things to be so different? What was wrong with the life we had here?

There was no sense thinking about it. I buttered one of my fresh-baked muffins as a quick snack for Dad. He ate it and headed back outside to start the milking early. I went to help him, hoping the work would keep my mind off things, but the wind was picking up terribly, and walking through the blowing snow just made me feel worse. This wasn't going to be a fit night for anybody to be out.

Dad had told me that Frank's trip to Camp Point should take about ten hours, but I wasn't sure how much that would change considering the snow. The whole thing just made me mad. At Sam. Why convince Frank to drive 230 miles when surely, after all the time they'd lived there, they could have found an acquaintance close by to help them?

But I knew it wasn't really Sam's fault even though the idea had been his. Frank had wanted to go, and he'd been glad to do it alone. I wished I understood, but I didn't.

Snow was blowing in through cracks in the barn wall, and I prayed Frank was already in Camp Point or soon would be. Better for him to be with Sam than to be alone along the road someplace if this weather kept on. Just the thought made me shiver.

"I saw Donald Mueller in town today," Dad remarked suddenly.

I looked up from my milking. The mention of that name made me feel strange inside, and I didn't answer.

"He was asking about Frank, how long he'd be gone."

"How did he even know he was leaving?" I had to ask, my heart suddenly hammering viciously.

"Apparently he saw Harry and Sam the other day and they mentioned the trip. He seemed very interested, I'm not sure why."

"He's a pig," I said halfway under my breath.

But Dad heard me and gave me an odd look. "Everything all right, pumpkin?"

I sighed. "He was one of the boys that used to pick on Frank something terrible."

I almost went on to say that Donald used to pester me too, but I didn't tell that part. I didn't want to think about it, because he was obviously up to his old tricks. Why couldn't he leave well enough alone?

36

"Sam and Thelma'll be happy closer to the deaf school," Dad affirmed then. "I think it's a good move for them."

I just nodded. Of course that was right, and nobody could really argue. Sam had a good-paying new job. But even though it was still in Illinois, Jacksonville seemed like a world away. And Camp Point was farther still.

My milk cow raised her back leg up and down, impatient because I milked slower than Dad did. "What's your hurry?" I asked her irritably. "You're not gonna go run the pasture in this weather anyhow."

Dad looked over at me again. "Need help, pumpkin? I'm almost done here."

Dad had been calling me "pumpkin" since I was tiny. But lately, it seemed like he'd done it less and less. Until today. Twice in just a few minutes. Maybe he was thinking of me as his little girl again for some reason. Maybe he was wondering about Donald Mueller too, since he'd brought it up. Maybe I should tell him about the invitation. But surely it wasn't necessary. Nothing would come of it. Donald was just a presumptuous dunce who mistakenly thought Frank was a weakling. He wouldn't have dared ask me to the dance if I were engaged to any other young man in town.

I rose from the milking, trying to turn my thinking to other things. I didn't want to have Donald on my mind for another minute. Dad carried both our milk pails to the house. Neither was full. Milk was down for both cows.

The wind was brisk, tossing snow in our faces on the way to the porch. The end of our lane was drifting shut. If the sky didn't clear by morning, we'd be snowed in. There'd be no going to town and no way to know whether Frank had gotten to Sam's house safely. But there wasn't any reason to doubt. I could easily picture him comfortable in a chair with one or two of the kids cuddled on his lap. Maybe he was already there, in out of the blowing cold.

4

Frank

In the frigid January air, I did what I could to help the family in that wrecked car. The man looked dazed, and his wife was bleeding from a head wound. I searched in the vehicle but couldn't find nothin' to hold against it to stop the blood. I'd forgotten my handkerchief again, and there wasn't nothin' else handy but Sarah's homemade scarf. Surely it wouldn't bother her too much that I used it for a temporary bandage.

The little girl in the backseat was scared for her mother. She had the strangest eyes I'd ever seen—cloudy, half-closed, and turned two different ways. At first I thought she might be hurt too, but her father checked her over and said she seemed all right.

I couldn't leave them in the bitter cold to go look for help. I wasn't sure where to go or how long I'd be. The man told me that the closest doctor was in Morrisonville. It wasn't one of the town names on my route, so for a minute I felt strange and unsettled like I might have lost my way. But he said it was only six miles down a side road.

Frank

The woman didn't want to go to the doctor, mostly because she wasn't wantin' her little girl to stay scared for her. She kept insistin' she was all right, but her husband was pale and shaky, and I convinced him that they all ought to be looked at. When I helped them to my truck I realized that the little girl was blind.

Mrs. Wortham's blanket came in handy to spread over the woman and daughter. I drove the whole family carefully on that snowy side road to Morrisonville, glad I'd put the tire chains on miles before. I couldn't help thinking that God had put me on that lonely road to do what I could for these people.

At the doctor's office, both of the parents needed attention, but there was only one doctor and nurse on staff. I ended up lingerin' with the little girl because they asked me not to leave her sitting out in the hallway alone.

I'd never prayed for strangers quite like I did then. The little girl sat in a chair beside me. She'd been clutching at a cloth bag since we left their car, and now she clung to it tighter the way she'd clung to her mother's hand in my truck. I thought of Sam's little boy Albert hugging close to Thelma's side sometimes, and wondered what life would be like if you couldn't see what was going on around you or hear what other people could hear.

I'd never figured to be in such a spot as this. I needed to get back on the road, but I couldn't leave yet. Out by that lake I'd asked God to use me and use this trip if he would. But I certainly hadn't expected somethin' like this.

The little girl didn't say nothing at first. And I didn't say nothing to her. The nurse went past us to call for some relatives on the telephone, but then she went back to the examination room without speakin' to us at all.

I considered what Sam'd think if I was late gettin' in. He didn't have a telephone at home, so I'd have to call Thelma's uncle and leave a message if I was held up too

39

long. I started itching to leave, but at the same time I knew I should stay. This little girl's parents and the doctor hadn't wanted her in the room to hear all of what was goin' on. So the most important thing I could be doin' right then was to make sure she wasn't left sitting alone till somebody else got there.

I knew I was right when she asked me in a quiet voice to pray for her folks. I already had been, but I was glad to oblige her out loud. She was being brave for a kid who couldn't a' been more than nine or ten.

I don't know how long I stayed. The little girl told me her name was Mary and her parents were Warren and Jeanie Ensley. We still hadn't heard how her folks were by the time her aunt and uncle arrived, but when they got there the nurse came out and said Mary's mother was doing all right. She took Mr. Ensley's brother aside and told him something that didn't seem to be good news. Mary wanted me to pray again, and so did her relatives. They seemed to think I was a minister, and even though I tried to tell them I wasn't, I still prayed with them because it was the right thing to do.

They wanted my name and address when I left, so I gave 'em one of the WH business cards Mr. Wortham'd made up a long time ago. Then I could finally get back on the road. The snow had started up again, the wind was getting worse, and I'd lost a lot of daylight. But I was still glad I'd been able to help.

Retracing my route back to the main road north, I realized I prob'ly wouldn't make it to Camp Point tonight. The sun was almost to set. But the road was still passable. I decided to press on and get as far as I could.

Before long, the wind was whipping snow as the night's darkness closed in. It wouldn't be safe to keep going much farther. This day hadn't turned out the way I'd planned. But it didn't bother me because I was so sure I'd been doing what I should.

At Auburn, I stopped to find lodging and got directed to the Commercial Hotel on the town square. Kinda hated to spend the money for a room, but there wasn't much choice. The lady there didn't have no problem letting me use the telephone to call Thelma's uncle, and he promised to deliver my message that I was held up by the weather. After that, I went to my room, ate more of the food I had along, and plopped onto the bed, determined to be up and gone by daylight.

But night brought a winter storm the forecasters hadn't known to predict. Buckets more snow, and whipping wind to boot. By morning the streets were closed, and the wind was pilin' up drifts tall as a hay wagon. I was stuck.

5

Sarah

There'd be no going to town today. In other circumstances, I would've liked the pretty snow decorating our
trees and fence lines, but right now it was depressing.
We heard on the radio about a train being stalled, but
it wasn't Sam and Thelma's. Hopefully, they'd be having
breakfast at home, with Frank in the middle of things.
I guessed they'd know the weather was bad here if they
tried to call and couldn't get any answer.

"Will the service station be open at all today?" I asked
Dad.

"I expect. But Charlie's probably out now with the
push-plow on his tractor. He may not be there till afternoon."

"I wish he'd bring his push-plow by here."

"Hershel Mueller'll plow this road as soon as he can,"
Dad answered.

It wouldn't be soon enough for me. But being here
where we couldn't hear the telephone ring might be
better than being there if it didn't ring. What if Frank

hadn't made it to Sam's last night? What if he *still* wasn't there?

I tried to quit thinking like that. Frank was probably playing with the kids or helping Sam and Thelma pack boxes already. January was an awful time to be moving, but Sam's new job would be starting next week, so it didn't make sense to wait.

I pulled on my coat and boots, grabbed a basket, and went out to collect the eggs. A hymn came to mind, and feeling grateful for that, I started humming it under my breath. It was one of my favorites. "Blessed Assurance." But it didn't seem quite right to sing it out loud in the morning's quiet.

I walked around the side of the house and through the gate into the chicken yard. The hens were cackling and fluttering about, stirred into a nervous frenzy again. Maybe they remembered yesterday's scare as plainly as I did. But before I could even get to the chicken-house door, I saw paw tracks. These were almost as big as the tracks I'd seen yesterday, but it couldn't be the same dog. These tracks were fresh, on top of the new-fallen snow.

Just thinking about encountering another dog like the first one made me more than a little anxious to get done and back in the house. I hurried through collecting the eggs and setting out feed for the hens just as fast as I could. No dog came around, but I heard barking again in the distance.

That was a rotten day. Snowed in at home, we had plenty to do, but I was longing to get out and get the word of assurance from Frank that I'd wanted so badly.

We finally saw Hershel Mueller, Donald's father, with his snowplow on the road just before dark. Dad said we'd be able to get out tomorrow if it didn't snow again. I couldn't wait. Not quite two days was all the time Frank and I had been separated, but the knowledge of the miles between us made me miss him all the more.

We heard barking we didn't recognize again at bedtime, and it bothered Katie considerably. She wasn't wanting to meet up with any other strange dogs anytime soon. But that wasn't what kept me from getting to sleep that night. I couldn't stop thinking about my wedding, only five months away. I wondered if Frank thought about it as much as I did.

When I finally got to sleep that night, I dreamed that Frank and I ordered a Sears and Roebuck house like one a friend of ours used to live in, and set it up in Dad's cow pasture. I was getting ready to plant a strawberry patch and a dozen rose bushes when the dream ended abruptly with our rooster's crowing.

The first thing I did was look outside. Clear skies! And the wind hadn't brought much drifting in the night. I could still see the path Dad and I had shoveled in our drive yesterday. I knew we could finish enough this morning to get out to the plowed road and get to town.

I hurried as quickly as I could through breakfast and chores. Mom and Katie were planning to bake bread while we were gone. I started thinking about Frank's birthday and wondering what I could do with him so far away. If he were here, I'd cook a special meal for him and make his favorite dessert, a gooseberry-apple pie. And then present the gift I'd bought to read him: *Walden* by Henry David Thoreau. But that gift would have to wait until we were together.

Dad and I worked quickly at the rest of the shoveling, and all the while that hymn "Blessed Assurance" kept running through my head just like yesterday. I could remember Emma Graham singing it so many times. She was the woman who'd given us this farm, and I'd considered her a special friend even though I was still so young when she died. I wondered what dear old Emma would think of me being engaged to one of the Hammond boys. I doubted she'd be surprised. She'd seemed to know all along that our two families were meant to be more than just neighbors.

Dad and I headed to town as early as we could. I think he was hoping for a telephone call almost as much as I was, but when we got to the station he got right to work as usual. There was nothing for me to do but wait, no telling how long. But surely Frank would call as early as he could, since he hadn't been able to get through yesterday when he was supposed to. I'd brought my embroidery along, knowing I'd be stuck in town until Dad got off work. But it wasn't easy to concentrate. So I prayed that Sam would be mindful and not keep Frank busy away from a telephone.

I tried to focus my mind on the embroidery—a double rose pattern on a set of tea towels for Katie. But looking down at them in my lap made me think of Frank's birthday again. What could I do for him if he was still so far away? I didn't want to just send him the book I'd gotten, because I wanted part of my gift to be reading it to him. If he wasn't home by then, I'd have to think of something else.

Might he like his initials embroidered on a set of handkerchiefs? I doubted he'd care, but it was all I could think of.

Hours crawled by. I worked and prayed, stared at the phone, and then prayed and worked some more. I finished one of Katie's tea towels and started on another. Dad stopped for a sack lunch with me and then got right back to work on an old car he was fixing for Charlie. Why didn't Frank call? Surely he knew we must be anxious after two days. Did he just assume the weather was so bad we'd be stuck at home again? I doubted that, unless things were far worse where he was. We rarely stayed snowed in for very long, partly because of my father's determination and partly because of Hershel Mueller's diligence as the road commissioner.

I sighed and threaded my needle with a short length of yellow thread. Thinking of Hershel Mueller made my mind turn unpleasantly to Donald. He'd always been far too bold, even after it should have been apparent that I was interested in Frank.

"Come on, Sarah," he'd dared to tell me once. "You wouldn't be happy with a Hammond. Especially not that dim-witted Franky. Can't you see that? What would it hurt to give somebody else a chance?"

I wouldn't even speak to him after that. I wanted nothing to do with anyone who had a low opinion of Frank—sometimes not even Frank's sister Rorey, who'd written me a long letter last Thanksgiving, asking if I was truly serious about our engagement.

> *You know Frank as well as I do. He's good with wood, but he'll never make a business work on his own the way his head's off in the clouds half the time. And can you imagine reading orders and everything else for him for the rest of your life? He'll be dependent on you or your parents, Sarah. Is that what you want?*

I'd been positively furious over that letter, and it wasn't easy to get past those feelings even now. Rorey was too much like her father. Neither one of them had ever managed to see the blessing Frank had been to my family, and his own, nor the humble brilliance that was hidden behind his silvery eyes. Rorey was ignorant. Blind, not to see how truly extraordinary her brother was.

The clock ticked away, and I began to pray again for the phone to ring. When it finally did, I nearly fell, I jumped out of my seat so fast. Dad let me answer it.

"Hello. Marathon Service Station."

"Hello. Who is this? Sarah?"

It was Sam, not Frank. My heart was doing flip-flops. "Yes, it's Sarah. Can I talk to Frank?"

Silence. And then Sam's voice, hedged with uncertainty. "Actually, I was calling to see if you'd heard from him."

Those words knocked the wind from me, and I could barely answer. "He's not there yet?"

Dad turned around.

"No, I'm sorry," Sam answered with hesitation. "We've been worried. I hoped he'd found an opportunity to call you."

"He was supposed to call you too, if anything held him up!"

"I know. That's what's bothering me after all day yesterday. He did try Uncle Milty night before last to say he was slowed down by weather. But he didn't call again so we expected him yesterday morning. Been weighin' awful heavy that we ain't heard nothing more all this time."

"W-where was he?"

"Uncle Milty don't remember the town. Is your father close by?"

Without a word, I handed the phone to Dad and sat back down, feeling numb. Frank was missing! Somewhere between here and there. And because of Thelma's uncle's poor memory, we had no way of knowing how far he'd gotten.

In the snowstorm, or on a patch of unfamiliar road, something bad must have happened. And not a little problem, either. Something big enough to keep Frank from a telephone all this time. He was supposed to have been able to call yesterday! He should have been to Sam's house the night before that! A day and a night had passed, and where was he? What could have happened?

6

Frank

Roads were closed in and out of Auburn all day yesterday. The winds were wild, pushing the drifts around unpredictable. Electric power was out, and phone lines were out too. I tried at least six times to place a call, but there was no getting through until the storm damage was repaired.

The hotel owner was gracious, letting me stay longer than I'd told her without adding to the price. She'd brought candles to my room and made sure I had a hot meal. I was fretting so much over what Sarah must be thinking that I would have left that afternoon if there'd been a way. But I couldn't see six feet in front of me outside, and the roadways weren't clear. No choice but to stay put. Despite the worries, I knew Sarah and her folks would want me to wait, hard as that was.

At least I'd gotten through to Thelma's uncle once so Sam would understand the situation. Maybe he'd managed to reach the Worthams, if the telephone lines were all right to Dearing. I hoped he'd think to call them. I hoped they weren't frettin' over this.

That next morning, I'd tried to work the telephone again, but with no better luck at it. Auburn's lines were just dead. But the roads had been plowed some, so I started out against the protests of the hotel owner and one of her neighbors. They thought the gray sky looked like more snow. But I couldn't wait any longer.

I started out confident that I'd get to Camp Point before noon that third day even though I had to drive slower than I wanted to. But before I got to the next town the truck started spitting and sputtering, trying to stall on the road. I had to pull over best I could to figure out what was the matter. Water in the carburetor, maybe. Should a' thought of that while I was in Auburn, with all the blowing snow there'd been. Warm engine could easily melt snow to water and give me problems.

There was water in the bowl under the carburetor, all right. I set to work taking the bowl off to empty and then putting it back together again. But after all that, the truck didn't want to start, and when it did, it sputtered some more and then died. *Lord, I need to get to a telephone. Here it is morning, and Mr. Wortham's bound to be at that service station again, maybe Sarah too, waiting for a call.*

I pulled the collar of my coat up and the brim of my hat down and set to work again in the cold, glad I hadn't forgotten my gloves. Would a' been nice to have Sarah's scarf, but I couldn't recall what we'd done with it, whether it had been left in the Ensleys' car or had gotten to the doctor with us. I doubted it was even ten degrees out, and the wind put a real bite in the air.

I ended up having to take the fuel filter off the truck and clean it up, and that was a far longer job than what I'd wanted. I did the best I could at the repair and then had the problem of getting everything set in place again. The old gasket had fallen apart, so I took the tongue from my work boot to cut another one to size. Had to take a wheel off the truck to get at some axle grease to set the gasket and filter in place. And in all that time, I didn't see even one other vehicle on the road.

Somebody was on the porch of a farmhouse close by, but I didn't pay much attention and thought they must have gone on in. After a while, as I was scrunched down replacing the wheel, I heard a voice calling, faint at first. I stood up, wondering where it was coming from.

"Mister! Mister!"

The voice got louder. A boy of maybe seven or eight was at that old farmhouse across the field, waving real big at me and hollering. I waved in response, thinking that would be the end of it. But his movement changed when he knew I'd seen him. Now he was trying to wave me in.

"Mister! Please help!"

He jumped off the porch and ran several feet forward.

"Please, mister! Please!"

I had no idea what was going on at that house. I was in such a hurry to get back on the road that I didn't even want to think about it. But I couldn't bring myself to turn my back on that pleading kid. *Lord, help. What are you doing with me on this trip? Seems like everything's gone out of my hands.*

"Mister! Mister!" the boy kept yelling. And I left my truck and tools where they sat along the road and set out across the snowy yard.

"What's wrong?" I hollered, but the boy didn't answer. He just kept waving me forward.

"Come in! Please, come in!" he begged when I got closer.

"Why? What's wrong?"

"My mother. An' my brother and sisters—they're freezin' cold an' sick. Please help."

He looked scared. And pretty cold himself.

"Please come in," he said again.

"You got a pa?" I asked as I followed him.

"H-he went t' St. Louis. He's s'posed to be home to-night. But we need help *now*."

He looked like he was gonna cry. I'd prob'ly guessed his age pretty close. And I didn't think I had any choice but to at least talk to his mother, if I could. Maybe there was something I could do, even if it was just to take word into the next town for them, to have the doctor sent out. I could hear what sounded like at least two babies crying inside.

The boy ushered me in quick, and a woman's voice spoke up before I even saw her. "Sir, we've got the chicken pox. You might not want to take another step."

"I've had it," I told her. "It won't bother me."

She sat on a chair with one foot propped on a footstool. Her face showed five or six red pox marks, no more than that. But her eyes looked sunk and red, and the ankle of her propped foot was real swollen. From another room, the sound of the crying continued, along with another plaintive voice. "Mama . . ."

"I'll be there in just a minute, sweetie," she answered the calling child, looking up at me with stark uncertainty.

Then I noticed she was wearing a coat. It was barely any warmer inside than it had been out. "The children all sick?" I asked.

"All but me," the boy who'd called me answered. "I had the chicken pox when I was little. I been trying to help, but I don't know what to do."

"You got wood?" I asked, noticing the fireplace filled with only ash and dying embers. I looked for sign of a coal stove or any other source of heat and spotted a grating pretty quickly. Coal furnace, prob'ly, but the iron grate was stone cold. "Out of coal?"

"We thought we had enough. My husband's bringing

more when he comes, but I had to use the last this morning." Her eyes filled with tears. "I'm so sorry, sir. I hate to beg help of anyone. But Bennie and I prayed. We asked God to make a way, and then Bennie saw your truck stop on the road. Please, just make us a fire, if you will. There's more wood in the barn, but it needs to be split. I was going to get it, but I fell on the ice this morning. I've tried, but I can scarcely bear any weight—"

One of the children in the next room wailed.

"I had to put them to bed," she explained. "All wrapped in blankets. It was the only way I knew to keep them warm. And they're so uncomfortable with the pox . . ."

She started trying to get up, but the pain was obvious. So was the strain of all this in her face.

"I been bringin' in what wood I could," the little boy told me with tears in his eyes. "But . . . but the little pieces is all gone, and I can't lift the big ones."

"Please," the mother begged again. "Please just make us a fire."

She looked awful, like the wear of this was already far too much on her. And she had a bad sprain of the ankle. That was really clear. They were in awful shape.

"I'll make a fire," I reassured her. "Don't try to get up. Your big boy and I'll bring the babies in to you once it's going good and startin' to warm in here."

I headed out straight for the barn.

"Bennie, go . . . go and help him," I heard that mother call behind me. And I wondered about a father who'd leave his family in such a mess, but maybe he didn't have any notion that all this was going to happen. Wouldn't do for me to judge without knowing the matter straight.

Bennie showed me to the ax, hatchet, and handsaw, all of them badly in need of sharpening. And there was plenty of wood, all right. Most every bit of it needing split. From the other end of the barn, I heard a cow lowing. But I ignored it and started in immediately, dull ax and all, to split some of the driest stuff I could find, to get the quickest fire I could with only a little kindling.

I'd have to split more for them. And carry plenty in. No doubt about that, but I stopped for now with just enough to get the fire blazing. The little boy helped me carry what he could, so we both went back inside with our arms full. One of the other children was up. A red-headed girl with hundreds of spots. I guessed her to be five or six years old, and she was absolutely miserable. Unable to wait for her mother any longer, she'd come out with a blanket wrapped around her. Now she just stood there and cried. She had a bad case of the pox, I could tell. And she was so cold her lips looked blue.

God, help them.

I stirred the coals and found a few more glowing embers than I expected. There was part of a catalog next to the fireplace on top of a basket of pinecones. I tore off several catalog pages, scrunched them in my hand, and set them on the coals along with some of the cones. Blowing real hard, I finally got a flame that licked and started to spread. I put the little pieces of bark and kindling I'd stripped off on top of that, then some other wood, small stuff first. Pretty soon the fire was crackling and roaring, and I had the big boy help me make a bed of blankets for the little ones close in front of it, and then scoot his mama's chair close beside them.

The other two children couldn't have been more than about one and three. They had pretty bad cases of the chicken pox too, but I noticed that none of the children had the cough I was hearing in their mother now. She was worn down sick with it settling in her chest some, and I was concerned because that kind of thing not taken care of can turn into full-blown pneumony.

"Thank you," she said. "We're so grateful for the small relief."

"Too small so far," I told her. "That fire won't last long

without more wood to keep adding. Will you all be all right in here if I go and split some more?"

She nodded. "Yes. Yes, thank you."

Once again, little Bennie followed me, but I wanted him to gain some benefit of the fire's warmth too, so I sent him back in with the first armload split and told him to stay inside in case any of the others needed anything. "Your mother hadn't oughta be up," I told him. "Fetch anything she needs an' put another log on the fire if it gets low."

I split enough more to make all the armload I could carry and was about to head back to the house with it when that cow let out an awful mournful sort of bellow. And I'd heard that kind of complaint before. I went to take a look, and sure enough, she was bulging with milk and awfully uncomfortable. Apparently, the lady hadn't wanted to mention that and seem to be begging for more help, but it'd do them and the cow a lot more good to have the milking done as not. So I took more wood inside and asked where to find the milk pail.

The lady's eyes flickered with a kind of fresh hope. "You don't have to do that, sir. I was going to. And Bennie was going to try again at the milking too. It's just so awful hard for him to get very far with his little hands not used to it."

"Won't take me long, ma'am," I said with a sigh. "I've done it plenty of times before."

As I milked, I wondered if they had food in the house. None of the children had complained of being hungry, but maybe they were too sick to care, or well-trained enough not to beg and complain in front of strangers. It was awful heavy to me to be taking all this time, knowing I was already a whole day late calling and Sarah might be waiting at the station right now. But I couldn't leave this family in a shape like this. I knew she'd understand that. If things had gone on with the house so cold as it was, those little ones or even their mother might have taken the hypothermia. They might have died.

I was glad to bring the warm milk in to them and suggest that they all oughta have a cup. The woman, who said her name was Vera Platten, insisted that I have some too. So I did, just a little, not wanting to take more than a swallow from them. Mrs. Platten cried about my help, feeling bad to need it and grateful I'd give it freely. She told me twice that she wished she could pay me, but I told her to forget it, that I couldn't accept anything from them for this.

I split a third armload of wood and brought it in, wondering how much they'd need to carry them through until the man of the house was home. There'd be no telling, since I had no idea what time he would come. It started really bothering me what could happen to this family if I left them alone and the husband was delayed.

Mrs. Platten's cough sounded pretty awful, and the little ones were still uncomfortable too. I fetched in a bucket of water and set a teakettle full by the fire to heat, hoping to find something to put in it for them. "Got any kind a' tea leaf?"

"I'm so sorry," Mrs. Platten answered me. "We haven't had regular tea in such a long time. I probably can't offer you anything you'd care for."

She'd misunderstood me completely. "I don't want nothin' 'cept to get some made for you. Got any herbs? I could look 'em over and see what's best."

"Top cupboard on the left," she answered me. "We grow or forage our own. It's so much cheaper."

That was nothing new to me. My family and the Worthams had been gathering tea herbs for as long as I could remember. I'd never had much store-bought tea except at outside functions. So none of the contents of Mrs. Platten's jars were strange to me. Sassafras. Chicory. Chamomile. Red sage, rosemary, comfrey. I could tell most by the look, the rest by the smell. I picked the comfrey because I'd seen Mrs. Wortham use it when someone had a cough. There was a little baking powder in the cupboard with the herbs, and a little sugar. Salt and pepper and a near-empty bag of cornmeal. Not much else.

"Do you have honey, ma'am?"

"I don't need it sweetened."

"Maybe not, but honey's good for what ails you. When Mrs. Wortham makes a cough syrup, she always uses honey. Lemon's good too, if you have it."

She was quiet, maybe not knowing for sure what to think of me, a stranger rustling around in her kitchen. Maybe I shouldn't have snooped, but I opened the cupboard on the right too and was dismayed to find nothing at all but a single jar of home-canned tomato juice and half a loaf of homemade bread. There was a potato bin close to the back door, but it had only four potatoes in the bottom. Unless they had something stored someplace else, they were almost out of food.

"Have you all had breakfast?" I asked.

Bennie nodded and his mother confirmed the answer. "You don't have to stay," she told me, her voice suddenly sounding scared. "You've done enough."

"Truth is, ma'am, I don't wanna stay," I admitted. "But I ain't gonna be able to drive off in good conscience and leave you like this. Three armloads a' wood ain't gonna last you long in this cold. And you got too much to deal with on top a' that, with your sick babies and yourself being sick, plus the ankle sprain. I could go, if you tell me where to stop to send the doctor out to you, or some other help from town. I'd feel all right 'bout that." I couldn't even mention the food. Everything else was bad enough.

But she shook her head. "We . . . we don't need the doctor. The chicken pox—it'll pass."

"There's your cough too," I prompted her. "And your ankle."

She looked like she might cry again. "We can't pay the doctor. And it's nothing serious. I'll be all right."

"Got kin I can fetch? Somebody else you know?"

She shook her head. "You've done so much already. We'll be all right till my husband comes home."

"When's he due?"

"Tonight, I hope."

There was too much uncertainty in that for my liking, but I didn't question her further. I just fixed her cup of tea and went back outside to split some more wood and think about this. That woman looked weaker to me than she let on. Or at least tireder. Maybe she'd been up half the night with a sick child. Or two. Or three. Maybe she'd been sick several days. Plus the fall this morning trying to get firewood. And if she was like Sarah's mother, she prob'ly hadn't been eating enough in the hard times, just to leave more for her babies.

I couldn't help feeling riled inside. Somebody should have seen to things better than this, if there was any possible way. Somebody at least should have had most of this woodpile split long before this.

I knew plain enough that they didn't have no telephone, but I was aching to get myself to one. Why couldn't the lady have given me the name of somebody in town so I could go, relay the word, and know someone would be heading out here to help? I couldn't leave them like this. But it pained me awful to stay, knowing I was worrying my loved ones if I didn't get word to them.

I whacked at that wood like it was gonna help matters for me to let myself get angry. Didn't look like I had much choice in the matter. I at least had to do this much. At least get 'em a decent woodpile to last through the day and night. My conscience wouldn't allow any less. Just thinking of that miserable little girl with her lips blue from cold made my gut squeeze.

But what about food? There was a chicken house off to one side of the barn, but I hadn't heard a squawk to know whether they even had chickens. I prayed so. That biggest kid could gather in what eggs there might be, if that was the case. And they had the rest of the milk. Not much else to last 'em very long. One meal, from what I'd seen. I prayed there was a pantry shelf some-place with plenty more on it, but the house was small, and the kitchen was tiny. I hadn't seen anyplace but the cupboard for food.

Lord God, what are you doing? First you take me past a wreck on the road and now this! It's not exactly what I had in mind when I prayed you'd use me and use this trip. Lord, help. I don't know what more to do here. And I want to get back on the road. But can I? In the face of this?

There had to be some assurance somehow. Some way I could know I wouldn't be leaving these people to freeze or starve if Mr. Platten didn't get home and they were alone again tomorrow. Truth be told, it wouldn't seem right for them to be alone even an hour, with the only able-bodied among them no more than eight years old. Three sick little ones. And a mother pretty near at the end of her rope. It wasn't right. It made me sick inside it was so all-fired wrong.

Sometimes this world stinks, I complained to God. *There's good people, children, that are blind, or deaf, or hurting. And people like these that are dirt poor and don't know what to do about it. God, what are you gonna do? What do you want me to do?*

I prayed that God would send Mr. Platten, wherever he was. Or their kin. Or somebody. I filled my arms with split wood again and carried it to the house, thinking to ask Mrs. Platten again if there wasn't somebody I could fetch for her or get word to. Surely even a neighbor would care enough to be neighborly and help them manage until Mr. Platten got home.

But she said they hadn't lived here all that long and she didn't know anybody they could call on.

"I gotta try," I told her.

She looked so sick. She couldn't hardly answer me except to take to crying again. "You've already . . . already answered our prayers. We thank you so much. We . . . we can make it now . . ."

One of the little girls took to crying too, and Bennie went to bring his sister to their mother's lap.

"Maybe she's hungry," he suggested with his sad eyes staring up at his mother's face.

"It's not lunchtime yet," she said real quiet, even though it had to be getting close to that time by now. The little girl buried her face in her mother's blouse and kept right on fussing.

"If she's hungry, it'd prob'ly do her good to go ahead an' have something to eat," I told the woman. "I can get it if you want. So's you stay off your ankle."

She turned her eyes to me, and the fear was in them again. But she didn't answer.

"Don't have much food, do you?"

She shook her head.

"How long's your husband been gone?" The question must have sounded fierce. I could feel the anger inside me, hard as I tried to squelch it.

She lowered her head. "Six days. He—he's bringing groceries too. Surely he'll be here tonight. We'll be all right until then—"

"You almost weren't all right!" I burst out. "Do you understand that? It was so cold in this place I don't know what might have happened—"

"I know . . ."

Her voice broke again, and I knew I shouldn't be scolding her. It wasn't her I was riled at anyway, but her husband, for leaving them so unprepared. But who was I to know his circumstance? Maybe he was held up by the storm. At least he'd be bringing food and coal. Soon, hopefully. But what if it wasn't soon?

"Are *you* hungry?" I asked Bennie. Instead of answering me, he looked at his mother.

"I can make a pot of soup with what I saw in your kitchen," I told them. "Plenty enough for all of you. Just like my mama used to make. Creamy tomato with the rest of the milk and the juice I saw. Hits the spot when it's cold like this."

Vera Platten reached a shaky hand in my direction. "God bless you," she whispered.

I didn't linger for no more words than that. I just threw a couple more logs on the fire and then went for the kitchen to find a pot and start mixing the soup. It'd boil too fast over the fire if I set it close, but I wasn't about to let the fire die back when it was the only heat they had. There was still a awful chill in the place anywhere but right near.

Bennie followed me and watched me open their last quart of tomato juice. "Are you some kind of angel?"

"No, sir. Just a frustrated fella tryin' to get to Camp Point, Illinois."

"Where's that?"

"Maybe eighty miles west a' here."

"Did your truck break down?"

"Had fuel pump trouble. I got it fixed though. Just got to tighten my wheel nuts to get back on the road."

"Please don't leave till my papa gets here."

I looked at his pleading face.

"Mama's been sick all of yesterday and today. I was scared."

I tousled his hair a little. "I can understand that. I would a' been scared too."

"When you was out choppin' wood, Mama told me you

60

oughta be going, that you was a stranger an' we couldn't keep you from your travels no longer."

Stirring milk into the pot, I sighed. "She's right. I don't belong to stay. Don't you think it'd be better if I drove into town and sent somebody to look after you? Or maybe another house close by? Haven't you got kin?"

"Not around here."

"You must know somebody. Don't you?"

"Miss Mendelson, the schoolteacher. I know her, but I ain't been in her class since before Christmas."

"Where does she live?"

"I don't know. I only seen her at the schoolhouse. I ain't been goin' back yet because of the weather an' Mama needin' my help."

"You've been good help today. Where's the school-house?" It was a thought, a hope. It was maybe noon on a weekday. But would school be in session?

"I don't think there'll be nobody there today."

"Is there a farm close by? Who's your nearest neigh-bor?"

"The Clarks. But they ain't very friendly. I don't think they like us much."

"Which way?"

"Down the lane away from the road and into the tim-ber about a half mile. I know because I walked there with Papa once. We offered to work for 'em fixin' fence or whatever they wanted. But they shooed us away."

Half mile. So close. "You tell me if there's anything else I need to know 'bout gettin' there. After I get your food made, I aim to pay 'em a visit. Maybe they'll come till your father gets home."

"Papa wouldn't like that. Mama neither. They never been nice before."

"You need help right now, from wherever you can get it."

I took the soup pot to the fire. With salt and pepper

and rosemary and a touch of cornmeal to thicken it, it wouldn't be exactly like Mama's, but it'd be passable good and plenty creamy. Thank the good Lord they'd had that much in the house. With a slice of the bread from the cupboard, they oughta all be satisfied for a while. Then with the fire built up and more wood handy, I could head to the neighbors and beg their help with all this. I had to be going. I had to. The day was progressing, and I didn't wanna be another night on the road, especially without gettin' to a telephone.

I served all of 'em close by the fire. I think Mrs. Platten was expecting me to claim a bowl of soup for myself, but I couldn't do that. I pulled my collar up and my hat down and headed out. A half mile. Down a snowy side road I could hardly see. Taking the truck would be impossible, so I'd have to walk it in the cold.

I felt bad steppin' off the porch and seeing little Bennie's face staring out the window. I was sure he was scared I'd leave them. Maybe he'd rest easy seein' I wasn't goin' near the truck. They were better off now than they'd been before, that was sure, but it wasn't near enough.

I wished I coulda drove. It woulda been so much faster. But the drifts were bad and there was no way I coulda got back there. It was hard enough on foot, and my leg started bothering me, making my limp that much worse.

Down a hill and on the other side of some trees, I saw a house with smoke trailing from the chimney. Deeply relieved, I hurried my pace the best I could. And somebody must have seen out the window. The door opened before I got to it. An old man with a white beard stood starin' at me like I was some kind of creature he'd never seen before.

"What're you doin' down our lane?"

"I come from your neighbor's house, sir. They're sore in need a' help."

62

"Which neighbors? Who sent you?"

Please, Lord. Please give him a heart of sympathy.

"I come from Plattens'. Mr. Platten ain't home, and the Mrs. and kids are all sick 'cept the one little boy—"

"Well, what do you need from me? Who are you? Some kind of kin of theirs?"

"No, sir. I was stopped along the main road, fixin' the fuel pump of my truck, when the little boy come out of the house wavin' and yellin'. They're out a' coal. The house was cold. And he was scared because the rest of 'em are sick—"

"What kind of sick?" a woman's voice asked me. A teeny white-haired lady stepped up behind the man.

"The little ones have the chicken pox. The mama too, but she's got a awful cough and a sprained ankle from a fall on the ice. I split 'em some wood to get a fire goin' in the fireplace. They're expectin' Mr. Platten back tonight with coal and groceries. But they need help till then. Somebody to sit with the little ones and keep 'em warm so that mother can rest up and mend. They were in a bad way, and they hadn't oughta be alone."

I looked right at the lady, begging her in my heart to respond. But it was the man who spoke first.

"Norman Platten don't have a lick of sense, leaving his family without coal nor wood, and them sick too."

I'd thought the same thing, but still I felt I had to defend the man. "They might not a' been sick when he left. And he's aimin' to bring back what they need when he comes. Could be he had to go take care of that, and he didn't realize how things'd get while he was gone."

The woman disappeared behind the angle of the door.

"Please help them," I begged. "The little boy tells me you're the closest neighbors."

The man was still looking at me pretty straight. "And you're just a stranger off'n the road?"

"Yes, sir, and needin' real bad to get goin' again. I was supposed to be to my brother's yesterday, but the storm held me up at Auburn."

"Yep. Pretty fierce piece of wind we had."

I stared at him. He only stood in the open doorway, not answering a word to my plea for help.

"Marvin Clark, you can get your coat on or stay here alone," the woman said from somewhere I couldn't see her. "There's a sick mother with a sprained ankle and ailing children to think about. I'm going to go with this young man if he'll help me, and do what I can till the father gets home."

"God bless you, ma'am." The relief was so deep in me I almost couldn't say anything more, but I thought of something real sudden, and I knew I had to ask it. "Can you spare a sack of food? I made 'em some soup just now, but they ain't got much a' nothin' else left if Mr. Platten's held up gettin' back to 'em. Not even enough for a decent supper tonight, I don't think."

"God love you, young man," Mrs. Clark answered me. "You always this concerned for strangers?"

"Don't usually need to be."

She hurried to the kitchen to fetch some food to bring along. Mr. Clark just stared at me. "My wife hadn't oughta be walking a half mile through them snow drifts."

"I understand. An' I'm sorry, sir, but I didn't know who else to ask."

"It's cold in that house?"

"Not as bad as it was. I got the fire goin' good and wood enough to keep it that way for a while. I'll split some more before I leave."

"Shouldn't be our affair to see to another man's family. Seems like he could've taken care a' things better than this."

"I don't know, sir. Maybe he's been short of work and had to go some distance to find anything. I'm trying not to judge. I just don't want to think of that family sufferin'."

Mr. Clark looked down at his boots. "My wife's liable to have her hands full with all them sick youngsters. Maybe I best come along to keep the fire up for her and see to anything else. They got chores done?"

"I milked for 'em. But there may be more needin' done. Mrs. Platten's feeling awful bad to need the help. But she can't do much of anything right now."

He got his coat. Mrs. Clark joined us, looking almost twice as wide as she had before, bundled in her big coat with two scarves—one for her neck and one for her head. I took the sack of food to carry for her, and we trudged back through the snow. The Clarks were both a lot shorter and older than me, and we didn't move as fast as I would have liked, but I thanked God the whole way that they were willing. *Bless them. Oh, Lord, bless them and send Mr. Platten home quickly. Let this be the start of good neighbor relations between these families. Thank you!*

I felt released. I felt free, certain that everything would be all right now and I could go. But I still needed to split some more wood, just to be sure, and I worked at it as fast as I could as soon as I got back. Mr. Clark couldn't work so fast as I could and there wasn't but one ax, but he took the hatchet and split up kindling and a pile of smaller stuff while I worked. He and Bennie shook my hand when it was time to go. Mrs. Platten asked my name, and that was the first I realized I hadn't told them till then. She seemed to think I must be a minister, like the Ensley relatives had thought, and I wondered what there was about me to give folks that impression. I hadn't even prayed with these people. Not out loud, at least.

All I had to do was tighten down a wheel on the truck, and I could go. Thank the Lord. I prayed I could find a telephone and get through to the Marathon station in

Dearing before Mr. Wortham left for the day, if he'd been able to get there at all. I prayed Sam wasn't stewing too bad over not hearing any more word since the first message. And most of all I prayed that Sarah would have peace, because I knew she'd be scared for me if she had any idea I hadn't called.

My brothers would prob'ly think I'd gotten lost, but not Sarah. She surely had more confidence in me than that. But that would have her thinking far worse things. About the storm. And some of the awful wrecks we'd heard about.

Give her the peace that passes understanding, Lord, I prayed. *Help her remember that perfect love casts out fear.*

7

Sarah

Charlie Hunter came to the station about three in the afternoon so Dad could go home. I'd known it was almost that time, but when I saw him march through the door my heart sank into my shoes and I didn't want to leave. *Frank's got to call! He's just got to!*

Dad had some work to finish up on Mrs. Patterson's old Ford, and Charlie didn't mind him staying till he got the job done. It was a little relief, even though I knew it wouldn't take long. I couldn't concentrate to embroider anymore. I just sat by the telephone. *Call*, I begged Frank in my head. *Oh, please. Be able to call.*

I stared at the map of Illinois pinned on the service station wall. Mentally, I'd traced Frank's route across it several times today. How far had he gotten? Where could he be? A thousand jumbled thoughts raced through me, a hundred explanations, almost all of them bad. One painful understanding just wouldn't leave me alone. He would have called already, if he could have.

I could feel the awful pinch of dread deep inside. I

tried to push it away, but I wasn't sure I could. Everything about this hurt right now, my heart most of all.

Peace.

Just one word. But it rolled inside me along with the words of that familiar hymn. *Blessed assurance, Jesus is mine! Oh, what a foretaste of glory divine! Heir of salvation, purchase of God, born of his Spirit, washed in his blood.*

I didn't stop and figure out why that hymn would enliven me just then. But I felt so much better just to let it float over my mind and heart. *Frank is still in God's hands, and that's the safest place to be. He's all right. He's got to be all right.*

I hummed the hymn out loud, needing it to soak even further into me and dispel the gloom of fear with the light of praise. I could trust. I could. That God works all things for good for those that love him. And Frank and I both loved him. We were "born of his Spirit, washed in his blood." And that made us safe. Blessed. Eternally. No matter what happened. I could rejoice for that, and believe that everything would be all right.

"This is my story, this is my song, praising my Savior all the day long . . ."

I sang the chorus softly to myself while my heart thundered seeing Dad wipe off his hands. He was ready to leave. But I didn't want to go. Not yet.

In just a minute, Dad was getting his coat and bringing me mine. That choked feeling of dread tried to come back, but I pushed it away. *This is my story, this is my song . . .*

Dad hugged me. I could see the concern in his eyes, and I knew he'd been thinking about Frank the same as I was, and that he'd loved him even longer than I had. Frank was family already, and had been for years, in Dad's eyes. "Believe," he whispered. "He's all right."

We put on our coats. We stepped out into the cold air.

Dad took my hand, something he hadn't done in a long time, and I recited his words again in my mind. *Believe. He's all right.*

I took a deep breath, letting the hymn float over me again.

And the phone rang. I could barely hear it. I wasn't sure I really had. But Dad and I both spun around and saw Charlie through the window, rushing to answer. He waved us in, and we ran. It felt like the sun breaking through storm clouds, like a ton of lead being lifted off my heart.

8

Frank

I wished I could hug Sarah right over the phone. She cried, she was so relieved to hear from me, and I felt awful bad to have scared her. I told her about the wreck and the snowstorm and the family with practic'ly nothin', and she said I'd done the right thing bein' a help.

"Maybe God had you there for them on purpose," she admitted, though I knew she wished I was back home.

It'd be late now before I got to Sam's, and Sarah and her father were already ready to go home. So I promised to call the service station tomorrow just to leave word that I'd gotten in all right. Sarah was relieved by that. She was worried that the weather might give me more problems, or who could tell what else, but I assured her I'd be all right. Wasn't easy gettin' off the phone, but I had a lot more miles to put under me.

"I love you, Sarah Jean," I told her.

"I love you too. Please be careful."

It still seemed a marvel that Sarah would have such feelings for me. I was incredible blessed, no doubt about that. And I hoped I wasn't stretchin' her love and tolerance by doing what I was doing. But I had to be the best I could for her, and I didn't think I'd ever really discover what that was at home.

Right after the call to Sarah, I talked to Sam at his uncle's store, and it was a good thing I did. They'd been worried sick that I was wrecked along the road somewhere. I knew they was anxious for me to get to them tonight. And I was just as anxious to have this trip settled.

But I'd barely eaten anything that day. I drove till the hunger drawed me to a roadside café in Jacksonville, where I ordered tomato soup because I was still thinking of the Platten family. With the soup in front of me, I prayed for them and the Ensleys. The Lord works in mysterious ways, his wonders to perform. And it struck me as mysterious that he'd have me meeting up with two families in need thataway. Sarah was surely right that he'd led me on purpose.

Felt good to have hot soup and coffee in me, but I was in a hurry to be back on the road. I crossed the Illinois River at a town called Meredosia and got gas in Versailles. It was gettin' dark around me, but the road stayed passable and I kept on through Hersman and Mt. Sterling. I was near to the end of my memorized route.

Before the next town, I saw a fella walking on the road in an army uniform. My gut feeling was to stop, but I almost didn't do it. After all that had happened so far on this trip, who knew what I'd be letting myself in for?

But he stuck his thumb out, and I couldn't pass him by. Here was a young veteran, maybe not even home for long, out here along the road on a cold night. Wouldn't be right not to at least take him a few miles.

I found out all he needed was a ride to Clayton, the very next town down the road. I was glad I'd stopped. He directed me to the café right across from the square and offered to buy me a cup of coffee for my trouble.

But I was keen aware how close I was to Camp Point and I didn't want another stop to give me a chance at being delayed again. So I just let him out and went on. Only six more miles. Man, oh, man, it was going to be a relief to be there.

I was feeling the cold pretty fierce that last stretch of road, but I was feeling satisfied too. Maybe I was two days late, but I'd done it. Camp Point in the moonlight was a pretty sight to me because a' that. And even in the dark it wasn't hard to find Pickinpaugh Motors, nor Sam's house. And they must a' been watching. Just as soon as I killed the engine, I heard a squeal from somebody little, and Sam come running out to meet me with four of his six young'uns. It was good.

9

Sarah

I lay awake that night sorting through everything Frank had told me in his call. Two different families would have been in desperate straits if he hadn't happened along. I had to accept that the Lord was working good in this trip, even though I didn't like it. And I prayed Frank was in a warm bed now.

What else do you have in store for us, Lord? What are you trying to tell me?

I couldn't stop thinking about those hurting people. Frank knew what it was like to have little, and to be in pain. He'd known what to do, and he'd done it well. I shouldn't have let myself fret so much for him, but I didn't know how to help it. I'd probably stay fretting, at least a little, until he was safe back home.

Now I was anxious to get tomorrow's assurance that he'd truly gotten to Camp Point. I prayed to never again have to feel so scared for him. Thoughts of his return trip tried to cloud my mind, but I shoved them aside. *He is in the Lord's hands. Everything will be all right.*

I lay a long while listening to some unknown dog barking again. It must have been very late when I finally got to sleep. And then I dreamed of snow, acres and piles of it, interrupting our June wedding.

In the morning I was in a hurry to get through chores so we could leave for town. Dressing quick and then pulling on coat and boots, I rushed out to gather the eggs for breakfast. But as I got close to the chicken house, I saw a new shadow. Something big with an awkward gait was coming around the corner near the fence. I froze, but it kept on coming. A dog. Every bit as big as the one I'd had to shoot three days ago. But this one was brown and mottled gray, mangy and skinny with a huge smashed-in-looking face. It saw me and stopped in its tracks.

Not again! I felt all trembly. *Is it mad? And here I am without Robert's rifle!*

I tried to think fast, wondering if I could get into the chicken house before this beast would have a chance to get hold of me. It was the ugliest dog I'd ever seen in my life, with a bowed leg in front and huge slobbery jaws. We just stood and stared at each other for a moment. Dad was in the barn. Would he hear me if I called?

But this dog hadn't bared its teeth. Its neck hairs weren't ruffled. Maybe it wasn't dangerous. It was just staring at me, as if it were trying to figure out what to do the same as I was.

"Go away," I told it. "Go home. Leave us and our chickens alone."

But it seemed pretty plain that this dog didn't have a home. It was in poor shape, looking half starved or more. It cocked its head at me and plunked down in the snow as if it were too weary to stand up anymore. I wasn't afraid then, but I still felt a little uncomfortable with those big brown eyes staring at me.

"You are ugly," I told it. "And uninvited. Where'd you come from?"

74

Another strange dog! I wondered if there might not be a pack of wild dogs around here close. But this one didn't act wild. At least I didn't think so at the moment. And we'd had strays wander through before. Just not within two days of each other.

"Did you know that big monster that was here the other day?" I asked the dog in front of me, even though I knew I was being silly. The dog cocked its head again and then laid the big bulk of it down across its forepaws and gazed up at me as if it were waiting for something special.

"My folks might not want to feed something as big as you," I said. "Doubtful you'd earn your keep."

He only watched me, and I sighed. "Will you let me get in the chicken house? Just stay right there if you're not going to go away. Leave me alone and let me do my chores."

He did. That big dog stayed exactly in that spot till I'd finished gathering the eggs and had given the chickens their feed. And when I was ready to go back to the house, he got up to follow me.

"Oh no, you don't."

But there was no preventing him, much as I tried. He followed me all the way to the house and even up onto the porch. He would have come inside except that I managed to get the door shut quick enough. He surely was persistent. Thank God he wasn't threatening.

Katie said we should shoo him away, but she didn't open the door to try it. Mom peeked out, looked at the creature, and was immediately sympathetic.

"It's so thin. Probably hoping we'll spare a bite."

"Are you going to feed it?" I asked, not sure how I felt about that. It might stick around if we fed it. And I usually liked dogs, but I wasn't sure how I felt about this one.

Mom shook her head. "Your father will be in from the barn soon enough. We'll see what he says."

Katie waited anxiously for Dad to come in from milking. She was not keen on that dog, I could tell. But she usually liked animals almost as well as I did. Having such a close call with that other big dog might have had even more effect on her than I knew.

Dad was awhile coming in from the porch. He was talking to the dog, just like I'd done. He came in and set the milk on the table. "Well, at least we know what's been keeping us up at night."

"He's huge," Katie said immediately. "What if he was running with the other one?"

Dad went to the washbowl and soaped up his hands. "He seems friendly enough. But at this point, I guess there's no way to tell."

"There's no sign of disease, is there?" Mom asked.

"No. But I don't want you girls close around him much till I get to know him a little better. Maybe he'll wander off on his own."

"If he doesn't," Katie protested, "how do we keep from being close to him if he's right on our porch?"

Dad nodded. "He wants company, all right. Was glad to greet me. Would have been happy to come in." He wiped his hands and then sat in the nearest chair. "I'll have to think about that pretty soon if he doesn't wander off."

I thought the big dog would surely mosey away after a while, since we hadn't fed him. But Dad and I were almost ready to go into town, and he was still in the same spot, right outside the door.

Dad sighed and turned to Mom. "Give me the scrap bucket, Julia, and throw a crust of bread and the leftover scrambled eggs into it. I'll put him in a barn stall and tell it around that he's here. Maybe somebody'll claim him."

"What if they don't?" Katie asked with concern.

Dad had a ready answer. "I'll keep him in the barn and watch for a couple of weeks, just to make sure he's all right. If he is, then he can start getting used to the place if he wants to. It'd be all right with me to have a dog around again. So long as he leaves the chickens alone."

Katie wasn't thrilled, but she didn't argue. She just gave me a letter she'd written to her beau, Dave Kliner, and asked me to mail it for her while we were out. It was a little strange for her not to go in to work for so long, but the five-and-dime was closed for some changes to the building, and Katie was using as much of the time as she could to work on a quilt for the Ladies' Society benefit at our church.

I was supposed to be helping, but I hadn't done at all well lately with my mind elsewhere, mostly on Frank. Mom and I had cut out the pieces for my wedding dress, but we hadn't started sewing it yet. Mom said winter was the time for handwork, when there wasn't so much work with fields and the garden and all. But other than Katie's tea towels, I hadn't gotten very far with anything. I probably had "marrying nerves," as our neighbor Mrs. Post would say. She'd asked me before Christmas if I was feeling them yet. It'd hit her six months early, she'd said, and she could hardly do anything the whole time but stew.

I didn't think I was that bad off, just more of a worrier than usual because of Frank's trip. I got my coat on again and tried not to think about it.

I promise to trust you, Lord, I prayed. *And I promise to trust Frank, no matter what comes. Even if I do have "marrying nerves."*

The weather was warmer today, and Dad and I were quiet driving into town. I couldn't help thinking again about the people Frank had met. His willingness to help strangers reminded me of the conversation I'd had with our pastor not long ago. He always talked to both parties when a marriage was decided upon. But what he'd had to say to me was surely not typical.

"Frank is a special young man, and I've always thought it would take a special girl to be his wife. There's more in Frank's future than his woodwork. He has a heart for people, Sarah. A rare caring that is the very best qualification for ministry."

He'd asked me if I thought I could handle it all right if someday Frank was called to preach. And I'd told him it couldn't possibly bother me. I loved Frank, and no kind of calling would change that. Besides, I already had a brother who had started preaching, so it was not such a strange thought to me.

But now I knew that at the time I'd given that assurance I hadn't really thought it through. Of course I still believed my answer was the right one. But how would I feel if Frank told me he wanted to go to the mission field like Robert? I'd never thought such a thing could happen. I'd always been sure Frank was a homebody like me. But no one knows what the years may hold. At this point, I wasn't even sure about tomorrow.

❦

Frank called right on time, and I was thrilled there'd been no more trouble. They were starting the moving that very day, and they would try to get as much done as they could before Sam began his new job next week.

"Maybe moving won't take as long as they thought," I suggested.

"Maybe not," Frank answered. "But Sam wants me to put a stair rail in at their new house, plus fix a couple of other things. He'll keep me busy awhile, no doubt about that."

I wanted to ask if he'd met Thelma's Uncle Milton yet, but I couldn't. The thought made me feel a little green inside. We knew nobody in Camp Point except Sam and his family, and they wouldn't be there after they finished moving. There was no reason even to think about the place.

At least it was a relief to picture Frank safe and sound at Sam's house. We went by to see Frank's older sister Lizbeth before we went home and told her all about his trip. She was glad to hear. Apparently she'd been fretting as badly as I was, but her little girl, Mary Jane, was down sick with bronchitis so they hadn't been able to come and inquire.

"We should have known," she told me, "that if Frank met up with any trouble it would be somebody else's. He had plenty of faith for that drive."

Of course she was right. And I knew she hadn't meant those words as any kind of rebuke, but I took them to heart anyway. I should be able to have as much confidence in him as he had in himself. Even more. And it should be easy. He'd never given me reason to doubt.

Dad and I were home by noon, and Katie'd made so much progress on her quilt that instead of helping her then, I got out the pieces to my wedding dress after lunch and began sewing the bodice. Oh, it was going to be beautiful. I decided I'd better sew up the dress shirt for Frank to wear too, and add a bit of my lace at the collar and cuffs if he'd let me. I'd seen that done before. Anna Leapley'd been very proud of the way she and her husband matched so beautifully at their wedding.

But Frank didn't want a big deal made over things like that. Just us and the preacher at our wedding would be all right with him. But it wouldn't be right not to have my family and his brothers and sisters. And our church family. And that's a crowd already, so what's a few more? We'd be inviting over seventy people by the time we were done.

"Hitched in style," that's what Anna Leapley called a big church wedding. And that'd be all right with Frank too, he'd told me once, so long as we were joined by God.

Katie admired the start I'd made on the wedding dress and promised to help me when the benefit quilt was done. As usual she went to check the mail. And when she came back she had a letter for me amidst the stack, from Donald Mueller. I threw it away without reading it. She looked at me oddly, but I didn't even try to explain.

10

Frank

It was nice to see Camp Point in the daylight. Sam said he thought I'd really like the store, and since that was figuring in my mind more than anything, I was glad to take a look at it.

Pratt's Heating and Lighting. The building was two story and on the main business street, with an awning over the front door and a back door leading out to a dirt alley. It shared walls with a restaurant on one side and a dry goods store on the other. Just like the name might indicate, it held little more than stoves, furnaces, and a big variety of lamps, mostly electric.

Sam explained that Thelma's uncle paid him a regular wage to run the store, on the condition that Sam would make the bank payments and eventually own the place, but "Uncle Milty" would continue to reap from the sales until the property was paid off. I thought that strange and asked why Uncle Milty didn't sell it to him outright and walk away from the business of it, if he intended it to change hands anyway.

"He don't want to walk away just yet," Sam told me.

"He likes to come in and talk to folks as the owner when he feels like it. Lot of people don't even know I was supposed to be buying it. He says by the time the note's paid, he'll be full ready to retire. Just not quite yet. But he only comes in two or three days a week. An' he's never been hard to deal with."

I looked forward to meeting Milton Pratt, but I told Sam I wasn't sure I could make the same agreement he had. He nodded his head in understanding.

"I just need somebody to take up those payments," he explained. "You and him can come to your own terms."

"But who's legal owner?"

"Both of us, I guess. Till the bank's paid. Then it was going to all come to me."

I thought on that as I looked around a little more. Sam had told me he'd liked the steady wage, that he was making more here than he had in Dearing. The arrangement had worked out fine for him while he needed it. But I didn't think I could do things the same way. If I was gonna buy and run a store, especially with my own crafted pieces, I'd want to straight-out be the boss, no questions asked. I'd have to buy the place outright or it might get awful complicated with him looking at what was my profit and what was his.

Most of the ground floor was storefront with just a small room in the back. The upstairs was empty except for storage. Sam suggested that I could live up there. He said Mr. Pratt used to before he bought his house, but it didn't look like it'd been lived in for a long time. There were only two rooms.

I didn't tell Sarah Jean much about the place when it came time to call, and she didn't ask. I thought it best to talk to Mr. Pratt before I went into much detail. Sarah and I made an appointment to talk again in a few days, and then Sam said he'd show me more of the town.

But I couldn't get my mind off the store. It might work, depending on the terms Mr. Pratt would want. But the back room was a much smaller workshop than I wanted. The store area in front seemed big because I'd never had anything like that to show my work in. But it was almost full already with goods I didn't care about. The two rooms upstairs would be all right for just me, but I'd still have to think about a house for Sarah. If I was to agree to this. And that was a very big *if*.

Sam and I drove slowly down the street in my truck, with him pointing out the different businesses, especially the ones run by folks he'd come to know. He was having a great time, and I knew he was hoping I'd get excited about the store, but I couldn't help feeling disappointed. I guess I'd wanted it to stick out to me as special, like a place that was just the right fit for me, and that hadn't happened. But why was I wanting something to work out clear up here? No wonder Sarah wondered at me.

Why Sam wanted it, I well understood. It was a way to keep peace with his uncle, who was accusing him of leaving him in a lurch. And a way he could tell himself he was giving me a great opportunity too.

He took me pretty much all over town, starting with the businesses. The railroad track ran through the middle of town with Railroad Park, a piece of ground on both sides of the tracks, for a town square. Most of the businesses sat facing each other on opposite sides of it. The depot was toward the west end.

He showed me houses south of the tracks first and told me part of the southwest area was called "little Dublin" because of the Irish immigrants who, often as not, had worked for the railroad. Most of the biggest houses were north of the tracks, especially on Ohio Avenue.

There was a sizable park clear at the north edge of town, but we couldn't drive into it because of the snow. Sam said it was called Bailey Park and it'd be nice come spring. The pond reminded him of our pond back home. And they had a big boulder hauled in that all the kids liked to climb on, including his Georgie.

Fine, I was thinking. *It's an all right place to live. But Mr. Pratt'll have to have some mighty pretty words to keep me interested in that store of his. Seems like I'd do as well or better back in Mcleansboro.*

I decided to straight-out ask what Sam hadn't told me yet. "So when am I gonna meet Mr. Pratt, anyway?"

"I don't know. He's eccentric sometimes. Hasn't told us when he's coming over, but he knows you're here. Maybe he'll show up about suppertime. He'll prob'ly wanna talk business first thing, but don't worry. I'll walk you through everything step-by-step and then make sure you understand any papers 'fore you sign 'em."

I wasn't sure how I felt about that offer. Sam seemed to think I was going to need explanations, not just someone to read, and that irked me.

Sam was supposed to open the store back up after lunch and work a couple days trying to clear inventory and settle his business before leaving. He asked me to go with him after we'd eaten, on the chance I might meet Uncle Milty. But he didn't show up.

Just listening to Sam, I learned a lot about the goods in that store. He showed me the ledgers he was working in and told me that whatever way I'd used back home for recording orders and sales prob'ly wouldn't work well here.

"I know the Worthams kept the WH books," he said. "Sarah could handle that well enough here. Ain't much to it. But I can help you till the wedding, and if she don't wanna keep on afterward, I can visit and catch you up sometimes till you're able to hire somebody regular."

I didn't even answer him. Sarah was already helping me with books sometimes. She and I had talked about there being even more of that one of these days. She didn't mind a bit, and I didn't mind asking her because we'd be a team. But there wasn't no way I'd ask my older brother to do it. Did he really think I couldn't figure out a way to get things done in a business without him? Of course I'd need help, but not his. He had enough to think about with six kids and a job of his own.

There weren't very many customers that day, and eventually I went back to Sam's house, where I could help Thelma pack. I begged some boxes for her from the local grocery stores, and that first day we made a lot of progress on the small stuff. While we were packing boxes, Thelma was the one to bring up another surprising idea.

"Franky, we've had people interested in this house, and we need to sell it quick. But if you want it, you an' Sarah, we'd give you special terms. You could pay us direct and not have to go through the bank."

The offer made me feel strange inside. "I would a' thought Sam'd mention that."

"He would've eventually. Takes him awhile sometimes to get round to everythin' he's thinkin'. He didn't wanna seem pushy. But he said I could ask you about it myself if I wanted to."

I shook my head at my oldest brother. He must've had all this planned out. Prob'ly thought this was just the kind of life I needed and he was doing me a big favor to hand it over. But it almost made me mad, because of what it surely meant. He didn't think I could buy a home any other way. And he didn't think I could take on a business without him helping work out the details.

If Thelma wondered why I was quiet the rest of the time till Sam got home, she didn't ask. But I felt like throwing their things in the back of my truck and hauling them to Jacksonville as quick as I could so I could just go home. Here I was wanting to manage on my own, and my brother was only wanting to make it look like I was while he arranged the whole thing.

This must have seemed like a great solution to his own problems to get a buyer for the house and the store. And he could still feel like he was giving me what I wanted, setting me up where everybody'd think I was independent. He knew how I felt about that. I'd told him that I didn't wanna go through life leaning on Sarah's parents, or Kirk and that farm, for anything. I had to find a way to put down roots and make it on my own, away from all the watch care.

Even Sam's. I figured I'd be telling him soon enough that Camp Point wasn't for me. Maybe I'd take another look at Mt. Vernon. Or Marion.

Dearing and Mcleansboro were just too close. I hoped that Sarah would be able to understand that, and I knew I'd have to talk to her about it real soon now that it was clearer in my head. I loved my family. And I loved hers. But I couldn't be sure they wouldn't always be checking on us and treatin' me like a kid if we stayed close, just because everybody took me to be different. I knew they meant well and they loved me. Especially Lizbeth and the Worthams. But I had to step away. At least for a while. To prove I could. Or I might never be satisfied with myself.

❧

Mr. Pratt came for supper just like Sam predicted. It was plain he wasn't happy about Sam leaving, and the first thing he did when the talking started was to offer Sam a raise to change his mind. I don't think he liked the thought of talking to me. He didn't seem to want nothin' to do with me at all. Sam had said he was just eccentric. But I found out he was also pretty blunt.

When he got around to talking to me, he had one initial question. "How will you run my business if you can't read the paperwork?"

Sam jumped in before I could answer. "I told you, Uncle Milty. Wait'll you see his handiwork. It'll bring customers from miles around. And he's got a sharp mind for business. A real good memory. And a bright young woman itchin' to marry him that's well able to take care of all the books."

Sam glanced at me quick but went right on talking. "He's good with people, and his furniture'll give the store the spark it needs. Ain't nothin' quite like it around here."

Mr. Pratt nodded just a little and asked the next question straight to Sam. "When do I get to see it?"

"There's samples still on my truck," I broke in. "I'll get 'em if you wanna look. But you oughta know that the only way I'd consider runnin' your store is if you sell to me and step away."

"He will," Sam spoke up quick. "Just like with me. He's not around much. Don't wanna be. I've been the manager."

"That's not what I mean," I said, looking at Mr. Pratt.

He nodded, and I was pretty sure he understood me. "Let's see your handiwork," he said simply. "I've sure heard it bragged on enough times."

I brought in the cedar chest, the tot's chair, and the carvings. Mr. Pratt liked them all. And then he asked to talk to me alone. Sam didn't like that a bit, I could tell. But I appreciated it.

"Your brother's leavin' me in a bind," Mr. Pratt admitted. "I can't run the store myself anymore, but I don't want to see it close. I'm willing to take a chance on you, but it don't seem like either of us are too sure about this yet."

He stopped and cleared his throat. "How about we just try things, say for six months to a year? I'll rent you the place. You can buy my inventory or sell it for me on commission and fill the rest of the place with your work.

If you decide you like the store, we can talk about you buying then. Or if you'd rather at that point, you can just walk away, no strings attached."

I wondered at him, why he seemed so desperate. He didn't know me at all except by Sam's word. What did he think he needed? Ongoing income from the place? "Excuse me, sir, for askin'. But wouldn't it be easier for you just to list it for sale in the local paper and find you a buyer right around here?"

"I don't want an outright buyer. Not yet. I'm fond a' that little store, and I don't want to part with it completely till I'm good and ready."

I sighed. "I doubt I'll be interested. But when will you be ready?"

"A year or two. I'll know. But till then I'd rent it to you. It'd be the same as yours. I'd step aside just like you want, except for collecting rent. An' all the profit would be yours, except for what comes of my inventory. But you'd get no wage like Sam does. That'd be your price for havin' me stay clear. What do you think?"

"Honestly, Mr. Pratt, I think you could put your terms for a renter, if that's what you want, into the newspaper and find some young fella eager for the chance. I'd recommend it to you, 'cause I'm not prepared to promise you anythin'."

He was angry. I could tell it in the little twitch of his eyebrow and the way his knuckles tightened across the crook of his cane. "Sam told me you were a willing worker and liable to jump at the opportunity. Didn't he offer this house to you like he said he was going to? Contract for deed? You can't beat the deal he'd give you just for being his brother. And this is a good house. You could raise a family here and have a good business just walking distance away."

"Maybe so," I acknowledged. "But I have no intention a' buyin' this house."

"Why not?" He seemed truly surprised. "Did you tell Sam that?"

"Not yet."

"There's not a thing wrong with it. Or my store either."

"I wouldn't claim there is. Except that I'd like the right to choose a home and a business for myself."

He laughed. "You're not hankering for the help as much as he's hankering to help you."

"I guess not."

He thumped his cane on the floor. "Well, Frank Hammond, I guess maybe I like you a little, even if you won't help me out. Sorry I forgot part of your message when you were on the way here. Those things happen when you get up in years."

He didn't seem all that old to me. And I didn't know what he was talking about. But I nodded. "It's done. Nothing to worry 'bout now."

"You do fine work. Would be an asset to the store like your brother said. Think on it at least, will you? We can talk again another time."

"I'll pray on it," I told him. "But I don't expect to wanna stay in this town, or to take up where Sam's leavin' off. So I hope you consider advertisin' for somebody else to run your store."

He barely grunted at that and was ready to leave. And Sam was pretty upset when he found out how our conversation had gone. He started to get after me for not thinking this through, but Thelma was much more conciliatory.

"Sammy, you can't blame him for havin' misgivings," she said. "We're so far away up here from everything he's used to. Give him some time. He don't have to decide tonight, anyway."

Sam nodded solemnly and apologized to me.

They don't understand, I couldn't help thinking. *Not even close.*

I played with the kids until it was time to put them all to bed, and then I went to bed early myself. Tomorrow we'd start moving things to Jacksonville. Sam'd be along on the first trip and then after he went back to the store, I'd go ahead and haul some more by myself. The sooner we got all this done the better.

11

Sarah

The night of the Lion's Club Carnival and Dance came and went, and I didn't go. I wondered only fleetingly what Donald Mueller would think of my absence, and then I turned my attention to my wedding dress again.

It felt good to be working alongside my mother, her skilled hands with mine producing something I'd be so happy to wear. The dress was going to be beautiful, but the details were so intricate that it was a good thing we'd started early.

Dad drove me into town again when the day came for Frank's next telephone call. I could barely sit still knowing he'd have something to say about the store by now, so it was awesome relief when he told me he didn't want it. I was so thrilled I barely heard what he said next.

"I've gotta talk to you 'bout something real important, Sarah."

"Important? What?"

There was a pause, and I knew he was gathering his thoughts. "I can't live at home anymore. I need a place that's just ours."

"I know. We've talked about that. A place where you can restart the business on your own."

"Yeah. But not Dearing. Not Mcleansboro."

My hand around the phone receiver shook. "Why not?"

"It's too close. Almost the same as home."

"But that's why I like them."

"Maybe Marion, or Mt. Vernon," he said slowly. "At least we've got some time to work this out."

"I thought you wouldn't mind living closer. We were looking at houses."

"Maybe this is why we didn't find one. It just ain't right for me."

It was a moment before I could answer. "Why, Frank?"

"I gotta make it on my own."

"But you've been doing that for years!"

"Not the way most folks'd see it."

"Who cares?" I blurted. "We don't have to pay attention to what other people think."

He was quiet. Too long.

"Frank? I'm trying to understand, really I am."

"I guess this isn't such a great thing to discuss over the telephone. I'm sorry."

My heart thundered, hoping he'd see. "You don't have to apologize. But why wouldn't you feel like you were on your own around here? You do your own work and make money at it. Everybody knows that."

He sighed. "I know what you're sayin', Sarah Jean. And maybe that oughta be good enough. But I need to stand on my own faith, my own effort, clear away from relyin' on help."

"Your family and mine have relied on you every bit as much as you've relied on them," I tried to explain. "That's what families do."

"I know." He sounded frustrated. "But you know I'm

looked at different. I need you to pray for me. Maybe I got nothin' to prove to nobody but myself. When it comes down to it, I guess all I need is the Lord's guidance. He knows the best place for us to get a start."

"Then that's what I'll pray, all right? For him to show you what would be the best place."

"All right."

My stomach tensed a little. Surely that meant I'd have to be open to the result of my prayer. God could send Frank to Kalamazoo, or to some island like he did Robert. But surely he wouldn't. God would know that wasn't right for us. He could give Frank peace about being close to home. He could open Frank's eyes to the way other people saw him—as a strong and capable young man worthy of the same respect as anyone else.

There was no shame in making a home close to where we grew up. No shame at all, even if we were neighbors to family. Frank was a hard worker. How could anyone think he wouldn't be standing on his own two feet?

We got off the phone, and I prayed right away for Frank to have peace in his heart. Maybe it was harder than I realized to be a young man thinking about providing for a family and making a decent home.

Dad fed the big dog as soon as we got back but still left it in the barn. He said it was looking better just to have regular food and seemed content to be in out of the wind. He'd asked the neighbors and several people in the service station if they had any idea who the dog might belong to, but nobody had any notion where it had come from.

I guessed we'd gotten ourselves another farm dog, whether he'd prove useful or not. Nobody really called him ours, but I supposed it would be official the day Dad let him have the run of the place. I'd gone and looked in on him a couple of times, and he did look better. We certainly wouldn't have to worry about coons or any other critters if he stayed around. He had a face that would scare off anything.

Kirk and Bert came over that evening because they knew we'd planned to talk to Frank that day. "Did he say anything about the job offer?" Kirk wanted to know.

"He's decided not to take it," I told him but was quickly dismayed at the reaction I received.

Kirk nodded his head knowingly. "What'd I tell you?" he asked his little brother Bert. "Way too far away. No way he'd take that kind of chance. Not without Sam in the same town. If he does any more job-looking up there—you wait and see—it'll be in Jacksonville and not Camp Point."

Bert nodded too, and I was incensed at both of them. "What makes you say that? The building's not right for what Frank needs in a store! And he wants to own it outright instead of renting like Mr. Pratt wanted. He didn't decide against it because of the distance!"

The very thing that still troubled me about the whole matter was what these two apparently didn't see. I wished Frank *had* turned it down because of the distance.

"Sure, there may be other reasons," Kirk acknowledged with a strange smile. "But Frank knows it wouldn't work to set himself off away from everybody, at least until he's got you with him. No way he could've accepted a job like that yet."

I could've screamed at him. How dare he hold such an attitude! I'd just gotten finished trying to assure Frank that nobody we knew could be thinking like that. And here were his own brothers. I'd been telling myself that such shortsighted opinions of Frank had died with his father. But Frank had known better.

"He could've taken that job if he'd wanted to," I insisted. "And he'd have done well at it! He's honest, with common sense and experience! What makes you think he wouldn't do fine away from home?"

Bert put his hand on my shoulder. "Kirk don't mean to upset you, Sarah. But you gotta admit he's talkin' realistic. We don't mean nothing bad. But you know how Frank is. A good worker, but it wouldn't take long for him to run into problems without somebody to help him with paperwork and such. And what if he gets carried away thinkin' deep and don't notice his customers? You know what I'm talkin' about. We all love him, but every one of us has seen him at those times. Lizbeth says there's no reason to think Frank can't be a success, but that's so long as he's around folks that understand."

I just stared. Lizbeth? She'd always been so wonderful toward Frank, far better than the brothers sometimes. If any of them, especially a sister, were to express doubts about Frank's ability, I would've expected it to be Rorey, who scarcely ever had a good attitude about anyone anyway. But Lizbeth? Never. I was stunned. And almost as much by Bert. He respected Frank so much. Looked up to him. I'd thought.

I turned away from them. This was exactly what Frank had been talking about! His own family didn't think he was able to make a go of things alone, and he was thinking he had to prove them wrong. No wonder he'd gone to find out about that job.

My eyes filled with tears. Life could be so simple without other people's foolish ideas. If they just believed in him the way they should, maybe he'd be content to stay close to home where I wanted to be. They were driving him away, and they didn't even see it!

"I think you're blind," I spat at both of them, squelching the tears before I turned around. "Frank was the one who held things together during the war. He kept up your farm and helped us too, even with his business on top of that! He's helped my father at the service station when they were full with repairs. The neighbors call on him when they need a hand. Even the pastor, when he had to be gone, asked Frank to step in and speak for him that Sunday—"

"He was pert' near a wreck then," Kirk put in with a laugh. "Awful nervous."

"Of course he was!" I snapped. "Wouldn't you be? The important thing is, he did it! He did a fine job! Everybody said so. And you couldn't have done it. Neither of you! You've got no right to talk like he can't handle what he faces, no matter where he is."

"We're sorry," Bert said quickly. "Never meant to upset you."

Kirk didn't say anything at all. I looked at Mom, who was across the room frying cabbage, and I wondered if this was exactly what she'd meant about letting Frank be his own man.

I prayed differently now. For God to touch Frank's family to see him the way they should. And for Frank to have the confidence and strength to make the decisions he should despite their thoughts.

But when I was alone that night, I started wondering even about myself. I really liked to read to Frank. I liked to help him with paperwork and things. And I could remember coming upon him more than once when he'd seemed so consumed in faraway thinking that he didn't notice my presence, even when I spoke. Could I be a little like Kirk and Bert, in hoping he'd stay close to home? I'd been practically frantic for him when he was on the road. Would I have been so worried if it was my brother or my dad making the same trip?

It was hard to think like that, hard to confront the doubts in my own head. It made me think again of the question Rorey'd asked in her letter: *"Can you imagine reading orders and everything else for him for the rest of your life? He'll be dependent on you or your parents, Sarah. Is that what you want?"*

I'd thought I wouldn't mind a bit because of how much I loved him. I'd thought that doing things for Frank would make me feel all the more needed and we'd be a team. But was I selling him short too, even thinking in such a way? It wasn't what he wanted, to be dependent on anybody at all. Even me.

Father, help. You have the answer, and I promised to trust you. No matter what, I will. But I promised to trust Frank too. And I do. I try. So is it being realistic to think of his limitations, like Bert says? Or is it just unfair?

12

Frank

In the four days since I'd gotten to Sam's house, we'd made a lot of progress getting things moved. Mr. Pratt wasn't happy with Sam or me, but there wasn't anything to be done about it. Sam had to do what was best for his family, and I did too, even if I only had me and Sarah to think about for now. I knew neither of us would really be happy running Mr. Pratt's store. We'd be better off picking the place that was really right for us from the start. I had some definite ideas, and I took to praying about it.

I need a bigger workshop, Lord. Even a bigger storefront if possible, and a back or side door big enough to load or unload all kinds of things. And a nice house right next door, that would be ideal. With plenty of yard, and even a garage.

It was Monday, and Sam was starting his new job tomorrow. We'd be spending the night for the first time in the new house. The kids were all excited, running every which way, especially up and down the stairs, which I wasn't keen on because I hadn't had time to fix them a rail yet. Thelma finally corralled the whole troop and got them settled down to read or color pictures while she finished supper.

Albert seemed more nervous than the other kids about being in the new place. I wondered how much he'd been able to figure out about what was happening. The move itself was surely clear enough, but not the reason for it. I wondered if he knew about the deaf school, or if he'd understand where Georgie and Rosemary'd be going when they started at their new school next week.

I let him sit on my lap while he drew Crayola pictures. He liked to draw people. Babies without legs. Boys and men with blue pants and really big ears. And all the girls with long curls like Rosemary's. If a picture didn't suit him, he'd scribble over it in black and start another one. I thought he was mighty good for his age and a lot tougher critic of his own work than he oughta be.

Dorothy and Pearl were coloring too, but Georgie was whittling off to himself and Rosemary had settled down with a little book her teacher had given her before Christmas. I watched her for a while the way I used to watch Bert or Emmie read at home. She laid her bookmark across the page and lowered it a little every time she got to the end of a line. Mrs. Wortham had suggested that to me once, to help me keep from losing my place on the page or getting overwhelmed by such a jumble of words. It hadn't helped much because my eyes didn't seem to know what to do with a whole line, especially if there were more lines above it.

There must be something I could do to read a book on my own someday. I pictured myself with my nose buried in a thin book like Rosemary's. I could imagine even harder books, like the ones by Charles Dickens that Sarah had read to me recently. They'd looked impossible with all that small print and so many lines jumblin' together. But if I was to cut a piece of paper with a window in it to block off everything but one line on the page, and then add a strip of paper to slide over and show only one word at a time, maybe that would work for me. I could break down a long word into syllables if I had to. It'd be like turnin' a whole page of print into a pile of Mrs. Wortham's word cards. And then it wouldn't seem so bad. Tedious, maybe. But not impossible.

I oughta try it. On a kid's book first, even though I'd rather jump into reading the Bible or a newspaper if I could. I smiled to think of myself with a newspaper tucked under my arm or a Bible on a nightstand, and the good feeling inside that must come from having actually read it on your own.

But suddenly I felt somebody's hand nudging against my shoulder.

"Franky?"

I turned my head. Sam stood looking at me with a funny expression. Albert was gone off my lap. Rosemary was gone too.

"Franky, it's time to eat. Where've you been? Thelma called twice, and even Albert responds to hand motions."

"Just thinkin'," I answered him, a little disgusted that he prob'ly thought he'd caught me in one of those "spells" people talked about. My brothers all seemed to think I just blanked out sometimes, or had my head in the clouds like Pa used to say.

"You all right?" Sam asked me as I stood up.

"Of course I'm all right."

"What're you thinkin' about?"

I didn't wanna tell him. I figured he'd find it pathetic. Or funny. "Nothing much."

"Lot a' concentration for nothing much."

I ignored him and went to the table. Thelma was serving roast beef, and she was mighty proud of the way it came out with her new oven. She was pleased as punch with this new house, I could tell. But I knew I needed to be spending the time while Sam was gone to work tomorrow getting that stair rail built. Too many little kids runnin' around here to put it off. I told them I thought the little ones oughta sleep downstairs for safety until I got that done. Thelma agreed with me, and since the kids all wanted to be by me, we ended up camping in the living room that night.

Next morning I woke up before light thinking again about reading. In one of my toolboxes I had some stiff paper that I used for patterns, so I got a piece, put a light on in the kitchen, and cut myself a rectangle with a window and a smaller piece to move back and forth. The house was quiet. I picked up the book Rosemary'd been looking at yesterday, wondering if I was bein' a dreamy fool thinking I'd ever really read.

I just picked a page—wouldn't matter where I started—and covered all but one line. It looked like a crazy string of letters, so I hid all but one word and started in.

It was easier than I expected, one isolated word at a time. Reading a whole book this way'd take forever, but at least I seemed to be making progress. But when I lifted the paper to look at the line I'd read, the letters almost got lost in the jumble again. Why should this be so hard? I could hardly count the lines on the page 'cause they ran together so bad. I might have kept working at it, but sudden footsteps jarred my thinking. I slammed the book shut.

Sam was standing in the doorway, looking at me with a peculiar smile. He'd seen what I was doing, no question about it. "You still keep tryin', huh?"

"Yeah. I guess."

"Makin' any progress?" He walked to the cupboard and found a tin of coffee.

"A little."

"Really? Any good stories in that book?"

"Didn't get very far." I stood up, not wanting to talk any more about it.

"Want some coffee?"

"In a while." I put Rosemary's book away for now so I could think about the business of the day.

Sam was ready to get me started on his new house. Before he went to work that morning he showed me where the lumberyard was. I picked out all the wood I'd need, hauled it back to Sam's, and started building the stair railing. I'd never worked on such a project with kids climbin' over everything, but I let them be as long as they left the nails and tools alone. Nine-year-old Georgie wanted to help, and I tried to show him how he could, but he really only wanted to pound nails, so I cut some scrap pieces for him, showed him how they fit together, and marked where the nails should go. He'd have himself a little stool when he got done, if he'd been paying attention.

Pretty soon Albert got in his way, and Georgie got upset. Looked like Albert wanted to try his hand too. At his age, I would've. And I figured six was old enough to start, so I set him up with scrap pieces and nails to make a stool of his own.

Thelma got mad at me when Albert hit his thumb. She said I had no business givin' him a hammer and nails when he was so little and couldn't hear me tell what to do.

"He don't need told," I tried to explain. "He was watchin' Georgie, and I pointed it all out."

She put a cold cloth on Albert's thumb and tried to get him to color again. But he wouldn't sit still till he got that hammer back in his hand and set back to work.

"That's the spirit, kid," I told him. Thelma glared at me, but she let it be.

The longest part of making that railing would be carving the individual balusters. Sam and Thelma wanted

102

them nice, so I got a basic rail in place with temporary support first so the kids'd have something between them and the stair edge, and then I set to work carving. Sam wasn't particular on the design. "Something with leaves, maybe," he'd told me. I thought about making each baluster look like it had a leafy vine around it, but I didn't want to spend that much time, so I decided on a simple leaf design at the tops. As it was, it'd take me better'n a week to get them all carved, and we still had at least another load a' things to haul from the house in Camp Point. I thought maybe if the weather was nice, I'd take the truck tomorrow and load up the rest by myself.

When Sam got home he was pleased with my progress but sober about something too. Soon as we had a minute alone, he sat himself down and looked at me kind of hard.

"Who's Mary Ensley?"

I was so startled I didn't know what to think. "How'd you know about her? Don't think I mentioned her name."

Sam crossed his arms and looked disgusted. "Franklin Drew, it ain't right for you even to be thinkin' on no other girl."

"She's only 'bout Georgie's age," I explained quick. "Remember the family that had a wreck? Mary Ensley's the blind daughter I told you about."

He pulled a piece of mail out of his pocket. "How could a little blind girl write you a letter?"

"Maybe her mama helped her with it. Or her teacher."

"So why's she writin' to you?" Sam pressed even after I'd gotten the letter into my hand.

"I don't know."

I hoped it was printed in big letters and I'd have some chance of deciphering at least part of it myself. But it was written in the flowing cursive of an adult, the very hardest script for me. It all looked like curling vines with leaves every which way. "Guess you'll find out why she wrote," I told Sam. "If you wanna read it to me."

He did, and right away. But the letter wasn't what either of us could have expected, and it left me not knowing what to say. Mr. Ensley had passed away from complications with his heart. Mary was thanking me for helping them, and asking me to pray for her and her mother. Sam noticed immediately that at the end of the letter she called me "Reverend."

"She thinks you're a preacher?" he protested. "Did you tell her that?"

"No."

Seemed to bother Sam that I'd left that impression, but I didn't know why they'd thought the way they did. Bothered me a lot worse to think a' that little girl's father dyin'. Mr. Ensley's shaky hands and pale face were plain in my mind. Didn't seem right that he could be gone when his daughter still needed him so bad. I prayed like she asked me to, but it was heavy on my heart that she'd said she didn't know nobody else to ask prayer from. Her teacher'd helped with the letter; she oughta know someone. But maybe not. I wished I knew a preacher in their area to send 'em to.

Sam asked me what the Worthams might a' thought of me gettin' that letter. I didn't know if they'd recognize the name or not, but it wouldn't a' been no big deal to them. I was just glad they'd forwarded it on so I'd know to pray.

Thelma sat with me after supper and wrote what I wanted in a return letter to Mary and her mother. Sympathy for their loss. Explanation that I was a wood carver, not a preacher. And a promise to continue prayin' for them anyway, as any believer should. At first I thought that was enough, but then I had Thelma add the twenty-third psalm at the end, because I figured it might be some comfort.

The next day was clear and sunny. Sam left for his second day at his new job, and Thelma was busy as always with her kids. I took the truck back to Camp Point for the rest of their things. It was a nice drive. I'd spent so much time with Sam's kids and all their lively noise that the time alone in my truck was a welcome change.

I was thinking about Sarah, wishing she was with me. Maybe when we were together again, I could have her work with me on spelling words and word cards like we used to do when we were younger. Surely I could get to reading at least a little better, even if I was still slow. Part of me scoffed inside, because I'd worked so hard at it and accomplished so little over the years. But there had to be a way.

My thoughts turned from there to Mr. Pratt's store. Sarah'd been so relieved for me to turn it down. I prayed again that she'd be able to understand that I needed to be somewhere besides Dearing or Mcleansboro. I hated that there could be a rift between us over anything at all, and this issue might not be an easy one to resolve.

Then I thought of the Scripture in Ephesians: "Husbands, love your wives even as Christ loved the church and gave himself for it."

Considering that made my heart heavy. Sarah loved her folks. She wanted to stay close to home. How could I take that from her, no matter what I felt? If I loved her enough, I oughta be able to live where she wanted to, make a living, and find a way to be happy, even with my brothers and all looking on. Even if they was to whisper behind my back that I was there 'cause I couldn't a' made it anywhere else.

I tried to quit thinking like that. Sarah was right that it didn't matter what anybody thought. All I was responsible for was to do my best at pleasing the Lord and loving my soon-to-be wife. I tried to picture a nice shop on the outskirts of Dearing, with a house beside it and a tree with a swing in it for the kids we might have someday. It was an all-right picture. We could be happy anywhere. But there was a strange emptiness to it that I didn't understand.

But then I thought of another Scripture, this one from Proverbs. "In all thy ways acknowledge him, and he shall direct thy path." That was what was missing. I couldn't plan this on my own, because surely God already had a plan for us. Maybe he already had a place in mind.

Where do you want us to settle, Lord? I don't have a lot of time left to figure this out. I should prob'ly be knowing already, to put Sarah's heart at ease. But I don't know what's best the way you do. Show me, Lord. Direct my path.

I got to the town of Clayton, where I'd dropped off the soldier on my first time through, and decided to stop at the little café on the main street where he'd wanted to buy me a cup of coffee. A bit a' coffee would taste good right now, and there wasn't any to be had at Sam and Thelma's old house anymore.

It was a comfortable café, but I didn't stay long 'cause I was feeling an urgency to get Sam and Thelma's moving done. Somehow heaviness settled on me the rest of the way to Camp Point. Felt like I oughta get away from here as soon as I could to start searching for a home somewhere else. But at the same time I hesitated, with no idea why. *Lord, help me. I want your leading. Your will.*

Driving into Camp Point this time was strange. It hadn't oughta have seemed so familiar so soon. I pulled into the drive at Sam's old house and went right to work, trying to keep from thinking too much about where we oughta settle and what I oughta do with myself after this.

Thelma's sewing table was the first thing to load, along with a pair of bedside tables. I packed boxes under and around them and then set a few more boxes on top of the

first ones, almost filling the back of my truck. I had to tie
the ottoman and a couple of extra chairs on top. I set a
box with glass things in the front seat and then checked
the house over to make sure I'd gotten everything.

I was upstairs when somebody pounded at the door,
but they didn't wait for me to open to them. I could hear
them inside before I got all the way downstairs.

"Yoo-hoo!" a woman's voice was calling.

"I'm right here. Can I help you with something?"

It was a portly neighbor I'd only seen once before. She
seemed disappointed that Sam and Thelma weren't with
me. "Do you think they'd mind if I look around?" she
asked. "We just found out that my niece Charlotte and her
family's going to be looking for a house down here."

"They wouldn't mind. They's wantin' a buyer."

"You wasn't makin' plans for the place yourself
then?"

I wondered if Sam had mentioned that notion around.
"No, ma'am. I got no such plans."

"All right." She nodded, and then went traipsing all
over the house, looking everywhere it's possible to look.
Even under sinks and on closet shelves. She found two
toys and an old glove, and I threw them in one of the
boxes. We'd been thorough enough that there was nothing left in the whole house after that. Made for a strange
feel, when it'd been so full before.

"Are you the brother that's good with wood?" she suddenly asked.

"Folks say I do all right."

"I got something I want you to see. My husband's at
home, and he'd be thrilled if you could fix it. Been in
his family for years."

She motioned me to follow her next door, but I hesitated.

"Come on. We won't bite. We just wanna know if
Grandma's china hutch can be restored."

I followed. Surely wouldn't hurt to offer an opinion. And that hutch was the prettiest I'd ever seen. Old. With beautiful wood and hand-carved cupboard doors that must've taken a lot of hours and some real inspiration. But one door was cracked, missing a handle, and chipped at one corner.

"We want it to look good as it did new and original. Can it be done?"

"Yeah. But it ain't simple. Have to replace the whole cupboard door and that means matchin' the wood and duplicatin' the fancy detail work."

"Could you do it?" the husband asked.

I almost told him no. Didn't make sense to add a extra job when I was hoping to leave soon as I got done with Sam and Thelma's house. They could find another wood-worker. But despite all logic, I didn't feel like turning 'em down. I ran my hand over the fine workmanship and caught myself wanting to see if I could copy the beautiful designs, though that didn't make sense at all. I had enough to think about.

"What do you say?" the man prodded me. "Our daughter's getting married, and I'd love to pass this on to her completely restored. We can pay you well."

I almost managed to say no, but when I turned and saw them both looking at me, I went ahead and made an agreement. They were excited. It was an heirloom worth a lot of money, and they were willing to pay me well for my work. But what would Sarah think about a delay?

Surely it wouldn't take long, I reasoned with myself. And I could use a little money coming in while I did Sam's work. He wasn't paying me nothing but board.

The lady wrote down Sam's new address to give to her niece, and then I took the damaged hutch door with me back to my truck. The loading had gone quickly. I was ready to go back. But instead of starting the truck, I just sat for a minute thinking everything through. Sam might have a buyer for his house now. I could have told the lady no, that I was interested in the place myself. But because I didn't, it might sell to that niece of hers. I'd closed one door on myself, and then opened another by agreeing to linger long enough to fix the hutch. I guess I wasn't sorry for either thing, but I did wonder at myself a little.

Strangely, I wasn't sure I felt like going back to Jacksonville with the load yet. But what was there to stick around for? I heard a train whistle and pictured a big old engine and its string of cars cutting through the middle of Railroad Park with the businesses all standing at attention on either side. Maybe the windowpanes in Mr. Pratt's building would rattle when the train whistle blew again. And I would never know what it might feel like to watch the train go by from inside that old store.

I wanted to see the place again, I didn't know why. I didn't want Mr. Pratt for a landlord over me, nor Sam thinking he had to help me get a business off the ground. Whatever I decided to do, I needed to do it without either of them trying to run things for me. But instead of starting off east for Jacksonville, I drove up slow to Camp Point's business district, wondering why I would even want to.

There were some nice old buildings. The bank. The dry goods. The big grand building called the Bailey Opera House.

What am I wanting, Lord? What are you *wanting? What am I hanging around here for?*

I parked in front of Pratt's store. It wasn't the right place for me. There was no yard beside it where I could work outside in good weather and stack wood when I needed to. The door in back wasn't big enough to be able to load and unload very easily. They must have squeezed every one of those stoves in the front, and it would have been a tight fit.

109

With a sigh, I started the truck again, but I still didn't feel like heading back. Instead I drove to the entrance of that big park at the north end of town. I stopped as close as I could, thinking about the pond Sam had told me about. I couldn't drive to it because nobody'd done any shoveling here, but I got out and started walking. Maybe being in a park with the winter-barren trees swaying would remind me of the timber back home. I'd always liked to walk there and pray. Maybe that's what I needed now.

I found the big boulder and a shelter house but kept walking, not content with that. In a circle of trees I found the pond. It wasn't very big and it was frozen, with a dusting of snow over the ice. I wished I'd brought a stool, so I could sit and look out over the quiet for a while.

What should I do, Lord? I don't wanna cause Sarah no heartache, but I'm not ready to go back home. No time soon. I want something new. Something I'll have to face up to, just you and me. Is there something wrong with me about that?

The wind picked up, and again I missed havin' Sarah's scarf with me. I lifted my coat collar to thwart the wind and realized that I'd left my hat and gloves in the truck. Sarah'd shake her head at me. She'd think I needed her here to remind me of things like that. And she'd be right.

Despite the cold breeze, I stood looking out over that frozen little pond. Though I was more than two hundred miles from the timber where my folks were buried, I thought of them and it almost felt like I was there again. In a way, it would be sad to live far away from those graves. But it could be a good thing too. I'd felt such heaviness there sometimes, like I was carryin' extra weight.

I thought I'd have the same heaviness in Mr. Pratt's store or in Sam and Thelma's house. Maybe it was just because they knew so much about me. I liked workin' with strangers 'cause they weren't as likely to see me as different and think I needed their help or sympathy. Sam loved me. He was always good to me. But he treated me like an oddity. Maybe he still believed what Willy used to say, that my head don't run in the same direction as other folks.

Back home I could tell how much my customers had heard about my peculiar thinking or trouble in school by how much hovering they did over their order and how careful they were to repeat things two or three times to make sure I got everything. Some of the people that knew me best treated me the most like a kid, that's what it was. And I didn't want it to bother me. I'd tried not to let it, but I'd grown to resent it anyway.

Father in heaven, help me forgive if there's need a' that. I don't wanna be bothered by nobody.

I thought I should get going, but no one had said any particular time they were expecting me back. So I lingered on, picturing Sarah Jean standing beside me with her hand in mine. She'd like this spot in the spring, even though it might not be so quiet if neighborhood boys come running through.

I walked back to the boulder and leaned against it. Wasn't no surprise that kids'd like to climb such a big old stone. If I was a kid, I'd have tried it. The thing stood most of my height and more than five times my width. I would a' liked to have seen the effort it musta took to get it here.

Smiling a little at my foolish excursion, I turned to walk back to the truck. I oughta be carving the rest a' those pieces for the stair rail and get that job finished. And now I had another job waiting. Sarah wouldn't care for me obligating myself even that much here.

I took to wonderin' what it'd be like if she was with me. Maybe we'd go see if the Bailey Opera House had real opera, or find something else we could do together that we never done before. But it was crazy thinkin' like that. I wanted a change, but she'd only want to go home. How were we gonna reconcile such opposite feelings?

On my way back through town in the truck, I tried to pray some more. But I hadn't gone two blocks when I noticed an old gent in his driveway, struggling under the hood of his car. I stopped to help him 'cause he looked so bent and tired that I wasn't sure he'd manage very well on his own.

"What's your name, young fella?" he asked when I'd got started checking things under the hood for him.

"Frank Hammond."

"Frank. Fine name. I knew a preacher once by that name."

Don't know why I felt like talking to him, but I did. Maybe just for the diversion. "I mighta been named for Benjamin Franklin," I told him without any reason at all. "One of my sisters told me that."

"Would've been a fine choice. Did your folks like history?"

"I don't really know, sir."

"Do you?"

"Well, yeah. Dependin' on the sort."

He looked a little puzzled. "What sort, then?"

I hesitated a little, knowing from experience that if I answered that question honest I'd be entering an area where at least some folks'd find me peculiar. But I took a breath and forged ahead, figuring I'd never see this old man again anyway, so it wouldn't matter. "I'm partial to the history of Bible lands," I told him. "And European history where it leads to understanding of the events of the modern day."

He stared for a moment. "I've met up with a scholar."

I laughed. "No, sir. I'm just a farm boy."

112

"From what farm? If you were local, I'm sure I'd have seen your face around here before."

"I'm not local. 'Bout 230 miles from home. I'm just up here to help my brother with some things."

He glanced at the load on my truck. "But you took the time to stop and help me?"

I didn't wanna tell him that he'd looked like he sorely needed it. Maybe that would bother him, even though he was really old. "I figured it was the thing to do."

He nodded and smiled a little. "Are you are a Christian man, then?"

"Yes, sir."

"A true servant of the Lord is a servant to his people." He seemed to be quoting from something. I wasn't sure his source.

"Yes, sir," I agreed. "Like it says in the fifth chapter of Galatians to serve one another."

Didn't take me long to find out that the trouble he was having was in the points. I got my tools to grind them out for him, and then his car seemed to be running all right. But he was in no hurry to leave for wherever he'd been going. "Have you been to the Bible lands?" he wanted to know.

"Oh no," I answered with surprise. "I never been outta the country. But I've enjoyed learnin' such things from books. The history adds a little to the understanding a' Scriptures sometimes, just to be able to picture the way things was at the times the words were written."

"Have you studied the subject extensively then?" he was asking with real interest.

"No, sir," I answered quick, feeling suddenly ashamed. "Not near so much as I'd like to." Had it been dishonest to mention books to this man? He'd surely think I meant that I'd read them myself. Listening to Sarah reading to me was surely not what he'd call "studying."

I wiped my hands on my old coat for want of a grease rag. Once again, I'd forgotten to put on my gloves.

"A pleasure to meet a Bible scholar and historian," the old man said. "Would you like a cup of tea for your trouble?"

"No, sir, I've got to get going. Got to drive to Jacksonville by this evening."

"Do you speak?" he asked abruptly. "At churches?"

"Well . . ." I stammered, flabbergasted at the question. "I did one time, but—"

"How long will you be in the area?"

"Don't know," I said, still feeling shook, he'd surprised me so much. "Another week. Maybe more."

"We would love to have you visit our church. I'll write the directions for you. If you're needed in Jacksonville tonight, you'll surely miss our midweek service, but if you're free on Sunday, we'd love to have you." He pulled a pad of paper and a short pencil from an inner pocket and started scribbling the address.

I just watched in silence. Had it been my imagination, or had this complete stranger almost asked me to preach?

He handed me the paper, and I shoved it in a pocket without even looking at it. He offered me his hand. "A pleasure to meet a young man of God."

"Pleasure to meet a godly elder." I tried to return the compliment with a steady handshake.

We parted ways then, me heading out of town, and him driving only so far as a local bank. I wondered at that encounter something immense, and the oddest thing about it was the stirring inside at what he'd called me. "Young man of God." I really wanted to be that. I wanted to go and visit his church. I even wanted to get up and share a word or two. And then I thought I was crazy for it. What in the world was I thinking?

114

13

Sarah

I'd written to Frank more than once already, and I was very glad to get a letter from him, in Thelma's hand, telling me what they'd been doing. It made me smile that he'd had Thelma repeat three times that he missed me.

But the same day I got a third letter from Donald Mueller. I threw it away unread like the last one and began to hope there would be another community function soon and Frank would be home to take me for everyone to see. Maybe then Donald would give up his foolishness.

I thought a lot about the things Frank had told me in our last conversation, about his need to make a life somewhere else. I still wished I could get his family to think differently, or Frank to not care. But he had to be his own man, as Mom had said, and I had promised the Lord that I'd trust him. I prayed for the trusting to get easier, but as the time neared for our next appointed phone call, I felt just as anxious as before. Surely Frank would tell me he was almost ready to come home. Deciding where we'd go from here would be so much easier face to face.

I rode with Dad to the service station, and when it came time for the call, Frank sounded different. He didn't talk about moving this time. He told me he was hoping Sam and Thelma would start going to church. And there was a church he wanted to visit back over in Camp Point; I'm not sure why. He was working on his reading again, making what he hoped was progress, and I told him I was proud of him for that.

"I wish you were here." The sudden sadness in his voice stopped me to silence. "Sarah Jean," he went on, "I wanna share every minute with you. It don't seem right to have to miss each other right now, but I guess there's some things I gotta work out, me and the Lord."

A strange feeling came over me when he said those words. "Like what?"

"Like what I'm s'posed to be doin' next. Pray for me, Sarah. I have a funny notion the Lord's gonna surprise us."

"I can't wait till you get home," I answered. But the words sounded empty, and the strange feeling only got worse for the rest of our conversation. I was practically shaking when I hung up the telephone receiver.

"What's wrong, Sarah?" Dad asked right away.

"Nothing." I tried to smile. "Just missing Frank, that's all."

But that wasn't all, and I shouldn't have lied. I couldn't get Frank's words out of my head. *Pray for me. The Lord's gonna surprise us.*

Where would we go from here? What would Frank choose to do? He wasn't asking for my input, only my prayers as he worked things out between himself and the Lord. But it was my life too. How did other women handle such uncertainty? My brother's wife hadn't complained when he announced that he was called to the mission field.

116

And I didn't remember my mother questioning Dad about our move to Illinois. Why was I the only one so selfish?

"Perfect submission, all is at rest . . ." The words to that hymn entered my mind unbidden. And for a moment it just didn't seem right. How could submission be fair? Why couldn't I just make the decisions I wanted to make and have what I wanted?

But I caught myself quickly. Jesus had said to his Father, "Not my will, but thine be done." If *he* yielded his own will, who was I to think I ought to hang on to mine? Frank wasn't seeking his own heart but God's in the matter. So it all came down to whether or not I was really willing to keep my promise.

We'd said nothing about Frank's birthday, only days away now, except to agree on another telephone call then. By that time, Sam and Thelma might already have a telephone installed at their house. I'd mailed Frank the embroidered handkerchiefs and a card two days ago. But I decided to write him another letter too.

Sitting at the service station desk, I almost started the letter in my usual cursive hand but then changed my mind and started to print, neatly and carefully, in case Frank wanted to try to read the letter for himself. Kirk would probably have laughed at his efforts. Rorey too. But I really was proud he would keep trying.

I was in the middle of the letter when Donald Mueller drove up to the gasoline pumps, much to my dismay. He had a fine-looking car and a proud smile when he saw me inside. He started into the station immediately and left Dad outside pumping his gas.

When he came bursting in, he was grinning ear to ear. "Sarah Wortham, how's life treating you? Are you still engaged?"

I had no patience for his stupid intrusion. "Of course I am! And that is the rudest question I have heard in a long time."

117

He just laughed. "Understandable, don't you think? You're the prettiest girl in Dearing, and the smartest too. Wish I knew what you want with Franky Hammond."

"I want to marry him, that's what," I snapped. "Go away. And stop sending me letters. I don't read them. You're wasting paper."

He acted as though he didn't hear me. "Ain't there no way to make you stop and wonder if you've made the right decision? What would it take to get you to give me a chance?"

How dare he? I wanted to throw something at him, but I didn't. "My father's waiting for you to pay for your gas."

"Let him wait. He hasn't washed the windshield." He smiled a huge crooked grin. "What are you so riled at? You oughta be pleased that I still think you're pretty, even if you do act like you hate to see me."

I took a breath, trying to calm the fire in me. "You haven't said a decent word since you came in here. Worse than that, you have no right to ask for my attention when you know I'm engaged."

Dad was starting toward us. I was glad.

"But isn't Franky still out of town?" Donald asked quick while he had the chance. "I thought you might think things through a little. Are you sure you're gonna have what you want outta life with him? Let me talk to you some more. Will you just consider going to lunch—"

"Go away! You're an absolute dunderhead!"

He laughed again. "Even your angry words are cute."

Dad walked inside then, thank goodness. His voice was quick and somber. "Donald. That'll be $2.67."

"Uh," he struggled finding words in front of my father. "Plus a Coca-Cola. I came in to find a soda and warm up a little."

Dad got him his soda pop without a word, and Donald

paid and left without daring to address me again. But Dad must have seen how agitated I was. Maybe my cheeks had flamed red like they did sometimes.

"What'd he do, pumpkin?" Dad asked when he was gone. "Put Frank down?"

"Yes. But worse! He asked me out. I could have thrown something at him."

"I'll be more careful next time you're here. If he shows up, I can keep him outside with me."

He got us both a soda pop and came to the desk to write down the sale. He was quiet, but I wasn't ready to be quiet yet.

"It's so unfair. People talk about Frank like he's impaired or something. I could just scream! But it's not just Donald. Some of Frank's own family—they talk like they don't expect much out of him, when I know better. What's wrong with people?"

Dad sat beside me and sighed. "Lack of understanding, Sarah. That's all. And Frank *is* a puzzle sometimes. I don't always understand him myself."

"But you don't put him down! They're just being dunces."

Daddy smiled a little. "It probably won't help to say so to anyone's face. Or call them dunderheads either."

"You heard that?"

"At least that part. And his reply. Maybe I should've thrown him out on his ear."

❧

I was relieved to go home that day. Mom would be pleased to hear that Frank was working on his reading. I expected that she would be full of questions about our phone conversation. But when I went in the house, she had news of her own.

Rorey'd sent a letter announcing that she was getting

married to Eugene Turrey. And they'd set the date for just three days before our wedding.

"What is she thinking?" I asked Mom, trying to stay calm. "Doesn't she know how much trouble Eugene has been? He's never respected her family, or even her all that much. And why so close to our wedding date? Did she do that on purpose?"

"You never know about Rorey," Mom said with a shake of her head. "We can ask when they get here. They're coming for a visit. Sometime next week, I guess."

I groaned. Rorey used to be fun, when we were really little. But Rorey grown up was a whole other story. And Eugene had been an aggravation for as long as I'd known him. They both seemed like spoiled, obnoxious children who wanted to focus everybody's attention on themselves. Rorey could be downright hateful. And Eugene was as bad as Donald Mueller. He used to torment Frank something fierce, and he'd tried to ask me out on dates when we were younger too. Thank goodness I never went.

It didn't seem to bother Dad about Rorey marrying Eugene, or them coming here. He just went out to do chores as usual and said I might as well stay in where it was warm. When he came back to the house he told us the big dog had disappeared out of the barn stall, and the news was a disappointment on a day like this. If Eugene Turrey or Donald Mueller were to show up, such a big ugly beast would have been nice to have around.

14

Frank

Sam reluctantly agreed to go to church on Sunday as long as it wasn't far, so we attended the closest Jacksonville church we'd seen. Thelma served us chicken dinner afterward. But I couldn't keep my mind off that Camp Point church. Why would the man want me to come? The church wasn't really in town, just close to it. I'd had Thelma read the address for me, which included directions along a road called the Cannonball. Sam said that was the one going straight north, past Bailey Park. The man had written the service times too, and they had a Sunday evening service.

I decided I'd go. Just for a little visit. Just to quench my curiosity. But Sam was not happy about it.

"Are you crazy? Driving to Camp Point tonight after dark? Come on, Frank. I thought you had good sense."

"You're the one that asked me to drive all the way up here," I reminded. "You must have been confident I could do that. And the road to Camp Point's familiar now."

"The Cannonball isn't. And it's over fifty miles to get there, Frank. After dark, for no reason."

"Church is a reason. And I've drove in the dark before. At least it ain't snowin'."

He shook his head and called me stubborn. And I left without supper so I'd have plenty of time. I didn't mean to get him upset. I wasn't sure why I felt so compelled. But I did. I wanted to see that old man one more time and find out what Central Bible Church was like.

Thinking about it while I drove down the road, I guessed it must have seemed like a pretty crazy thing to do. I'd already been to church today, and to a nice one that was convenient to my brother's house. There wasn't a shred of logic to going fifty miles tonight. But I wasn't about to turn back.

"In all thy ways acknowledge him, and he shall direct thy path."

There was that Scripture from Proverbs again, jumping in my head. And then I thought of another one. "A man's heart deviseth his way; but the Lord directeth his steps."

That was Proverbs too. Chapter 16.

"Do that, please, Lord," I prayed. "Direct my steps."

It wasn't hard to find the road I needed once I got to Camp Point, but finding the church was a good deal harder because I had to turn down a side road and it was nigh impossible to be sure which one to take in the dark. I finally asked at a farmhouse for directions. That got me there, and I was still early enough that there was only one other car parked outside. I recognized it immediately. The old man. He was already here. I almost jumped from the truck and run in, but I stopped.

Maybe he liked to be early. Maybe he liked to have a little time for prayer in the church alone. Some folks did. I'd done it myself before. So I waited until somebody else showed up.

They trickled in slow. And I waited, feeling something

almost prickly inside. I had to pray before going in. Finally I got up my courage and stepped from the truck.

Several heads turned when I came in. The old man was up front, and he smiled real big when he saw me.

"Young brother Franklin," he said, walking over and offering me his hand. "What was the last name again?"

"Hammond."

"Oh yes. Welcome."

He wasn't the preacher, he said, but he was preaching tonight. Once the singing was done he did a fine job. But toward the end he suddenly stopped and asked me if I had anything to say.

They were folks I didn't think I'd see again. Couldn't hurt nothin' to share a little of what was on my heart. So I stood up where I'd been sitting in the back row.

"I been blessed," I began a little nervously. "Can't tell you words that's enough for how good God is to me. When I was little I used to think people'd make fun a' me all my life and I'd never amount to nothin'. But God's took hold in so many ways."

I looked around a little. All eyes were on me, but I wasn't nervous anymore. "He's given me gifts in my hands to earn a living. He's given me the prettiest woman you ever could see to love me and soon become my wife. Even so far from home I find him dealin' with my heart and directin' my steps. All the way to this church. I'm glad I come, 'cause I believe he wanted me to. That's really all I got to say right now, just to express my thankfulness."

I sat back down and the whole church was quiet. But not for long. Pretty soon a elderly lady got up and expressed her thankfulness, too, for the health she had, and for caring neighbors and friends. After her was a tired-looking mother with five little ones around her. And then more of the folks. Don't think that church knew there was gonna be a bunch of gratitude expressed that night as part of the service, but it was a good thing, and I was glad I was there. Afterward, before I could get in my truck, the old man asked where I was headed for the night.

"Back to my brother's. In Jacksonville."

"Quite a drive for so late."

"I know. An' if I don't get goin', he'll be up wonderin' if I've wrecked my truck or got myself lost."

"It's nice to have folks who care."

I smiled. "Thanks for puttin' it that way. I feel a little too watched over sometimes."

He almost laughed but changed the subject immediately. "Are you a war veteran? I hope you don't mind me wondering—a young man with a limp."

"No, sir. But I would a' liked to gone."

"Ah." He nodded. "The limp was older than the war."

"Yes, sir," I answered, thinking that an odd way to put it, and strange for him to think he needed to know.

"I appreciated the church service," I told him. "You had good words."

"So did you. It's been a very long time since we had such sharing. Thank you."

I didn't see any special reason I oughta be thanked, but I didn't argue.

"Would you come back and share a message next Sunday night?"

I should've known he might ask, even though there was no reason he should. "I'm not a ordained minister," I told him plainly.

"I understand. And it's all right. The church won't mind a lay minister as guest."

He was persistent for some reason, thinking I oughta speak. I hardly knew what to tell him. "Uh—I'm not really a minister at all. An' I don't know if I'll still be in the area next weekend."

He didn't seem to hear the first half of what I said. "Well, let me know, will you? If you haven't gone, we'd love to have you come and share from the Word."

He handed me a piece of paper again. This one I presumed would have a telephone number or his address.

"Uh—I've got to pray about this."

"Very good." He smiled at me. "That's a smart response."

I drove away, not sure what to think. I'd felt so absolutely directed to come here tonight. But now this? I'd been a nervous fool speaking at my own church. How much worse would it be here? I kept hashing the notion over in my mind, all the way home, so much that I didn't even notice going through some of the small towns on my way back to Jacksonville.

Sam was put out when I got back because it was late and he'd stayed up to watch for me even though he had to get up early.

"You coulda gone to bed," I told him. "I made it fine."

"It's not so simple as that," he complained. "You're a little brother, and I needed to stay up till I knew for sure. I hope you never decide to do that again."

Maybe that was my answer. What good would it do to drive all the way over there and rile Sam? I wasn't a minister. Why did people keep gettin' such a notion? They needed to find a real preacher, and I needed to keep my mind on my work where it belonged.

15

Sarah

Sunday night I dreamed that Frank and I were walking in the snow and Donald dropped out of a tree and took my arm. Frank didn't even notice as we continued along, until Donald had me turned down a side path to his elderly aunt Mabel's beautiful home, right on the main street of Dearing.

I woke up sweating. Frank had been preaching in the dream. That was the only response he gave over me walking off with Donald. He'd just turned his head and started preaching. I wasn't even sure to whom.

I felt sick about that dream all morning. Why would my mind play such cruel tricks? I wouldn't walk anywhere with Donald. And Frank wouldn't fail to notice. It was all completely preposterous.

I'd almost put it out of my mind when Mom sent me to check the mail because Katie was back to work. Waiting in the box was another letter from Donald. I wished I could twist it to bits and leave it lying in the dirty slush alongside the road. I wished I could kick Donald Mueller in both shins and make him leave me alone. But as I held that letter in my hand on the way to the house, strange feelings, strange thoughts rose up in me like I'd never known before.

What could it hurt just to open the letter and read it? I'd thrown the others away. To be fair, shouldn't I read just one?

No. It was senseless temptation. Foolishness.

But maybe Frank wouldn't care. He won't know. And even if he did find out, he wouldn't think it was any big deal.

I scrunched the envelope in my hands. How could I be thinking such thoughts? I had absolutely no reason to read the letter. No obligation. I didn't have to be fair to Donald. He wasn't being fair to me or to Frank trying to push himself in this way.

He has a job right in Dearing, my thoughts persisted. *And his aunt's house has been up for sale for three months. He could get it easily.*

My eyes filled with tears, and I started to run. I couldn't hold this letter another minute, but I couldn't just drop it on the ground either. What if it blew around until a neighbor picked it up and read it? What if they thought I'd invited Donald's attention? Why would I even think of reading it or let it enter my head where Donald might choose to settle?

"I'm sorry," I whispered as my feet flew across our snowy yard. "Oh, God, forgive me."

I was sure such thoughts meant that I had an unfaithful heart. A wicked, treacherous heart that would allow me to entertain notions about Donald just because he was likely to stay in Dearing. I bounded onto the porch and flew inside, horrified at myself. I had to get rid of the letter. I had to. Instantly. Because if I held it in my hand much longer I might open it, I might actually read it. *Oh, God, forgive me!*

I ran straight to the kitchen woodstove, flung open the

fire door, and shoved the crumpled envelope inside, almost losing my mitten in the process. And then I slammed the door shut and gulped down a big breath, feeling better already. What on earth was wrong with me? It was like I'd just been loosed from an encounter with the devil himself. I was scared to get such a glimpse of myself.

"Sarah, what in the world is the matter?"

I hadn't even noticed my mother sitting at the table.

"Uh . . . Mom, I . . ." What could I say? My hands were shaking. Out of breath, I just plopped into a chair.

"What was that letter?"

I had to tell her. To do otherwise would be to feed the doubt, the temptation, that had so horribly thrust itself upon me, real or not. "It was from Donald Mueller. I—I didn't open it."

"Donald Mueller? Why would he be writing? You don't think you should've found out?"

Oh, my innocent mother. "No. This was the fourth time. I opened the first one, because that was the only one with no return address. And it was an invitation—an invitation to a dance."

"When was that?"

"The letter came the day Frank left." My eyes filled with tears. "Then three more. But I can't open them. I don't want to read them."

Mom got up from her chair and moved toward me. "Why didn't you say anything?"

I felt numb suddenly in the pit of my stomach. Why? Could it be that some faithless part of me had wanted to keep the secret? "I—I don't know. It was too embarrassing to talk about. He—he knows I'm engaged. I didn't want anybody to see the letters."

Mom leaned and gave me a hug. "Under the circumstances, you're right to throw them away. But there's no reason to be so upset, is there? If you continue to ignore him, he'll surely get the message."

I didn't answer, and she looked carefully into my eyes. "Why is this bothering you so much, honey? Has he done something to frighten you?"

"N-no. I mean, I don't know why he's doing this. I just wish he'd stop."

"Tell your father. And Frank. A clear message from either of them ought to be enough to put an end to things." She hugged me again. "All right?"

I nodded, my heart thundering crazily. How could I tell Frank? Would he doubt me?

"If you get another letter, I want to see it," Mom said then, and I saw the rare flush of anger in her features. She was rightly appalled at Donald's advances. What would she think if she knew my thoughts today?

I worked alone all I could after lunch. I cried. I asked God to forgive me, maybe fifty or sixty more times, for not only my thoughts about the letter but also my dream. What did it mean? When I thought I was trying to bolster my trust in the Lord and in Frank, was my heart looking for a way out and trying to lead me astray?

Mom told Dad about the letters when he got home. And he was bothered enough to offer to go over to the Muellers right away and warn Donald to leave me alone. But I didn't want to make trouble for my father. I didn't want to create a scene. So I told him not to go. It was all right. Maybe the letters would stop. If not, I could just keep throwing them away. Donald's efforts were pathetic and useless.

Dad smiled about that, but he didn't promise not to do anything. We ate quietly and I wondered if Dad was thinking about Donald showing up at the service station. I wondered if he'd told Mom about that, or if he questioned in his mind why I hadn't mentioned the letters to him then. I didn't really know why, except what I'd told Mom, that it was just too embarrassing.

Katie had nothing to say about all that, and I appreciated her efforts to lead the conversation into more pleasant subjects. But that didn't stop me from fretting about it still. Frank would have a Scripture to quote if he were here. Something completely applicable to the situation. But the only Scripture I could come up with was a passage in Jeremiah that Robert had brought up once in Sunday school: "The heart is deceitful and desperately wicked and who can know it?"

I tried to remember what our Sunday school teacher had said about that. Something comforting, surely. But I couldn't recall, and I was far from comforted. Would I be able to talk to Frank about this? If I didn't and he learned it from someone else, what would he think of me?

He couldn't be indifferent the way he'd seemed in the dream. That was nothing but my imagination running away. He might be angry at Donald. But surely he would be sympathetic and comforting to me because I hadn't turned away from him. I hadn't even considered that. Had I? It was only the devil's temptation, playing tricks with my mind because Frank was so far away.

I needed him here. I needed his gentle words, his reassuring touch. Then the gloom and doubt would be washed away in an instant, and everything would feel right again. I didn't have such struggles when we were together.

Come home, Frank, I willed in my mind. *Please hurry and finish whatever it is you're still doing and come home.*

16

Frank

I spent Monday and Tuesday working on Sam's house, carvin' on stair posts and fixing two different sticking closet doors. Thelma wanted to know if I could make her some new kitchen cupboards because the ones they had were far too small. I measured and planned and went back to the lumberyard for the wood I needed. After careful scrutiny I even found a piece of walnut that would work for fixing that china hutch for the folks next to Sam's old house.

I worked at the hutch door that night and all the next day, fetching three-hundred-grain sandpaper and emery cloth from the local hardware, putting on the original aged hinges, and carefully matching the stain. It felt good to set the finished door up away from the kids to take back to Camp Point in the morning.

"Beautiful work," Sam told me. "But it ain't practical to be running that far after a small job."

"A favor," I explained. "For your old neighbors."

"Same as strangers to you." He shook his head. "Oh

well. If you wanna spend your pay on the gas to drive over there, it's up to you."

I didn't have any choice now. The next day, Thursday already, I was glad to be on the road to take the hutch door home. It was wearing on me that I hadn't given that little church an answer. Wasn't right not to tell them anything. I should've said no to the man right away. Now I knew I'd still be up this way over the weekend because I wasn't done with everything, but driving the distance just wasn't practical, like Sam had said. He'd be sore at me all over again if I did the same thing this Sunday. I hadn't even mentioned it to him, nor pulled out that second slip of paper 'cause I didn't wanna hear what he'd have to say. But today I'd be in Camp Point anyway. So this was a fine opportunity to find the old man and politely turn him down.

Sam's old neighbors were happy with my work. They paid me and sat me down to a cup of coffee and an apple Danish. But my satisfied feeling left just as quick as I remembered what I had to do next. I wasn't looking forward to telling the old gentleman no, but it had to be done. I'd been praying on it through the week like I'd told him I would, but without any answers.

Pulling the slip of paper out of my pocket, I wondered how to ask these folks what it said without them knowing I couldn't read. I hadn't wanted to ask Thelma because I wanted to leave her and Sam out of it. And I'd tried to figure out the three lines myself, but it was no good with the handwritten script.

I took a deep breath and reached the paper across the table to the kindly couple. "Can you tell me how to find this place?"

They didn't direct me like I'd expected, down Ohio to the driveway where I'd met the old man. Instead, the address was for the bank on the main business street where he'd been going that first day. Maybe he worked there. Or owned the place.

Good thing I was from out of town, or those folks would a' wondered at me having trouble with an address so simple as that. I went to the bank feeling nervous and asked the first teller where I might find the man I was looking for. He'd told me his name was Willings. She knew right away who that was and took me to a side room. The old man stood up as soon as he saw me.

"Franklin Hammond, I've been wondering about you."

With my hat in hand I stepped forward, trying to settle the right words in my mind before I said them. "Sir—uh, I'm not a preacher, like I told you. I'm just a farm boy."

"I'm one of those myself." He smiled. "Good many people around here are."

"What I mean is, I don't feel qualified. It don't seem right. And I'm staying clear over to Jacksonville right now. I should have given you my answer right away."

"Yes?"

He'd have understood. I could tell that. But just when I was ready to say what I'd planned on, that I just wouldn't be able to do it, something come over me and I couldn't get the words out.

"Yes?" he said again.

And durned if I didn't tell him that if he still wanted me I'd try and do my best just this once. He was pleased. And I felt like I'd dug a hole and proceeded to fall into it. What in the world was the matter with me?

I wanna do it, I found myself telling my own heart. *Just this once.*

I left that bank thinkin' I must've gone plum crazy. Sam would think so. No doubt about that. Maybe Sarah would too.

❧

When I got home an' told Sam I was goin' back to that church, he looked at me like I'd lost every bit a' sense I might ever've had.

"I'm gonna speak," I explained. "Got asked last week, but I hadn't really decided till today."

"Franky, what if it's snowing? You can't predict that."

"I'll go early if it looks like it'll get bad. An' I'll get a room for the night so you don't have to wait up wonderin'."

He shook his head. "You're full a' surprises. What're you gonna come up with next?"

"I didn't know I was gonna come up with this."

He plopped down in his favorite chair and stared up at me. "Since you seem to already have a church over there, maybe you oughta reconsider Uncle Milty's store and our house. Maybe it's a sign that you should stay."

"I don't know about that." My mind whirled thinking about his words. Would Sarah think this meant I was wanting to stay?

"I'll take payments on the house," Sam explained again. "You won't never have to worry about paperwork for a bank loan. And Uncle Milty understands. He'd work with you on that property, an' I'd help."

"I don't wanna do things that way."

"Why not?"

I woulda thought he'd understand, but he didn't. I'd have to spell it out. "Cause you're trying to make it easy for me."

"That don't make sense, Frank! That's what brothers are for."

"You ain't this way with all your brothers. You didn't ask Harry up here. Or Kirk. Or Bert."

"They ain't suited to the store. You know that. And besides, they wouldn't be as much help with my house. Them stairs look like a rich man's now."

"I'm glad you like 'em," I grouched. "But it don't change how I feel."

Sam frowned at me. "I was hopin' you'd want our house. I need a buyer."

"I know. But what about the neighbor's niece?"

"Far as I know, they're still interested. But I was kinda waitin' on you—"

"Go ahead an' sell it to 'em. You need the money more'n I need to owe you."

That was pretty much the end of what we had to say to each other. I got myself to bed early that night, but I lay awake a long time thinking about Sarah. Would it upset her about me preaching over there? I didn't think so. Maybe she'd understand me just wantin' to help that church once like I'd been asked.

As I was laying in the dark, my mind started circling through Scriptures about trust. That'd be my topic Sunday night, I was pretty sure. Relying on God, not man. A message as much for me as anybody else.

✿

The next day was my birthday. Thelma made a cake and Sam's kids give me a whole batch of homemade cards and pictures. Sarah'd sent a package that they'd hid back till the time. I was excited to talk to her again, but when the time came for our telephone call and I told her I was gonna be speakin' at that church she cried. She said she wasn't unhappy, or even surprised. So I wasn't sure I understood the reason for the crying then, but she couldn't explain.

"Don't you worry," I assured her. "I'm not gonna buy nothin' up here nor settle anyplace without talking to you first. I wanna do for *you*. Not just myself."

"I love you, Frank," she said real quiet. "Happy birthday."

I felt like kissing her. I wanted to. It seemed like awful long since we'd been together, and I wanted real bad to hold her again. "I love you too."

I had the feeling that there was something else she wanted to say. But maybe I was wrong, 'cause she didn't get to it even when I asked her. I knew we oughta get off Sam's telephone line, but it was hard. I missed her more right then than I had any time. But it wouldn't be long before I could go home. I was done with the stair rail and the closet doors. I'd fixed an attic step and a piece of broken woodwork below the window in Georgie and Albert's room. Once I was done with Thelma's cupboards, I could leave.

"Next week," I told Sarah. "Maybe Tuesday I'll head out. I'd say Monday, but I better spend some time tomorrow preparing for that church. I might not get the cupboards done till Monday. Wish you were here to read me some Scriptures."

"Frank, you remember Scriptures faster than I can look them up."

"I still like to hear it fresh."

"You'll do fine. Maybe Thelma can help."

"Maybe. But I still wish you were here."

We said good-bye soon after that, and I thought of the long drive to get home. Despite the snow and the miles, I was looking forward to it for the chance to be with Sarah again. Seemed like I was missing her even in my dreams.

17

Sarah

Frank was going to preach! Just like our pastor had predicted. Even if it was just once to fill in like he'd done for our home church, I knew it was the beginning. Surely he had the calling. Thoughts of my silly dream tried to present themselves to my mind, but I shoved them away. He was coming home!

I was thrilled but at the same time trying not to be scared. He might be called anywhere to preach now. There was no telling. And I—I might be looked at as a minister's wife! Me! With all my foolish foibles. Could I really handle this? Now I understood why our pastor had felt the need to ask me.

What if Frank really becomes a full-fledged minister? People expect things of a minister's wife. It would be so easy to fall flat on my face!

Despite my uneasy feelings, I was determined to accept whatever Frank chose to do. That would be my "perfect submission," and I was overjoyed it wouldn't involve a move to Camp Point. Maybe we'd live in Mt. Vernon or

Marion like he'd suggested. Maybe he'd eventually pastor a church.

He'd be home next week, and I felt like dancing around the house. Until the mail came again. There were just two letters, but both of them made my stomach sour. One was from Donald Mueller again. I just gave it to Mom without a word. The other was addressed to Frank, and it was the second letter he'd gotten like this. Mary Ensley. A girl from one of the families Frank had helped. He hadn't said a word about the contents of her first letter. Now why was she writing to him again?

I showed the envelope to Mom, and she said we might as well hold it since it might not get to Jacksonville by the time Frank left if we sent it on now. I wished I could open it, though I knew those feelings were wrong.

Don't be a goof, I told myself. *Mary Ensley must be the blind girl Frank told me about. She's probably just thanking him for the help.*

But that could've been in the first letter. What need for a second one?

I felt miserably guilty over those simple thoughts. It was scary to realize that just as I could entertain unfaithful thoughts, I could harbor jealousy and mistrust toward Frank. There was no reason for it. None at all, and I felt like a fool. Yet the feeling persisted. *Frank's attention, his love, is not all centered on me. Even if it is done innocently as he ministers, he will be giving his heart in other directions. How will I live with that?*

I tried singing "Blessed Assurance" again, to take the words to heart:

"Perfect submission, all is at rest. I in my Savior am happy and blest, watching and waiting, looking above, filled with his goodness, lost in his love . . ."

Somehow, instead of inspiring me, the lyrics made me lonely. Especially the line "watching and waiting." Why couldn't I dwell on the "lost in his love" part? Why would I be having such selfish worries? I wanted my life to be the Lord's as much as Frank did, didn't I?

Mom said Donald's letter was short and arrogant, claiming I wouldn't know what I was missing if I didn't meet him in town "just to talk." I'm sure she and Dad wondered about me that night. I should have been over-flowing with joy and excitement that Frank was coming home. Why wasn't I? What had changed? Nothing in me, I hoped. And yet I knew that Frank wouldn't be the same. The distance, and especially ministering to needs, would have worked something in him that I hadn't been with him to share. He was preaching now. Receiving let-ters from people in need that I didn't even know. I felt like he'd traveled hundreds of miles in his walk with the Lord and left me far behind. Would he see it that way? Would he know my shortcomings?

"This is my story, this is my song. Praising my Savior all the day long . . ."

I tried to sing. I tried to rejoice, but the worry roamed free inside me, and I couldn't chase it away. *He doesn't want to need me, or anybody. What will that mean?*

Saturday, Emmie Grace came over and worked with Mom, Katie, and me baking bread for the coming week for both our houses. Mom was humming almost the entire time, and so was Emmie.

"I knew it," Emmie told me as the dough was rising. "I knew Frank was going to be a preacher too."

"He was careful to tell me that he's just filling in," I cautioned. "Just a guest for one Sunday evening."

"It's a start." Emmie smiled. "You know there must be a reason they asked him."

Unlike her brothers, Emma Grace had boundless confi-dence in Frank. After all, he'd held her hand and comforted her through so many hard times when she was little. In a way, Frank was more like her father than their father had been, even though they were only eight years apart.

"We should make him a cake when he gets home," she suggested. "It can be a party."

I knew Frank wouldn't want any big deal made over him, but a cake among family was a nice idea. I readily agreed, and we decided to bake it on Tuesday, so it would be ready Tuesday night or Wednesday, whenever he got in.

The next morning at church I asked for prayer for Frank because he would be speaking that night. Our pastor was very pleased.

"I wish I could be there," he said.

"So do I," I told him, but I was glad it would only be one time up there. Then maybe he'd do more speaking around here where Emma Grace and I and all the rest could attend. I could hardly wait till he was home.

When evening came and I knew it'd be time for Frank's service, I couldn't stop thinking about him preaching. It had gone so well the time he'd done it at our church. Surely this time would go well too. I wasn't worried for him. Just a little for myself. I'd once heard our pastor's wife tell my mother that people look at a minister's family differently. Expectations are higher. They automatically think you to be holier than average folk, though the notion is ridiculous when you think about it. We're all just people, prone to mistakes. No getting around that.

I went outside with Dad when he was milking. He looked older than he used to, with a touch of gray at the temples. I couldn't help asking him the question on my heart. "Dad, will it be strange when Katie and I are moved out?"

"Very strange," he answered solemnly. "It already is with Robert gone. But hopefully you'll visit often, and we'll visit you too. It's just part of life."

He was filling water troughs when I left the barn to check the chickens and make sure they had feed and water for the night. They were fine in their roost, all but the one Mom called "Silly Hen," who liked to perch on the windowsill or a ceiling rafter.

It didn't take me long to get done in there. Stepping from the chicken house, I started to sing a hymn again. The moon picked its way from behind a cloud. Suddenly from out of nowhere, giant paws were all over me. I almost screamed, but then I realized what this was.

"Big dog?" I shoved hard. "Get down."

He obeyed me, but not before slathering his tongue in a sloppy dog kiss across my cheek.

"Dad! Guess who's back!"

The big dog bounded around me twice and then ran to meet Dad as he came out of the barn. Dad stood stock still at first, and then greeted the big critter with a friendly pat. "Well, Horse. You're looking good."

He was. And happy too. He was thrilled to see us, and even happier when we got him some food. "Horse?" I asked Dad.

"Sure. People used to ask me if I'd ever get a horse. And he's so big. It just seemed to fit."

"So is he ours?"

"I guess. If he wants to be."

Mom came out to greet the dog, glad to see him looking so well. Katie wasn't as happy. She stood in the doorway, but she didn't come near. I understood how she felt, at least a little. But I was glad to see the big animal back. And he was just in time.

The next day a strange car pulled into our drive and the dog let us know in no uncertain terms. It turned out to be Rorey with Eugene Turrey. They'd come like they promised. But Horse didn't think they belonged. He barked and growled awful, especially at Eugene, until Mom managed to call him off. I couldn't help being a little surprised because the dog had always been so gentle for us.

I think Eugene smelled of liquor, and the dog didn't

like it any better than I did. If Mom realized, she didn't
say anything, but sat them down at the kitchen table
for a cup of hot cocoa. Rorey was wearing a dress that
she shouldn't even have tried squeezing her bosom into.
She talked on and on about St. Louis and how great
the city was and how much they loved their apartment
and Eugene's job and such. And I found it all very hard
to listen to. They were already sharing an apartment;
they had been for a long time, without even stopping to
consider that a shame.

I knew the Scriptures said not to judge. But it also said
to be separate and not live like the ungodly of the world.
Rorey didn't care. She'd never cared what the Bible had
to say. She used to tease Frank over quoting it when we
were kids and would get downright mean about it. So I
shouldn't have been surprised when she reacted with a
scoff when Mom told her Frank had preached in Camp
Point last night. It wasn't big enough news to warrant
more than a moment of her attention. She started talking right away about some friend of Eugene's who was
part of a honky-tonk band.

And then out of the blue she told us she wanted to
have her wedding right in our yard, because it would be
beautiful in June with all the greenery and flowers. She
wasn't even asking, just informing us, like it was something we should have thought of ourselves. Mom didn't
promise anything. She only said she'd talk to Dad about
it when he got home from work. But in *our* yard? Three
days before my wedding? It almost seemed like she was
purposely trying to be difficult. I was glad Frank and I
were planning to be married in the church. At least she
wouldn't be disrupting the preparations there.

She talked on and on about the band-member's girlfriend, whom she planned to invite as a bridesmaid,
and another new friend that worked in the butcher shop
below their apartment. And then suddenly they were

ready to leave again, to go visit Eugene's family and some of his friends in town.

"Have you stopped to see any of your brothers and sisters?" Mom asked Rorey before they got out the door.

She shook her head. "I figured you'd probably want to have them all for dinner tomorrow, since we're here. We can see them then." And they scurried to the car. Mom had to yell at the dog again to get him to leave Eugene alone.

I stood on the porch for a minute watching them drive off, scarcely able to believe Rorey's crassness. How could she have gotten so ill-mannered and disrespectful? My mother and father had done so much for the Hammond kids, and the rest acknowledged and honored them in their own ways. But Rorey seemed to think she could walk in here and use them for whatever was convenient to her.

Mom turned her attention back to the laundry, not letting Rorey's appearance interrupt any more of her day. But I thought of Frank, due to be on his way home tomorrow. I was almost ashamed to think it, but I hoped Rorey and Eugene would be gone by the time he got here. They both liked ridiculing him, pushing for a reaction. Mom hadn't told them he'd be back, and I was glad.

I prayed for no problems or delays on Frank's return trip, and for peace when he got here. There were so many things to think about. Not just Rorey and Eugene, or Kirk and Bert and their attitude. There was also Donald Mueller. How would Frank react to that? Did I even need to tell him? I hadn't been able to bring myself to when we'd talked on the phone on his birthday. I hadn't wanted it wearing on him as he prepared his sermon.

I wished I could get rid of the feeling that everything had changed. I wanted the world the way it used to be when we'd had nothing but farm chores and a few wood orders to think about, and then settling down in the evenings with Mom's reading or Dad's stories. But we weren't kids anymore. Frank had moved on. My parents, and these farms, were not the center of his life anymore. For better or for worse. And I wasn't sure what that would mean.

18

Frank

I woke up Monday morning anxious to get back to Jacksonville so I could get my work done and get home to see Sarah. I'd paid for a room for the night in Camp Point even though I prob'ly could have stayed with one of the church folks. I didn't want to impose on any of them, but one sweet old lady'd asked me to stop by before I left town so she could give me a pie. I'd protested, but she said she liked to bake pies for folks and I'd cheat her out of a blessing if I didn't let her.

So I got dressed, reciting in my head the directions she'd told me. She lived on the west side of town, a couple blocks up from the train depot. I prayed for her and her church, not expecting that I'd ever be back there. Then I prayed for Sam and his family. None of us would be seeing them again till the wedding.

The sun was shining bright. Would have been a perfect day if it wasn't so cold again. I went whistling out to the truck, carrying my old suitcase. One more day finishing up Thelma's kitchen cupboards. And then I'd be driving again. Maybe if I got done quick enough, I could leave tonight.

The sweet old lady's name was Hannah Haywood. It wasn't hard to find her house, small and neat with empty planter boxes lining the porch. I imagined she had them filled with flowers in the spring and summer, and maybe her whole yard too.

But as I stepped out of the truck and closed the door, I turned my eyes for just a moment to the house across the street. Two story, white, with a nice garage and a really big yard. Another building stood in the lot next to it. A business building, but obviously empty, it had two big windows up front and a double side door prob'ly wider than my truck. There was a sign out front. My gut churned a little as I struggled to focus on the letters in the top line. F-O-R S-A-L-E.

The effort to read that much was exhausting, and I didn't even try to read the words below it. Mrs. Haywood had already stepped out to her porch. She was surely wondering why I was just standing so long staring across the street.

"That would make a fine shop for somebody, wouldn't it?" she said. "It's bigger inside than it looks. The back room is big too."

I turned and stared at her, not even able to answer.

"Hope you like gooseberry pie. I had so many berries canned. A neighbor has a bush, but she wasn't using any. Said I could have all I wanted. Would you like to come in out of the cold for a cup of coffee?"

I nodded my head, but she kept right on talking.

"I enjoyed what you said last night. Hope you enjoy the pie. Those berries might be some of my last, you know. They're moving before long, and I suppose that'll be the end of the gooseberries for me. Don't think I'll put in a bush of my own. Never had to, so long as I've been here. The lady who lived there before them shared with me too."

146

She opened her door wide and motioned me forward. I went, but I wasn't sure how to respond to all of her talk. The shop was for sale. A neighbor's house too? I should get myself out of here. I shouldn't linger even long enough for that cup of coffee, lest my thoughts get to turning in strange directions.

But I went ahead after the woman because I'd told her I would, and when I stepped up on her porch, I turned my head to look at that building one more time. It could be perfect. If the back room really was big enough for my workshop, it was just what I'd been looking for down in Dearing and Mcleansboro. And there might be a house available right close too.

Oh, Lord, here? Should I get my mind off this quick? Help me. Direct my steps.

Hannah Haywood chatted pleasantly while I drank my coffee, but I doubt I heard most of it. She cut me a piece of her pie, and it was good, but I couldn't keep my mind on that. If I was to inquire about that place, what would Sarah think? Would it be foolish of me to want to see inside?

Finally I told Mrs. Haywood that I really had to be going. I had a long way to drive back to Jacksonville, and quite a bit of work yet to do. She had to remind me that she wanted me to take the rest of the gooseberry pie, and I thanked her again. I would've gone on and driven to Sam's house then, trying not to give that building another thought. But when we got outside, a man was just stepping out of his car and heading toward the two-story house.

"There's my neighbor now," Mrs. Haywood told me. "They say they're moving this spring. I sure am gonna miss 'em." She waved real big at the man, and he waved back, stepping onto their porch.

"Um—Mrs. Haywood, do they own both the house and the commercial building?" I dared ask her.

147

"Yes, they do. Thought they might put a auction place in there, but it never worked out with the job Mr. Bellor got."

I carried the pie to my truck. I set it absently on the seat and thanked her again. And then I turned and looked at that building some more. I should drive away. I really, really oughta drive away, before I gave Sam and Sarah and everybody else cause to wonder at me again. I took a deep breath.

"Mrs. Haywood, do you think your neighbor would mind showin' me the place?"

My heart started pounding. Here I go again, doing just the opposite of what my head was trying to say. Just like that church.

"Well, no," she said immediately with some surprise in her voice. "Of course he wouldn't mind. They're wanting to sell it. They're moving up to Hancock County, closer to family. He's going to work for his father, I think."

I turned and looked at her, feeling tense and hesitant.

"Go on over and ask if you want," she prompted. "He surely won't mind. He's probably back home for a bite of breakfast. He does that sometimes. Leaves real early and works just up town, you know. Next to the Pig Parlor. Go ahead and ask."

"I . . . uh . . . wouldn't want to interrupt a man's breakfast."

"Nonsense." She smiled real big. "His wife Tilda told me how badly they're needing a buyer. They've got their eye on a house near Carthage already, as I understand it. Quite a thought, you and that place! Didn't I hear you're getting married? There's a lot in that house to like."

My heart was still pounding. What was Sarah gonna think? With my insides feeling bunched tighter than a straw bale, I went on across the street, and Mrs. Haywood followed me.

148

Mr. James Bellor didn't at all mind showing me the property, even though it meant he'd have to carry his breakfast back to work with him instead of sitting down with his wife and children. He opened the store and ushered me inside, turning on an electric light that startled me because I hadn't expected it.

"Would make a nice business," he said. "Plenty of show room up here. What kind of work do you do?"

"Wood," I answered. "Furniture and carving."

"Oh, then you'll appreciate the back."

Before we'd spent two minutes in the front of the shop he was heading me toward a double doorway in back. And that room was every bit as big as the front. With shelves and cupboards built in at the walls and a back door as wide as the side door I'd seen. I stood scarcely listening while he told me when the place was built and what it had been used for before.

"I'm not wanting too much for it," he said. "Because the roof needs work. You do that kind of thing?"

"I have. Back home."

"Well, then that won't be a problem. Did you notice the yard? Big, ain't it? Goes clear to the corner."

I nodded. I'd noticed that.

"Previous owner put in town water to the little washroom back here," he said, opening a door to show me. "Are you interested in the house too?"

I swallowed down something in my throat. "Maybe."

"More to look at over there. Wanna go see?"

I went. Feeling shaky, half crazy, or maybe even cruel, I followed as he showed me room after room. Kitchen. Sitting room. Dining room. Two bedrooms upstairs and one down. The place could use a lot of work, I could tell that. But nothing I couldn't do. What would Sarah think? That I'd lied to her about being ready to leave this town? That I was being a fool and not thinking of her feelings?

149

"This place needs roof work too," Mr. Bellor admitted. "I'll have to be honest with you about that. Needs quite a bit, to be real honest. But if you're handy, maybe it ain't a problem. Wanna see the cellar?"

I nodded. Mrs. Haywood had stopped in the kitchen to talk to Tilda Bellor. I could still hear them, goin' on about gooseberries and peonies and hollyhocks and such. There was a nice furnace in the basement, the kind that could be converted for coal oil or wood. Upstairs there was one fireplace. And a new kitchen stove that Mrs. Bellor was quick to point out she wanted to take with her.

I took a deep breath. Indoor plumbing. Electric. Plenty of room for a family, inside and out. They had a big, big yard with nice trees and a wide-open spot in the back. "What are you asking?" I had to know, though I almost hoped the figure he told me would be too high to even consider.

It wasn't. It was actually quite a bit less than I expected, well within the range of what Sarah and I had worked out would be manageable if we needed to get a bank loan.

"Let me think—let me pray on this," I told them. And then I couldn't stay even a minute longer. I had to go, away from those folks, someplace alone. I felt like I could break down like a fool and cry.

I went to that frozen pond in Bailey Park. I sat in a snowbank, not caring if I got wet or cold, leaned back, and stared up at the crystal clear sky.

"What is this, Lord? What am I doing here? What do you want? Is this some stupid accident, me finding that place? Now what do I do? It's got everything I wished for! Is it nothing but temptation?"

I didn't have an answer. I didn't even want to get up out of the snow. But Sam and Thelma would be expecting me, and one way or another I still had that work to finish. So I drove back to Jacksonville with my thoughts tossing every which way. I was supposed to be leaving tomorrow. None of this was making any sense.

Thelma wanted to know how the speaking went at the church. It wasn't easy to turn my thoughts to that enough to even tell her. She must have known I was thinkin' deep on something because instead a' stayin' right there talking to me or lettin' the children climb all around while I worked on the cupboards, she took them upstairs with her and let me work alone.

Sarah had read me a quote in a newspaper once, that the secret of success in life is to be ready for your opportunity when it comes. But was this the opportunity I'd wanted? Should I jump at it the way I was itching to, or was I just being an idiot? I didn't know Camp Point that well. I didn't know if my store had a chance here or not. So many things could happen. What if folks were right and I really couldn't manage on my own?

Poor Sarah. She didn't know what she was getting herself into, marrying up with me. I didn't even know what I was gonna do from one day to the next. We hadn't arranged no other telephone time because I'd thought I'd be leaving. I needed to talk to her, but if I called the Marathon station, she wouldn't be there. Maybe her father would be. Maybe I could arrange a time tomorrow.

I should go call. Right now. Thelma'd let me. But I couldn't quite bring myself to do it. Sarah wanted me to head back tomorrow. I wanted it too. Didn't I?

As soon as I got those cupboards done I took a long walk. Thelma asked when I got back if I was feeling all right.

"Yes," I told her. But I couldn't explain. Not a word of it.

When Sam got home, I packed all my things, ready to leave in the morning. He wanted to play checkers, pop popcorn, and listen to the radio, spending time with the family on my last full night with them. But it was hard to keep my train of thought on what was going on around me. Two or three times, maybe more, somebody spoke to me and I didn't even notice until they got to repeating themselves or come up and touched my arm.

"What's the problem tonight?" Sam finally asked me. "Somethin' on your mind?"

"I need to go back tomorrow."

"We know that," he said with a funny look. "We've all been knowin' that since last week. It's been good to have you. Wish I could keep you longer. But I understand that you wanna go home. I would too if my girl was there."

"No." I shook my head. "You don't understand. I need to go back to Camp Point tomorrow."

"What? Why?" Understandably, he looked confused. "Not that church for some reason? Tomorrow's Tuesday. Surely there ain't no services on a Tuesday."

"No. It's not about the church."

He brightened. "You wanna talk to Uncle Milty again?"

I shook my head. "I appreciate him. I like him all right. But his place just ain't for me, Sam. I couldn't feel right about it."

"Well, then what in blue blazes are you talkin' about?"

I couldn't tell him. I don't know why. I almost did. But then I just couldn't. Maybe he'd step in to try to help me. Maybe he'd tell me the whole thing was stupid. I didn't know. I didn't wanna find out. "I just need to go back there. Just one more time. Just to be sure."

"And what are you tryin' to be sure of?" he asked me with the question big in his eyes.

"I'll go early. Real early. And I'll stop back here before I go on. I promise. And I'll tell you then."

He shrugged. "Guess it wouldn't do me any good to press you for details or tell you not to waste your gas again, huh? You're a genuine puzzle to have around. I sure hope Sarah knows what she's gettin' into."

That was the end of it then because I wouldn't talk no more. Truth was, I wished I could forget it all, and at the same time I was glad I couldn't. I had to talk to Mr. Bellor again. And maybe Mr. Willings at the bank too. He would know a lot more about Camp Point than I'd been able to learn. He would know the businesses, what they had plenty of and what they needed more of. He would know the people too, whether times in this area were treating the folks good enough that they'd be able to consider the kind of extras that I could make. I knew real well that when times are hard, people don't buy furniture, let alone the fancy carved kind.

But I could do a lot of other things. Like the repair of this-and-that around a home. I already knew from experience that making it known I was willing to take on those kind a' jobs'd contribute a lot to making things work, even in lean times. Almost half of WH business over the years had been fixing things for people. Mr. Wortham'd said everybody used to do that kind of thing for themselves, but it wasn't quite that way as much no more. Sometimes folks just liked my touch. Making something old look new, or making something plain look extra special.

Sam didn't talk to me much in the morning. He ate his breakfast and shook his head at me before he left for work. "You'll waste half the day goin' back over there. I hope you're at least gonna call Mr. Wortham when you're ready to head that way so he knows when to expect you."

"I will."

"You oughta tell him you might be staying another night with us. You won't have time to get home today if you don't leave before noon."

"I'll call him when I know what to say," I answered, and left it at that.

I hardly noticed half the miles I covered on my way

back to Camp Point. It did seem foolish. I'd have to fill up with gas again. I sure was wasting a lot with all this back and forth. Mr. Bellor wasn't home. I'd missed his breakfast time, but his wife told me where to find him at his work downtown, and his boss let him have the time to take me through his place again. It was available right now, Bellor said. The shop was standing there empty, and he wouldn't mind if I wanted to get into it and get a start on my business right away. But we'd have to wait with the house until they got moved. Sometime in April was what he expected.

I talked a long time to Mr. Willings. I prayed with him. I went and walked by the pond again and prayed some more. I was so anxious I couldn't hardly see straight, knowing what I wanted to do. But I couldn't do it. Not yet. Because I'd promised Sarah I wouldn't take no big step without talking to her first. So I went back to the bank. Mr. Willings let me use his telephone.

I told Mr. Wortham I wouldn't be able to leave today. I asked him to bring Sarah with him to town tomorrow so I could have another chance to talk to her. It was real important. And then I called Sam and told him I wouldn't be back to Jacksonville either. Mr. Willings had offered to let me stay the night and I was gonna do it. I needed to be right here in Camp Point when I talked to Sarah, and I needed Sam not to be in the middle of it.

Mr. Willings said he'd be pleased to have me move to town. But he couldn't guarantee his bank would provide a loan because someone else was placed over such decisions, and he wouldn't get involved on my behalf. I told him that was how things oughta be. I didn't want no free ride from my brother, and I didn't want it from a new friend who'd asked me to church, neither. If I couldn't satisfy the bank without no special favors, then I didn't belong to be doing this. I'd talk to them tomorrow. Maybe. After I talked to Sarah.

154

I could scarcely sleep at all that night. I didn't wanna make Sarah cry, but I was afraid this was gonna do it for sure. I'd yield to her if she hated the thought of this badly enough, I knew I would. I'd give it up and go home. But I found myself hoping she'd consider, hoping she'd understand the thundering excitement this was working in me like nothing ever before.

This would be all on my own. I could work in this town and get established in the months before the wedding. It might be the only chance I'd ever have to prove to myself that I could make a go of things if I needed to, even before Sarah came to be by my side. It'd be something I'd always know then, and everybody else'd know if they took a look, that I could truly make it with nobody to lean on but God.

I prayed, since I couldn't sleep. I prayed and cried and half thought I was crazy. But I wanted this. So awful bad, I wanted this. Everything I'd found out today just fed the longing in me all the more. This was meant to be. It was right for me. If only Sarah could see it too.

19

Sarah

Tuesday started out a great day. The sun was shining. Perfect travel weather for Frank. I wouldn't have to worry about him being stuck somewhere in a winter storm. Mom and Emma Grace were bustling about, happily baking Frank's cake plus plenty of things for dinner with a houseful of Hammonds, and Eugene. Despite Rorey's rudeness, Mom seemed more than willing to host them, just as Dad was willing to allow them to have their wedding in our front yard.

Katie was working at the five-and-dime and though I sometimes wished I was still working at the Mcleansboro library, on this day I knew I wouldn't have been able to concentrate. Surely Frank had already left. He was on his way home.

I gift-wrapped the book I'd gotten for his birthday and drew out a pattern of the dress shirt I wanted to make him for our wedding. Mom knew I was a little past myself in excitement to see him again. Except for dusting she didn't give me a thing to do.

Bert came over early. He and Emma Grace were both

worried about how their older brothers were going to react to Eugene. It wasn't just him running off with Rorey that bothered them, though that certainly didn't help matters. None of the Hammond boys had gotten along with Turreys since the Hammonds' barn burned several years ago. Eugene's brother Lester, along with Rorey, had been at fault and tried to coward out of it. And even though Lester had died in the war, everybody remembered the huge fight between Willy, Kirk, and Harry and four of the Turrey boys, including Eugene.

But Mom wasn't concerned in the slightest. "If they haven't put it past them by now," she said, "at least they'll behave themselves in our house."

She was surely right. Kirk and Harry wouldn't cause any trouble in my parents' home, and Willy, the worst hothead, wouldn't be around. As for Eugene, hopefully he'd have the sense to be decent, especially since he wouldn't have his brothers along. Still, it would make for an uncomfortable dinner arrangement, except for the buffering presence of my parents.

I didn't expect Frank to call Dad today. I figured he'd just be driving. But when Dad got home from work he sought me out first thing, before chores, the mail, or his cup of coffee. And I saw the concern in his face, like what he had to say might be upsetting.

"Frank called to tell me he hasn't left yet. He wants you to come into the station with me tomorrow so he can talk to you about something important."

The lightness I'd felt all day fled in an instant. Hasn't left yet?

I could think of only two kinds of delay he'd need to talk to me about. He was called to preach and needed to speak at that church for another meeting. Or he'd changed his mind about Sam's house and Mr. Pratt's store.

The rest of the evening I was in such a stew I could

hardly eat, even with everybody there. Of course there were questions at the table about Frank, but I answered them as briefly as I could, or not at all and let Dad answer for me. Everybody could probably tell I was bothered, even though I tried to hide it. And the whole thing seemed to amuse Rorey as soon as she found out that we'd expected him to leave today.

"You don't never know what you're gonna get with Frank," she said. "Not from one minute to the next."

"I wouldn't say that," Mom disagreed quickly. "He's proven himself to be faithful and reliable. No doubt he's occupied with some good work. He'll be back when he can."

I appreciated Mom's assertion, but I wished everyone would stop talking about him. Soon enough they did, but the conversation just got worse.

"We're going bowling with Donald Mueller and his cousin tonight," Eugene spoke up, turning his head to look at me. "He suggested you and Katie might want to come along. What do you say?"

"No possible way," I grouched. I couldn't discuss such a thing. I couldn't even sit there while someone else discussed it, so I just got up and started clearing from the table whatever dishes people weren't using anymore.

"I can take care of that," Mom told me.

"I want to."

"What about you?" Eugene was asking Katie. "You can still come."

Katie wasn't engaged, but she was serious enough about her boyfriend to be fiercely loyal. She made a face and glanced in my direction. "No, thanks. I'm planning to stay home and help Sarah sew on her wedding dress tonight."

We hadn't made such plans in advance, but I appreciated the gesture. Perhaps she'd chosen the words as a stark reminder of my status and the folly of the invitation. But she was true to her word. After cleanup was done and everybody was gone except our family and Emmie, we pulled out the fabric for my wedding dress and went to work. I could tell that Emmie Grace was worried about Frank and hoping we knew more than what we'd shared at dinner. But there was nothing else to tell her, so Mom kept her busy while Katie was keeping me busy, and we got through the evening.

I didn't sleep well that night thinking that our future might be pinned on what Frank had to say tomorrow. I tried to pray about it, but I didn't know how.

Trust. The word kept coming back in my head.

I'd promised to trust. Was I doing that? Or was I failing miserably? *Lord, help me. I want to trust you. And him.*

When the rooster jarred me awake before the morning sun, I lay in the stillness trying to think things through. Maybe the same church or another one had asked him to speak again and he'd felt led to agree. Maybe they wanted revival services, or a longer fill-in during a pastor's absence. I could accept that. I could be proud of Frank in that. But he had no other reason to stay in Camp Point. After what he'd told me about Mr. Pratt's store and his feelings about Sam's offer, I felt certain he wouldn't have changed his mind about those things. That couldn't be it.

I got dressed, peered out the window, and was instantly struck with dismay. Snowing again! How could it be? The weather'd been so much nicer yesterday. For a moment my heart was in flutters, but surely it wouldn't last. Dad would be willing to take me into town despite the snow. He knew Frank would never, ever say something was important unless it truly was. We had to be there for that call.

But Dad was cautious. "Weather's looking iffy, pumpkin," he told me as I came into the kitchen. "If it gets worse we won't be able to go."

I wanted to argue that we had to try, but I knew there was no use to that.

Dad took a sip of his coffee and sighed. "Charlie warned me not to come in to work today. He'd heard it was going to get bad again, but I was hoping he'd be wrong."

"Maybe it'll quit," Mom suggested. "You don't have to leave for another two hours."

But if it didn't quit, a lot of snow could come down in that time. Gloomily I did my part of the chores, praying the snow would stop. With growing exasperation, I could see my chances of getting to town for the phone call slipping away. Frank would understand. He would know that's just the way it is sometimes in winter. But I hated it, nonetheless. We had what looked like six inches more on the ground already, and it showed no sign of stopping.

"I'm sorry," Dad finally told me. "It wouldn't be safe to get the truck out."

Of course he was right. It would be foolhardy to try taking the truck to town in this. The sky was gray-white all over, and the snow was coming down stronger than before. We hadn't seen anybody out with a snowplow yet. We could get stuck on the road or stuck in town. I felt like crying. But I could tell this bothered my father almost as much as it did me.

I gave up. As it came closer to the time when we should be leaving and the snow just kept on, I went back to the work on my wedding dress, resolved to use the time wisely. Dad went out earlier than anyone usually did to check the mail, and suddenly he came bursting back in, hollering.

"Sarah! Sarah, get bundled up! Orville can't wait for long!"

Orville? The mailman? He was on time, and that must mean he was doing the route in his sleigh. Dad must have begged me a ride. He must have begged *us* a ride. It was clear pretty quickly that he was going too.

He had his coat on already but was gathering up blankets to wrap around us.

"Layer up," he told me.

And I smiled. "I love you, Daddy."

"I love you too. Now hurry up."

With coats and boots, double mittens, scarves and hats, and our arms full of blankets, we trudged out to the road to meet Orville Mueller's sleigh. It didn't occur to me that Orville was Donald's cousin until I saw Donald sitting up front in the sleigh with him. I looked at Dad, but he only ushered me on without a word. No wonder he was coming along. There was no way my father would send me off alone with that hooligan and his cousin after what had been happening.

Donald looked at me close, but he didn't say anything. I hoped Dad had told them why we wanted to get to town so badly. I hoped Donald realized that the chance to talk to Frank was well worth any kind of hassle in any kind of weather.

I knew what this meant to my father. We'd be stuck in town till Orville finished his mail route. And since we were interrupting to get him to haul us to the station, finishing would take him longer than usual. That would leave my father responsible for the mail being late to every person after us. He'd even be responsible if Orville's boss got upset. I guess we'd owe him a pretty large favor.

We climbed in the sleigh and bundled the blankets around us. I took Dad's hand. "Thank you," I whispered.

"You and Frank," he whispered back, "you're worth it."

Orville got his horses going to get us into town as quickly as he could. It was cold and the snow just kept up, but thank the Lord, we'd be getting there anyway. Hopefully soon enough. That was the thing that worried me. What if we got all the way there but missed the telephone call? Frank probably wouldn't try repeatedly because if we weren't there the first time, he would expect that the weather kept us from coming to town at all. And we couldn't call him because he hadn't given us a number to use.

Dad had a watch along and he glanced at it from time to time. I knew he was thinking what I was. What if we were too late? We'd have put Orville and ourselves through this trouble for nothing. And yet we had to try. *Come on, faster*, I wanted to urge Orville's horses. But I knew they were doing the best they could.

Why hadn't we been able to get a telephone at home yet like so many people we knew? Of course I knew the answer to that. The company was just slow getting the line out our direction. It was coming. This very summer, maybe even sooner. But that did us no good now.

I got awfully chilled, but Dad made sure I was well bundled to keep the snow and the cold out as best we could. "We'll make it on time," he assured me as the town drew near. "We're doing all right, I think."

But I knew we wouldn't have much time to spare. As soon as the sleigh stopped at the station I jumped out quick without waiting for help. And I slipped on the ice almost right away, but I didn't care. I jumped right back up and ran for the front door. But Dad had to unlock it. Charlie was probably out with his snowplow again. If we hadn't come, Frank wouldn't have found anybody at all.

Donald Mueller hadn't said a single word on the whole ride. That seemed almost miraculous, except that my dad was along. And I think he'd told them what we needed. Donald surely realized by now that I was a closed door to him. I hoped so.

Inside the station I tore off a layer of blanket and mitten, expecting the telephone to ring any second. But Dad informed me we had four whole minutes left. I sat down with a smile. *Thank you, Lord!*

Frank was almost three minutes late. By that time I'd already started pacing in nervous anticipation. When the phone finally rang, I nearly jumped out of my skin.

"Hello?"

"Sarah. I'm glad you could come in again. I hated to trouble you."

He had no idea, but I didn't tell him about the sleigh. "It's all right. I'm always glad to talk to you."

"I have something I need to talk to you about."

"That's what Dad said. What's happened?"

My insides were in knots. Surely he'd tell me about how the preaching went, about being asked back, about feeling the call on his life just like our pastor had predicted. But he said nothing of the kind. Instead he started in about some other store building and a beautiful house next door and how it was all just like he'd pictured it and he could start his business right away if the bank agreed. And if I agreed.

I was speechless. Absolutely bewildered. He'd told me he was ready to leave there. He hadn't wanted even Sam's offer of a house, which would have cost us less than what he was talking about now. Why was he doing this?

"Don't you want to come home?" I asked, and I could hear his deep intake of breath.

"Sarah Jean, I'm tryin' to explain that. Sure I want to, to be with you. But if we decide to do this, it'll have to wait. The owner says I can start up the shop in just a few days so long as the bank's in agreement. I could be in business here and get established before the wedding. And get the house fixed real nice for you ahead a' time. It's beautiful. I think you'll love it, I really do. It's a little like your mom and dad's house, but a touch bigger, and

the yard is big and nice. Plenty a' room for a garden.
And flowers—all the flowers you could want."

"Frank, it's two hundred miles away."

"It's right next door to the shop. Just the kind a' building I need. With another big yard. A real nice storefront.
And you should see the workshop. I'd have room, summer and winter, even if I had four or five projects goin'
at once. I could live in the place until I can get into the
house."

I bowed my head, hiding my eyes newly brimming
with wetness so Dad wouldn't see from across the room.
Frank was talking about not coming home at all. Not
until the wedding. And then? "Oh, Frank. I thought you
were so sure it wasn't right for you up there."

"The other place wasn't."

He wasn't listening to what I'd really meant, and I
couldn't say anything more. Our silence hung in the air.
I'd promised to trust him. Straight out. No specifics or
exceptions. But could I?

"Sarah, I love you," he said real quiet. "I just want you
to consider it, that's all I'm askin'. I don't have to tell 'em
today. I'll give you whatever time you want. And if you
just can't see clear to the idea of makin' a life up here,
then I . . . I can tell 'em no."

I'd never heard his voice like this before. Bold and
excited. Yet timid and uncertain at the same time. He
really wanted this, I could tell.

"What does Sam think?"

"He don't know nothin' about it. And I ain't tellin'
him, Sarah. He'd want to come to the bank with me and
everything, and I'm not havin' it. I gotta do this on my
own. Do you understand?"

He had such a depth of emotion in his voice. It made
me a little afraid. "You wouldn't want me at the bank
then, either, would you?"

He was quiet, but only for a second. "Sarah Jean,

forgive me. I can't do this without talkin' to you. I can't do it without your okay, 'cause it's your life too. But no, I wouldn't want you there. Not right now. I need to do this myself if I can. And if I can't, then I need to find that out now and quit foolin' myself. This is the only time, Sarah, for me to know for sure I won't just be leanin' on you—"

"Franky, you never lean on anybody! Except God! Don't you realize how everybody's leaned on *you*? Your whole family! They never would have made it through the war and losing your folks—not half so well. And me—I'd be a wreck without you! Don't you know that?"

He was quiet, a much longer time. "No. I guess I don't."

I should have jumped in with more assurances, but I couldn't find my tongue, and before I knew it he went on.

"You been readin' for me. And seein' to plenty a' things to help me out. Your mother and Thelma too. Even Bert and the rest. I'm not sure anybody really thinks I can get anywhere without that. And maybe I can't. But I wanna try. If I fall on my face and make a mess a' everything, I could still come home and tell everybody they was right all along. Then maybe I'd pick up WH where I left off and live close by your folks if you'd still have me. I'd do the very best I could for you. Every day a' my life."

"Oh, Frank."

"I love you so much, Sarah. I wanna be better than that for you. Do you understand? I'll always need you. But I want you to be able to lean on me, not the other way around. I wanna work and make something for you that our families don't have to fix for us. I love them too, but if I let them do any a' this for me, I ain't sure I'll feel like I'm worth all a' what you are to me."

My heart was pounding in my throat and I could scarcely breathe. "Frank—you don't have to prove your worth. I love you the way you are. I always have. If that's what this is about—"

"It's about what I think's right for us," he said then, still sounding timid. "If you'll have it. I ain't sure I ever felt like this about nothin' before. Like I've been directed. Like circumstances brought me up here and led my heart 'round till I could find this place. I can picture us here."

When I tried to speak again, my voice sounded quivery. "B-but the closest relatives'll be more than fifty miles away."

"I know. And I think that's what I need. At least for a while."

Again, there was silence between us. I thought of Kirk on the morning Frank left, nudging him, calling him a knucklehead, and telling me he'd be back. I thought of Rorey's awful letter and Bert's words about what was realistic. None of them believed he could do this. He hadn't even told Sam, because Sam wouldn't think he should even try. Not alone. Not the way he wanted it.

Oh, Lord, he really can't read well enough yet! What will happen when they give him papers at the bank? What if they turn him down because he has trouble filling out what they need from him? He'd be absolutely deflated. Why is this so important? Why so far away? What should I tell him?

"I gotta leave it up to you, Sarah," he said then. "It wouldn't be right to do this if you're against it. I want you to be happy."

I closed my eyes against the tears in them. *Oh, Frank. How can you tell me all this and then say it's up to me? How could I deny you for my own comfort's sake?*

Trust. That's what I needed. I didn't want to cry, not in a way that he'd hear me, but I couldn't help it. I tried to stop. I tried to pull the receiver away just a little so he wouldn't hear, but I didn't want to miss a word that he might say to me.

"Sarah? Oh, Sarah, I'm sorry. I shouldn't lay all this on you. It's just wrong. I know what you want—"

I took a deep breath, trying to shove my voice through the tears. "I-I want you satisfied."

"I can come home," he said quickly. "I can just forget all this. Please don't cry. There'll be something—something down there—"

His voice was shaky. And I couldn't bear it anymore. "Frank! I want you satisfied! I want you to do what you know in your heart is best. You're more important to me than the farm. I can't keep the same life we had when we were kids. Do what you need to do! Please."

He was quiet so long I thought we might have been disconnected. Finally, when he spoke, his voice sounded far away and yet still somehow strong. "Are you sure?"

"Yes." I took a deep breath. Trust. I'd promised. *Lord, help me be able.*

"Are you really sure? I won't get the terms Sam offered me. I won't get Kirk nor your father to co-sign for me neither. Did you know they both offered to do that when we were lookin' at houses down there?"

"No."

"They did. Because Wilfred Patterson at the bank has a nephew that went to school with me, remember?"

"Yes."

"So they all think I belong in a loony bin or in some government program to help the feeble-minded."

"Oh, Frank. Not that bad."

"You think not. He said plain out I'd need a co-signer or they wouldn't have no confidence in me. Your father told me he said that. But I'm gonna go in the bank up here and be flat-out honest with 'em, and I'm gonna get me a loan if the good Lord wills."

I felt a surge of something warm inside me. "I believe you will."

"But only if that's what *you* want. I mean, I know you wanted to live down there. But if you can see it clear . . . to give this a chance . . ."

For a fleeting second I wondered what a difference there would be to our future if I just told him no. It was just too far. *I* wanted to lean on family, even if he didn't. That would be far easier, but I couldn't say it. I couldn't dash a hope like that. "Yes. Talk to the bank. Give it a chance. I love you."

"Oh, lordy, Sarah. I love you too. You are the absolute best—"

"Tell me about the house some more."

We talked on a very long time. And by the time we finished, I felt good about the choice I'd made, so long as I didn't think too long and hard about the details. Debt. So far from home. So far from the safety net my parents had always been for both of us.

Seven thousand dollars was a lot of money to commit. But a very good deal for the property we'd be getting. If Frank could make the business work. *Lord, let him not be disappointed.*

Dad found work to do at the station, since we'd be stuck here for several hours. I sat and prayed for a while because Frank was going to talk to the bank this very day if he could, and I had a strange mix of feelings about it. In a way I would still be relieved if nothing worked out up there, and yet I knew I would be saddened and disappointed for Frank now too.

As the time wore on, I got restless. If he had anything more to report, Frank would call before we expected to be leaving, but that could be hours away.

We'd been in such a rush to leave home that I hadn't taken time to bring any needlework, and we had nothing with us for lunch either. So I decided to bundle up and walk a block down the street to Dearing's little library for a book of poems, and on the way back stop and get us each a sandwich at the café halfway between. Dad was hesitant about me heading out in the steady snow-fall, but it was such a short way. He had me call first to make sure the librarian was there. She was, because she lived only two blocks away and hated to close for anything.

Dad saw to it that I had my coat buttoned and my hat, scarf, and mittens in place, as though he had forgotten I was almost twenty-one. He gave me a big hug and added a blanket around my shoulders when I turned to leave. I wondered if he was already thinking about what it would be like with me gone away to Camp Point. I was.

The snow was noticeably deeper, and the air felt frigid. I was very glad there was no biting wind. In beautiful weather, the short jaunt from the Marathon station to the library would have been over in no time, but today time seemed to flow differently and the town hardly seemed real. Everything was pretty, like the inside of a Christmasy snow globe. But there was hardly anyone out, and I was glad to reach the library steps.

Mrs. Kittering was pleased to have the company. She asked questions about my family and chatted with me most of the time I was there. I looked at several poetry books before selecting one that featured Elizabeth Barrett Browning. I'd always loved her work, and it was small enough to fit in my coat pocket so I could keep it protected from the snow.

No vehicles were parked outside the café. I would have guessed there were no customers. But as I got close, the door opened and a lone young man stepped out to the porch. He turned and looked at me, and I froze in my tracks. Donald Mueller.

"Well, Sarah," he said with a smile as he stepped from the café toward me.

"I thought you were with Orville on the mail route."

"He dropped me off not five minutes after you."

"I need to get some sandwiches. Get out of the way." My words were abrupt, harsh. Quickly I added, "Please."

He chuckled. "So did you hear from Frank?"

I nodded, not wanting to talk to him.

"Is he coming back? Rorey said he was due in last night but he hadn't left yet. Is he having trouble with his truck?"

"That's none of your business."

"Didn't forget the way, did he? Boy, what would he do? Can he find Dearing on a map, do you think?"

"Shut up and let me by."

Only one narrow path was shoveled on the sidewalk, and Donald was standing in it. I tried to go around him, even though it meant plodding through the deeper snow, but he sidestepped to stay in front of me.

"Is he gonna stay? What'd he say, Sarah? Did he leave you behind for whatever job it is he's thinkin' about up there?"

"No. Get out of my way. Please."

"You seem upset about something. I can tell. Is everything okay?" He reached his hand toward my arm, and I pulled back.

"You're what's upsetting me! Leave me alone!"

He looked strangely sad. "Just think about it, Sarah. Do you really want to leave everything you know? And follow him willy-nilly who knows where?"

I stared at him. How could he seem to know the questions in my heart? It was as though his words were designed to shake away the certainty I'd felt over what I'd told Frank. Of course it was right that Frank should have this opportunity. How could I deny him something so important? And yet, here was the tempter, asking me again what *I* wanted, suggesting that I back out of a promise and follow my own will.

170

"Let me by," I warned. "Or I'll scream. And don't think nobody would hear. I can be loud if I need to be."

"I would never threaten you," he said, the sadness even stronger in his eyes.

"Then move." I struggled in the deep snow to go around him again, and this time he let me by. But he followed me toward the café door.

"Sarah—I've liked you a lot since tenth grade. I figured you'd give up on Frank eventually, but . . ."

He hesitated and I kept on walking.

"Orville said if I was ever gonna have a chance, it was now or never to get your attention. I care about you, okay? I don't want you to be hurt or drug off someplace by somebody that don't know what he's doin' half the time. I got a good job, Sarah. I'm gonna buy my Aunt Mabel's place right here in town."

Just like the dream. With my heart pounding fiercely, I rushed to open the café door. *Shut up!* I wanted to shout at him. *Leave me alone!*

I hurried inside, but he followed me. There was a woman with graying hair behind the counter, and I got her attention immediately. "Two roast beef sandwiches to go, please. And may I use your telephone to call the Marathon station?"

She looked at me oddly. "That's only two doors down."

"I know. But I need to call anyway. Right away."

She glanced at Donald but gave me a nod. "Aren't you Sarah Wortham?"

"Yes, ma'am."

"The telephone's in the back to the right."

"Thank you."

I hurried to call my father, and while I was back there I heard the waitress talking to Donald, but I couldn't tell what she said. When I came back to the front room, he was gone.

"He left you a note," she told me.

My heart was still pounding. Had she been conspiring with him? Why? "I don't want it."

"He said you wouldn't. He said he didn't mean to scare you. He just wanted you to know how he felt."

I plopped into a chair and felt like crying. "Why would you relay his message? I just want him to leave me alone."

"He's a good kid," she said then. "A bit misguided sometimes. But he means well."

"How do you know what he means?" I felt like I was shaking inside.

"I'm a good friend of his mama. We talk sometimes."

I was horrified to think it might be talked around town that Donald Mueller had a crush on me. What if it got back to Frank? Oh, for gracious sakes! Rorey and Eugene surely knew already. And they'd make the most of it if they could.

Dad got there before the cook had the sandwiches ready. He took me in his arms and held me for a minute. "He seems to be gone, pumpkin."

"Was it stupid to ask you to walk me the rest of the way?"

He shook his head. "You did the right thing."

Try as I might, I couldn't keep the tears from welling up and overflowing then. This was just too much today. I wanted to go home, curl up, and cry.

"He didn't mean you no harm," the waitress said as Dad paid her for the sandwiches. "He just wanted the opportunity to talk."

I hadn't seen such a fierce face on my father for a long time. "You can tell him I'll be calling the law if he comes near my daughter again. And I'll be after him myself if I see so much as one more letter."

I didn't have the appetite for that sandwich. I would never have expected Donald to push things so far. He'd asked me out on dates plenty of times when we were in school, but I'd always turned him down and thought that was the end of it. Now he was a grown man, twenty-three like Frank, and he hadn't let it go.

Dad was worried for me, I could tell. I told him everything Donald did and said, and though he wasn't really threatening, I'd been scared just the same. And Dad was mad. That waitress had probably told Donald he'd better clear out before my father got there, and she'd been right. Who knew what might have happened?

We talked some more about Frank's decision and my answer to it. Dad was sure I was right to be supportive, but he knew it was hard too. Especially when I'd been expecting Frank home. After a while, Dad tried to get back to work on an old engine while we waited. I pulled out the poetry book and tried to read, but I just couldn't concentrate.

I dreaded riding home with Orville now, even if Donald wasn't with him. And Dad must have thought that through. He wiped his hands on an old grease rag and tried calling Charlie Hunter's home telephone. He wasn't there, but Dad told his wife that we needed a ride if he was able to give us one.

I sat and prayed. Forcing Donald from my thinking, I ran through the conversation with Frank again in my mind. And then a thousand jumbled memories rushed through me. Of Frank the day his leg got broken, being brave despite the pain. Of his brothers and other boys tormenting him endlessly, calling him retarded and scatterbrained and crazy. Of sitting under the apple tree with him while he calculated sums he couldn't do on paper. And then listening with wonder while he told about the cherubim described in the book of Ezekiel and about molecules and elements, and how that excited him when he thought of the Lord God forming Adam from the dust of the ground.

It was stupid for Donald to try to get my attention. Frank and I had shared so much for so long. Heartache and loss. Good times and bad. I couldn't feel for anybody else what I felt for Frank. Not ever.

I still remembered the day we'd talked in the timber when the war was young, when he'd asked me to always be his friend. It'd been easy to promise that I would, even though the things we were going through and about to go through weren't easy at all. I knew I'd loved Frank even then, before either of us had known to admit it, because he was honest enough to bare his heart and humble enough to admit his own fears.

Lord, help me not to doubt, not to fear, despite the squeezing press of nerves I feel inside. Frank trusts you. He believes you're leading him. Help me to have peace in that, no matter what comes. Help me to fulfill my promise and really, really trust you, not just go through empty motions or empty words.

Dad kept busy, going from engine work to cleaning up in the service garage. I tried reading another poem, got halfway through, and had to stop again because my thoughts just wouldn't leave me alone.

That waitress had called Donald a kid. He was acting like a foolish kid, no question about that. But what about me? I'd never really wanted to grow up. So the step Frank was trying to take was as much for my benefit as it was for his. If we stayed here as I'd wanted, maybe we'd never grow into whatever purpose God had in mind for us. I might have been content with that, but Frank could never be.

Despite the wisdom of that reasoning, I began to sense the stirring of the same seed of doubt. Donald's words echoed in my heart even as I tried to chase them away. *Do you really want to leave everything you know? And follow willy-nilly who knows where?*

174

Here it was again. The temptation. A way out. Not just in my head anymore, but blatantly offered face-to-face. I could have a life here in Dearing if I turned away from Frank and his dreams.

There should never have been a struggle in my mind over that. I loved Frank. What might the Lord have in store for us? Why would the tempter be trying so hard? Perhaps I'd never know the answer, but I did know that I'd made a promise. And going back on it now would be turning not only from Frank but from God.

I will trust you, I affirmed again in my mind. *I will trust Frank. No matter where it leads me.*

Somewhere I'd heard a Scripture that says we wrestle not against flesh and blood, but against principalities and powers. I didn't know why that should apply to me, and yet that day I felt like I was wrestling indeed.

20

Frank

At the bank, Mr. Willings pointed out the man I needed to talk to. I had papers Mr. Bellor had given me, telling details about the property and what he wanted for it. He was ready to sell as long as I could get the help I needed from the bank to pay him.

Lord, work your will. I took a deep breath and knocked at the man's office door though it was standing open. He was a young man, younger than I would have expected to find in his job. He looked up and motioned me inside without saying anything. I waited while he shuffled papers, put some away, and then finally asked what he could do for me.

"I need to talk to you about a loan," I said. "I want to move my business here to Camp Point."

"What kind of business?"

I handed him a WH card, took another deep breath, and did my best to describe to him the kind of work I'd done and hoped to continue doing.

He looked over the papers about the Bellor property and started asking me questions about my previous income and assets. I told him how much I'd been bringing in, how much I'd saved back, and how much I thought I could put into a down payment, even what I thought I could handle for a monthly payment and how long I figured it'd take me to pay it off.

He smiled and turned to an adding machine sitting on his desk. "I've been used to doing the figuring myself for most folks."

"Seemed reasonable to have an idea in advance," I explained. "So I'd know if it was worth your time for me to even come in here."

"What interest rate are you allowing yourself?"

I told him the last figure I'd heard and admitted it might not be accurate because I'd gotten it in Mcleansboro two months ago.

"Mcleansboro? So why do you want to move up here?"

"I'm startin' a new life. Gettin' married. And what I've seen of this town leads me to believe I could make a go of it here."

"Why is that?" he questioned on, and I felt sunk a little. Seemed like he was going to be hard to convince. I wasn't sure he was even taking me at my word.

But I told him why the shop was just what I needed and that Camp Point didn't have another one like it, nor Clayton either, which was close enough to draw at least a portion of my customer base from. I told him about the historic homes I'd seen and that I knew how to restore features should anyone in the area need that done. And I'd found a church here I liked and had done work locally already.

When he told me my income wasn't as high as he'd like to see from a loan applicant, I explained that I hadn't counted the farm income and that up here my work time wouldn't be divided putting hours in for a joint venture with my brothers.

"They can handle the farm without me now, and I'll be able to put full time into the business. I understand Quincy's the biggest town around here. Haven't had time yet, but I'm planning to drive over there and see if I might interest some of the shops in consigning some of my work. That'll generate more sales, once I get it going."

"You're a confident young man," he said without looking up from his adding machine.

"It don't pay to be otherwise."

"Why not move into Quincy if you anticipate sales there?"

"I'm a farm boy. Smaller town suits me fine. Big yard and a wide corner lot is almost like havin' a field. There'll be room for plenty a' garden."

He looked up at me with another smile, this one a little different than the others. "Your figures are reasonable. And it'd be nice to see somebody make a go of that property again. I'd like you and Mr. Bellor to meet with me tomorrow, and we can start drawing up the papers."

That simple. I almost couldn't answer. But there was something else I had to tell him, and I prayed it didn't mess the whole thing up. "About the papers. When it comes time for all that, I'd appreciate it if you had a secretary that could read 'em out for me. I'd pay her for the trouble. I understand better picturin' things in my mind than I do tryin' to hold it in front of me, and I wanna make sure I have a full grasp of the details."

He looked at me a long time. "That's the prettiest way I've ever heard of admitting that you can't read."

Even though I felt like I'd been kicked, I made myself answer him steady. "I can read, sir. Just not well enough yet, and I know better than to allow that to be any hindrance to my understanding a' terms. I want things done right."

He nodded. "You're brave as well as confident. I've

worked with a number of men who don't read, and most are not so ready to admit it."

I bowed my head. "It'd be foolhardy to pretend, sir, or to sign anything I wasn't clear on."

I thought he might start asking how in the world I thought I was gonna manage a business then. I could imagine getting his ridicule and a rebuke before he just shook his head and dismissed me. But it didn't happen that way. He told me his bank's current interest rate and how that would alter the monthly payment amount I'd figured. And then he asked me how I'd learned to calculate such things.

"I looked at properties close to home some. Didn't find the place I wanted down there, but I paid attention to what the fellow from the bank said about how payments is figured up."

He didn't answer me anything about that. "I'll talk to Mr. Bellor. Can you come back tomorrow at two o'clock?"

"Yes, sir."

That was it. I was on my way to buying that piece of property, and it felt like a gift from heaven. How could it have been so easy? Of course, we weren't half started, but he didn't seem to have no problem with me asking to hire a secretary to read for me. I wondered for a minute if that would really be so different from having Sam here to help me, or Sarah. But it would. I knew it would. If I had to bring kin along, it'd be like saying I couldn't do it without 'em. But paying the secretary would just be business. The banker even seemed to understand that.

I paid for a room for a week even though I didn't like spending the extra cash. I knew I could prob'ly stay with Mr. Willings, but I didn't want to be leaning on his kindness if I didn't have to do things that way.

I did use his telephone to call Sarah back. I told her everything that banker had said. She seemed glad, she

179

really did, even though she'd been crying before. She said she was happy to be part of the life I chose, whatever it was. And I told her I couldn't imagine being more blessed. God gave me a gift when he turned Sarah's heart in my direction. No doubt about that. I didn't think there'd ever be a way I could thank him enough.

When I finished that call, I knew I'd have to make one more. To Sam, who'd be expecting me back through Jacksonville today or tomorrow if I didn't tell him otherwise. I really didn't want to explain anything to him because he might want to get himself here in time for the meeting tomorrow. But surely he wouldn't be able to on account of his job. And anyway, I could tell him plain I didn't want that.

He was mad. He said Uncle Milty would be too, about me buying but not from them. I hadn't even thought things through to anticipate that, but Sam was really angry.

"I would have signed a note just between you an' me, Franky. You could've been in my house already! Now we still don't have a sure buyer, and you're going to somebody you don't even know."

"Their place fits me better," I tried to explain. "The house and the shop both. And both yards. It's just what I need."

But he wouldn't hear me and called me selfish and ungrateful. I apologized, even though I didn't think I needed to. The way I saw it, I never had any obligation to buy from him or from Milton Pratt. I'd never made any promises.

"You're just asking for heartache being so bullheaded," he told me. "If you don't wanna work with me and Uncle Milty, why should I run all the way over there to help you? We coulda already had things squared away a whole lot easier."

"Sam, I ain't askin' for help. There's no need you runnin' over here."

"You ain't askin' for help?"

Why that hadn't sunk in, I don't know. "Nope."

"Is Sarah coming up?"

"Not yet. We got no plans for that till after the wedding."

"Franky, you're crazy! When are you signing papers?"

"I meet with the banker again tomorrow. Not sure how long it'll all take. But the owner led me to believe that I could be in the commercial building as soon as next week if all goes well at the bank, which is what I expect."

He was quiet for a moment. "You're blowing your money staying in town over there, aren't you?"

"I'm paying for a room, yeah. But I don't consider the money blown. I'm gettin' a start."

"God love you, Frank." His voice sounded softer. "I wish you'd listen to me. You're gonna get yourself roped in over there and end up half broke and disappointed."

"No. It won't be like that. You'll see."

"I hope not. For Sarah's sake most of all. You're bein' a fool. Renting Pratt's would make more sense. It'd be easy to step away if things don't work out. And buying from me there wouldn't be no problem if you had trouble. I'd be patient when you need it and find another buyer if it ever come to you wantin' to go back home."

It was hard to keep talking to him. "I know what you had in mind, Sam. And I don't want your guarantees. You can call me bullheaded all you want. I still love you. But I aim to make a life on my own. I just called so you'd know I won't be back over there no time soon."

"Are you gonna tell this to Uncle Milty, or should I? He's still got his heart set on somebody running his store for him."

"I'm sure he can find somebody. A young fella I met at church is ready to start lookin' for a job. I might mention it to him."

"Don't know if Uncle Milty'll like that or not."

I shook my head even though Sam couldn't see it. "I'd just as soon be his friend, you know that, but I never signed on to spend my time tryin' to please him."

He laughed, just a little. "I shoulda known with you. If there's one thing you always been, it's unpredictable. Lord knows where you'll end up."

"You're right," I answered solemnly. "I expect he's the only one."

❧

Laying awake in bed that night, I prayed for Sam and Mr. Pratt. I prayed for Mr. Bellor and the banker and that meeting tomorrow. I prayed for Mr. Willings too, and his church. When he'd learned I was thinking to stay, he'd been real happy about it. He asked me to speak again. He said their pastor was in the hospital and he'd been doing his best to fill in and find speakers when he could. I prayed for that pastor, even though I didn't know his name. From what Mr. Willings said, he wasn't far from going home to be with the Lord.

I started re-thinking everything while I was laying there. Sam thought I was a fool to do things this way. I didn't agree. Not the way he meant it. I had to find a way to do on my own without my brothers stepping in thinking they needed to. But here? Sarah was being mighty good about it. But was it really right?

I couldn't hardly sleep. I got up and walked around my little rented room, praying about this whole thing. What was I thinking, anyway? I didn't even know any-body here.

But that's the kind of challenge I knew I'd been longing for. To put myself in a spot and make things work, just to prove I could. Was that selfish pride? There wasn't nothing stopping me from makin' a go a' things down by Mt. Vernon somewhere. Sarah'd like that better. Why here?

It all come down to what the Lord wanted for us. And me yielding my heart to realize that nothing was going to work for me anywhere without him in the middle of it. I couldn't stand on my own two feet without his foundation under me and his strong hands holding me up. I told him I was sorry, just in case I'd lost sight of that. I told him I was willing to quit now and go home, or anywhere else he might want me. And right then while I was praying that, I had the strangest feeling I was supposed to go see Mr. Willings again. Now.

But that was crazy. It was almost midnight. He'd think I'd lost my mind if I come banging on his door right now. And I didn't know anything I needed to talk to Mr. Willings about anyhow. I tried to keep on praying. I even sat on the edge of the bed, thinking I'd lay back down and try to get some sleep. But I couldn't get it out of my mind.

Go see Mr. Willings.

"He's gonna think I'm crazy," I told myself. "He's gonna wonder if I been out drinkin' or somethin'."

But I put on my coat and I went, slow, trying to talk myself out of it the whole way.

There was a light on in his house. At least I might not be waking him. But I still felt bad going up to the door. What in the world was I gonna tell him? I knocked, feeling ashamed to ring the doorbell. I knew he was a widower and lived alone, so I wouldn't be waking nobody else, but I thought it better to just knock once or twice. If he didn't hear me, I'd go.

He heard me. He come to the door a lot quicker than I expected, and he was dressed like he was ready to go someplace. Of course he was surprised to see me.

"Franklin Hammond. What can I do for you tonight?" He seemed troubled.

"I'm not knowin' nothing I need you to do," I told him. "I just couldn't get it out of my head wonderin' if there's something *you* need."

He just looked at me a minute, and then he opened the door wider. "Come in."

I didn't know what to say. He was awful quiet. I followed him to his sitting room, but he didn't sit and neither did I. Instead, he took hold of his Bible and a pair of reading glasses from a corner table and then turned and looked at me.

"I do have a need. Our pastor's wife called. She's convinced that he's about to pass, and she would like me to be there. But I have difficulty driving so far at night. I told her I might have to wait till morning, bad as I hate to when she's asked for me."

He looked down at the floor. I didn't know much of anything about him or his pastor, but I could tell they must have been good friends. "Would you like me to drive you? You'll have to direct me, 'cause I got no idea where they are, but I can see fine to drive at night if that's the trouble."

"The St. Mary's hospital in Quincy, son. And I'd greatly appreciate it. The good Lord must have sent you. I was wondering if there might be someone I could call on as late as this."

"I'll get you there. My truck's right outside." *Thank you, God, for speaking to my heart*, I prayed in silence. *Thank you for getting through my thick skull enough that I could listen.*

He had his coat on quick and was ready to go. I reminded him he oughta take a hat on account of the cold and then remembered I'd forgotten my own. Again.

We were pretty quiet on the way to Quincy, and I was glad we hadn't had more of the kind of weather Sarah and her folks had gotten down there. Mr. Willings only spoke when he had to direct me, till we were past three other little towns. Then he cleared his throat and started talking a little more.

"Pastor Ells has been a blessing to so many. I'm glad to have known his friendship since we were young men. I'm glad to have known his heart."

There was nothing I knew to reply to that, so I only listened. And in a moment, he went on.

"Sometimes when someone passes away it feels like the close of an era. I suppose this'll be like that. And I may feel like I'm living past my time."

"I don't think anybody does that," I had to answer. "All our times are in the Lord's hands."

"Yes," he said solemnly. "Of course you're right."

I kept thinking maybe that pastor wouldn't die tonight. Maybe it wasn't the Lord's time for that yet. But sometimes it is. I'd been through enough to know.

I wasn't sure how we'd be received coming into the hospital in the middle of the night. Ordinarily, I think they would have turned us away till morning. But there was a nephew downstairs waiting, hoping Mr. Willings would be able to come, and they'd already gotten permission from the staff on the pastor's behalf.

I felt very out of place. I didn't know any of these people. I offered to stay in the truck, or at least downstairs. But Mr. Willings insisted that I should come along. I was a brother in Christ, he said. The one chosen to be with him tonight.

First thing we did was pray for the family. And then Mr. Willings went in the room to see his old friend. I stayed in the hall. Everybody did, except Mr. Willings and the pastor's wife. They stayed in the room a long time, and then we prayed some more while others of the family took their turns to be at the bedside.

We'd been there almost two hours when the pastor left this world. It was bittersweet, so much sadness put together with the family singing hymns, and the comfort of knowing the blessings that man'd gone on to receive. I prayed quiet most of that time, not sure why the Lord had seen fit to include me in this.

The pastor's wife was strong. I knew it must have been an awful blow, but she was handling it a whole lot better than many people handle such things. My pa had fell apart when Mama died, and then when my brother got killed, he was so bad he just couldn't go on. I prayed for this lady and her family. She was old and really little, but sturdy. In some ways she reminded me of Emma Graham, the neighbor lady who'd done so much for us and left her farm to the Worthams. I still missed her sometimes, because she didn't treat me no different than the rest of my brothers, except maybe to give me a little extra attention now and then.

That'd been so awful long ago. Before my blasted limp, and a whole lot of loss. I sighed, pushing away those kinda thoughts. This man'd had two sons and a daughter, and they were all here. I prayed for them, pretty much knowing what they must be feeling at a time like this. *Lord God, give them peace.*

When there was nothing else to be done and Mr. Willings was ready to go, the newly widowed old lady came up an' give me a hug. "God bless you, young man," she said.

"Thank you," I struggled to answer her. "God bless you too, ma'am. I'm real sorry for your loss."

"My loss is Herman's gain," she replied, squeezing tight onto her dampened hanky. "Thank the Lord for the promise of heaven." She seemed to be searching me. "Are you the one that spoke at the church last Sunday night? I heard you did a fine job."

"Thank you, ma'am. That was me."

"Do come back. I'd be pleased to hear you."

I nodded. She went on down the hall with one of her sons, and Mr. Willings and me went back outside to the truck.

"Are you too tired to drive back?" he asked me. "We've been up most the night."

"I'll be fine."

I wasn't too sure about the first turn out of Quincy, but after that it wasn't hard to retrace the way I'd come. Good thing, because Mr. Willings fell asleep in his seat. I was beat by the time we got to Camp Point but not about to show it. I woke Mr. Willings and helped him inside. I wasn't expecting it, but he asked me to stay. He said he didn't feel like being there alone right then, even though he knew he wouldn't be doing nothing but sleeping.

In the morning he called the bank and didn't go in. I'd stretched out on his couch just to be close if he needed something. He'd seemed awful feeble on the way in the house last night. I wasn't sure if it was the sadness or the weariness, but I was glad to stay because I was concerned for him. He moved slow that morning too, and he had a lot of telephone calls to make. Everybody from the church needed to know. There'd be a funeral, and the church women'd be called on to feed the family afterward.

I felt out of place all over again, but Mr. Willings didn't want me to leave just yet. In between telephone calls, he started to fix sausage and eggs, but then somebody called him, so I took over the cooking. I wanted to have some way to help him out. I made him a cup of coffee, found some bread, and toasted a couple of slices of it. So when he was through on the telephone again I had a plate ready for him.

"You are a godsend, do you know that, Franklin?"

I guess I didn't. I was just dealing with the situation best I could. And wondering at him calling me "Franklin" all the time. No one else ever had, except my pa when he was angry, but he'd always thrown in my middle name too.

We sat and ate, and he thanked me for taking him to Quincy last night.

"You already thanked me," I reminded him. "I need to thank you for breakfast."

"That's been as much your doing as it was mine."

We ate quiet for a while, and then he looked at me with a real serious expression. "I would like you to pray about something, please. Last night before he passed, Herman and his wife asked me to consider pastoring the church in his stead rather than leading the church in a search for someone else. I'll have to speak to the congregation, but I intend to do as most of them wish, even if it means accepting such a call."

He studied me for a second. "I'm aware this may seem hasty, but either way I'd like you to consider speaking regularly for us on Sunday nights, at least for a time. It would be a great help."

"I'm not sure I'm qualified."

He nodded. "Perhaps not as much as you'll eventually be. But you're certainly called."

Tingling jitters went shootin' inside me. I'd never been sure of such a call. Not for preaching at least, despite what other people seemed to think. "Um . . . I don't know, sir."

He nodded again. "That's all right. Just pray about helping us for a while, since you expect to be in the area. That's all I ask."

I agreed to pray about it. I really couldn't do nothin' else. He was concerned about keeping me up so much of the night when I had to meet with the banker again today. But there wasn't anything to be done about that, and I wouldn't have changed it. He prayed with me, that the Lord'd grant favor in my business dealings, and I came away from his house thinking sure that God had me in Camp Point for more than my own independent ideas.

"Your will be done," I said when I was getting in my truck. "Direct my steps. And my heart."

I went to my rented room to clean up and change clothes. Then I drove by the property again to take a closer look at the foundations. When the time came to go to the bank that afternoon, I was crazy excited but tried not to let it show. The loan officer's name was Cyril Hayes. He told me he was willing to give my business a chance. So he approved my loan application and had his secretary read me the papers.

When we were all done, he said he loved fine wood and would like to see some of my work if he could.

"Got a cedar chest with a few pieces inside it under a tarp on my truck," I told him. And he was eager to step outside with me and take a look.

He bought the toddler chair on the spot and ordered another one. Said he had twin baby girls that'd grow into them before you know it. Then he looked over the eagle and asked if I thought I could do a desk-sized horse just as nice.

"Yeah. I've done horses before. Pair of 'em on bookends for the mayor down in Dearing."

He wanted to take the eagle inside and show his co-workers. I got a lot of nice comments, and when he was ready for me to put the carving away again he said the bank'd be honoring Lance Willings soon for years of service.

"We've already been discussing a suitable gift for him, and his love of horses has come up more than once. I wanted to show your work around today because we may choose to commission a horse carving, the finest work you can do."

"That would be a pleasure," I told him, hoping for the opportunity to make something special for Mr. Willings. Maybe I'd do it even if the bank chose not to order from me.

I left there with my mind awhirl. I'd made a new sale.

And way bigger than that, I'd got the loan approved. It felt like a gift from God.

I wished I could talk to Sarah, but I'd told her not to go to town today if the weather was bad. They had Mr. Willings's telephone number now. We'd be talking soon. But I wished I could hear her voice. I was still a little worried for her.

Lord, give Sarah a heart of peace and joy in this. Bless her real big. She's such a blessing to me.

I drove by the Bellors' place real slow and stopped to look for a minute. This was gonna be mine. Ours. I couldn't wait for Sarah to see it. She'd fall in love with it, I knew she would. And I had a lot a' work to do gettin' the business established and makin' the place the best I could for her between now and June.

For the first time I wondered what I should call the business here in Camp Point. WH, which stood for Wortham and Hammond, might still be appropriate since I was marrying a Wortham, but it was prob'ly time for something new.

"He that tilleth his land shall have plenty of bread," the Scriptures say. And I had a storefront to fill. I'd be tillin' away a lot a' hours just on that, not to mention the roofs and everything else the property was gonna need. I couldn't remember ever feeling so excited. This was an answer to prayer, sure as I was alive.

21

Sarah

Two opinions wrestled inside me that afternoon as I knew Frank would be seeing the banker again. "Lord, work all things smoothly if it is your will," I prayed. But almost in the same breath I said, "Close every door if that would be better."

Emmie, Bert, Harry, Rorey, and Eugene were all at our house again, and unfortunately Frank's decision was the topic of conversation.

"I didn't see it comin'," Bert said. "Don't know what to think."

"I'd like to know what *he's* thinkin'," Harry replied.

"Just quit," I said to both of them. Emmie Grace's eyes filled with tears, and I gave her a hug. I was about to promise her that we'd welcome her in our home, but Rorey broke in before I had the chance.

"Looks like you got a choice to make now, Sarah," Rorey suggested smugly. "You ain't married yet, you know."

"Might be greener pastures closer to home," Eugene added.

Emmie was stunned. "What do you mean by that? Are you tryin' to say they might not get married?"

"They're talking nonsense," I assured her. "Because they don't have sense enough not to listen to idiots."

Rorey's eyes flashed. "That's the rudest thing I ever heard you say."

"You deserve it if you think I'm going to turn my back on Frank."

Mom interrupted the conversation to serve up tea and cake. Rorey and Eugene were leaving in the morning. I tried to put aside my frustration at them and be civil, but they were irritating to their very last moment with us.

"Frank missed out on his cake," Rorey observed, helping herself to a generous piece.

Emmie was very upset. "We'll make him another one," she answered sourly.

"Might be hard to do. Never know what's gonna happen now."

Eugene gobbled down three pieces of cake. I couldn't even eat one. Mom did her best to keep the rest of the talk light until Eugene got up to get their coats.

"We'll see you in June," Rorey announced. "Thanks, Mrs. Wortham, for hosting our wedding."

"You'll need to get started seeing to the details," Mom suggested.

But Rorey was rather flippant. "You pretty much know what to do."

Mom shook her head. "Maybe so, but it's not our job to do it. Have you been thinking about a dress, flowers, invitations—"

"A little. We have plenty of time."

"Not so much when you consider everything. Especially the dress."

"C'mon, hon." Eugene hurried Rorey before she could answer. "Clem'll be waiting."

Clem was one of Eugene's brothers. They were all going out drinking on Rorey's last night here, though she could have stayed with us or gone in to see Lizbeth like she'd been asked. But Rorey wasn't one to do what she was asked at the expense of a night out. She pulled on her coat, hugged Emmie, and then turned to me.

"Buck up, Sarah. Maybe Frank'll have this out of his system before June. And if not, well, at least he's working. Sure hope it isn't too big a debt."

Bert nudged her and shook his head. "It'll all come out fine. Frank's heart's in the right place. He's bound to make good."

I was surprised Bert would say that, but I appreciated it, and so did my mother.

"I'm certain of it," she added. "There's no reason to speak negatively. God has a purpose in all things, and I expect Frank and Sarah to be blessed."

"Funny name for a town," Rorey remarked. "Camp Point."

Eugene took her hand and they proceeded out the door with a chuckle. I ignored the comment and didn't bother with a quick good-bye. Emmie thought they might stop here again in the morning before they left for St. Louis, but I knew they wouldn't. They were too busy thinking about themselves and their own fun to bother.

❧

I hardly knew what to do with myself that afternoon. It seemed that life had flown out of control and there was nothing left but a whirlwind of circumstances. Frank so far away. Rorey's foolishness. Donald Mueller.

Emmie and I tried to be cheerful, but she seemed to be having as much trouble as I was. "I miss Frank so much already," she admitted. "I'm gonna miss him all the more after the wedding. And you too."

I knew she would, so I told her what Frank had said, that she could come up there with us if she wanted to. I understood now what Frank had meant when he said that having his kid sister along would be different, even if he needed to be away from the rest of the family. Emmie was only fifteen and without her parents. She wouldn't think he was leaning on others. She'd be leaning on him.

Katie seemed to realize that today working on my wedding dress was not the thing to do to ease my mind. She seemed at a loss, but Mom got us started making cookies. Snickerdoodles and date rounds and oatmeal raisin drops. Dozens of them. We'd send Frank a package, and Willy too. Bert started a letter at the kitchen table, to keep Willy informed, but he was reluctant to include details about Rorey's marriage plans.

"Maybe she'll change her mind," he suggested hopefully.

"Not if she has any inkling that we want her to," Emmie replied.

"She does," Harry said. "Kirk let her have it in no uncertain terms this morning and she cussed him good. Glad you all weren't there."

Emmie shook her head. "But she thinks it's all right to tell Sarah to reconsider."

"That's Rorey for you," Bert concluded, and turned back to his letter.

He and Harry wolfed down as many of the cookies as my mother would allow. And while I busily kept shaping more, my mind wandered to Frank again. What would he be doing tonight? Was the Lord truly at work in this decision? To what end?

"Blessed assurance," I started to sing as I got another cookie tray ready for the oven. "Jesus is mine! Oh, what a foretaste of glory divine . . ."

Katie joined me with her soft voice. And Mom turned toward both of us and smiled.

"Heir of salvation, purchase of God, born of his Spirit, washed in his blood . . ."

22

Frank

I hadn't eaten anything since breakfast with Mr. Willings, and it was getting into the evening now, so I went to Miller's restaurant on the square for a sandwich. I would have gone back to my room then, but I had the feeling I oughta check on Mr. Willings again. He'd looked so feeble, maybe on account of the grief. I just wanted to ask him if there was anything else I could do.

But he wasn't alone at the house that time, and I didn't want to intrude. About then I realized what I guessed I'd known all day and never thought about. This'd be the night for midweek service at the church. Mr. Willings hadn't said anything otherwise, so I assumed they'd still be having a service of some kind. Maybe it wouldn't bother nobody if I was to show up.

I went and cleaned up again best I could. I didn't know what time the service started so I went out early just in case with Mrs. Haywood's pie pan, even though she'd said it was an extra and I didn't have to return it. Nobody was there. There wasn't moon enough to shed much light on the church, but I got to looking at the place while my headlights were still on. It could sure use a fresh coat of paint come warm weather. And the outhouse in back was standing crooked and needin' shoring up pretty bad. One of the rails by the church steps was leanin' out a little too.

I wondered what they'd think if I offered to take on a little of that work. I hadn't seen but two young families at the Sunday night services, and there wasn't no father in attendance with one of those. But maybe that was on account of the weather lately. There might be a lot more on Sunday morning. But what I'd seen of the church folks so far was more old people than young. Maybe they could use the help.

I walked around the snowy church grounds, praying for the whole congregation. I loved our pastor back home in Dearing. It'd be an awful blow to lose him, so I knew this congregation might be feeling terrible heavy tonight over losing their pastor.

If the good Lord willed, I could see myself helping these people at least some of the time. But it was easier to think of painting or shoring up the outhouse walls than doing more preaching. I wasn't sure my speaking oughta be called preaching at all. Sharing, maybe. Or just bringin' a few thoughts out of the Scriptures for folks to consider. I didn't fiery preach, like Pastor Jones back home. I didn't get so carried into the message that it seemed it wasn't just me talking no more, the way it was with him.

Oh, but that'd be a joy, I suddenly thought. *To know beyond any doubt that it ain't just me. To feel what Pastor Jones calls the "unction" working inside.*

I wondered how it was with Sarah's brother Robert. Strangely enough, I'd never heard him speak. He'd only done it twice in the States. He'd been called straight to the mission field. And just a little, way down deep, I envied him 'cause he knew he was called, beyond a doubt. 'Cause he was able to go so far and be so sure of himself in serving the Lord among folks he'd never seen before.

Is that what you want outta me, Lord? Here?

I imagine it must've seemed strange to the first folks who pulled in to find me walking around the churchyard in the dark. I didn't have no way to explain myself. I just went inside and sat down quiet in the back row. I was still thinking on Robert and his wife going to serve the Lord in the Pacific islands. I'd a' loved to join 'em, but I didn't figure I had much to offer.

Lord, use me. Somehow. I know I may be an odd kind a' vessel, maybe with some damages needin' repair, but you made me for a purpose. Use me however you see fit.

More folks had come in, and I scarcely even noticed until one little old sister bumped against my foot when she come to shake my hand. I knew I'd been thinking past where I was sitting, not even noticing the other folks around me till now. My brothers woulda thought I was off in the clouds again, but she didn't seem to notice.

"Mr. Hammond, how nice to have you back."

"Thank you." I felt kinda trembly. I don't know why. I wondered if everybody knew already about their pastor's passing. Prob'ly so. You could tell it in the faces. An' I felt driven up front. Seemed crazy. But nothing had started. Mr. Willings wasn't even there yet. I felt driven to not just stay and pray in my seat. I needed to go to the altar, but what would these folks think?

Despite my doubts, I went up front, praying in my head while people started settling in behind me.

Lord, help. I don't know what you want of me. Help these folks. They's sheep without a shepherd, at least till the decision 'bout Mr. Willings is made, and even then, they'll be missing the man they prob'ly all loved pretty dear.

I pictured how I'd felt after Mama and Mrs. Graham died so close together. Lost, like there was nothing left to hold the world together. The first disciples must have felt that way and even more when the Lord was crucified. All the hope they had in this life and the life to come was hung in the balance.

The world is full a' grief, questions, and pain. But you didn't make it this way, God, I know. Sin made it this way, and you made the answer to sin. Plant your answer in me like a livin' seed. Let it take off and grow and vine out and touch everybody around me. Plant your answer in these people too, so they can see clear to your peace and rejoice in all you've done for them.

I could see it in my mind. Folks growing in a loving understanding of Jesus, their hearts big enough to take in everybody and every situation they met. If people was to live with Jesus working alive in 'em every day, if they was to live like Jesus would live, the world would be a different place. There wouldn't a' been no war. There wouldn't be nobody hungry as long as somebody else had bread.

For a few minutes I was still vaguely aware of movement and voices behind me, but I lost track of that and I lost track of where I was.

I could tell people these things—I could tell people if they lived like Jesus the world would be different, at least their own world, right around them. With the devil like a roaring lion, there was bound to be trials just like Jesus predicted. But they'd never be the hopeless kind 'cause they'd be wrapped in God's purpose and peace.

Was this a call? Was me kneeling down here in the front of this church knowing what I could do to make even my own world better, was that the Lord calling me up to present his will? Was I supposed to preach it? Live it out in the open? Or both?

I remembered the day Sarah's Uncle Edward hit me with his car. The pain of that break in my leg was so bad I couldn't hardly think, but there was a funny kind of

peace despite it all, because I knew I'd been doing right.
I'd been telling him about Jesus, even though he was an
ornery rascal. I'd been washing his car for him, because
I wanted to show him that Jesus and his children do
things for folks outta love.

My pa didn't understand it. He didn't understand a
bit of what I was thinking back then, and I really didn't
understand it all either. But Jesus had put some kind of
knowing on my heart of how important it was for me
to try livin' like him, even when it got hard. I wouldn't
never say I'd done well at it. Maybe I never would. Prob'ly
nobody truly could 'cept Jesus himself, but that weren't
the point. I was just s'posed to try, as much as the early
disciples did. They preached and they gave, they worked,
loved, and traveled all for Jesus's sake and died because
they wouldn't give it up.

They even had wives, some of them. So it said in 1
Corinthians. But it didn't say what the wives thought
about it all. What would Sarah think if I laid everything
aside the way they did?

She'd fit right in to the Lord's service here. I could
imagine her hugging on the dear sister that had lost her
husband and these folks that was without their pastor.
I could see her making friends with Hannah Haywood
and letting her use all the gooseberries she wanted off
our bush, even picking and stemmin' 'em for her besides.
I could see her singing in the church, belonging even
better than me, because the only thing really peculiar
about Sarah was her choice of me for a beau.

She was perfect for this place, or anywhere else we
could choose to go. Pretty, smart, and kind, she was like
an angel out of heaven. *Lord, she's part of the way you're
equipping me, ain't that right? You got your plan for her
too. I can't hardly wait till we're married.*

Suddenly the Ensleys come to mind, and I prayed for
them. Then I prayed for the Platten family and other

poor folks I didn't even know. I prayed for people I'd met on the trip and people I'd met since coming up here. I prayed for the teachers and students at the deaf school and for my nephew Albert, just starting out with his education adventure.

I prayed for Sam, that he'd be real blessed for caring about me, even if the caring did step over into frustration for me sometimes. I prayed for the rest of my brothers because they were the same way and sometimes worse. I prayed for Willy, off in the service, and Rorey, who'd left everything familiar, including church, to go gallivantin' in the city with Eugene Turrey. I prayed for Robert and Rachel and the folks they ministered to, and other ministers brave enough for missions overseas. I prayed for President Truman and other leaders because it was the right thing to do.

I don't know when I'd ever had praying come over me like that. I was on my knees so long I couldn't even feel my right leg no more. I couldn't usually stay down on both knees very long on account a' that leg, but this time I did. I heard singing. I heard footsteps. Finally, I turned myself to sit, knowing it'd be a minute 'fore I got the feeling back enough to get on my feet.

The church was almost empty. Mr. Willings sat in the front pew, just watching me, his eyes glistening tears that give his whole face a shine.

Where did everybody go? Did they leave on account of me? I didn't know what kind a' service they had for midweek—regular preaching, or Bible study, or what. Had I put myself in the way?

I almost couldn't breathe, just looking at him, but he didn't say nothing to me.

"Sir—sir, did I do somethin' wrong?"

Slowly, he shook his head. "No, son. There's no wrong about praying."

"I mean, right here. Now. Maybe I shoulda stayed an'

200

done my prayin' back in my room. I didn't mean to stop the service."

He smiled, just a little. "You didn't stop anything. It went right on. Maybe the best we've ever had too."

I felt so strange and weak that I didn't think I could've stood even if my leg was ready. I'd missed it? The service had not only started but got all the way through, and I hadn't even noticed? Lord God, my brothers were right! There was something about me almost half outta my mind or something. Why didn't I hear 'em? How could it happen?

"I . . . I'm sorry. I must a' been a awful distraction up here."

"No, Franklin. You were no distraction."

He didn't say nothing else, only rose to his feet. I tried to rise too, but I couldn't get my knee workin' good yet. "I'm sorry, sir," I said again, my heart pumping something thunderous. "I'm gonna hafta sit a minute, till the tingles clears up an' I can work the knee a little better. But then I'll clear out—"

"Franklin, did you hear me say you've done nothing wrong?"

I couldn't help it. I didn't know what was coming over me, but I started shaking. I started crying, and I couldn't get myself to stop. "I—I jus' wanna do what's right. I wanna help, an' I come in here like a fool an' lose my head jus' like always! They're all gonna think I'm crazy, just like my brothers figure. I can't do nothin', I can't be nowhere very long 'fore it comes clear what a crazy thing I am—"

I expected him to just walk off and leave. He prob'ly should've. There wasn't no call for me to be such a mess. But he didn't leave. He come up to the altar and he sat right beside me. He didn't say nothing, just put his hand on my shoulder. And the words flowed from me before I could stop them.

"Mr. Willings, I'm sorry. But I guess if you're wantin' me to keep speakin' to your folks here, you might as well know how I am. I just . . . I just can't be like other folks. I never could. I wouldn't never mean to do what I done, settin' myself up here in front of everybody like a fool. I didn't know the service started yet. I woulda stopped—I promise you I would've, if I'd a' just known. I'd a' gotten myself back there to that back row where I belong—"

"Son, was the Lord talking to you up here?"

His question made me feel all the more shaky. "I don't know. I can imagine it was like that. I know he was dealing with my heart."

"Then you belonged where you were, don't you think?"

"But the service . . . and the people—"

"You didn't hinder anything. It seemed to be what they needed. Nobody really had the heart for a service as usual tonight. Sometimes it's hard to step into the same routine in the face of the grief that shakes us. We were served better following your example. Did you know you weren't alone at the altar?"

I shook my head.

"We prayed. Almost the entire service time. It was just what we needed. More than one person told me that. We'll be all right, as a church. Nobody was troubled by what you did."

I closed my eyes. The tears were less, but they wouldn't quit completely. I still felt ashamed, but at the same time I knew it was right. And God had broke me open a little bit. I guess maybe he wanted Mr. Willings to be able to see inside.

"Do you know it's all right not to be like other people?" he asked me.

I stared down at my work boots. "Sometimes I know that. Other times I don't handle it very well. I guess you can see that."

"May I ask how the Lord was dealing with your heart?"

"About teachin'. With words, but by example too. About livin' like he lived, and lettin' him live in us. I had a powerful need for prayin' too. I don't know that I ever felt it so powerful before."

He looked forward across the empty pews. He sighed. "The Lord giveth, and the Lord taketh away. Blessed be the name of the Lord."

Them words almost set me to shaking again. "You ain't talkin' 'bout me, are you? Bein' given? And your pastor bein' taken away?"

He looked at me. "I don't mean that you belong to us here. That's for you and the Lord to decide. But you've been a gift. You've been a blessing."

I shook my head. "Nah. You all have blessed me, makin' me think there's some reason for my craziness. There ain't no sense doin' what I'm doin'. I'm two hundred miles from home. My brother don't need me here no more. I oughta go back. How come I can't?"

He smiled again. "You don't want to. Or the Lord doesn't want it. That's between you and him."

"No wonder my brothers think I need t' be watched over half the time. I don't even know what I'm doin'."

"It appears to me that you know better than you give yourself credit for. There's no shame in being set apart."

I bowed my head. "You don't know all a' what I mean, Mr. Willings. This ain't the first time I've lost track a' what's goin' on around me. Sometimes I put things together in my head in such ways I forget what else is goin' on."

I glanced up to him, and he was watching me patiently. But I knew I wasn't finished. Maybe the Lord wanted me to lay myself open in front of him. "That—that ain't all either. I know I ain't ignorant. At least I wanna think

I'm not, but there's somethin' else you oughta know. I don't carry no Bible. Ain't no use 'cause I can't read it yet. Maybe there's somethin' wrong with the way I think, 'cause I know I see all right."

I looked down, quaking a little over the reaction this would bring. Who ever heard of a man of God who didn't read the Word? And now the banker knew, and Mr. Willings knew. All of Camp Point'd know before long, and maybe things would be just like back home. Maybe I was kidding myself about making things work here. Maybe I was bein' a fool. But I couldn't hide something that important from Mr. Willings when he placed such confidence in me. It wouldn't be right.

"You couldn't read the notes I gave you?"

I shook my head.

"What about the history books you were telling me about?"

"I didn't lie, if that's what you mean, sir. My—my fiancée and her mother, they read 'em to me, at different times. I'd like to get hold a' some more."

"Bible too?"

"Yes, sir. I-I wish I could read it for myself. I work at it. But they done the readin'. An' I listened good, to the preacher back home too."

He was quiet. I couldn't tell if he was angry that I hadn't been more honest before. Maybe he wondered how I could be such a fool as to try to buy property up here in his town. Maybe he'd repent for asking me to speak here, I didn't know. None of it would surprise me. Maybe I deserved it all. "I'm sorry," I said again. "I shoulda told you sooner. You got a right to know what you let behind the pulpit."

He looked at me pretty oddly. "Why do you put it that way? What I let? Like you're more creature than man?"

Something about that stabbed deep. I felt a shooting

strangeness inside me. "I'm—I'm nothing much, sir, and I guess you oughta know. I'm off in the clouds, peculiar and absentminded, not much good for nothin' some-times—"

"Is that you talking, or your brothers?"

Suddenly it was hard, fighting up against tears again. "I don't know. Maybe it's my pa."

"It's not the Lord. Of that I'm confident."

"I oughta go. Maybe I can get my leg under me now."

"Franklin—Brother Hammond—do you remember 1 Corinthians, chapter one?"

"Yes, sir. I think so."

"Can you quote it? Right toward the end of the chap-ter? Verse 26 or 27. 'But God hath chosen . . .'"

He stopped, like he was waiting. And I felt the quiver-ing inside me again. *Lord, what are you doing with me tonight?*

I remembered the Scripture he was talking about, even though he hadn't quoted very far. I knew what came next. "God hath chosen the foolish things a' the world to con-found the wise; and God hath chosen the weak things a' the world to confound the things that are mighty . . ."

I looked up at Mr. Willings.

He nodded. "Can you go on?"

I swallowed hard. "And base things a' the world, and things which are despised, hath God chosen, yea, and things which are not, to bring to nought things that are: that no flesh should glory in his presence . . ."

Mr. Willings seemed to be almost shining again—just a touch of dampness on his cheeks reflecting the golden light of the church lamps. "I think you were just confess-ing to me how you feel foolish and weak, even despised, maybe by your own heart sometimes. I would say then, that according to the Scriptures, you are ideally qualified in God's eyes. Undoubtedly chosen."

I smiled, just a little, and then I could feel it spreading all over my insides. It prob'ly wasn't right to laugh, but I did, a tiny bit.

"Don't you suppose that God made you exactly the way you are on purpose?" he asked me. "He knew what he wanted to use in this day and time. You're a remarkable young man, and he's planted the Scriptures in your heart where they can't be set aside on a shelf."

I nodded. *Lord, thank you.* "He—he's called me. Just like you said. I don't know for what all, I just know he wants to use me, an' I wanna be used."

"That's the beginning, son. You're right where he wants you."

He shook my hand but kept hold, and I realized he was thinking to help me up. "How about a bowl of chili?" he offered. "Neighbor of mine made it. Won't take long to heat up."

I struggled to my feet, the leg still tingly, my knee feeling weak. But inside I felt like I was soaring, like something was broke free. "That'll be real good," I answered. "Thank you."

23

Sarah

It was strange when January ended and February began with Frank still not home. Now I knew he wouldn't be, not till a visit at Easter. He got the loan and closed on the store building. Lizbeth was so flabbergasted that she never said much about it except that she was proud of him.

He moved into the back of the store and got a little countertop electric burner so he could cook. He had a telephone put in too, despite the expense, because it would help the business and make things more convenient for us to reach him. He also got a post office box. That seemed so final. He'd really moved.

And I would be moving too. It seemed everything I did now was to prepare me for the day, even the mundane, everyday things. While gathering eggs, I would think of the big yard Frank had described to me and wonder if we'd have chickens of our own. Stirring a pot on the stove, I stopped to consider how much less we'd need when it was just the two of us.

I sewed tea towels for us now, and embroidered pillowcases to put on the bed we would eventually have. Some days I spent hours on my wedding dress, but other days I couldn't seem to work on it at all as I sifted through my nervousness and mixed-up feelings.

The big dog Dad called Horse became a comfort during those times. He would come to me whenever I was outside and stay as close as he could, as though he were charged with it as a duty. I petted him and told him my troubles, confessing the weaknesses I told nobody else but God.

"I still haven't told Frank about Donald," I admitted one day. "I haven't wanted to bother him with such a stupid thing when he's working so hard. Do you think I'm right about that? At least Donald's been leaving me alone, so I guess it isn't an issue anymore."

The dog gazed at me sympathetically and then leaned his head against me, which could almost knock me over when I wasn't expecting it. Bert had looked up pictures and declared that the dog was a mastiff, a very large breed.

"I bet you wouldn't like Donald if you met him up close," I chattered on. "Be sure and let me know if he comes around here. I notice you never bark at Kirk or Harry or Bert anymore. Just troublemakers like Eugene."

I was just talking because it felt good to talk. The weather had warmed enough that the snow was almost gone. I'd come out to dump the scrap bucket and bring in a fresh pail of water, but I wasn't ready to go back inside yet.

"What do you think, dog? Is home really wherever you make it?"

Suddenly he stiffened. I could feel a difference in his muscles even through my wooly layer of mitten. "What is it?" I hardly dared to ask out loud. Looking around the yard, I didn't see anything different at all. "Do you smell a fox?"

He almost pulled away from me but seemed to hesitate at the last minute and then scoot closer to my side. I put my arms around him. "What is it?"

He was staring at the road. He didn't bark or move another muscle, he just stood in wary attention and watched as Orville Mueller's mail truck sauntered its way down our lane with two heads inside. Was Donald with him again? I got up and moved to the back porch where I knew I was out of sight of the road. Horse kept at my side the whole way.

"Thank you. I'd rather not have them see me outside." I petted the dog's head. "Do you always watch the mailman?"

I'd never paid attention to how Horse reacted to Orville before. Could he possibly know that he had somebody with him today? Maybe it wasn't Donald. After all, Donald had a job in town somewhere. How could he have the time to ride along on the mail route? It must have been his day off, that time he'd done it before.

Horse didn't bark, just kept his alert. I was sure he'd settle down and relax again as soon as Orville drove the truck past our mailbox and on down the lane. But he stood stock still, and then suddenly sprung into action like he'd been wound up and let loose. He went tearing out across the yard barking and carrying on. And at the same time I could barely hear the sound of tires easing up our drive. They were pulling in.

I dashed inside. "Mom! Orville's coming to the house. And he's got somebody with him."

Mom glanced out the window with a shake of her head. "Surely Donald has enough sense—" She stopped herself mid-sentence. "Maybe it's just Orville with a letter that's charge-on-delivery."

But I could see out the window too, and now I could tell for sure that it was Donald in the passenger seat. He stayed put and let Orville get out of the truck and come to the house alone.

Mom had to step out to shush the dog and call him aside so Orville could get to the porch. He was delivering a package for Katie that wouldn't fit in our box. A birthday present from her boyfriend. From inside the house, I listened with relief to the brief words between Orville and my mother, and I thought he was going to turn away without incident. But he suddenly stopped.

"Uh . . . Mrs. Wortham, my cousin asked me to please let you folks know he's sorry for scaring Sarah in town the other day. He'd . . . uh . . . he'd like the opportunity to apologize to her in person."

My mother sounded gentle yet emphatic. "You may tell Donald that his apology is accepted, but Sarah doesn't want to talk to him. We're sorry if his feelings are hurt, but he'd be better off turning his attention elsewhere."

"Um, he wouldn't mind if you were right there to listen in on what he had to say," Orville persisted.

Mom's answer made me smile. "I'm not interested in listening in. But my husband would be. So I suggest that Donald take the matter up with Mr. Wortham directly if he wants any more to do with Sarah."

This time Orville turned away. "Uh, yes, ma'am. I'll tell him."

Mom held the dog till Orville was in the truck, then she came in with Katie's package. I hugged her.

"Maybe Donald'll finally leave me alone."

"Let's hope so," Mom agreed. "He certainly is a persistent fellow, putting his cousin up to such a request."

She put on water for tea and I set the package on the table for her. It wasn't heavy or especially big, just too wide for the mailbox. My curiosity about it should have crowded away any further thought of Donald's latest vain effort, but Mom's words stuck in my mind. *He certainly is persistent.*

Why? Why on earth would anybody be so completely bullheaded? I was engaged, for heaven's sakes! I'd turned him down or ignored him I didn't know how many times. Why didn't he just get the message and give up?

Then I remembered something he'd said. *"I care about you . . . I don't want you hurt . . ."*

Could that be true? Really?

It was a numbing thought, and I had to get away from it as quickly as possible. I turned the radio on, but to my dismay it was more static than music and I had to turn it off again. So I turned my attention back to Katie's package. "What do you suppose Dave has sent all the way from Wisconsin?" I asked, hoping to stir a conversation.

"We'll have to wait and see." Mom was pulling tea herbs from the cupboard and didn't look my way. "Katie's going to be surprised. It's the first time he's sent a gift."

I grabbed the honey jar and a couple of spoons and sat in the closest kitchen chair. "Are they getting serious?"

"I think so." Mom turned around. "It's beginning to look like it."

She passed me the spearmint and chamomile, and I set them on the table. Mom reached for cups and I watched her. People said I looked like her, and I knew I did a little. But Mom seemed to have changed lately. The little lines at her eyes and the corners of her mouth never used to be there. Was it aging her to think how close we were to the day when none of us kids would be home? Or was I just noticing such things more because I'd been so aware of my own growing up?

Things were about to be so different. Everybody would be grown and on their own before long, even Emmie.

"Mom, do you think you and Dad'll be lonely after Katie and I have married and moved away?"

She was checking the water to see if it was hot enough.

211

"Let's not hurry Katie, honey. But when the day comes, I don't know. It will seem strange. But there's always plenty to do around here. And your father and I enjoy each other's company."

If only Frank had found a place as close as Mabel Mueller's house in Dearing. Only fifteen miles! I almost told Mom that I wished we were going to be living nearby so I could see her more, but I knew she'd tell me that Frank was doing the right thing and deserved our support.

She always seemed cheerful about Frank's decision and the idea of our life together so far away. I figured she understood him, maybe better than I did. But it had to make her at least a little sad to think of Robert overseas, me about to be in the northern part of the state, and Katie maybe ending up in Wisconsin. It made *me* sad.

I spooned dried spearmint leaves into the tea strainer over my cup and sighed. Life bumped along too fast to let people get a comfortable hold on things sometimes. When I was little, I used to think that Katie, Rorey, and I should all grow up to live next door to each other. I no longer felt that way about Rorey, but with Katie it would still be nice. Especially if we were both close to Mom and Dad. But such wishful thinking only led to foolish, wayward notions, and I found myself daydreaming about houses in Dearing. It was such a nice town. Not as nice as our farm, but I'd always liked it.

Mom poured my tea water and her own. She sat down and pushed tea leaves away from the edge of her strainer with a spoon. "You needn't worry about us, you know," she assured me. "Once you're married, if we get lonely we're liable to show up at your doorstep for a visit."

"I hope so."

"It'd be quite an adventure, actually. Might be fun."

I smiled. I really could picture my parents doing that. Even unannounced. It was something rather delightful to look forward to.

I turned my thinking to Frank as we sipped our tea. He'd be just as thrilled as I about a visit from my parents. He'd have so much to show them. I tried to picture the place the way he'd described it to me, but I really couldn't. I did know that he was in a store that wasn't very full yet, but he was already open for business, making things right out in the open where people could watch. Plus he took orders. And did repairs. The shop was surely very nice, but from what Frank said, the house was even better, with plenty of room for overnight guests.

It felt good to find myself thinking about Camp Point in positive ways. Frank'd said business might seem slow for a while, but he was doing all right. A store in Quincy had ordered two of his cedar chests for their showroom and another store in Paloma wanted one too. I couldn't be surprised. He made the most beautiful cedar chests I'd ever seen. Everybody who saw them would want one of their own. At this rate, it might take him a long time to get his own storefront full.

I wondered if I would make friends as quickly as Frank had. He'd told me about Mr. Willings from the church and an elderly lady named Hannah Haywood, a brand-new neighbor, who helped with his letters to me. I liked her already, because she always included a nice little note of her own.

There were good things about Frank's move. Kirk acknowledged that he had real "guts" and plenty of brains to even make a start. I was proud when I heard things like that. And sitting with Mom over a cup of tea, I found it easier to level my thinking and relax. The idea of moving didn't seem so strange right now. Just an inevitable part of life. I prayed to keep this frame of mind and not let fretful thinking bog me down again. I was in for an adventure, so I might as well enjoy it.

Emmie came over that day when she got out of school. By then, Mom was making noodles and Emmie was glad to help her. Bert and Harry joined us for supper, and even though it wasn't her birthday yet, Katie went ahead and opened the package. It was a fat photograph album in a binder that could be opened to add more pages. Her boyfriend, Dave, had started the first page with a picture of himself at home and one in the service, plus a picture of him and Katie together when he'd visited last November. She said she loved the album because it was ready to fill up with memories. And I wished I had one with pictures from when we were kids.

We popped popcorn that evening, and Dad played checkers with Harry while the rest of us sat around the table with pens and paper. Mom was working on a letter to Robert, Katie was writing to Dave, and I started another letter to Frank. Emmie was copying several of Mom's recipes, and Bert was finishing an article he was working on for the Mcleansboro newspaper. I liked evenings like this, except that it would have been even better if Frank were sitting here too, carving one of his angel figures or something.

I wondered if he missed us as badly as I missed him. I wondered what he did up there evening after evening all alone. In a way, I would feel comfort to leave here and be with him as soon as possible, just so nobody would have to be by themselves.

February flew by us, and March rushed in. Dad started taking fewer hours at the station, getting ready for spring planting. And the telephone company was making preparations for stringing wire out our way. Frank was still speaking at that church. Mr. Willings had become the pastor. And I was getting so eager to see Frank at Easter that just the thought of it consumed a great deal of my attention.

Rorey's plans vexed me, though it didn't seem to bother

Frank when I explained. She still wanted her wedding in our yard, which was complicated enough. But I was most exasperated that she insisted on having it such a short while before ours. I'd asked her to consider changing her date but she refused, even though preparing for both weddings was going to throw everything into a tizzy. We'd chosen our date first. Why did she have to do this? I couldn't help thinking that she was wanting to turn as much of the attention on herself as she could.

Frank didn't care. He said if she was determined to get married then the date was up to her. And if people were too tuckered out after her wedding to celebrate ours then we'd just be blessed in the quiet. But I knew that'd never happen. Everybody'd do both, which would have my mother whirling busy, since she was something of a mother to Rorey too.

As if Rorey's timing weren't already bad enough, in the middle of March I got a letter from her. I knew I wouldn't like it when she said at the beginning to please not get mad, just consider what she had to say. Knowing Rorey, that meant she was about to get obnoxious, and it didn't take her long.

I hope you're doing a lot of thinking while Franky is away. I didn't wanna upset you while we was there, but there's something I have to ask. Don't it bother you what people will think about you marrying someone you grew up with? I mean, we're all practically brothers and sisters. I've been asked if your parents adopted all of us, especially Emmie cause she's youngest and Franky cause he's mostly lived at your house since he was fifteen. Don't that make him almost your brother? People I know think so.

By the time I got to that point, I was already mad. What was wrong with Rorey that she would try again with her stupid arguments to convince me not to marry her brother? Was it me she despised, or Frank, or both? I didn't really want to read on, and maybe I shouldn't have, but I did.

> *You're scared of change, Sarah. You like Frank cause he's familiar. You never gave no other boy a chance cause you wanted things to stay the same. But it ain't a healthy way to look at life. How do you know he's the one for you? I couldn't have married Robert. We were over to your house and at your table too much. He seems like my brother too. And Franky's been over there more than the rest of us. You just want what's comfortable, like a little kid dragging a old blanket. Why don't you take a chance? Be brave enough to give somebody else an opportunity before it's too late.*

I crumpled the letter in my hand. How dare she? She didn't mention Donald Mueller directly, but I knew what she was getting at. Had he put her up to this? Or was she hard-hearted enough to come up with it on her own?

How could I respond? I was in the kitchen alone reading the letter. Should I show Mom and Dad? How would they react? What would Frank think, or Lizbeth, or Emmie?

Everybody else had seemed happy all along that Frank and I had chosen to be together. Rorey was risking angering more than just me by writing this letter. Why didn't she care? Did she seriously think I'd listen to her and start dating now? How could she want me to?

She was just hateful, vicious, and cruel. She always had been, throwing my doll down the stairs when we were little girls, and years later lying to blame Frank for the barn fire that was her and her boyfriend's fault. I didn't know how she could grow up so mean, but she had, and she was meaner now than ever.

Of course Frank was familiar, but I loved him for plenty of reasons besides that. And he'd stayed at our house more than the other Hammonds because their pa didn't want him home. Where else would he go? He was already working with my father, and he slept in the woodshop almost as much as in the house anyway.

Nobody'd been adopted. They'd had their pa till Frank was eighteen, and then it was Frank who moved back to their farmhouse to care for the younger ones. Of course we were all close, like family. But we weren't blood kin, and nobody else saw anything wrong with Frank and I deciding to marry. Leave it to Rorey to invent something like this to try to mess up our happiness.

I grabbed paper and started a letter in reply, but I felt like I was just spitting fury.

How could you be so hateful? I'm going to marry your brother regardless of what you think, and you and Eugene and Donald Mueller can all go suck eggs. Don't you dare write me another letter suggesting I date somebody else, or I'll . . .

I couldn't finish. There wasn't any use. I crumpled my letter up with Rorey's and threw them both into the cookstove. Maybe the best response was none at all. Even telling anybody else would just flame tempers, and what good would that do? It was going to be hard enough for everybody as it was to accept Rorey and Eugene marrying, and their abrasive, intrusive presence at our wedding time. Why make it harder? If I kept quiet, maybe she'd forget her nonsense. Or at least have the intelligence to keep her mouth shut.

Only later did I stop and think that Mom had seen the letter when I first brought it in the house. I prayed she wouldn't ask what was inside, but that evening she wanted to know if Rorey had said anything specific about her wedding plans.

"No," I said simply, hoping she wouldn't ask further.

"I was hoping she'd tell us what she'd decided about a wedding dress, and her guest list, decorations, and such."

"Nothing about her wedding, Mom."

"Well, she doesn't write a letter often. What did she have to say? May I see it?"

My stomach tensed. "Um . . . she was just kind of rambling. I burned it."

I bit my lower lip and looked away, wondering how Mom was going to react. We normally shared letters from Robert or Rorey or Willy. And burning it would have seemed strange even if we didn't.

To my surprise, Mom didn't press me further. Maybe she knew something had upset me. It might have been plain on my face. But she didn't ask. Until bedtime. And then she had only one tender question.

"Is everything all right, honey?"

I didn't want to say anything, but part of it came rolling out before I could stop it.

"Rorey thinks I ought to date somebody else, Mom. She says I never gave anybody else a chance and I ought to before it's too late."

Mom shook her head. "That's why you burned the letter."

"Yeah! What's she trying to do? Why would she want to break us up? It's her own brother!"

"Rorey's behavior toward Frank has always been puzzling, honey. Just like her father's."

"I know. But this is just stupid. Maybe it's because Donald Mueller is Eugene's friend. I didn't want to tell you. I didn't think it would help matters to get anybody else as mad as I am."

"I can understand that. But I'm glad you said something." She gave me a hug. "Rorey can be a trial sometimes, I'm well aware. And if Donald asked her to intervene for him, they're both just being foolish. Did she mention him directly?"

"No. She didn't give any names. Are you going to tell Dad?"

"Probably."

"Do you think he'll be mad?"

"Disgusted, more like. At Rorey's impudent behavior."

"I started to write back, but I'm not sure what to say."

"That's all right. Maybe you don't need to answer. I'll write and ask her how she's coming with her wedding plans. And crow a little about how happy you and Frank are with each other."

I smiled. "Okay. Thanks."

That should have been the end of Rorey's dumb ideas bothering my mind, but late that night I woke up remembering Betty Weir from the bank asking me once if Frank was my adopted brother. People knew he'd been around my family for years. Not only since he was fifteen, but since his mother died years before that. People had seen us with the Hammond kids, and had seen Frank working alongside my father and assumed they were father and son. Might it seem odd that we would want to be together? *Was* it odd?

Could Rorey be right? Did people think Frank was like my brother? But why would it matter what people thought?

I tried to dismiss such thinking, but it was hard to quiet the awkward, accusing voice that suddenly pestered me.

You are afraid of change. That's why you wanted to marry Frank and didn't think of other boys. You thought

*he would be just like this farm. Comfortable. You thought
everything would stay the same.*

It wasn't true. It couldn't possibly be, because my
feelings for Frank were so much deeper than that. I
hadn't wanted to date the boys from our one-room school
because I'd seen them be cruel and unkind, mostly to
Frank. But I'd never seen Frank treat anyone the way
he'd been treated. He was stronger. Quieter. And far more
empathetic. Special, just like our pastor had said. It was
grossly unfair to think I only wanted to be with him
because I was afraid of the unknown.

I didn't know why I was having such a ridiculous men-
tal battle. Maybe it was a test, to see if I was strong and
sensible enough to stay with the commitment I'd made.
But what bothered me most was that nothing should
be bothering me about it. I was weak, pitifully so, to be
feeling tested at all. Why would I doubt my own motives
and my love for Frank? It didn't make sense.

"Father, help me," I prayed. "Am I really afraid of the
unknown? I want to love Frank the way I should and
let him be his own man the way Mom said. I want to
put my life in your hands and not worry for tomorrow. I
promise again to trust you. Help me do better. I promise
to trust Frank too, and not let these crazy thoughts, or
foolish people, come between us."

I lay still in the darkness. I could hear Horse's distant
barking outside.

Why? I kept wondering. *Why have my thoughts been
so back-and-forth? What would Frank say if he knew even
half of all this?*

I should tell him. I should confess it all. He had a
right to know. Not just about Donald, but about Rorey,
and especially my struggles. But how could I tell him?
What if he thought I wanted to put off the wedding or
back out of it altogether? What if *he* decided we ought
to wait? I didn't want that at all.

It was wedding nerves. That's exactly what was plaguing me, just like Mrs. Post had warned me. I'd brushed off her notion as something that wouldn't concern me, but I should have listened. No wonder she'd had a hard time concentrating enough to get anything done. I was having a far worse time than I could ever have expected. And it certainly didn't help matters to have Rorey and Donald plaguing me with their stupid ideas.

Everybody gets scared. Everybody gets nervous before their wedding. And being scared turns your thinking on its ear. But things would be all right. No need to trouble Frank with a bunch of foolish concerns. He had enough to think about running a business. *Our* business. It was going to be fun.

I was so glad we were scheduled for another telephone call the next day. I couldn't wait to hear Frank's voice. We started off talking about things on the farm and Frank's Easter visit coming up soon. I felt so happy that he'd be here for a few days. But while he was telling me about his week, I suddenly wondered about the letters we'd forwarded to him, from Mary Ensley. Was he writing to her? He'd never explained. I'd never asked. Should I?

Then out of the blue, he had an announcement to make. "Sarah, I've got to tell you the greatest thing. That little blind girl, Mary Ensley—she gave her heart to Jesus."

I was speechless, feeling suddenly caught in unfairness, questioning the letters when he'd been faithfully ministering.

"She's been goin' through a rough time since her papa died," he continued. "Did I tell you that? I tried to be encouraging after the first letter, but then she wrote back askin' all kinds a' questions about God. I told her what I could an' asked her to find a minister in her town. I'm glad she listened. He led her to trust in the Lord, and I believe her mama's gonna turn to God too in time. Pray

221

for her if you will, Sarah. It ain't been easy for 'em since the accident."

I didn't know how to answer. "I—I will, Frank. I'll pray for her."

"Is somethin' wrong?"

"N-no. It's just . . . I'm proud of you, bringing a child to the Lord."

"It wasn't me. It was that minister in her town—"

"Who wouldn't have been involved if it weren't for you."

I could almost hear the smile in his voice. "One plants an' another waters. I guess it all comes together."

"I love you so much." It was probably silly, but my eyes started filling with tears, and he seemed to know right away.

"Are you sure nothin's wrong?"

"Oh, Frank! I feel so unworthy. While I'm struggling, you're busy at the Lord's business. I wish I could be more like you."

"Why are you strugglin'? What's wrong?"

I could hear the concern in his voice. I knew I'd have to be careful what I said, or he'd drop everything and rush home early. It'd be good to see him, to feel his strong arms around me, but I didn't want it to be because I was so weak he couldn't do anything different. "I'm all right," I said quickly. "I think I'm just nervous. About the wedding and so many changes. I wish I was as strong in the Lord as you are. I wish I could minister too. But I feel like I'll be very little help in that way at all."

"You'll be perfect," he said, the smile back in his voice. "I know you will. I've seen you plenty strong."

I had no idea when he could mean, but I didn't ask.

"The changes'll be good, Sarah Jean. I wish you were here already. The church people is anxious to meet you. I've told 'em so much about you they love you already."

"Goodness, I hope I don't disappoint."

"You won't. Ain't no way."

He was so confident. *Lord, help me be like that!*

We couldn't linger on the phone long. He'd be visiting soon enough. I could hardly wait, and he said he was just as anxious. It was bittersweet, hanging up the receiver that day. How could I be so blessed and yet so ignorant that I often lost sight of the blessing? Lord, help me indeed.

At home that night, I made coffee bread and thought of Frank way off by himself so cheerfully serving the Lord. It was right not to worry him with my petty doubts, at least not over the telephone. And when we were face to face, the uncertainties would fly away like chaff in the wind.

24

Frank

I kept trying to handle what mail I got by myself, but despite all my work at it I still had trouble. So I ventured across the street to see Mrs. Haywood every few days, and she would read for me and serve pie or cookies. Then I would return the favor by helping with her yard work or whatever else she might need done. She was seventy or eighty years old, maybe more, without any family close by. It bothered me to ask for her help, an' I kept feeling worse about it until she got after me.

"You know what I can't do?" she asked one day. "I can't move my heavy furniture to clean behind it, but you moved it for me the last time you were here. Do you think I should be downcast over that? I'd rather be grateful. God made people to need each other so we'd pull together and not be so lonesome. I look forward to you coming over. It brightens my day."

I felt better about it then. It was a different thing for me, to think of my inability as a blessing to Mrs. Haywood. But she was a widow living alone, and she really liked to be needed. So I thanked God that my lack could be an avenue of help to her, and that was a big step for me, one I'd never quite taken before.

I was happy working, and spending a lot of my time alone. I didn't get many orders, not yet. I concentrated a lot of time on getting things made to display in the store, though I knew I'd be bringing what I had in the old WH workshop when I came back up after Easter. I sold a table here almost as soon as I'd finished it, but not much else out of the store, not yet. Some folks called me for things I didn't expect. Could I take down a tree limb, or rehang broken-down shutters? I fixed porch steps on one house and patched a hole in the floor to match the existing hardwood in another.

Not much money coming in, and I knew when I had a family here to support I'd need more. But there was just enough now, it seemed, to manage to keep myself going and pay what I had to pay. That was a blessing, and I felt good about it.

Soon as the weather was good enough, I spent two days patching the store roof, and another patching the roof of the house too, even though the Bellors were still living in it. They were decent neighbors, but I was eager for them to move so I could set to work in my spare time getting the house ready for Sarah. Until I could do that, I spent some weekend time working on the church. Painting would have to wait till it was warmer. But I shored up the outhouse to level and fixed that wobbly rail out front.

It wore on me every Saturday about speaking to the church on Sunday evenings. And I couldn't eat much Sunday dinner for thinking about having to get up in front of everybody again. I still didn't feel adequate, but I kept doing it and they kept wanting me to, and I kept feeling blessed afterward every time. Sometimes Mrs. Haywood read Scriptures to me in preparation, which she insisted I shouldn't feel bad about, because she needed to hear it too.

225

Finally the time came for my trip back home. Mrs. Haywood hated to see me go. She said she'd miss me even though I'd only be gone about five days. Since he couldn't go down with me, Sam ran me through my route over the telephone just in case I'd forgotten some of the towns. But I'd driven it once and didn't expect any trouble.

"Looks different in the spring," he said.

That didn't sound very confident, but I didn't let it bother me. I had a wonderful time with the drive, and the most wonderful thing of all was the sight of Sarah running out of the house to meet me when I pulled into their driveway. She was so excited she couldn't hardly talk, just hugging on me and crying and laughing all at the same time. I squeezed her tight and gave her a big kiss. I don't think her father minded. At least he didn't say anything about it.

He wanted to talk. That was clear real quick, though he didn't take me off from the others till after I'd had a chance to eat something, hug on Emmie and Lizbeth, and greet Harry, Bert, and Kirk. Then after Kirk'd had a chance to tease me about my haircut and whatever else he could think of, and Lizbeth's little girl'd had a chance to cozy up and show me a picture she'd made, Mr. Wortham asked me to come outside and see their calf. I knew what he wanted. Maybe everybody else did too, because nobody come along.

"How's the business treating you?" he asked after I'd admired his new Guernsey heifer.

"It's been all right. Slow start, but I'd have to expect that."

"Paying the bills?"

I smiled a little and nodded my head. If it was anybody but Mr. Wortham, I might not feel like answering. Wouldn't be their business. But he was as good as a father to me, and I knew he was looking out for his daughter. I could tell he'd been doin' a lot of thinkin'.

226

"Would you object to a visit in a couple of weeks?"

"No." The offer took me completely by surprise. "No, that'd be nice, though I ain't in the house yet. Kinda limited in the shop, but you're welcome."

"Sarah would like to come with me. I know she would, but before I could tell her for sure one way or the other, I needed to talk to you."

"It'd be great to have you. I could introduce you to people and show her around the town—"

"That's what I thought, and it would put my heart to ease, Frank. I hope you understand. She's still my baby."

I'd never heard him call her that. He looked almost far away now, and though I could picture that I understood, I knew I really wouldn't, not till I had a child of my own about to marry and move away.

"I'll take the best care of her. I promise you, if things get hard up there, if I can't make it work, I'll move home. We'll visit every chance we can get. Lot more'n Sam and Thelma do, I promise you. An' you can come up there. We'd love to have you, whenever you want."

"I know all that. And I wanted you to know that I think you've done the right thing, even if it isn't the easiest thing for any of us."

Those words meant more to me than anything else anybody could say. And there wasn't much more to our conversation. There didn't need to be.

I loved hearing Pastor Jones on Easter Sunday and having a chance to talk with him over dinner and afterward. Mrs. Wortham had invited them and all my family to spend the afternoon. I missed having Willy, Rorey, and Sam around, though they all were supposed to make it here in June.

Even more, though, I missed Joe. The time that had passed since his death didn't really lessen the feelings, but I knew he was in heaven with Mama. I believed that Pa was too; at least I had great hope in it.

Sarah and me went for a long walk, through the timber and along the stream. We visited my folks' graves but didn't linger there very long. I held her hand as we went back across the timber again. We didn't say much. She gave me a book by Henry Thoreau that she'd been saving back since my birthday, and she said something about having another surprise for later.

We found a pretty spot and sat on a log. She leaned back against me and read Thoreau's first chapter. I'd heard about this book from a former schoolteacher and I'd been wanting to get my ears around it whenever I could, but the rest'd have to wait.

We'd already talked over some things, along with Sarah's mom, so we pretty much knew everything we needed toward our wedding. I gave Sarah what money I could to pay for things. I wouldn't have felt right for the Worthams to have to take care of it all, even though they were the bride's parents.

I guess the biggest thing we didn't know about our wedding time was how much Rorey's plans would end up affecting ours when it came right down to it. She hadn't told them much of anything that she wanted yet.

In a way I hoped Rorey would re-think and not get married at all. But I realized that she prob'ly hoped the same for Sarah. I was concerned about Eugene being an unbeliever and not very reliable, but Rorey was concerned about me being too scatterbrained and illiterate to be a good provider. I prayed that Eugene and I could both prove the doubters wrong.

Leaving again was sad, even though I'd be seeing Sarah again when she came up to Camp Point in only two weeks. I found myself hoping to find the Bellors already moving when I got back so Sarah and her dad could stay in the house while they were there. Emmie clung on me a little before I drove away. Me settling somewhere else seemed to be harder on her than anybody, and I felt bad for her about it. But I promised to come down a lot and that she could come up there any time she wanted and stay as long as she liked.

Kirk asked me who was reading for me up there. I didn't feel the need to answer. I just asked him who was gettin' everybody up early and keeping the barn stalls clean and the tools sharp now that I wasn't around.

It hadn't occurred to me to sharpen things for people, but Mrs. Wortham had asked me to do her scissors and kitchen knives while I was down. Once I got back to the store, I'd have everything I needed with me for that. Might make a few cents here and there on the side if I was to let people know.

I loaded the rest of my tools and a rocker, a pair of matching chairs, another cedar chest, and eight or ten carvings from the workshop. They sure would make the storefront look better. Leaving Sarah was the hardest thing. She didn't cry, but I knew she was close to it. She'd told me she believed in what I was doing, that she understood why it was right for us. But I knew it was still hard for her to see me go, and to think of being away from her folks once we got married.

Not everybody's blessed with folks like hers. I'd hugged on Mrs. Wortham and she'd hugged on me like we were already kin. And we were, really. Sometimes I dreamed of what I'd be like if I'd never known the Worthams, and it wasn't pretty.

It wasn't easy sayin' good-bye, and Sarah and I lingered arm in arm longer than we should've. But then it was time to be back on the road.

I put miles under me as quickly as I could, and stopped in Auburn for a bite to eat down the street from the Commercial Hotel. It was a clear evening now, and there were flowers in the square.

I thought of the Ensleys and the Plattens as I drove on, but I didn't try to look them up. Sam had invited me to stay the night so I hurried on to Jacksonville and got there before the kids got to bed. They seemed to have fun climbing on me, and I didn't complain. Albert had a tutor now who also spent time teaching Thelma hand signs so she'd understand the things Albert was learning to say. I was fascinated, and had Thelma teach me what she already knew. Albert loved it. When I left, he used his hands to tell me he loved me. He'd been catching on quick, just like I knew he would.

Camp Point looked the same as I'd left it, and it was with a strange feeling of loss that I got back into my work schedule. I'd gotten used to being mostly alone, but the Easter vacation had me out of the habit. Now I was missing Sarah awful bad. But she called the first day to hear my voice and know I'd gotten there all right. That helped a lot.

She said they'd have the telephone line to their house before the wedding. I was glad. That would make talking to her folks so much easier once we got back home here. Sarah brought up the idea of a honeymoon again. At first we'd decided against going anywhere on account of the time and expense, but she told me she'd like to do some little thing at least. It would be a lot of fun.

"What would *you* like to do?" she asked. "Is there someplace you'd like to see?"

I knew right away an answer to that. "It wouldn't be a little thing, Sarah Jean. But maybe for someday. I'd like to visit water so big you can't see the other side. Where you can go out on a boat till you don't see no shore no matter where you look."

"Franky, we should."

"The ocean's a long way."

"There's a place closer than the ocean."

The Great Lakes, she was talking about. Lake Michigan especially, because it was the closest. Sarah was a little nervous about the notion of going even that far, but she favored the idea anyway. "Let's at least think about it, all right? You're brave enough. It would be quite an adventure."

We agreed to think on it and pray on it. She said she'd ask her folks to pray on it too. I would've loved to jump in and tell her we should do it. But I wasn't sure yet about the money. It might not be the most responsible way to behave just starting out.

Mrs. Haywood was so glad I was back that she cooked me a whole meal. She was thrilled that Sarah was coming for a visit and offered to put her up at her house since the Bellors hadn't moved yet.

We'd lost an elderly member of our congregation while I'd been gone. Mrs. Haywood told me about it and said Mr. Willings was taking it hard.

"He'll be glad you're in town. The funeral is tomorrow, and he thought you'd want to be there."

I did, even though I remembered how hard the funeral for Pastor Ells had been. This one, for a sweet elderly lady, was very quiet, with hardly anybody in attendance from outside the church. Pastor Willings did a very good job. Speaking at funerals must be the hardest of all the various duties of a pastor. I knew it wore on Mr. Willings to be a pillar of support for everyone else when he himself was also grieving. I didn't learn until after the funeral that the woman who died had been a cousin of the deceased pastor and Mr. Willings's childhood neighbor. That bothered me for his sake, and I looked in on him several times over the next couple of weeks because I was worried for him.

He taught me how to play chess one night. I'd played checkers with my brothers plenty of times when I was a kid, but never chess. I thought I'd be pretty poor at it, but Pastor Willings said I did fine for a beginner. The little carved chess pieces got me thinking about making my own style of set. He said it was a great idea and I oughta get one on display in my store as soon as I could. He thought I'd get orders for that, for sure.

Secretly I worked on the horse carving that the bank had commissioned. And I made shelves for one wall in the store front, though I hadn't had time to fill them. I advertised in the *Camp Point Journal* the kinds of things I made and the kinds of repairs I did, as well as knife and tool sharpening. To my surprise, that got people bringing me things to sharpen almost as soon as the paper came out, so I had plenty of work.

I hadn't seen anything at all from Milton Pratt since the night I turned him down about his store. But I knew he lived around here somewhere, and I went past his empty building uptown every once in a while and thought about him. I hadn't meant to do him wrong. I hoped he didn't feel that I had. But everything about the Bellors' place was what I needed, even down to the neighbor across the street, and I was certain that of the two I'd made the right choice.

Mr. Pratt surprised me one afternoon by marching right into the store. I didn't recognize him at first. He walked in leaning heavy on his cane, ignored my greeting, and started inspecting everything I had in there. I just let him look. Finally he come close to inspect what I was working on, my wedding gift for Sarah, and I took a better look at him and realized who he was.

"Kinda empty in here," he told me.

"I'm workin' on that."

"You know what you need?"

Inventory, of course. We'd just established that fact. But I waited to see what he would say.

"You need six or eight stoves and a whole row of lamps up against the wall."

I had to set down the chisel I'd been holding. "That's not exactly what I'm working toward here."

"I can see that, but you've got the room. And I've

got renters who don't want what's left of my inventory. They're putting in fashions, and they want everything out of their way."

I almost turned him down flat, but I had to remind myself that things were different now. This wasn't Sam's arrangement, and I was already the boss here, which wasn't gonna change. Maybe I could help him, and it would make the place look stocked like a business ought to. That could help both of us, if we could agree on details.

"Ain't got the ready cash to buy your stock outright, Mr. Pratt, but I could sell it for you if you give me a commission rate. Then all you'll have to do is get it here and come and collect when I make a sale for you, or I can bring you your money if you'd rather."

It didn't take us two minutes to make an agreement. He said he'd be happy to come and collect, but he didn't have a way to move anything. Could I do it with my truck? I agreed, hoping I wouldn't regret this. His remaining stock wouldn't fill the place, but it would take up plenty of room. Hopefully, it would sell pretty quick, and as each piece left I could fill the empty spots with more of my work as I got it finished.

Carving took time. Especially the detailed figures and the finer large pieces of furniture. Realistically, I knew it'd be months before I could make enough to really fill the store, and that was only if I didn't sell many of the pieces as I was going along. So I could see Mr. Pratt's inventory as a blessing. For both of us. And maybe another friendship too. He said we oughta seal the deal over a sandwich and coffee at Miller's, and I agreed. While we were there, he introduced me to everybody in the place and told them what we were planning to do.

Sarah and her father were due in only three days. But I spent one of those days moving stoves and lamps in my truck. Mrs. Haywood thought the whole idea was wonderful. Mr. Pratt was on hand to watch me and give me quite a bit of opinion, and while he was at my shop again, Mrs. Haywood brought us lemonade.

She took it on herself to write on paper the agreement between Mr. Pratt and me. That was the first time she thought to question how I was keeping books. When Mr. Pratt was gone she asked how I was handling that. By then I knew her pretty well. I showed her my ledger book. It wasn't real good, I knew that, but I could make sense of it, and I knew Sarah would be able to because she was used to how I'd done before.

But Mrs. Haywood was pretty stumped. I had simple symbols for everything. The work I did, every kind of furniture, days of the week, even utilities and other expenses, so I had some record of everything coming in and going out. She thought it confusing and completely dependent on my memory, which was right.

"Takes me a long time, especially with invoices," I admitted. "But I been settin' a mark down prompt an' not missing nothin' so far as I know. Sarah'll write it all down her way after we're married, an' it'll be clear to anybody. But I'll still hafta keep track a' the day-to-day for her, so I know I gotta make it work."

"You're something of a marvel, you know that?"

I told her Sarah's system was prettier. She didn't figure totals in her head like I did, but it didn't take her near so long to write them down.

"I can't wait to meet her."

"You'll like her. Everybody does. She's real special."

"She must be," Mrs. Haywood said, taking a long look at one of my carvings. "She's found a way to hook a real prize."

I shouldn't have said nothing at all, but I was surprised enough that the words come out before I could stop them. *"Me* a prize? Are you kiddin'?"

She laughed. "Don't you know what a catch you are?

A handsome young man, so smart and talented. You're an artist, plain and simple. And you've stirred plenty of talk among the young ladies in town. It's a good thing that girl of yours is coming up to be seen with you. That'll calm things at least a little."

I didn't know what to say. I'd never had the interest of no girls except Sarah. She was the one that got other people's attention. I knew there were prob'ly boys back home that would still try to woo her if they could. But me? The girls hadn't never looked my way because they remembered me as a backwards misfit like when I was little. That was a hard picture to change. But here, I was the stranger. That explained a lot, because mystery adds its own interest.

"I thought you'd want to know the kind of talk that's started about the new bachelor in town," Mrs. Haywood said. "Don't be surprised if you get the young ladies coming in viewing your work."

"Thanks for the warnin'."

"What's this?"

She laid her hand on the large piece of walnut leaning against a workbench. It was only half shaped, with the beginnings of the flowers I envisioned chiseled into the center. "It's my wedding present."

She looked at me funny for a moment and then smiled. "For Sarah, you mean."

"Yes, ma'am." It would become a tall double-arched headboard with a full bouquet of mixed flowers, their stems all intertwined. I'd known for a long time that Sarah would like a handmade headboard on our bed in our new house together, and I knew she'd like this. But I'd have to hide it when she come up.

"Beautiful," Mrs. Haywood told me.

"It ain't yet. But I aim to make it that way."

She said something about Sarah being mightily blessed

and then asked me if she'd ever told me about her late husband. She had, but not very much.

"He was a carpenter. Helped to build quite a few of the houses in town. He would have loved your work." She smiled. "He was also the handsomest man that ever lived."

I smiled too. It was nice to think of Mrs. Haywood still so much in love with her departed husband. Sad, of course, but somehow blessed all at the same time. She offered to bring me a cup of coffee and a piece of pie, but I turned her down and took her out for a sandwich. And she said she could help me with my bookkeeping until the wedding.

"Only if you let me pay you."

She shook her head. "Wouldn't take me long and I'd enjoy it."

"I ain't workin' nobody for free."

She looked over her glasses at me. "All right then. A sandwich every week and you come over and move my furniture whenever I want to clean."

Because it was Mrs. Haywood and we already had a pretty good arrangement between us, I couldn't do nothing but agree. I was obligated to let her help, she said, because I was already doing most of her yard work and errands and that was more than enough for the reading she did. She agreed to do something else for me too. Sarah and her father would want to look over every inch of the store and the house. I needed a place to hide the headboard while they were here.

"They won't be into my things," she said, "even if they're in my home."

She offered to let me hide the headboard in her basement, and once I got it over there she covered it with a couple of sheets. Then I just had the regular tidying to do, getting the sawdust swept out of the workshop and everything looking as nice as I could. I already had a feather mattress in the corner to sleep on as long as I was living in the back shop, and I thought I'd see about borrowing another one from Mr. Willings so Mr. Wortham could stay in the shop with me.

"Why don't you both just come here?" Mr. Willings offered when I asked him. "You're not quite equipped for guests till you can get in that house."

I wasn't sure how I felt about that. I didn't know what Mr. Wortham would think either, so I decided I'd just leave it up to him. I told the Bellors when my company'd be coming, hoping they'd have things cleaned up and looking nice, but I had no control over that. They'd been to Carthage, Mr. Bellor told me, to see about the house there. It was April already and he was leaving his job here and starting his new one in May, so they oughta be moving. But there'd been problems with the house they'd thought they were getting. So now they were looking at another one.

"I know," he said with a worried look. "Our papers say you take possession May first. We're just hoping, praying, that we can be in the new place that fast."

It wouldn't seem fast to me. I'd been waiting since February. But I could understand if they were dealing with a completely different piece of property now that things'd be delayed.

"You got time yet," I told him.

"Not enough, it doesn't seem like. We're packing. Won't take us long to move when we get in our new place, but the house we want is still lived in. We'll have to wait till they can move."

"Did they say when?"

"Not yet. Could you see clear to give us an extra month if we need it?"

I agreed. What else could I do? June first would still give me a little time with the place. I'd have over a week in June before I left to spend time back home ahead of the wedding.

237

Things were turning out differently than I expected about the house, that was for sure. But everything else was going well. Sarah called me to tell me they'd be leaving on tomorrow's train. She'd wanted her mother and Katie and Emmie to all come too, but they decided they'd do that after the wedding, once we were situated. The train would be at the depot tomorrow evening. I had such a fluttery excitement I couldn't hardly stand it.

They planned to stay three days, and Mrs. Haywood and Mr. Willings both said they'd like to feed 'em while they were here. But that was my job more than theirs. I figured I'd let them each cook us one meal if they really wanted to, and I'd take care a' the rest. I had a table and chairs now, and a couple of pots to cook with. We'd make it just fine.

I fixed the store to look as nice as it could. What carvings I had were sitting pretty on a shelf with four wall plaques hanging above that. The furniture was arranged along the south side and around the workstation I'd set up to sharpen things or sit and carve where I could talk to the customers who came in. Mr. Pratt's stoves and lamps were only along the north wall, and I was pleased with the way they added to the place, even though I hoped they'd sell for him quick.

It was hard to concentrate on anything the morning of the day they were due. I thought I oughta finish Mr. Willings's horse for the bank, but I didn't think I wanted to put my hand to something that delicate when I was feeling almost giddy with anticipation. Didn't want to work at something big inside, either, lest I get wood scrap all around. I might have worked outside. It was a nice day, and I knew any customers'd see me plain enough in the side yard. But I wanted to be sure I'd hear the telephone, just in case. The train might get delayed or something. I didn't wanna miss a call.

I decided to take walnut scrap and start whittlin'

those chess pieces Mr. Willings favored. They didn't have to be fancy, at least not my first set. I was working on a bishop when a skinny young lady come in. I hadn't ever seen her before. She didn't claim to be needin' anything particular, just lookin' around, so I told her to let me know if she needed help, and I went back to my carving. Pretty quick she was right next to my workstation.

"What's that?"

"Chess piece." I showed her the knight and pawn I'd already roughed out.

"I heard you were good," she said, leaning close with a smile. "I had to come and see for myself. You are very, very good."

"My fiancée's coming tonight on the train," I blurted out real quick, not a bit comfortable with the way she was lookin' at me. "We're gettin' married in June."

"Oh? That's nice." She didn't look like she meant that. "Where's she from?"

"Down by Dearing."

"Illinois?"

"Yes, ma'am."

"Don't call me ma'am! I'm only twenty. Call me Shirley."

I didn't call her anything. I just set my attention back on my whittling.

"Are you from that Dearing town too?"

"Close by. A farm."

"Could've guessed that. I like farm boys. They're always good workers."

"I've known exceptions," I said without looking up. "And plenty a' fellas from town that don't do no shirkin'."

"Oh, I know. I guess you're right." She went to eyeing a cedar chest, rubbing her hand along the lion's head carved on the front. "This is sooo pretty," she cooed.

"Thank you."

"My mother would love this. Can you come down on the price?"

"No. Sorry about that. Took a lot a' work. First time I ever did a lion on a cedar chest. I'm kinda proud of it."

She smiled in my direction and moved on to admire the rocking chair.

I seen a shadow of movement outside the front window, and Mr. Pratt pushed his way through the door. Just then I was glad to see him.

"Sold anything yet?" he asked immediately.

"Not of yours, if that's what you mean. Only been three days."

He walked over to look at his inventory like he was worried somebody mighta broke something. Satisfied that everything was all right, he came back over and sat in the nearest sale chair.

"Do you know how to play gin rummy?"

I looked up. Mr. Pratt was a character, I could tell that. I was going to have an interesting time with him. "No, sir. Heard of it, but never played."

"Ain't hard. Want me to teach you?"

"Don't have time for that. No thank you."

"How about checkers? What you makin'? Oh, sakes a' living! It's chess pieces. You're not one a' them, are you?"

"One a' what?"

"Chess enthusiasts. You know. Those that think themselves above everybody else. Now, checkers—that's a game for the common man. No pride involved. Same way with gin rummy."

I didn't answer. I had no idea where he was gettin' his information, but it didn't mesh with anything I ever heard before.

The skinny gal give us a funny look. She admired the carved eagle on a shelf and then pretended to be looking extra close at the cedar chest again. She left after that, and I was relieved.

"That wasn't your girlfriend, was it?" Mr. Pratt asked me.

"No. She'll be here on tonight's train. That was just somebody lookin' around."

"Oh. Got any coffee?"

"A little in a pot in back. But it's cold and strong by now."

"I don't care. It'll be all right if you heat it up."

I might've drunk it myself after a while. I didn't mind lettin' him have it, but the request seemed peculiar. Why wouldn't he rather go to the restaurant where other men in town seemed to like to gather and talk sometimes? He must have been lonely without Sam and Thelma's bunch to drop in on. But I wasn't sure how it'd work out if he started droppin' in on me.

I got him the coffee. I needed to empty the pot and wash it anyway. And then I considered that maybe the Lord had called me up here for the people, especially my elders. Here was another widower, like Pastor Willings. And there was Mrs. Haywood. She and other elderly widows made up almost a third of my Sunday night congregation. I was ministering to 'em regular, in more ways than one. I got called quite a bit anymore, if one of 'em needed something done and this or that neighbor or friend wasn't available. I guessed I'd have room in my days to fit Mr. Pratt in too once in a while, even if all he wanted was my old coffee and another look at his stuff.

"Sure would be nice if Lindbergh or one of them other barnstormers would come through here again," he mused. "I miss those days. Did you know Lindbergh brought his plane to a field not half a mile from here?"

"Charles Lindbergh?"

"Yes, indeed. It was 1925, I think. Friend of mine went right up in the air with him. You ever been flyin'?"

"No, sir."

"That's right. You wasn't one that went off to the war." He took a long drink of my stale coffee. I went back to my carving, and he sat and watched me for a while. "You know," he finally said, "I'm glad you didn't rent my store."

I looked up, not sure how he meant that. "Good. I'm glad we're both happy."

"I don't think I'd like chess sets in my windows."

I smiled. "Pardon me sayin', but I don't think I'd like 'em bein' your windows."

He nodded. "Yeah. Yeah, I know. You're the independent one. Sam says you'd rather drown than grab hold on a dock made by somebody else."

"It's not quite that bad."

"Um-hm."

He gulped at the coffee, which couldn't be very good anymore. "You gonna advertise my things?"

"I can. Next time I talk to the newspaper."

"When will that be?"

I thought a minute. "I already got an ad running that's got one more edition to go. I'll go see 'em after my fiancée's visit to start a new ad for a few weeks and mention your merchandise then."

He drained his coffee and stood up. "You're gonna need one of them stoves, you know. Mrs. Bellor's taking hers with her."

I wondered how he'd heard that and how many other people in town knew pieces of my business. But it didn't matter. "If there's a stove to be bought, I'll let Sarah do the pickin' out. Along with most everything else. That's only right, since I was the one to pick the house."

He didn't have much more to say, just thanked me for the coffee, took his cane in hand, and went back out to the street.

That afternoon I closed the store and went and got a haircut. Couldn't concentrate much more on work anyhow. I cleaned up and put on my Sunday clothes. I knew when the train was due to arrive, but I couldn't keep myself from being early. Just couldn't stand to wait no longer. Only stop I made on the way was at Jacob and Judy Hurley's house to offer a dime for a bouquet of flowers. I prob'ly wouldn't a' been so bold, except that Mrs. Hurley was right out in the flower patch and she started the conversation herself as I walked by.

This'd be the first time I ever walked to meet a train. All the other times we'd ever been was in Dearing for somebody going a long ways away, or coming back. Like the day Willy and Robert and so many other boys we knew had gone off to the war. And the day Robert come home wounded. I'd dreamed about seeing my pa off on a train, but that wasn't the way he'd left us. The dream was stubborn about it, though, coming into my head several different nights, leaving me standing by the tracks while Pa and the railcar faded off in the distance.

Lord, he didn't really leave my life even when he left, did he? Sometimes I think he's still with me every day.

On purpose I hadn't let myself think on what Pa would've said if he was around to see me marry Sarah Wortham. But those thoughts come rushing at me all at once now. He wouldn't object outright. Not to my face, at least. He might talk it over with Mr. and Mrs. Wortham and see if they could really accept such a strange turn of events. He might even try to talk them out of it. But he wouldn't talk to Sarah Jean at all. She'd been bold to him once, standing up for me and my brothers and sisters, and I couldn't think of one time after that when he'd said even one more word to her.

Pa still got in my head sometimes, telling me I didn't know what I was doing or I was the same old clumsy mess as ever. And preaching? That wouldn't surprise him. Not one bit, but that didn't mean he'd have accepted me to be any good at it.

Stepping up to the depot, I breathed a painful sigh. *Why'd you have to leave us, Pa? If you'd only stayed, sharing your grief with the rest of us, then we wouldn't a' had to be burying you too. It was bad enough about Joe. But you hurt us, Pa, runnin' off like you done. You made it worse.*

I wiped my brow, trying to push those thoughts away. I needed to get my mind on happier things. Wouldn't do to have Sarah Jean finding me glum-faced. She oughta know how glad I was to see her. I stood for a while against the outside wall of the depot, but then I started pacing on the platform. Soon it wasn't so early anymore, and after a while it wasn't early at all. I wasn't sure how long I'd waited. But when I finally heard the train whistle, my heart beat faster just thinking about holding Sarah Jean. I'd have to thank her father. I'd have to make real clear how much I appreciated him bringing her up here.

I knew he figured the trip was as much for him as it was her. He wanted to look over things and be able to tell Mrs. Wortham and his own heart that I'd done all right and everything'd be fine for their little girl. I took a deep breath. What would he think? My business had a long way to go before it was truly prospering.

Sarah was the first one off the train, looking fresh and perky in a pink jacket and pretty high-heeled shoes. Oh, I was glad she was here and folks'd see her and know that I was the one that'd made quite a catch.

I run up and took her in my arms. She dropped the bag she was carrying and hugged at me too. I didn't even notice her father at first, till I saw him alongside the train claiming their luggage and doing his best to leave us alone for a minute.

"Your father's a wonderful man," I whispered to Sarah.

"He says the same about you."

"I think he's the one I learned it from."

244

She smiled and kissed me right there in the open. Just a little kiss. But I knew there was folks that seen. "It looks like a nice town," she said, a little timidly.

"It is. I got so much to show you."

She looked around. "Where's the truck?"

"I didn't bring it. The store's close enough to walk." And then I thought, *What a stupid idiot I am*. I forgot all about them having luggage. Sure, we could carry it a few blocks. I could carry most of it myself. There wasn't that much. But what a picture that'd make for them to remember.

"Let me speak a word to the man in the depot," I told her real quick. "We're just down the street from the square. It's a beautiful evening. Maybe you'd like to walk to the railroad park and have an ice cream 'fore we go home. I can bring the truck up for the luggage later."

"Oh, a walk would be nice," she agreed. "We did so much sitting on the train."

Now I had to pray that the man in the depot would let me leave the luggage. He chuckled a little about it. "Got to get out on the town first thing, huh? It's all right. But I'll only be here a little while and then it's gonna sit outside. So don't wait too long."

Sarah loved the flowers I'd gotten for her. We all enjoyed the walk. But we took our ice cream with us to my store and didn't linger in the park because Sarah said she wanted to put my flowers in water before it was too late for them. I didn't have a vase, but I gave her a pickle jar I'd emptied and washed to use for a drinking glass.

"We could have sent more dishes with you," she reminded me.

"I been makin' it fine. Don't wanna get too comfortable over here in the shop, you know."

She looked around only a little before we went back after the luggage. Just Sarah and me. Mr. Wortham wanted to stay at the store.

I didn't know what he'd tell me when we got back. But when we came in, he was in the storefront with the electric lights on, sitting in my workstation. "I've been looking over your work, Frank. It keeps getting better. You outpaced me a long time ago. You're one of the best I've ever seen."

Mr. Wortham wasn't real frivolous with his compliments, but it was hard to let that one soak in anyway. "You taught me an awful lot."

He shook his head. "You did most of what I can do when you were ten years old. There wasn't much I could teach." He picked up Mr. Willings's horse. "You have a gift."

The praise was a little unnerving. "That piece is commissioned by the bank. It's gonna be the appreciation gift for forty years of service."

"Nice choice." He set it down. "Looks good in here, Frank. You must have been working day and night."

"I ain't been able to keep workin' on new stuff every day 'cause I've been sharpening for people, doing repair, and sometimes helpin' the church folks."

"How's that going?" he asked on.

I reached for Sarah's hand. "Good. I'm looking forward to you joinin' me this Sunday night when I speak."

If I said all, I'd have to admit I was terrified about it, not for them to meet the church folks, but for them to see me minister there. Of course I was excited about it too.

We walked over every bit of the store and went outside to look a little more at the house. But it was starting to get dark, and Mrs. Haywood came across the street and greeted Sarah and her father like they were long-lost kin. Mr. Wortham thought it ideal for Sarah to stay with her. But he didn't want to go to Mr. Willings's house. Not yet. He wanted to stay at least the first night in the shop with me.

Long after the stars were out and Sarah Jean was surely asleep on one of Mrs. Haywood's beds, me and Mr. Wortham lay on mattresses on the floor of my woodshop, staring up at the dark ceiling and talking.

He had more questions about the business and the house and where I stood financially. He had questions about the town and the church and my hopes for the future too. But after we went over all that, for some reason we weren't done. We talked about my brothers and the feelings that had made me want to look around up here. I told him about Mr. Pratt and why I couldn't make his plan and Sam's work for me. But mostly, we talked about the call of God and what it can mean. I told him about me and Mr. Willings in the church, the Scripture about God using the foolish things, and how deep I was wanting to be used.

There wasn't none of it that seemed to bother him too badly, but he already had a son halfway across the world. Prob'ly nothing I said could compare to that.

Finally, late into the night, we slept, and I dreamed about Mr. Willings's horse running across the open prairie, and the carved eagle rising free of its branch-like base and soaring across the moonlit sky.

25

Sarah

I sat on the bed in Mrs. Haywood's lovely guest room as early morning sun slipped between the window curtains. Surely I should be happy instead of feeling butterflies like this. Frank seemed so different up here. So energetic and purposed. He'd picked out a good store building and a house that seemed nice too, at least from the outside. He'd done an amazing amount of work in a short time.

Why did I feel like crying? He was happy. I had no reason to think he wouldn't be successful here. He was proving his point. But far more than that, he was being used by God. Mrs. Haywood had told me last night what a blessing he'd been to their church, speaking faithfully on Sunday nights and taking care of needed repairs to the building, not to mention ministering to various needs among the congregation. She said Mr. Willings had health problems and though he'd become a wonderful pastor, he wasn't able to carry all the obligations of the pastorate alone. Which made Frank a godsend.

And I knew what that meant. They leaned on him

already. They counted on him, and that was likely only to grow, not lessen. He was planted here. Rooted, spreading out, and blossoming. Would I be able to do the same thing?

I really didn't know. My mind said yes, and then again, I questioned.

Oh, Lord, I am such a ninny sometimes. I go back and forth so much! I want this for him. I want it for both of us. But then I turn around and feel like crying and hope he'll change his mind. But it's gone too far for that, hasn't it?

Frank leaving now would be like cutting away a piece of that church and asking them to go on with a hole in their hearts. And it would tear at him too because he'd established himself. He was needed. To ask different of him would be terribly unfair.

I rose to my feet and opened the ruffly curtains. I couldn't see the store where Dad and Frank would be because this was a north window and they were across the street to the west. But I could see just a bit of the house from here, and it was pretty in the early light. Frank had told me it would need work, but that was a good thing. It meant we got a better price, and we could fix things to be the way we wanted.

We'd be looking at the house more completely today. The Bellors were going to be gone, and Frank had arranged with them for us to be in the house while they were out.

He'd promised to show me more of the town too. And tomorrow would be Sunday. We'd get to see the church then, meet more people, and hear Frank speak. I should have been excited about all of this, but I was scared too.

I wondered if I'd been this apprehensive when I was five and my family left Pennsylvania to hitchhike across the countryside. We'd had nothing left when we arrived in Illinois, and maybe that was part of my problem, though

249

things had worked all right for us. I was young back then but not immune to the worries of those Depression years. The farm had become security to me. We could always get by there, even if we had nothing but what we could pick of the plants growing around us. Here in a strange town, what could we do if times got hard again? Maybe the idea of moving made me feel like I'd been reduced to nothing again.

Trust. The gentle reminder popped into my head.

"Oh, Lord, I know!" I whispered the words to the window glass and then turned around. Mrs. Haywood was up. I knew she was. I could smell whatever she was cooking, and it was wonderful. I should go and offer my help before Dad and Frank came across the street to join us.

But my thoughts wouldn't leave me alone as I brushed my hair at the dressing table. Of course I should trust. That's what everything came down to. But in a way I wished it didn't have to be that way, that we could just go through life having everything the way we wanted and never have to worry about the unseen. Then life would be like heaven, wouldn't it?

But maybe not. I wouldn't have to have faith. Nobody would. We might all be like pampered children so used to treats that we'd never think to work for them or say thank you. God was far, far wiser than I was in knowing that wouldn't be best for us.

As I set my brush down I wondered if Rorey ever worried about the future. She didn't seem to. She acted far too full of herself and her ideas of fun to consider what lay ahead. But I didn't want to think about her now. Here I was in Camp Point, my soon-to-be home. I had to find a way to be gracious and cheerful for Frank. He'd worked so hard.

I went to the kitchen, where Mrs. Haywood was making cinnamon rolls, eggs, and bacon. And a pie. "The pie's for your dinner later," she told me, even though I was sure Frank had said he was going to do the cooking for us for the rest of the day.

She let me help set the table. And oh, what a pretty table it was, with a linen cloth and napkins and gorgeous yellow rose china. I wasn't sure I'd ever seen anyone put on a fancy breakfast before. She said she didn't usually, but this was an extremely special occasion.

"I'm looking forward to having you for a neighbor," she said with a smile. "I hope you're looking forward to it too. Though of course I know I'm not the first thing on your mind."

I wanted to answer sweetly and positively. I knew I should. I even tried, but I couldn't seem to make the words come out. Not anything but, "Yes, ma'am," which must have sounded ridiculous.

She looked over at me but went back to sprinkling cinnamon sugar over her rolled-out batter. "Don't worry about being nervous," she said softly. "It's the most normal thing in the world."

Somehow I found my tongue. "It doesn't make sense to be nervous. Not for me. Frank and I love each other. I know we'll be happy. And he's doing so well here—"

I stopped. I really shouldn't be talking about this. I barely knew this woman.

"But it's new," she said. "So of course you're nervous. Should have seen me when I first got married and moved from my father's farm to a little house on the other side of town. I cried for three days. It wasn't that I didn't love my husband. But I was only fifteen and I didn't know how to be married. I didn't know how to do anything, and I was scared as the dickens."

"But I'm a lot older than fifteen," I told her. "And I have no reason to be scared."

She glanced over at me and nodded. "Except that it's a normal reaction to change. Outside of birth and death, marriage is maybe the biggest change there is."

251

I could almost wonder if this woman had been hearing my prayers. Were my feelings really normal? But even if they were, that couldn't make them right. Faith wasn't supposed to be bound up by fear. "I promised to trust," I told her plain out. "But it isn't always easy."

She'd rolled her cinnamony dough into a big log and started cutting off generous slices. "Is it trust of the Lord or of Frank you're having difficulty with?"

I wasn't sure I liked her asking such a candid question. But it wouldn't be right not to answer. "Maybe both. But neither, really. I do trust them. I love Frank. And he's so sure he was led to live here. I can believe him. I can accept that."

"You're just not sure about rejoicing in it, yet, huh? That'll come. Once you're together. You'll see. Best thing you can do for a man is believe in him. And he's a fine man to believe in. He'll take care of you. I have no doubt."

"Has the business been good?"

She smiled and spread melted butter over the tops of her rolls. "He keeps busy. Good bit of it's to be a blessing to people without asking for pay, but you might be surprised to know how he's gained by that. People know he's a nice, honest young man. He's already gained respect, even among other businesses. Did you know he joined the business association?"

"No. I guess he hasn't gotten around to telling me that yet." I set out juice glasses, wishing Mom had come along. I liked working beside her and having her there to talk to any time I wished. Never in my life had we been so far apart.

It'll be like this every day, the fretful thought invaded my mind. *Only you won't have your father here, or a train ticket to go home. This'll be your life, up here alone.*

I won't either be alone, I argued inside my head. *I'll be with Frank.*

Mrs. Haywood put the cinnamon rolls in the oven, and not long afterward I heard Dad and Frank at the front door. She sent me to let them in so she could drain the bacon. I hugged them both as soon as I opened the door. I don't know why. I just couldn't hold myself back from it.

"Sleep well?" Dad asked me, probably wondering at me seeming to cling to them.

I nodded.

"Gettin' along all right with Mrs. Haywood?" Frank asked. Maybe he was wondering too.

"Yes. Fine. She's a wonderful lady."

I wasn't sure of anything else to say, but there was no need. Mrs. Haywood had us all sit down for coffee and juice and served plates full of eggs and bacon. She asked Frank to bless the food, and he did without showing a shred of discomfort. We were scarcely started eating when she brought out the cinnamon rolls, piping hot and fresh from the oven. They were so good I told her I'd like the recipe.

The pie was gooseberry-apple and I knew she'd been talking to Frank enough to get to know him pretty well. Not many people ever made that combination, but he loved it. She insisted that we should take it with us when we left, and enjoy it along with whatever else Frank had planned for our lunch. It was her welcome gift.

After breakfast we went across the street. Stepping inside the house for the first time was a strange experience. Of course the Bellors' belongings were still everywhere, much already in boxes. But I had no difficulty imagining what the house would be like empty, and then filled again with our things. A rocking chair made by Frank should sit by the fire, with my best woven rag-rug on the floor beside it. If these curtains moved with the Bellors, I would make new ones. Blue, to match the blue highlighted in that favorite rug. We would put Frank's mother's clock on the mantel with a candle on each side of it. We would have other chairs, or maybe a love seat, and a bookshelf, and a radio.

This house was a little like Mom and Dad's, with two bedrooms upstairs and one down. But the sitting room was practically big enough to divide into two rooms, and there was an extra room besides, off in one corner. The house already had indoor plumbing. And a telephone line reaching from a pole out by the street.

Dad noticed things like the sagging basement steps and sticking doors that we would be able to fix once we moved in. Frank told us about patching the roof already. More than one room had bits of peeling wallpaper, but that didn't bother me. We could make this a lovely home. Eventually, we would.

Frank showed me where he wanted to put in a garden. "It's not too late to get something planted this year," he said. "I thought I'd start on that next week."

It gave me a good feeling to think about having a garden already here ready to come home to after the wedding. That, at least, would make being here seem not quite so strange.

"You want me to plant flowers too?" he asked. "Somethin' that'll be bloomin' in June or July?"

"You might not have time. I hear you've been very busy."

He smiled. "I can get somethin' in. Just for you."

He wanted to go for a walk again when we were done looking at the house. Dad stayed at the store. Frank and I hadn't asked to be alone, but he was giving us the opportunity anyway. He picked up what looked like a scrap piece of pine and asked Frank if he could whittle on it while we were gone.

"Sure. Use anything you want."

We walked past the train depot and back to the railroad park. Sitting on the rail of the bandstand Frank told me again that he loved me and was proud that I'd be his wife.

"And I'm proud of you," I told him with a kiss. "All you've accomplished here. It's . . . it's . . ."

"Unlikely?"

"Oh, Frank."

But he was grinning at me, teasing, and not upset at all.

"Maybe amazing would be a better word."

"Blessed," he told me then. "I think that fits."

We walked down State Street past many of Camp Point's shops and businesses. A lot of people knew Frank already and offered friendly waves. He showed me where the People's Bank was and told me the library was upstairs above it, but he hadn't been in it yet. We turned on Ohio Street, which Frank said Sam had called "the Avenue."

"Used to be where the rich folks lived, I guess," Frank said. "I think people are pretty mixed together anymore, though."

We walked for several blocks, past some beautiful big homes. Frank pointed out which one the pastor lived in, where we'd be eating Sunday dinner.

"Do you really think he ought to cook for us tomorrow?" I questioned. "He's got the sermon to think about."

"I told him the same thing. But he said it'd be fun. He plans to leave something in the oven the whole time we're at church and pull it out when we get done. He says he's done it before for folks."

Hand in hand, we strode as far as that street would take us and then turned west and continued to the entrance of a large park on the edge of town. Frank wanted to go in. So we walked toward the shelter house, enjoying the spring breeze. And then Frank surprised me with a sudden pull on my hand.

"Look at that big rock."

It was big, all right. Massive.

"Wanna sit on a boulder?" He picked me up, quick as a wink.

"Frank!"

"I can set you right on top."

Laughing, I let him do it, and there I was, perched precariously on a boulder. Frank backed up and ran at the rock with his limpy gait, zipping right to the top and plopping down beside me with a grunt.

"Whew. That wasn't as easy as it looked when I seen a kid do it the other day."

"Are you all right?" He'd landed pretty hard, and I thought immediately about his weak leg.

"Sure. I didn't plan this, you know. Just bein' silly."

"I like it. Nice place to sit. And a new experience. I can go home and tell people you swept me off my feet and I didn't get back to earth for . . . I don't know how long yet."

With his fetching dark hair rustling in the breeze, he leaned close and kissed me, but then we heard children somewhere close and we quit, lest they come into view and see us at it. Frank's pretty silvery eyes were shining in the sunlight, and he looked dreamy handsome. I wished we could stay together like this for the rest of the day. I didn't even care if we stayed right where we were on that rock, but the children we'd heard were suddenly in front of us, running toward the swings in our direction.

"Wanna see the pond?" Frank asked. He slid down the face of the boulder like he'd done this before, landed on his feet, and turned around. "Your turn. Slide down. I'll catch you."

The front of the rock was sloped enough that sliding down did seem natural. I didn't think the rough stone could be very good for the backside of our clothes though, but I slid anyway, far more rapidly than I expected to, into Frank's arms.

"Oh!" I caught my breath and still held on to him, even when he set me on my feet again. "Did I hurt you?"

He shook his head with a little smile. "You're not very big, Sarah Jean."

"Big enough to bowl you over, I was afraid."

"Not near."

He took me to see the pond, telling me he'd come out here first when the snow was still on the ground, and he'd found it to be a quiet respite. A good place to walk and pray. It was a pretty place. I liked it too, but on such a beautiful Saturday we couldn't expect to have it to ourselves. There were three big boys fishing. Frank knew one of them and gave him a wave.

"His family's started coming to our church," he explained.

Our church. The words gave me a peculiar sort of feeling inside. Did Frank realize how completely he'd adopted this new town? How long would it take me?

When we got back to the shop, Frank made us what he called "one-pot stew" and served it for lunch along with biscuits from Lawless's Market.

"I call it 'one-pot' 'cause I can only cook one pot a' something at a time," Frank explained. "I been makin' it a lot 'cause it's easier'n figurin' how to make something else with only one burner and no skillet."

I suggested we walk to the dry goods store and buy a skillet this very day. He agreed if I wanted to, and then he told me I should pick my favorite of the stoves in the front of the store. If Mrs. Bellor took hers along to their new house, he'd have the new one installed before he came down for the wedding.

"Maybe you need it in the back room here," I suggested.

"Nah. I make it fine. And this is temporary. Less than two months to go."

He was delighted with the thought, I could tell. I sat

257

on a chair he'd made, with my dish on a table he wasn't finished with yet, and enjoyed that stew immensely. It was some of the best I'd ever had. Between the three of us, we almost cleaned the pot out.

Dad had carved a little pine canoe in the time that we were gone and had started on a tiny wooden man to go with it. I'd always thought my father was good at such things, but he was right that Frank had gotten even better. This store looked like the domain of an artist.

As soon as he finished eating, Frank rose to a work desk and pulled a ledger book from his drawer. "You both bein' family and so close connected to the business, maybe I should show you my records so far."

"You don't have to," Dad told him.

"At least I wanna show Sarah. An' I don't mind you seein'. I got nothing to hide. You know me. There ain't gonna be no surprises."

But there was one. He'd made a simple agreement with Mrs. Haywood to help him with the books, and I could see where she'd made a small start. I was used to Frank's system, and when I considered that he'd been working here alone since February, I expected his books would be badly in need of an organizing touch. But they were clear and current, at least to someone who understood Frank's homemade shorthand. I was pleased.

But Dad looked more at the content than the system. "Looks like with expenses, you're coming barely ahead of breaking even."

"'Bout what I expected startin' out," Frank assured us. "I've had to buy wood till I can find a place to cut some of my own, and with turning on the town utilities, fixing the roof, and otherwise gettin' the shop ready, it's been costing me more to get goin' than it will to keep on."

Dad nodded, and I fought away an uneasy feeling. *Don't worry*, I told myself. *This is just like any business starting out. Frank's right. It'll get better.*

I started to clean up the stew pot and our dishes, but Frank wouldn't let me, at least not alone. So we finished the cleanup together, using the lavatory sink because there wasn't any other one. Frank would surely be glad to get into our house. It'd be taxing on the patience to live this way very long, even though the shop had running water.

I'd brought the book I'd given Frank at Easter. Thoreau's *Walden*. When we were finished cleaning up, I read a chapter aloud, and then we went to buy a skillet. It was kind of nifty picking out something together that we'd probably use for years.

Frank took us uptown for supper. I wondered if he ought to spend the money, but he said it was Saturday night and a very special occasion, having us here. He wanted to take us to a restaurant, to celebrate. Camp Point had seemed so quiet earlier today. But come evening it filled up and got lively.

"Saturday night," Frank said by way of explanation. "Everybody comes to town."

There were so many vehicles there were scarcely any parking places left along the square. And not just cars and trucks. A few people had come in farm wagons. One with a tractor. And two horses stood side by side, tethered near the front of the opera house.

"Lot of farmers around here," Frank said. "Just like back home."

There was a lot of music too. And dancing going on in at least one place we walked past. Frank didn't suggest going in. Instead we had a nice dinner in a restaurant on the square and then started across the park on our way back to the shop. There were people on the sidewalks and people on the bandstand.

"I don't come up here most Saturday nights," Frank told me. "Got work to do."

Did he come sometimes? I wondered. *Did he take to*

the jumping Saturday-night crowds of his new town as well as he took to everything else?

Just then, a young woman with a striped dress came out of a store with two or three friends and gave Frank a gigantic wave and a smile. He appeared not to notice, but she came straight in our direction, followed by her friends, all of them pretty and dressed like they were on their way to a party.

"Frank Hammond," the girl called as soon as she knew she was close enough to be heard. "Is this the gal you were telling me about? Can we meet her? Peggy and Janet didn't believe I'd actually talked to you enough that you'd tell me anything so personal, but I told them you wouldn't deny it."

I didn't like that young lady. She was far too forward for no good reason. Frank was polite enough to comply with her intrusive request, but no more. "This is my fiancée, Sarah Wortham. Sarah Jean, this is Shirley . . . uh, I don't remember if I learned your last name."

"Bates," the girl said with a smile, sticking out her hand. "I'm Shirley Bates. Pleased to meet you."

"Pleased to meet you too," I said and immediately felt guilty. That had been a lie slipping out before I could think about it. But what else could I say?

"So you're getting married in June?" she went on glibly when she should've been introducing her friends. "Only two months away. Does it worry you to be so far apart?"

"No," I answered a little too bluntly. "Why should it?"

"No reason." She turned to one of her friends and actually giggled. They said their names far too quickly to expect me to remember them, and I noticed they were looking at Frank most of the time. They hurried off down the street, but the encounter left me with a lingering discomfort.

"How long have you known them?" I asked Frank.

"Don't think I ever seen but the one before," he said. "She come in the shop to look around."

"Not only at carvings, I'll bet."

Dad looked my way.

"They were acting like schoolgirls," I went on.

"Yeah," Frank said simply. "Can't argue with that."

His manner and his answer didn't give me the assurance I needed. So I decided to ask a very direct question. "How many times have you been up here on Saturday nights?"

He stopped walking and seemed to be studying me. "Just once besides this."

"What happened then?"

"Nothin' special. Mrs. Haywood had a root beer float."

Dad smiled. I didn't reply. But I knew exactly what I was feeling. Jealousy. Big and ugly, not just toward those foolish girls, but also toward Mr. Willings, Mrs. Haywood, the church, even this whole town because they had Frank's attention when I wasn't around to claim it. And it might not be any different even when I was here.

"You want an ice cream?" Frank suddenly asked.

"Okay."

We stopped at the drugstore for cones, and when we stepped back out to the sidewalk, I saw the same three girls watching us from across the street. Frank noticed them too. "Maybe they ain't never seen a woman lookin' so fine as you," he suggested.

"They're not looking at me," I countered. "They're noticing my handsome beau and probably wishing I'd disappear."

I was surprised that Dad didn't reply to that, but he didn't.

"They're likely just curious 'cause we're strangers in town," Frank suggested. "Hard for me to picture anybody thinkin' me handsome. Tell you the truth, I always figured you to be so pretty there'd be danger a' young fellas better lookin' than me tryin' to sway you away."

My stomach knotted, and I glanced at Dad. "There aren't any better-looking fellows. And even if there were, I care a lot more about what's on the inside than the outside, anyway."

Frank didn't answer right away. He held my hand and took a lick of his ice cream cone. My heart pounded. Did he know about Donald Mueller?

He cocked his head and glanced toward me. "You care more 'bout the inside, huh?"

"Yes, of course. But I still think you're handsome."

"Well, then . . ." He grinned and his eyes twinkled. "Maybe I don't need to shave tomorrow."

"Oh, Frank." Relief spilled over my insides. "You'd better shave. For church."

He'd been joking with me. He was in such a light-hearted mood. I tried to act as though I were the same way, but the guilt of my stupid secret was a heavy weight to carry. Dad was probably wondering why I hadn't mentioned Donald's foolishness, unless he already had. And then Frank might be pretending he didn't know and waiting for me to bring it up. I'd have to tell him. But how would he react? He had so much to think about, so much to do, I hated to trouble him with something so childish. Donald Mueller could be taken about as seriously as those three giddy girls. There was really no use.

Dad was admiring some of the buildings and gardens as we walked. Frank finished his cone and started talking about furniture stores in the town of Quincy. It'd be silly to trouble the conversation now. We walked back to the store as the evening light faded. Dad asked a question about the church, and my thoughts moved there quickly. Tomorrow we'd be meeting lots of people, and eyes would be on me, watching the girl who was engaged to marry their beloved Frank Hammond. Would they think me worthy of him? Surely not, if they had any inkling of the things that went on inside my head.

I stayed over with Mrs. Haywood again that night. The next morning we went together in Frank's truck to the church. They had no piano or organ. Just the voices of the congregation blending together in songs selected from the hymnbooks. I loved it and it made me nervous all at the same time. I was used to the piano at our church. And our small but voluminous choir. Here, I felt like I could be heard so easily. Everyone could. Most of them didn't care and sang out freely, even loudly. Including Frank. But I felt so self-conscious. It was easy to tell that I was one of only a very few sopranos here, and that made my voice stand out all the more.

Still, the effect of all those unhesitant voices lifted together was rather joyous. I also liked the way people greeted one another, and us, with hugs and hand-shakes.

It was a nice service, and Mr. Willings had plenty of good things to say about faithfulness in all things, inside of church and out.

I still didn't feel right about the pastor cooking for us. Should be the other way around as far as I was con-cerned, but maybe the day would come for that. We spent almost all of the afternoon at the pastor's home, just sitting and talking, but as evening drew close, Frank started acting restless. He asked me to read Psalm 103. But after that he was so tense and jittery that he finally just left us there and went off walking alone.

"Not to worry," Pastor Willings said. "He's working out his message, that's all."

I did worry, a little. I'd never seen Frank so nervous, driven, or whatever he was, not even the time he'd spo-ken at our church in Dearing. Maybe it was because Dad and I would be hearing him for the first time in this new place with these new responsibilities. I hoped that was what it was. I hoped he didn't get so uncomfortably restless every week.

He couldn't eat with us before church. None of us needed much, but the pastor brought out fixings for sandwiches and a bowl of potato salad. I told him that Frank had said he would feed us that night, and the pastor smiled. "He probably doesn't remember that right now. Don't remind him."

Before we were even finished eating, Pastor Willings offered to take Dad and me to the church in his car if Frank wished to go on ahead. To my surprise, Frank jumped at the opportunity immediately and left as soon as he could get out the door.

"I know he likes to spend time at the church alone before the service," Pastor Willings explained. "He's got quite an intercessor's heart."

Praying for others, I knew he meant. But if I'd been the one speaking, I could imagine that I might be praying desperately for myself—for strength, wisdom, and the right words to say. I wondered if being called by God could be painful, as wrenching as it looked sometimes. So many expectations to live up to. So many needs, so many obligations, and such an awful lot to be responsible for. Being a minister must be the hardest job in the world.

26

Frank

Speaking tonight was tougher than the very first time. I knew Sarah Jean and her father better than any of the people up here. But just knowin' they'd be listenin' gave me worse nerves than I remembered ever having before.

Calm me down, Lord. They love me, and that ain't gonna change. There ain't nothin' to be so nervous about.

I paced around the churchyard and then went and paced inside. I didn't know what I was gonna say. The gist of it maybe, but certainly not where to start.

The folks came filing in like usual, a little bit bigger group than some Sunday evenings, maybe because of our guests. When Sarah and Mr. Wortham got there, I had the pleasure of introducing them again for the benefit of whoever hadn't been at church that morning to meet them.

After the singing, I tripped on the way to the pulpit and felt like a fool even though I hadn't fallen. With all the faces looking at me, especially Sarah Jean's beautiful smiling one, my stomach felt extra tight, so much that it was a little hard to breathe.

Start with a quote. That you can do, I told myself. *Psalm 103, that's what's been on your heart all day.*

"Bless the Lord, O my soul, and all that is within me, bless his holy name . . ."

There. That's better. Easier to breathe, easing into the familiar.

"Bless the Lord, O my soul, and forget not all his benefits: who forgiveth all thine iniquities; who healeth all thy diseases; who redeemeth thy life from destruction; who crowneth thee with lovingkindness and tender mercies . . ."

I went on. I went through that whole psalm, outlining all the benefits God has supplied by his grace, the greatness of his character towards us, and what our joyous response should be. To bless and to serve. The Lord Almighty. And the people he has positioned us to share our lives with. Because each of us has a purpose, a calling to fulfill in the world around us. No matter what our station in life, our age, our aptitude, our education. Everybody has a way they can bless, like Mrs. Haywood and her pies. Or Mr. and Mrs. Wortham and their gracious acceptance of Hammond kids invading their home for so many years of their life.

When I finished, everyone was so quiet. Of course, I'd experienced that before, but I might never get used to it. That tiny lull right at the end, just before the service is dismissed and the conversations start. I always wonder at that moment if anything I said has sunk in and become useful, or if everybody is thinking about the ride home, the waiting bed, and what the workday tomorrow might bring.

Before we dismissed, Mr. Willings suggested that we sing one more hymn. Usually someone from the congregation would call out a number from the hymnbook and there'd be rustling of pages while everybody turned to the right song. And the singing would start with only

266

one voice, then two, slowly building in volume as everybody joined in. But this time there was no rustling of pages. Sarah's timid voice began so quietly. A few others joined almost immediately, and then more, without benefit of our hymnbooks. "Blessed Assurance." And I'd never heard it sound more beautiful. By the time we finished, Sarah had tears in her eyes and I felt so incredibly blessed I could have kissed her, but I didn't. Not in the church.

It wasn't easy, seeing them off on the train the next day. I really wanted to keep them, if I could've. But I knew June was just around the corner, and then Sarah'd be with me to stay. I looked forward to them days, because after they left I was lonely. But I swapped work for the use of a garden tractor to turn a patch of ground in the yard, and I planted corn and beans and a whole lot else. That plus my regular work kept me pretty occupied.

Mr. Willings called me the Friday after Sarah left. He was sick, too sick to get to work or call on a family that had asked him to visit. "Can you go for me?" he wanted to know. "Just listen, if they want to talk. Pray with them."

I went to see that family, but it wasn't easy. And the hardest part was thinking of Mr. Willings at home in bed. I asked him if he wanted me to fetch the doctor, but he said he'd already talked to him and just needed to rest. That bothered me, a lot, but if there was something specific wrong he didn't tell me what it was. He got feeling better in about a week, but I kept up visits with people whenever he wanted me to.

A few folks took to calling me "Preacher," even though they called Mr. Willings "Pastor." I wasn't sure how I felt about that. I didn't mind helping. I was sure I was supposed to do that, but it was a little overwhelming to realize that people were seeing me as an actual minister in my own right. Far as I was concerned, I was still just a woodcraftsman willing to serve.

27

Sarah

I thought I'd already seen the worst of Rorey in her letters. But toward the end of April she sent another one asking if she could wear my wedding dress. I couldn't believe it. Did she think I'd decided not to use it? Or did she just want to grab the dress we'd spent so many hours on and wear it three days before me so I'd be the one looking like I was using a hand-me-down? What a lot of audacious nerve! There was no possible way I was going to let it happen.

Mom was calmer than I was about it. "Don't answer her yet. Wait three days till you've cooled off a little."

But I might just get hotter. Maybe that was why Rorey'd chosen her date, so she could use my things and act as though they were hers. What else was she going to ask for? She could be such an awful headache. Almost every time we heard from her she had something to say that just made me cringe. She and her boyfriend had good jobs, so they'd told us. So why couldn't they afford a dress, or at least the material for one? Mom and Dad had even offered to help, since Eugene's parents didn't have much and Rorey's were deceased. And Mom and I could have been spending some time sewing for Rorey, if she had only let us know.

We still could, maybe, though I wouldn't be feeling near so good about it now. Maybe that's what I'd tell her. Pick the material and pattern, bring them here, and I'll help with the sewing. But only if you work at it too. And keep your hands off my dress.

I had a sudden thought that really, really bothered me. What if Rorey and Eugene had sent Frank a letter too, asking for the use of his suit or who knows what else? He had such a big heart, he might agree and not even think about it. He wouldn't care about us using the same things afterward. He might just think nobody would notice, like he wouldn't notice. But I cared. And it was probably selfish of me, but it was my wedding and I didn't want Rorey stepping in and using us.

I asked Dad to call Frank and tell him not to agree to anything if Rorey and Eugene contacted him. I stayed mad all day. That night I prayed for Rorey, and I couldn't really stay angry while doing that, but I was just as determined to tell her no.

I didn't wait three days to answer. I wrote a letter of my own the very next morning and showed it to Mom before sending it, just to make sure it wasn't too harsh.

I appreciate your confidence in my choice of style, but this dress has been fit carefully to my specific figure and I just don't believe it would be right for you. We might not even be finished with the trim before your wedding, but if we are, I can't risk damage to the dress because there might not be time to repair it. Too bad your ceremony isn't at least a week after ours, then I would happily let you try it on after my wedding and see if it would work for you.

Mom smiled.

I went on to offer our help if she wanted a hand-sewn dress, even though it would hurry us a great deal now. And Mom added a reminder of their offer to contribute to the price of a boughten one.

I mailed the letter. And I got no reply at all. We continued with the preparations for my wedding, wondering what Rorey would be doing for hers. She hadn't told us anything about what she wanted except the date and the place. Mom sent her a separate letter with questions.

April was gone and then May went rushing by us, and I got more and more anxious. Frank would be coming early in June to spend some time with his family and help us with things before the wedding. He would be closing his shop for much of the month in order to do that, but I was glad. He and I had decided we would wait awhile before a honeymoon. That way, I could get completely settled first and we'd have time to save back money and get the store running the way we wanted.

But when I told Dad that, he said not to be too solid in our decision. A trip right away would be a nice idea, and he'd talk to Frank more about it when he came down. The way he said it sounded a little mysterious to me, and I knew he was hiding something, but he wouldn't tell me any more.

I was hiding something too. At least from Frank. I did show Mom, but I could scarcely hide it from her since she'd been home when the package arrived. A wedding gift for Frank. Selections from the Book of Psalms. Printed for children, so the type would be larger with fewer words on the page. I was hoping he would love it and be able to read it for himself.

On the twenty-third of May I got a very long letter from Robert and Rachel. They were doing well. But despite their hopes, they would be unable to return to the

States in time for the wedding. I sat and cried, right at the kitchen table with the unfinished letter in my hand. I'd wanted them here so badly. We were supposed to have everybody home.

But my only brother couldn't come. It took me a minute before I could manage to finish reading his letter. He was so sorry about this. He let me know plainly how badly he felt about it, but there was no way they could get here. The ministry was going well and he was getting around with only a cane now instead of the crutches he'd still used sometimes when they left. They'd seen sixty-four islanders give their lives to God. And Rachel was expecting a baby.

"Mom! Oh, Mom!"

She came rushing in from the other room not even aware of the letter because I'd been the one to check the mailbox. She saw my tears and seemed to pale in front of me. Unable to speak, I just handed her the letter.

She cried too. I didn't know if it was about the baby or them not being able to come. Maybe both. And then we hugged each other.

"He said they might be here in September," I reminded her, hoping the thought would cheer her if she needed it. "Maybe to stay for a while. Till the baby is born and strong."

What a thought! I was going to be an aunt! And not just because of Frank's nieces and nephews. This was different. My mother was going to be a grandma. She sat down.

"Go to the field," she said. "Get your father."

I ran the whole way. And that created such a curious picture that not only Dad stopped what he was doing, but Kirk and Harry too. Dad climbed down from the tractor and I told him all the news in one big breath. He pulled me tight into a great big hug. And then he picked me up and twirled me around. When he set me down, I

271

didn't know what to think. He looked different than he ever had before.

"Go on," he told Kirk and Harry. "I'll be back. Gotta go find my wife."

Kirk climbed into the tractor seat. Harry gave me a nod of the head, and Dad and I hurried back to the house, where Mom gave him the letter. I left them alone awhile. I just felt like it was the right thing to do. And Dad was a long time getting back to the field.

Life kept changing. Katie's boyfriend Dave came clear from Wisconsin to visit. He stayed with Kirk, since they'd been friends in the service. But he came over nearly every evening to go for a walk with Katie or ask her out someplace. It didn't take him three days to find a job in Mcleansboro, and only three days after that to find his own place to live. But he kept up the visiting, real regular.

Frank came home June ninth. By then we still hadn't heard any details from Rorey about her wedding. But she came rolling in on June eleventh in a jalopy with doors of two different colors and a horn louder than a school bell. Eugene was at the wheel, and they had two friends with them that we'd never met before. A girl in a terribly ugly dress and a man with slicked-back hair who was hanging on to the girl pretty close.

Rorey wanted them all to stay at our house till the wedding. We did need the time to talk to her, but Mom told her the bride and groom shouldn't stay in the same house ahead of the wedding. Eugene was about to drive off to his folks' place and leave everybody else, but the other fellow had liquor with him, and Mom told him he couldn't bring it inside. Dad had made that rule years ago because of Rorey's father and our Uncle Edward, but it was still in force. So that young man took his bottle and left with Eugene, and the girl went with them.

Rorey stayed so we could talk about wedding plans

with her. She seemed to think it was odd of us to feel uncomfortable with her lack of communication. And she was pretty aggravated about Mom not wanting Eugene to stay.

"I bet Frank's around here somewhere right now," she said with a pout. "Prob'ly in the workshop. I bet you let him stay."

Better him than Eugene and his rowdy friends, I wanted to say. But Mom had a much more effective answer.

"Actually, he's over with Kirk. He's been back and forth some, and he'll continue to be. But we can't have him staying here. We've got things going on that we can't have the groom in the middle of."

"Ooooh." Rorey turned to me with her eyes shining. "Can I see the dress?"

"No," I said before I could stop myself. "Not yet," I quickly added. "We're not done with the pearly buttons."

"Did *you* get a dress?" Mom asked her. We'd assumed weeks ago that she must have decided to buy one.

"I brought a pattern," she calmly announced. And Mom and I both could have hit the floor. Or the ceiling.

"A pattern?" I was absolutely flabbergasted. "Rorey, haven't you even started sewing it? You only have one week."

She looked at me like I was the one not thinking straight. "You said you'd help."

"That was back in April!"

Mom touched Rorey's arm gently. "Show me your pattern."

When Rorey went to open her suitcase Mom gave me a look that said she understood as well as I did what an impossible task Rorey was bringing us when we had so many other things to do. "We can look," she said softly. "And do the best we can. We can make something work."

I could've just screamed. I'd bet Rorey'd even planned this. If we were too overwhelmed for last-minute sewing, it would be so much easier to share one dress. Mine. But there was no way I'd do that. She could just wear her Sunday clothes! She was not stealing all of my work and planning!

The pattern she'd picked was beautiful. But outrageously complicated. Far harder than mine, and she was looking at me very closely, hoping for a reaction. I wouldn't give her one.

"We'll have to make some modifications," Mom said, looking like she was thinking deeply. "Have you picked out the material?"

Rorey gave me a sideways glance. "Not yet."

Mom suddenly didn't look a bit perturbed. "Well, then. We'll have to go to town this very day. Does the young lady you brought along know how to sew?"

She didn't. She didn't seem to know how to do anything except come around with Eugene and his friend when we got back from town and try to get Rorey to go out drinking with them. And Rorey went too, expecting Mom and me and Mrs. Post and Katie to make progress on her dress while she was gone. Until Mom put her foot down. The second night when Rorey was fixing to leave again, Mom took hold of her and laid it out straight.

"You are getting married in six days. If you want us to work another minute on that dress of yours, then you need to show us you really want it. If you leave tonight, especially to visit a tavern, we won't touch it again. And you can find yourself something else to wear and another place to get married. If you want a nice wedding on this property, then you need to give it your full attention."

Rorey was stunned. "But you know what to do."

"That's not the point."

"Why can't I just wear Sarah's dress? I lost weight. It'll fit. I thought sure you'd talk her into it because we don't have time."

Now Mom was as angry as I'd been. "That's not Sarah's fault or her obligation. You can wear your church clothes if we run out of time. And there's more besides that to think about. You have a lot of work to do, and I should think your friends would want to help."

"But . . . I told them you'd take care of everything. You always have."

Mom shook her head. "We work together here. You've known that since you were a little girl. But now you're a grown woman. And you know how to act like one."

"You don't want me to go out at all?"

"Not till the dress is done and every other detail of your wedding is taken care of. I'm not doing another thing for you unless you're working just as hard for yourself."

Rorey was mad. But she didn't say so. She went to the car and talked to Eugene and his friends and they left without her. She walked back in looking pretty upset.

"They really wanted me to go with them tonight," she told me privately.

"Too bad," I answered her.

She stared at me in shock. "Don't you like me anymore, Sarah?"

I had to sigh. But I didn't feel like being anything but honest. "I'll always love you. But I haven't liked your ways in a long time. I know you've been through hard things, but you're not the only one. You didn't have to get so irresponsible."

"About what?"

"Your wedding plans, for one thing. And the drinking. Didn't you learn what a problem that was when your father was doing it? Why do you want to bring more trouble on yourself?"

"We're just havin' fun."

"Like rolling downhill into a mud puddle. Maybe it looks like fun on the way down, but eventually all you've got is a mess."

"I don't drink like Pa did. I've only been drunk once or twice, and I'm always with my friends so we get home just fine—"

"You know better. That's all I'm saying. You know it's trouble, and you know that when there's work to be done, that's where you need to be."

"Girls," Mom said sternly. "There's a dress to be sewn."

Rorey and I both joined her in the sitting room. Neither Katie nor Mrs. Post said a word though I'm sure they heard everything. Rorey pouted, but she dove right into the work with a will nonetheless. She really did want her wedding to be nice, even if she had been hoping we'd just take care of it all.

Mom had redesigned the store-bought pattern. She took out the ruffly back and the sleeves that were fitted below the elbow and ballooned above. "You'll be cooler without all that," she said. "Would you like a shorter sleeve, or even sleeveless? It's supposed to be plenty warm."

Sleeveless, Rorey decided upon, because Mom convinced her it would be elegant. I knew Mom wanted to simplify our task as much as possible, but she was right. Sleeveless would look wonderful on Rorey, and she'd look trimmer without the ruffly posterior.

Mrs. Post was working on the veil. Katie was almost finished with the underlining. Mom and Rorey went to work on the all-important bodice, and I measured and cut for the long, flowing skirt. This was going to look nice, and Rorey would be beautiful. At least I thought so. She didn't seem convinced and even told us that one of her friends had said she should be happy to know Eugene must really love her, because he couldn't possibly be marrying her for her looks.

"It's surely true that he loves you," Katie said in response. "But I'll bet he considers your looks to be a big extra bonus."

Rorey really appreciated that. And it was very gracious coming from Katie, whom Rorey had rudely ignored for most of our growing-up years.

"When do I get to meet your boyfriend?" Rorey questioned her.

"Maybe tonight. He's had supper with Kirk, and he'll probably come after a while for a little stroll."

"You two should go out with us," Rorey suggested and then made a quick glance at Mom. "I mean when the dress is done."

"I don't know," Katie hedged. "Dave's not much like Eugene. Very private."

"We could leave Carol and Max at a different club."

Katie kept her eyes on her sewing. "I'll mention it to Dave. But I doubt he'll be very interested."

Of course I knew why not. Katie had already told me that her boyfriend was very religious. He wouldn't want anything to do with taverns and the kinds of clubs Eugene and Rorey went to. But Katie was being quiet about all that, not wanting to draw herself into the middle of things any more than necessary.

"How about you, Sarah?" Rorey suddenly asked. "Would you and Franky like to go out with me and Eugene?"

I figured I was already in the middle of things. So I didn't mince words. "You know that wouldn't work. Frank wouldn't like your idea of fun, and you wouldn't like him there with you."

"Why don't you all just have a picnic together?" Mom suggested. "Here. Tomorrow."

I was very surprised. And Rorey wasn't thrilled because she knew Eugene wouldn't be. He seemed to be avoiding us now, even though Mom had tried to invite him to dinner. None of us felt like we knew him all that well, though he had gone to the same one-room schoolhouse. He'd always been pretty much to himself, except when he'd joined his brothers to pick on Frank or mustered his courage at parties trying to get me to dance with him. I was so glad I'd never consented.

Reluctantly, Rorey agreed to Mom's idea of a picnic because it would give everybody a chance to get to know everybody. The whole family, and Rorey's other friends, would be welcome. That might be quite a goings-on, especially with Eugene around Frank and me again. I wondered how he'd act.

Sam and his family wouldn't get here until the day before Rorey's wedding. And Willy would be coming on the train that very morning. But besides that, everybody else was close enough to come to our impromptu picnic if they wanted to. Except Robert. That would leave a piece of my life and heart missing, but there was nothing we could do about it. We'd get word to Lizbeth. Maybe it would be fun, if Rorey and her friends could behave.

We kept on sewing but talked about the picnic at the same time. There'd be so much food to prepare. Rorey promised she'd help. Deviled eggs. Potato salad. Fried chicken. But goodness, how much chicken would we need?

"Just make everybody a chicken salad sandwich," Mrs. Post suggested. "Don't overwork yourselves, girls. We have a lot of sewing to do."

Then she offered to bring us a giant bowl of chicken salad in the morning. And she wouldn't take no for an answer. We thanked her. Over and over. The Posts had always been good neighbors. They'd gotten up in years and they'd slowed down a lot, but they were just as generous as ever.

When Katie's boyfriend came to walk with her, Frank was with him. They'd been getting acquainted, and I was glad. I'd had a feeling they'd like each other, and I was right. But I wasn't sure why Dave and Kirk were such good friends. Kirk was so different, but maybe he hadn't been in wartime. Maybe he wasn't different around Dave.

The four of us went walking together. And it was odd how Dave admitted right in front of Katie that though he hadn't proposed yet, he was wanting to soon. Katie wasn't surprised. They'd talked about it. And agreed together that they shouldn't become engaged till after our wedding since it was so close.

"We don't want to take attention off of you," Katie said.

"And Rorey," I muttered. But nobody seemed to hear me.

Frank said he wouldn't care at all. He didn't need the attention anyway. And I wondered if there was something wrong with me to appreciate Katie's sentiment so much, and still be so aggravated at Rorey. Was I just selfish and proud? Probably. Didn't Frank see it? Why in the world did he think I was the right match for his selfless, ministering heart? I felt miserable about that, turning it around in my mind, until Katie noticed how quiet I was.

"Everything all right, Sarah?"

I wasn't sure how to answer. "Um. Yeah. It's just we have so much more to do."

Frank took my hand. "Are you sure that's all?"

This was the absolute worst time, but with his silvery eyes looking at me with such tenderness in them, I couldn't stop myself. I started to cry.

We were close to a pasture fence, and Frank leaned against it and took me into his arms. "What's wrong?"

"Should we go on alone for a while?" Katie asked.

I nodded, though I hated to send her away. I didn't really know Dave yet. And I was terribly embarrassed, though he wasn't looking at me.

They walked on down the fence row, and Frank just held me close. I leaned my head into his shoulder and tried to listen for his heartbeat. *Oh, God, why can't I be more like him?*

"Can I do anything, Sarah Jean?"

I shook my head. "Just keep holding me."

"Do you wanna talk about somethin'?"

He waited so quietly. And it took me a long time to coax the words out. "I feel like a spoiled child that doesn't want to share. I don't really even want Rorey here. She seems to be one problem after another, like she just wants to ruin everything. But she's your sister. And I love her too. Why can't I be more like you? You don't get upset when they want to take some of our attention. You welcome it, because you don't care about attention anyway. But me! I want it to be *my* day. Just like I've dreamed since I was a little girl. I want it to be my whole *week*. And all of my preparations and things to be only for us. Not her. Do you hear how selfish I sound? It's terrible. I'll bet you're glad they're here."

I could feel him drawing in a deep breath, the lift of his chest, and then the gentle fall. "I try to be."

The words were sad, and I looked up at him, too surprised to answer.

"It's not Rorey that bothers me so much as Eugene. Pray for me. I think tomorrow's picnic's a good idea, but it won't be easy. I hope I don't let him keep me on edge. It's bothered me a long time 'bout him takin' her off down a terrible path the way he's done. She never did no drinkin' before. And Harry told me he asked if she was expecting, and she answered that she didn't know."

Silence hung between us for a moment, and I knew there was anger beneath Frank's surface calm. It seemed so out of character that I didn't know what to tell him. But of course, it was natural. She was a younger sister, after all. Why wouldn't he feel protective, even fiery under the circumstances? I wondered about Kirk, who had far less self-control than Frank did. How was he reacting to this? Maybe he was the one we'd better watch tomorrow.

"I know they both were upset when Lester died," Frank said softly, bowing his head. "Shoot, we were all struggling. On top a' losin' Joe, and Pa. And Robert gettin' hurt. We were all upset. Lord, I thought for a while that maybe she'd gone crazy with it."

I drew close again and squeezed him tight. How well I remembered those difficult days. I, too, had thought Rorey simply couldn't handle losing a brother, and then her father and her fiancé too. But Lester had been Eugene's brother. For Rorey to run off with Eugene to St. Louis had been a dreadful shock. "She made her own choices as much as Eugene did," I reminded him.

"I know. But Eugene only lost Lester. Rorey lost Lester plus Pa and Joe. He shoulda known she was vulnerable. He shoulda helped her mourn around family for a while instead of whiskin' her off to the city and fillin' her emptiness with a bottle. I guess it's a wonder she hasn't had a child before this."

"Frank—"

"There wasn't none of us blind, Sarah Jean, not even back then."

I sighed. "Is Kirk this upset?"

"You remember the fight he got in over the barn fire?"

"Oh yes. But that was Willy's idea, not his."

Frank nodded. "But he's boilin' just the same. An' he already told me to look out when Willy gets here. Bert's told him about things in his letters, an' he wrote back that he'd like nothing better than to beat the tar out of Eugene when he gets the chance."

"He can't! It'll be their wedding day!"

"Willy does pretty much what he wants to do."

"Oh, Frank! Kirk wouldn't help him, would he? Or Harry, or Bert?"

"I don't suppose Bert would. It's not in him, I don't think. And you know I can't."

"Maybe you can talk to them. Maybe you can keep them calm."

"I'm not sure I can." He sighed. "You're wondering about yourself, Sarah. But look at me. Up in Camp Point I'm known as a minister of the gospel, but part of me don't even want to keep 'em calm. Let 'em do what they will and let Eugene take his licks. He's brought it on himself, drivin' in here with his drinking friends and acting like we all owe him somethin'."

He squeezed my hand, and the strength in his grasp surprised me. His next words were calm, but I knew the anger was still alive in him. "He told Harry that Rorey's family wasn't doin' enough. We oughta pay for the dinner with his folks the night before the wedding and a hotel for him and Rorey afterward. Plus the wedding reception. He thinks we oughta pay for pretty much everything except that dress you all are making. And your folks helped pay for that."

"Maybe he lost his job," I suggested. "We know his family is poor."

"That's not all there is to it. We don't mind paying some, 'cause she's our sister and she's got no folks. But what about his part? When's he take up *his* responsibility? He's not even buyin' her a house. They've got some dingy rented apartment above a meat market where the bedroom smells like liverwurst and the rats run up and down inside the walls at night."

He pulled away just a little and grabbed the fence with one hand. "She'd be better off without him. Back home with Emmie and her brothers."

"But she wants this."

He bowed his head. "She never did know what was good

for her, Sarah Jean. Don't be mad at her. She's like a foolish little kid runnin' after the first fella with a lollipop."

I hugged him. But there was nothing I could say to make this better. We couldn't stop Rorey if she wanted to marry Eugene Turrey. Even talking to her about it might only make things worse, because it might alienate her from her family more than she'd already been. I knew Frank worried for her. It was quite a burden. I felt ashamed that I'd so often let petty things bother me.

"I'm hopin' Lizbeth's got some wise thoughts on all this," Frank said. "An' I guess I'm hopin' too that she can rein in Willy. He never much listened to me."

If anyone could, it would be Lizbeth. She was the oldest, except for Sam, and she'd been like a mother to the younger ones since their mother's passing.

Frank told me that my feelings toward Rorey weren't strange at all and I shouldn't feel bad for them. I wished I could tell him that there was so much more going on inside my head, but he already looked so sad I didn't want to make things worse.

"All you want is for Rorey to let you have your special time," he said with a sigh. "That ain't half so bad as hoping my soon-to-be brother-in-law'll get run out of town. But I guess I'm tryin' not to hope that. I been prayin' for him. Lot better if he'd come to know Jesus. That'd be the beginnin' of better days for Rorey, no doubt about that."

"She needs the Lord too," I said softly, feeling miserable to let him think I was handling things better than he was.

"I know she does," he answered. "You work on that, if you can, Sarah Jean, tellin' her 'bout the Lord an' his love for her. And I'll try, okay? I'll work on my brothers and even Eugene if I get a chance. It can be our project. Like a gift we give God at our weddin' time, even if we feel like doin' something else."

"I like that." I could see the passion beneath the surface of Frank's stormy eyes, and I knew I wouldn't be able to withhold things from him any longer.

"I don't think God faults us for our feelings," he said quietly. "It's what we do about them that counts."

He looked down the lane toward Dave and Katie in the distance and then took my hand. "Maybe we should join them."

But I held back. "Frank . . . there's something else I should tell you."

Immediately I felt guilty. His eyes dramatically changed, and I realized that even with all his strength and accomplishments, Frank was painfully vulnerable. He looked afraid—that I could still doubt him, or maybe even reject him. I drew him close and held him tight. "I love you."

"I know. At least I always did believe it so."

"Don't ever question that, please?" I looked up into his eyes again. "You mean more to me than anyone but the Lord himself, and I want to make sure you know that."

He drew a deep breath. "I feel the same 'bout you. But . . . but what was you needin' to say?"

"I didn't want to upset you. I didn't want to be a bother and make you think you needed to come down here and see to something that was really nothing at all."

"What?"

I hesitated, scared of hurting his feelings or giving him another burden when it was already hard enough about Rorey. But I couldn't hold back now. "Did Dad say anything about Donald Mueller?"

I wasn't sure what I was seeing in him. Sadness, anger, or confusion. But not quite any of those. "No," he answered simply. His grip on my hand tightened.

"H-he was bothering me for a while with letters, trying to get me to go out with him or meet and talk."

"How many letters?" Frank's face looked set, hard to read.

"Five, I think. I only opened the first because he hadn't put his name on the outside. Mom read one of the others, but I threw the rest away still in the envelopes. I just thought you'd want me to tell you."

"How long ago was this?"

Again, I hesitated. "The first letter came about the time you left."

He looked past me to the sky. "So did you meet with him?"

My heart almost stopped. "I wouldn't do that. Not on purpose. He showed up twice when I went to town with Dad, but I didn't want to talk to him. I didn't want to see him."

"Then what was it?"

"What do you mean?"

"Your feelings 'bout it all. I see somethin' in you. I'm not sure what."

I could scarcely breathe. "Franky—"

"Was you considerin'?"

"No! Why would you think that?"

"You didn't wanna tell me. You don't wanna show your whole heart . . ."

How could I deny? Frank could read me like other people read an open book. What could I answer? He was hurt. Not by my words, but by what I didn't say. The hesitation. The turmoil he must be seeing in my eyes. "Frank, I was struggling with things in my head, about not wanting to leave here and go so far . . ."

I told him everything. About the temptation, my dreams, my doubts. I told him about Donald at the service station and in front of the café, and my promise to God to trust. I was crying before I got halfway through, and his eyes misted as he listened, still holding my hand.

"I never wanted anything to do with Donald. It isn't

that. I was just so afraid of facing a strange place. But now I've been scared for you to see how weak I am. You've been serving the Lord while I've been nothing but a big baby over the thought of moving. There's so much that's wrong with me, Frank. Sometimes I think you'd be better off with somebody else."

He held me, kissed the top of my head. "Everybody has misgivin's, Sarah. An' weak times. Most every day I wonder what you'd want with me."

I had to look up at him. "You've been faithful. But I—"

"You been tested. Remember what I said—that God don't fault us our feelings, just how we act on 'em. You didn't ask for Donald's nose in things. You didn't go out with him. You decided to stay with silly ol' me."

"I decided to stay with the blessing of God. And you're such a big part of that."

"You was brave. To let me buy that place despite how you was feeling. If you'd tol' me all this, I'd a' come home."

"I know."

He leaned and kissed me. "Then quit worryin'. Okay? You made your choice. 'Long as you're still happy with it, I guess we'll be okay."

"I am. Very happy."

A fox ran across the field in front of us, and I could hear a hoot owl somewhere nearby. "I wonder what come into Donald's head to try with you," Frank said softly.

"I don't know. I think I'm downright rude to him. I wasn't sure how else to be."

"I think you done fine."

I wondered if I should tell him about Rorey's letter. It was the only thing I hadn't said. I didn't want him angry with her on top of his concern, but I didn't want any more secrets either. "Frank, Rorey thought it'd be a good idea for me to see someone else."

"She said that? Recent?"

"Couple of months ago. In a letter."

He sighed. "Well. I guess I ain't worthy of you in her eyes."

"That's ridiculous."

He smiled. "I'm glad you think so."

I felt like a load had been lifted from my shoulders, and in the moonlight Frank was looking more at peace too. He took my hand, and we walked on in the direction Dave and Katie had gone. I thought they would surely be inside by now, but they were waiting on the porch when we got back to the house. To my surprise, Frank confessed our struggle about Rorey and asked them for prayer.

"I can talk to Kirk," Dave suggested. "I'll try to cool his head a little. Fighting anybody's not gonna help matters."

Mom and Rorey were still working on the dress when we went in, but Mrs. Post had gone home. Frank and Dave had a cup of tea and then walked back to the other farm. Katie and I got back to sewing for a little while. But first I went to Rorey and gave her a hug. Frank was right. Despite our own feelings, we could give the Lord a gift: to love her. To try to win her, and Eugene, to the light of God's love.

28

Frank

The next morning I had a feelin' a' dread I tried hard to shake. Mrs. Wortham's picnic idea was a fine one. None of us'd spent much time with Dave, or Eugene, and it'd been awhile since we'd had opportunity to be with Rorey. But I had a feelin' the day wasn't gonna go smooth as planned, so I prayed there wouldn't be no hard feelings, no drinking, and no trouble.

It was a beautiful Saturday, exactly a week from our wedding day. I was glad for Lizbeth to come out early and talk with Harry and Bert. She would a' talked to Kirk too, but he was off with Dave the whole morning.

Emmie'd been busy making cakes for the picnic. She loved to cook, and her food was some of the best around, but she must've been feeling some of the same concern I was. She told me an' Lizbeth that she wasn't lookin' forward to this picnic, not like she knew she should.

"It's good to have Rorey home," she said almost tearfully. "But I don't feel like I know her anymore. It's almost like she grew up someplace else."

"She's not done with the growin' up," Lizbeth observed. "We just need to love her all we can."

Emmie made a face. "I s'pose that means we have to love Eugene too?"

"That'll help." Lizbeth looked at me. "And I know we're up to the challenge."

I took a deep breath, trying to chase away the awkward feeling I had inside. She was right. We were s'posed to love Eugene, challenge or not. Despite the past, the present, or anything else. But it was hard, rememberin' him and his brothers throwing mud globs at me after school, and especially thinking about Rorey now. What would her future be like if they continued without the Lord?

We took the wagon out to the pond for the picnic so Lizbeth's little girl Mary Jane could ride and we could haul along everything we could think of that we might need. Emmie's cakes, blankets to spread on the ground, Lizbeth's coleslaw and sweet pickles, cooked eggs, extra bread, two buckets of fresh water, and plenty of dishes and such. When we got there, Eugene and his friends hadn't come yet, and Rorey, Sarah, and Mrs. Wortham were still back at the house waiting for them.

"Maybe they won't come," Harry suggested.

"If they do, I oughta have paper and pen along," Bert put in. "This picnic could get int'resting enough for mention in the *Times Leader*."

Despite his young years, Bert contributed regular to the local newspaper, but I figured he was kiddin' us about this. Lizbeth and Emmie spread out everything that was already brought. Katie and Dave headed back to the Worthams' just to see if they needed help carrying anything.

We didn't have to wait long. Rorey and Eugene came walkin' arm in arm, and their friends Max and Carol were the same way, only Carol didn't look too comfortable traipsin' through the timber in her fancy dress and high heels. I was glad Sarah was sensible enough to know that everyday clothes and flat shoes were better for a picnic.

We had enough food to feed an army. Eugene stared down at it all like he didn't know what to do.

"Come and sit," Lizbeth invited them. "I think we have blanket space for everybody."

Carol didn't look pleased, but she obliged without sayin' anything, slowly maneuvering herself onto the nearest blanket. Max sat behind her and she leaned back against him. Rorey and Eugene sat beside them, and when Rorey leaned into him, Eugene gave her a kiss on the cheek. That was awkward to see, 'cause he looked so much like Lester and I could remember Lester kissing Rorey. It didn't seem so awful long ago, and I wondered how much Rorey thought about that. Hopefully not a lot, 'cause it'd prob'ly make her sad. She'd been convinced she was in love with Lester. And now Eugene. I hoped she really understood what she was doing.

Everything went fine through eatin', and then some a' the group went swimmin' in the pond. It was all so peaceful that Mr. and Mrs. Wortham went back to the house with some of the dishes. Nobody got riled till Eugene brought his dripping wet self to the blanket where I was sitting with Sarah and asked how long I figured it'd be 'fore she had her fill a' me.

I could almost see the steam rising in Sarah's eyes, but I squeezed her hand and answered before she got the chance. "I 'spect the Lord'll take care of us an' we'll manage together fine. I hope the same for your marriage."

He smiled big. "Do you now?"

Kirk stepped up. My brother'd taunted me plenty over the years and let other boys do the same, but it was clear he wasn't fixin' to let Eugene by with it today. Harry and Bert got out of the water. Dave was watchin' close, and so was Lizbeth.

"I wish the best for my sister," I said. "I'll be prayin' for both of you."

Eugene tilted his head a little, way too cocky to stop and think about me having three brothers close by. His voice came out hard, just like I was used to.

"An' why do you think we're 'specially needin' your prayers, Mr. Retard-Holier-Than-Thou?"

That was enough for Kirk. He got hold on Eugene's wet clothes and threw him to the dirt path. "Get outta here! You don't walk on our farm and insult my family!"

"Kirk," Sarah suddenly spoke up. "He surely didn't mean it. Probably just an old habit."

Eugene stared at her.

"You know, like biting fingernails or twirling hair," she went on. "We all know how Eugene used to tease Frank, like so many other boys around here. Maybe he can't help it if he hasn't been able to outgrow it."

Kirk smiled. "Maybe you're right. Takes some people longer'n others t' grow up."

Eugene was frowning, and Rorey had turned red as a beet.

"Frank was just saying how he hopes the best for you both, Eugene," Sarah said sweetly. "We'll gladly continue praying for you always, and we'd be happy to receive your prayers as well."

"Him?" Max laughed. "Pray?"

"Shut up," Rorey told him.

"You never know who the Lord'll see fit to touch and use." Sarah smiled.

Eugene moved away from Kirk and went to shove Max back into the water.

"He oughta apologize," Harry said.

But Lizbeth shook her head. "Let it go."

Sarah had cooled the fires, even in herself. I was proud. And things got almost back to normal. But the picnic didn't last much longer, at least for Eugene and his friends. Minutes later, they decided to go get a change of clothes and go bowling. Eugene was disappointed when Rorey told him she needed to stay and work on her dress. To everybody's surprise, he asked Katie and Dave to join them, but Kate said she was going to be sewing with Rorey, and Dave declined so he could spend the rest of the afternoon haying with Kirk.

I joined them at the work, along with Harry and Bert. Seemed like old times, us brothers working side by side like that. Only instead of Dave with us, it oughta have been Sam. Or Joe.

"Good thing Willy wasn't here today," Bert observed. "He'd a' lit into Eugene quicker'n we could do anything about it."

"Are you kiddin'?" Harry said with a sideways glance at me. "Maybe he'd agree with him. He's said plenty a' things about Franky his own self."

"If *you* said it he might go along, yeah," Bert went on. "But not comin' from Eugene. You remember after the fire. That was some fight, and Willy's said more'n once he'd like another chance at the Turrey boys."

"That was years back," I told them. "A lot has happened. Willy's grown up in the service. He served with Lester for a while. His feelings is bound to have changed."

"About Lester, yeah. But not Eugene. He was mad about him runnin' off with Rorey. It wasn't honor to Lester's memory nor to our family, especially so soon."

Words slowed as we progressed with the work needin' done, but I took to praying in my head for Willy and the weddings next week. Too bad Robert wasn't here. He'd always had a good influence on Willy. Kirk had let Sarah's words stop him, but I wasn't sure Willy'd do the same.

29

Sarah

On Monday morning, Frank drove me to Dearing to pick up the shoes I'd ordered and choose a pair for himself. I'd only been in Hollstetter's new shoe store once before, with Mom, to pick out the style to go with my dress. Frank wasn't keen on new shoes. He was comfortable with his old boots, but I'd insisted he needed a nice new pair for the wedding. He went to the men's section to try some on while I talked to Mrs. Hollstetter.

"Oh yes, they've come in," she told me. "I left them in back so we wouldn't sell them by mistake. I need to be leaving for an appointment, but I'll have my sales assistant bring them right up."

She disappeared, and I occupied myself looking at a display of purses made to match shoe colors. The store was quiet, and I was just thinking of joining Frank by the men's shoes when I heard a sudden noise behind me. Before I could turn around, strong arms grabbed me. Donald Mueller. He gripped my arms and leaned his face at mine, trying to force a kiss. I struggled, but I couldn't pull myself out of his grasp.

And then I heard another noise—the clunk of something hitting the floor. Frank was around the corner of the display in a second, and he lit into Donald faster than I'd seen anybody move. I'd never seen Frank fight. He hadn't even been close to getting mad over Eugene's spiteful words at the picnic. But he hit Donald, and he hit him hard. Donald fell back against a rack of shoes, and Frank turned his attention to me.

That was the first I noticed that Donald was wearing a vest with the store name on it. He was the sales assistant Mrs. Hollstetter had sent me. I felt like fleeing, even without my wedding shoes.

"Are you all right?" Frank was asking.

I nodded, still too stunned to speak.

"I just wanted to talk to her," Donald stammered, holding his jaw.

"That was no talk," Frank said fiercely. "Do you want me to call the law, Sarah?"

I stared at him, unable to answer for a moment. I didn't think Frank had ever hit anyone. In all the years I'd known him. Not when he'd been so cruelly teased or even when Lester Turrey beat on him and blamed him for the barn fire. But he'd never had to defend *me* before.

Slowly, I shook my head. "W-we don't have to call the law if he promises never to touch me again."

Frank was doubtful. "You sure you're all right?"

"Yes. I just want my shoes."

Donald stared up at both of us, still holding his jaw. It looked like he had a bump over one eye too.

"You heard her," Frank demanded. "Where's the shoes we ordered?"

Donald pointed to the display across the aisle from the purses. He must have seen me and set them down there, maybe thinking there was no one else in the store.

Frank picked up the shoes and took my arm. Donald pulled himself to his feet, still staring at us.

"You won't be gettin' up so easy if you ever come near her again," Frank told him. "An' you'll have a jail cell waitin'. You owe her an apology. Right now."

"I'm sorry," Donald muttered, looking pale. He would never have imagined Frank rushing so strongly to my rescue. And I hated to think what might have happened if Frank hadn't been there.

I gave Frank a hug, my eyes filling with tears. It was a good thing Mom and I had prepaid the order, because he was ready to go without waiting another second.

Later in the week, we picked up a pair of shoes for Frank at O'Flannery's in Mcleansboro. And I didn't see Donald again after that. Not ever.

30

Frank

Sam and his family came on Tuesday's train, and the kids were full a' bounce and noise. Except Albert, who greeted me with the same simple hand signs he'd used last time I saw him. I signed him back the very same thing—"I love you"—and he smiled. Then he made some other signs, and I had to ask Thelma what he meant.

"Come home with us again. That's what he's asking you," she told me, and it was real plain that it made her happy how quick Albert had taken to the sign language. He could talk now for the first time, at least to her and his tutor. Thelma'd worked hard to learn the signs with him, and Rosemary and Georgie had learned a few too, but Sam hadn't. "Too busy," he said.

"Teach me more," I asked Thelma, and she promised she would when the time allowed.

Wednesday was Rorey's wedding day. Kirk and I went alone to the train to get Willy. It made me think of the day he come home after bein' injured in the war. He'd been traveling with Robert, who'd been hurt a lot worse. We were all tense and excited then, both worried and relieved that they were home. And Willy'd been home twice since. He'd been fine, glad to continue with the service, planning to keep on for another tour of duty. Kirk had been happy to get out of the military. But Willy was different. He'd become a Marine sergeant first class, and it seemed to suit him just fine.

He was lookin' broader of shoulder than I remembered. And he was the tallest of us, 'less Bert or Harry'd manage to keep growin' and pass him by. He was in his uniform, and he smiled big when he saw us. He gave me a hug, which I hadn't known to expect.

"Has anybody asked Sarah if she's sure 'bout this?" he joked at me. "There's prob'ly two or three other guys that'd have her."

I thought of Donald Mueller immediately and felt my dander rise. But my brothers kept right on with their talk.

"Frank's got her hoodwinked," Kirk was saying. "And she's even happy about it."

Willy gave me a little shove. "I knew it'd happen, son of a gun." But his face and whole mood changed pretty quick. "Rorey still got her fool notion?"

Kirk nodded. "Yup. Five o'clock this evening."

Willy shook his head and grimaced. "She's outta her senses. How can she think about him?"

"She's just bein' Rorey," Kirk said.

But I had a different answer. "I think it's the only thing she knows to do."

"That's stupid," Willy said right away. "She could tell him to get lost, and then move back home where she belongs."

"I think she took off with Eugene to run from the grievin'. And if she don't stay with him, she thinks she'll feel lost where all the hurt can get hold on her again."

He gave me a funny look. "Franky, you got the most convoluted way a' thinkin' things through I ever heard of. She's just bein' a idiot takin' up with idiots."

Despite his harsh words, Willy didn't seem to have planned anything to spark any trouble or disrupt the wedding that would take place that evening. "Let 'em have their foolishness if that's what they want."

He borrowed Kirk's car to pick up Lucinda Tower for the ceremony. And he sat clear in back, silent as a stone, in his uniform, with nothing resembling a smile.

Rorey's dress turned out nice despite the short amount of time they'd had. She wasn't completely satisfied, but that was Rorey. She had Carol, Lizbeth, and Emmie stand with her, but she hadn't picked out matching dresses, so Carol was dressed in some kind of spotted thing I'd never seen anything like before, and Lizbeth and Emmie were in their Sunday best.

Eugene had two of his brothers and Max beside him, and they had a Turrey niece and nephew to be flower girl and ring bearer. It was a beautiful evening to be outdoors, but it still seemed peculiar to have chairs and everything set up in the Worthams' yard like this. There was a bunch of Turreys, and it was awkward watchin' my brothers tolerate 'em being here. And tolerate this whole proceeding. Mrs. Turrey cried and cried about her little boy gettin' married, even though she had five already married and three more still at home.

Rorey had Sam give her away 'cause Pa was dead, but I thought if Pa'd been asked, he woulda said that Mr. Wortham had earned the right. Funny thing about Rorey; she didn't use no Worthams in any way in her ceremony, even though she'd wanted it in their yard. But the reception wasn't to be here. The Worthams made most of the food, but Eugene had wanted the doin's at the community hall in town, with his sister-in-law in charge of the punch bowl and other drinks. I knew what that meant, and so did Sarah.

"Do you think we should even go?" she asked me.

"Might insult Rorey if we don't show up for a little

while, but we can leave early if you want. Might get a little crazy in there late."

All of Sarah's family and most of mine felt the same way about that. But we shoulda known it would have been wiser for more of us to stay to the end. Willy seemed to be having a good time dancin' with Lucinda, and Harry was spending an awful lot of time with Eugene's sister Rose. But after Sarah and I left, along with her folks, Lizbeth, and Emmie, the ruckus started.

Katie told us later that Willy cornered Eugene and shoved him against the wall, making threats of what would happen if he wasn't good to our sister. Sam tried to break 'em up, but they'd both been drinking too much, Eugene's brothers tried gettin' involved, and then Harry and Kirk flew off the handle and got in the middle a' things too. Sam lost his cool, and poor Dave had an impossible job tryin' to calm everybody down.

The way it turned out, Eugene got a black eye, and everybody else was looking pretty banged up too.

Rorey threatened to never speak to her brothers again, including me, even though I hadn't been there. But I shoulda been. Maybe that was why she was mad. I mighta been able to do somethin' to stop it.

I felt miserable bad over the whole thing. So did Katie, who'd had the misfortune a' having to see it all. I wasn't quite sure why Dave had stayed so long, knowing he was just as uncomfortable with the drinkin' as I was, but he told me later that he owed Kirk a lot, and he'd learned to watch out for him in his moments of weakness.

"Your brothers need prayer," he told me. "Willy's already a drinker, and Kirk was an awful drunk when I met him overseas. He might still be if he didn't have younger brothers and a sister on the farm. And Harry's not far behind."

Pa's legacy. Lord help us. Hadn't they learned? The war'd been hard. I couldn't fault Kirk and Willy for strug-

gling then. But I prayed it wouldn't go on. And Harry.
He well oughta know. He'd seen Pa's last days and what
a wasted wretch he'd become. I felt awful bad about all
that and spent a lot of the next day praying for my family, including Rorey and Eugene.

They'd took a trip into Mt. Vernon and was supposed
to be back Saturday for our wedding, but now we didn't
know what to expect.

We'd decided months ago to have my three oldest
brothers plus Robert as groomsmen, and let Harry and
Bert usher. And all three of my sisters, plus Katie, were
supposed to be bridesmaids. Then we learned Robert
couldn't come, so we'd put Harry in his place and decided to let Sam's oldest son Georgie be another usher,
even though he was only ten. But what would we do if
Rorey didn't show up?

Harry and Willy were banged up from the fight. Only
two more days to our wedding, and things weren't lookin'
exactly pretty. Sarah was something of a nervous wreck.
It didn't help that the lady who was supposed to make
our cake had to leave suddenly for Marion because of a
family emergency. Thank the Lord for Bonnie Gray, my
old Sunday school teacher and Robert's mother-in-law,
who said she'd gladly do the cake for us.

The pastor came out to see us twice. He'd come to
talk to Rorey and Eugene before their wedding too,
but Eugene didn't make himself available for any more
conversation than necessary. Seemed like Pastor Jones
had more on his mind than me and Sarah now, though.
I think he talked to everybody, especially my hard-
headed brothers. Willy wasn't sorry for the trouble
he'd caused, refusing even to acknowledge that he'd
started anything. And Harry and Kirk weren't sorry
for their parts either. They were only standing up for
family, the way they saw it. Never mind that Eugene
was family now too. They didn't care if he ever came

300

around. And they didn't seem to realize what a spot that would put Rorey in.

The Turrey family had a awful reputation in our area, even though a former sheriff was related to them. There were a lot of Turreys, and most of the boys had caused their share of trouble. But I loved my sister, foolish as she could be at times, and we wanted her at our wedding. So I decided to go visiting, to Eugene's folks, because maybe they knew where he and Rorey had gone. Maybe they could get word to them to let them know how much we wanted them to be there on Saturday.

I was gonna go alone 'cause Sarah was so busy with things. And I knew if I took any of my brothers that two or more Hammond boys showing up on the Turrey doorstep might look like a threat and end up causin' more trouble. But when I was fixin' to leave, Lizbeth was wise enough to realize I had something in mind, and she made me tell her what I was up to.

"Don't be crazy," she said immediately. "You do *not* go alone, Frank Hammond. They'll cream you but good, just for the chance to pay us back for the ruckus at the reception. I wouldn't put it past them to try to do something to cause trouble for your wedding too. And the chance to bust up the groom might be too good to pass up."

I shook my head. "What do you suggest, then? I wanna get word to Rorey. I'm sorry even if Willy isn't."

"I'm sorry too." She was thoughtful for a moment. "Maybe I'd better come with you. They're not so likely to think of fighting with a woman along."

I wasn't sure I liked the idea, but she was insistent. And she wasn't the only one. When she asked Emmie to watch Mary Jane while we were gone, Emmie wanted to give Thelma or Katie that job and come with us. "Both of Rorey's sisters," she said. "That ought to tell them something."

I didn't know if they were right about this, but I let

them have their way. We drove to the Turreys' in my truck, and Lizbeth quickly took charge. "Don't you get out first," she told me. "Let me go to the door."

She did, with Emmie a little ways behind her. But I wasn't about to just sit in the truck, so I got out and followed them. Eugene's brother Clem was the one to open the door, and when I saw his eyes I knew Lizbeth'd been right about me not coming alone. He looked right past the girls and straight at me.

"What do you want?"

Lizbeth answered quick. "We'd like to get a message to Rorey and Eugene, if you know where they're staying in Mt. Vernon."

"Don't even be thinkin' you're gonna bust up a honeymoon! I ain't tellin' you nothin'!" Looking fiery, he was about to slam the door, but Lizbeth was bold enough to step up and get herself in the way of it.

"You don't have to. Just if you know how, send them word for us. Will you do that, please?"

"Why should I?" He was looking at her a little differently. His brother Edwin and sister Rose came up behind him. I was glad to see Rose. She was a quiet girl, a lot slower to get riled than her brothers. She always had a sad look in her eyes.

"We want them to know how sorry we are for the trouble," Lizbeth explained. "Willy got out of hand, and we should've known not to leave him in a drinking environment. He doesn't handle it well. Kirk and Harry thought he was in danger with all of you there, but they should've just pulled him out of the fight and apologized."

"They was doin' what they could to bust heads," Clem protested. "Oughta see Eugene. He's black and blue. And he ain't gonna want no message from Hammonds. Rorey neither. She's had all she wants a' you."

"We're real sorry," Emmie said with tears in her eyes. "We love our sister."

302

"Funny way a' showin' it."

"We'd like the chance to apologize in person," I said then. "Sarah and I really want them to be at our wedding."

"Why? So your sturdy brothers can light into Eugene again? Only reason you don't fight is you're lame and weak."

"No." I shook my head, almost wishin' word had got around what I'd done with Donald Mueller. "That's not the only reason. What happened at the reception wasn't right. Like Lizbeth said, we shoulda known not to leave 'em there. They don't handle things the best sometimes."

"Like your pa?" he asked with such venom in his voice that the words were like a blow. I felt them deep in my gut.

"In a small way, maybe. But I pray they learnt their lesson. Please let Rorey know how sorry the rest of us is and how bad we want them to be there Saturday."

"Do you really want Eugene to come? Or just Rorey?" It was Rose asking, and the sadness in her eyes seemed twice as sad as usual.

"Shut up," Edwin said behind her. "'Course they don't want him. It's just words to look good."

"No. I'm serious."

For some reason Rose's eyes filled with tears. I thought of everything I'd heard about the Turreys lately. Their father and an older brother were in jail. Another brother's wife had left him, taking their children far away. Two sisters were estranged from the family, and their mother was in poor health. I remembered Rose from our school days, painful shy, the brunt of her brothers' teasing every bit as much as I was.

"I want you all to be there," I told her suddenly. "I mean it. Your whole family, 'cause you're part a' ours now. Tell Rorey and Eugene we'd like them to be there, and the whole family's invited. Please come."

"Are you tryin' to show 'em up?" Edwin asked with a quizzical expression. "Is that what it is? Make 'em see that you got a fancier wedding?"

"No. I just wanna include everybody."

Emmie looked a little scared, and I wondered what Sarah Jean was going to think. The whole Turrey clan? Was I asking for trouble? Sittin' some of these characters next to my hothead brothers in the close quarters of the church? Lord, have mercy. I didn't pray this through before speaking, and I sure hoped I wasn't gonna be sorry.

Clem smiled. "You want us there?"

"If you can respect that it's all to be held in a church," Lizbeth added quickly, giving me a sideways glance. "Everybody's got to respect the house of God. And that includes Willy and the rest of my brothers."

"You think you can keep 'em in line?"

"I will or they'll know what for," Lizbeth said. "If I'd stayed late there never would've been trouble. You can blame it on me. I shouldn't have left."

Clem cocked his finger at me. "You can take the blame if you want," he told Lizbeth. "But it's this 'un's idea to get us to his wedding for some reason or 'nother. If we show and there's trouble, he'll be the one I come after."

That was too much for Emmie. She burst into tears. "We don't want trouble! We're trying to get rid of the trouble. We just want peace between everybody! We just want everybody to be a happy family."

Rose got teary too.

"We'll see," Clem said ominously, pushed Lizbeth back, and slammed the door.

We all stood quiet for a moment.

"Well," Lizbeth finally said. "I'm not sure if that went well or not."

"Nobody's hurt," I ventured.

"Let's pray it stays that way."

We were almost back to the truck when the door opened again. I turned around warily, not sure what to expect. But it was Rose and her mother coming toward us, both of them crying.

"I'm so sorry too," Mrs. Turrey said, reaching her large arms in Lizbeth's direction. "There's been bad blood between our families ever since that fire . . ."

I thought of Bert and Mr. Wortham both being injured, and all that the fire had cost. Lester'd snuck over in the middle of the night to see Rorey, and the fire was just a foolish accident. He'd been slow to own to it. And some of my brothers were even slower to forgive.

"It's gone on long enough," Lizbeth agreed, giving Mrs. Turrey a hug. Rose stood by awkwardly until Lizbeth hugged her too.

I saw Clem watching from a window with a frown on his face, and I prayed for all of them. I couldn't predict what would happen, but I felt sure I'd done the right thing by offering the invitation. The apostle Paul said that he became all things to all men in order that he might win some. I didn't know that I'd win anybody, or even succeed at my attempt at peace, but at least it was an effort. And at least Rose and her mother found some relief and peace in that.

31

Sarah

We'd waited and planned for this wedding. We'd worked so hard. I wanted everything to be just right. Now three of the groomsmen were bruised and one of the brides-maids might not even come. And if she did—oh, Lord, she might bring her in-laws with her! Eugene's brothers, some of the meanest people I knew.

Why did Frank have to invite them all? Why couldn't he have at least asked me first? The church would have little room to spare as it was.

But seating was not the real concern. I'd despised being around Turrey boys since my first meeting of them, because they never seemed to make it through a day without tormenting someone or causing trouble some-where. I didn't want them in my church on my wedding day. Despite all the pious words I might have told Frank if he had thought to ask me, I deeply, truly did not want them. And the more I tried to tell myself that Frank had been right in what he did, the more angry I was at him about it. This was my wedding too! How could he invite a bunch of hooligans who had little interest in us except for finding ways to get back at Hammonds?

They hated Frank. What was he thinking even to go over there? They'd tormented him at school, and kept on tormenting him even when he didn't go. They had no respect for his kindness. And no respect for his brothers. It seemed all the Turreys wanted was to settle some imaginary score.

Almost eight years had passed since the fire, but the trouble hadn't quit because they didn't want it to, plain and simple. And I didn't want people like that around. I wouldn't even want Willy around if he weren't Frank's brother. At least Kirk and Harry managed to be sensible most of the time. I'd thought Willy was too, but apparently not about this.

Rorey was at the center of this now as much as before. She'd chosen to be with Eugene, but her brothers thought he'd only taken advantage of her broken heart and led her into trouble. I knew their concerns were real. I shared them. Willy had handled things all wrong. But was Frank's answer the right one? To bring everyone together again? It seemed like the most insane thing we could do, like pinning up a mountain lion with a bull moose and expecting them to get along.

Why didn't Frank see what a disaster this could be? The most important day of our lives, and he'd gambled it on the behavior of Turreys!

I tried not to show how upset I was. I prayed they wouldn't come. But an opportunity like this—I knew it would be too much for some of them to pass up. What would they do? Would they have some scheme to disrupt things? Or just wait till the reception and then corner Willy or Frank the way Willy'd done to Eugene?

I had the flowers to work on, but I could scarcely concentrate. I was getting more and more edgy as the time drew closer. *Lord, I know you gave Frank good sense.*

Why didn't he use it? I know I'm supposed to trust him, but how can I, when he can make a decision like this?

Like the stab of a knife, fear cut to my insides, tearing my thinking and leaving me with renewed, gaping doubt. *It's not just this*, my rambling mind started telling me. *Frank didn't think this through. He just waltzed in without counting the cost, assuming everything would be all right. And it's the same in Camp Point. He's taking chances with my well-being as well as his, and not even considering the consequences.*

"Lord, help me," I whispered more than once. "Help all of us."

Mom knew I had more than just wedding jitters. She acknowledged my disappointment about Robert not being here, and the uncertainty about Rorey, but she never let on that she thought Frank had done anything amiss by his invitation. Maybe the opposite. She'd been praying to get Mrs. Turrey into church, and she said it'd be a blessing if the wedding managed to bring her there for the first time in years.

Mrs. Turrey, fine, I thought. *It would be all right if it was just her. But she hardly goes anywhere without a son. Or two. Or more.*

I tried to pray. I tried to tell myself that my discomfort was nonsense, that of course I could trust Frank to know what was best, even for a situation like this. I'd promised to trust him, I reminded myself, and I hadn't included any conditions with the promise. *Lord, that was hasty*, my fearful mind argued. *After all, he's just a man.*

I'd never been so on edge in my life. When Saturday dawned I was completely miserable on what was supposed to be the happiest day of my life. I was glad not to see Frank in the morning, and I felt even more miserable for feeling that way. He'd only been trying to be kind. But at what cost? As a minister's wife, as Frank's wife, how many times would I have to look forward to my husband putting some delinquent, or several of them, ahead of my wants and needs?

He might give away anything. Or invite absolutely anyone right into our home. Could I really live like that? I tried to picture what it would be like to have Rorey and Eugene staying with us, or Eugene's brother Clem. Or a drunk off the street, or somebody fresh out of jail. The home that'd seemed to have such cheerful potential didn't seem so cheerful considering that.

The hours rushed forward and there was no sign of Rorey. The decorations were in place at the church. Everybody's dresses were in order, and it was almost time to go. But I hadn't been able to eat anything, and it was a hot day. I felt so light-headed I was afraid I might faint. Was everybody's wedding day like this?

I was so nervous and uncertain that when it came time to leave I just sat in the car and cried.

"What in the world's wrong, pumpkin?" Daddy asked me. He really had no idea. "Just nervous, I guess?" he asked on. "I couldn't say what it's like to be the bride, but I was nervous on my wedding day too. Everyone is."

That didn't help me a bit. Surely not everyone has to think about the possibility of a brawl breaking out, or her new husband sacrificing her peace of mind to placate a bunch of ruffians. I was scared. I was still mad. I wasn't even sure I wanted to get married anymore. Not today, with everybody watching my tears. Maybe we could wait till October when Robert was here. I'd feel so much better about that.

Dad went right on and drove us to the church even though I was feeling far from ready. He actually seemed a little amused, which made me all the more upset. At least Mom was taking things more seriously. She was tearful too, though I soon found out that it was for an entirely different reason.

"Honey, you're all grown up."

"Mom, I've been grown quite awhile now."

"I know. It just sinks in today, I guess. Seems like just yesterday you were only six, out picking flowers in the field."

"Mom . . ." She didn't understand either. And Dad was all the more amused. I could not have been more exasperated with them, even though I didn't remember being exasperated at my parents before. Everything was haywire today. Frank's stupid invitation had turned my whole day topsy. Things weren't supposed to be like this. I was supposed to be sweetly touched by my parent's reminiscing and have no worries over anything other than getting down the aisle without tripping.

What would life be like with Frank? And without the stable buffer of my parent's common sense? Was I really ready to make a life so far away? I didn't want to. I'd never really wanted to.

Oh, I was a mess. Shaking, teary. Mom and Dad snuck me in the back of the church, and I was more worried that no one see my face than the dress before the time.

"Try not to get yourself too wet," Katie told me with a sweet smile.

She wasn't even taking me seriously. Everybody thought I was just nervous.

Oh, Lord, I am *nervous! What in the world is the matter with me?*

Just a few weeks ago, things had looked so right. Frank's store was going well. He was smart and kind and so talented. Generous, loving . . .

And incredibly impulsive. To change his mind about Camp Point and decide to stay after he'd already told me he was leaving there. To take on preaching at a church, just because of meeting an old man in his driveway. To invite the Turreys to our wedding just because . . . because he didn't think to ask me about it. How much

310

more of that would there be? What was I getting myself into?

I knew people were filling the church. I could hear the murmur of voices as Mom and Lizbeth fussed with my hair and Kate and Emmie adjusted the ribbons on each other's dresses. Rorey's dress hung on the door untouched. There'd been no sign of her and I tried hard to tell myself I didn't care. Whether she was here or not, whether her in-laws were here or not, I didn't know, and I didn't care.

Pastor's wife was playing the piano softly. Soon the tempo and the song would change. Mom leaned and kissed my cheek.

"You look absolutely beautiful."

Tears filled my eyes again, and I tried hard this time not to let them fall. I had to get through this somehow. Frank was surely already waiting.

It was almost time for Mom to go to the sanctuary, and I knew Dad was right outside the door. But a sudden commotion outside made me jump, and Rorey came busting through the doorway, her face all flushed.

"Oh, Sarah—" She came rushing at me, grabbing me in a hug. "I was so scared we were gonna be late."

I couldn't say anything. *It's okay*, I was thinking. *That she's here, it's okay. It's good. She's Frank's sister. It's what we wanted.*

I didn't ask about Eugene or his brothers or anybody else. I just hugged her in return and cried, hoping she'd think it was because I was glad to see her. Lizbeth took charge right away.

"Rorey, if you're gonna be a bridesmaid, you've got to get into that dress quick."

She stripped on the spot. There was nobody there but us girls, and Lizbeth and Emmie helped her get herself in order while Katie fixed a piece of lace on my dress to lay flat. But the room had suddenly taken on a dark cloudy look, and I was so hot I almost couldn't stand it. My stomach felt like lead and my heart felt like it could leap clear out of my dress. Everything I could see had taken on a coating of sickening grayish swirls. I grabbed Katie's arm, and Mom got me a chair.

"Honey, are you all right?"

"N-no. I-I feel faint."

Katie started fanning me right away with a paper fan in each hand. Emmie ran to get me some water, even though I didn't think I'd be able to hold it down.

"Mama Turrey says the best remedy for the nerves is to pinch yourself good an' hard and imagine how happy you'll be when the whole thing's done," Rorey volunteered.

Mama Turrey says? Oh, I should just go ahead and pass out! Let everybody wait. Maybe they'd give up and go home.

Mom hugged me. We heard three knocks on the door. Mom's signal that it was time to start. But she didn't move.

Help me, Lord! I wanted this day to come so badly, and now it's here and everybody's waiting and I don't even want to move from this spot. Help me.

I leaned my head onto Mom's shoulder.

"Are you going to be all right?" she asked me. "It's okay. I felt faint on my wedding day too."

"You did?"

"Oh yes. I almost collapsed right at the altar, but I guess I shouldn't tell you that."

It was very hard to picture my peaceful mother in any state close to the way I felt. "You were just nervous?"

"Scared stiff, more like. Even though I loved your father and he had a good job, I was so unsure what the future would bring. How was I to know what sort of path he might take us down? I was tying myself to another person for better or for worse, and that could mean almost anything."

I took a deep breath. I understood. Very well. "How did you get through it?"

To my surprise, she laughed a little. "I went ahead and married him, of course. Because love and trust are stronger than fear. And you know how it's come out. We've been happy."

Love. And trust.

I know. I know, Lord. I trust you!

Mom kissed me and stood up. "Are you going to be all right now? You look a little better."

I nodded, hoping I wasn't wrong. And she went on out to her place at the front as the mother of the bride. I squeezed Katie's hand when I heard the music change.

Oh Lord, can I really do this?

Emmie, Rorey, and Lizbeth each went out. I knew exactly where they were and how far they'd progressed by the music. Daddy came and took my arm, and then Katie gave me a huge hug and rose to take her place too. She was crying, without a sound. Her dark curls framed her pretty face and her eyes glistened.

"I love you, sis," she whispered. "And you can do this."

"All right?" Daddy asked, helping me to my feet.

"I-I'm trying to be."

"You're beautiful."

For some reason, that just got me teary again.

"I love you, pumpkin," Dad whispered. "I want you to know that you made the very best choice for a husband, and I am very, very proud."

There was no way I could have stopped the tears then, but it was the best thing he could have told me. It gave me strength to walk out of that side room and toward the sanctuary door.

"Maybe I *wasn't* already grown up," I whispered to Dad.

"You are today."

The music changed again, and we walked in together. I thought I'd be looking around to see who all was there. I thought I might still feel angry, frustrated, and scared. But when I saw Frank's face, when I saw his eyes, I didn't notice another thing. The sanctuary could have been empty, or filled to brimming with Turreys. I didn't know. I didn't care. All I could see were his beautiful smiling eyes, seeming brighter than the sun shining through the windows.

Love. Trust. *Oh, God, how could I doubt? He loves me. I see it shining from his very heart. He will never, ever do me wrong.*

I could feel a song welling inside me so strong I almost felt like singing it. *Perfect submission, all is at rest. I in my Savior am happy and blessed . . .*

Yes, Lord, I submit myself to you. I trust you, just like I promised. I trust you to hold Frank and me both, and all of our days, in the palm of your hand.

I didn't feel faint anymore. The ceremony flew by like a happy dream, and then we were kissing. I held him so tight and didn't want to let go. And he held me with his heart pounding and his hands shaking and a smile so big it could have lit the room. Man and wife. What beautiful words. I think I laughed, and we went down the altar steps together and out. We were finally one.

I didn't realize until the reception that the Turreys had indeed come to our wedding. Not all of them, but a sizable representation. With Mama Turrey in the middle of them. She came to hug me before we cut the cake and told me she'd warned her boys that if there was any trouble, she'd take their father's belt strap to their backsides even if they were bigger than she was. Lizbeth must have given her brothers a similar warning. Hammond and Turrey young men stayed far afield of each other in that fellowship hall.

314

But the same did not hold true of Hammond and Turrey couples. Rorey and Eugene danced every song. And to everybody's surprise, Harry and Rose were together at this reception even more than they had been at Rorey's. They scarcely took their eyes off each other. And somehow, seeing that put peace in the rest of the Turreys. If Frank could want them here, and Harry could fall for one of their own, then maybe the Hammond men weren't so bad after all.

When I saw Mom and the pastor's wife sitting and talking to Mrs. Turrey, I felt silly for doubting Frank. He'd been right that they should be here. Even Willy looked like he'd put everything behind him to give his attention to Lucinda Tower again. Even so, Eugene was careful to stay out of his way. Clem too. And the Turreys all left early. Their Mama made sure, herding them out before we were even close to finished, even though there'd be no drinking here to complicate the evening.

We were expecting to have Lizbeth's house to ourselves that night while her family stayed with my folks at the farm. Then we would join everybody for church in the morning, pack our gifts and belongings, and head up to our new house.

But we had a surprise waiting among the gifts. A big brown envelope from Central Bible Church in Camp Point. Train tickets, round trip. And some spending cash besides.

Frank was speechless, and I was almost as bad. "W-we're going to Chicago?" I looked at Dad.

"Mr. Willings thought you ought to have a honeymoon," he explained. "And Frank hadn't taken any money for preaching, so the church wanted to share a blessing. It wasn't hard to figure out where to send you when you told me Frank might like to go to Lake Michigan one of these days."

Frank and I hugged. We kissed again. We'd been thinking to wait till next spring and try to manage a trip then. But this would be grand!

So we changed our plans. We'd be leaving tomorrow on the train for Chicago with only the things we'd need for that trip. And then, after four days seeing the Great Lake and the city, we'd come back for the truck and our belongings, and then go home. The Bellors had been moving their things the day Frank left, he said. And I suddenly couldn't wait to get into our house.

I was so excited at the reception that I forgot to give Frank his gift, but I decided it was better to wait until we were alone anyway. Frank had never been on a train before so that was a grand experience in itself. And I'd never been in a hotel room. It was like being royalty, with people just waiting to make you comfortable. Frank asked who to call to get a boat ride, and the man at the desk said he would take care of getting us a reservation.

"I feel guilty usin' the church's money for this," Frank told me when we got to our room.

"It was their decision. And from what Dad said, they collected it just for this."

"I wonder how they managed without me noticing."

I smiled. "It isn't very hard to keep a surprise from you." I put in his hand the package I'd been holding almost the whole train trip.

"What's this?"

"Another surprise, silly."

He looked so puzzled, maybe realizing for the first time that I'd had more than just a purse in my hands. He looked it over, but there was no clue on the wrapping.

"Open it up."

He sat on the edge of the bed, and I sat beside him. "Another book?" He was still puzzled.

I didn't answer. This gift would be one to speak for itself. He tore the paper away with extra gentleness, slowly,

316

as if he already knew this would be something he would treasure. I watched his face, scarcely able to breathe.

"Oh, Sarah Jean." I saw the moment of recognition. His bright eyes lit with joy. "I love you."

He pulled me into his arms, cradling the *Selected Psalms for Children* at the same time. He didn't say anything more for a long time, just opened the book to the first page and started reading carefully while I watched. When he got to the end of the second line he looked up and smiled. "Sarah, I'm reading a psalm."

"I see that."

"This is great. Does the whole Bible come like this? Big print, not too much on the page?"

"I don't know. I can check."

He went back to reading the familiar words, and it was bliss just to watch him. He'd always loved the book of Psalms. I knew he'd longed to be able to read it. And now he was. I felt so happy.

"I've got a surprise for you too," he said finally. "You'll have to wait till we get to Camp Point to see it, but I wanted you to know I was thinkin' of you."

He set the book aside and I lay in his arms. The first night in the hotel was something grand. But the next day was even grander. We had a ride on a beautiful boat that took us way out on the lake, so far that there was no seeing the shore behind us. With the sun shining bright in the blue sky overhead and nothing but water on every side, Frank looked absolutely swept away.

Holding my hand, he spoke softly in a faraway voice. "Who hath measured the waters in the hollow of his hand?"

"Is that from Job?"

"Isaiah. Chapter forty." He was looking dreamy, staring out across the water and the bright, open sky. "Lift up your eyes on high, and behold who hath created these things, that bringeth out their host by number;

he calleth them all by names by the greatness of his might . . ."

Suddenly, he reached his hand down to the rolling waves and sent the biggest splash he could straight in my direction. "'Oh that men would praise the Lord for his goodness, and for his wonderful works to the children of men'—that's in Psalms. 'They that go down to the sea in ships, that do business in great waters; these see the works of the Lord, and his wonders in the deep.'"

"So what was the splash for?" I had to question.

He smiled. "I'm just so glad you're with me. And I want to experience all I can." He leaned over again and soundly splashed himself.

We splashed each other, and then we kissed, not paying a bit of attention to our guide. But that old gentleman was very mindful of us.

"Newlyweds, huh?" he asked with a smile.

"Yes, sir," Frank answered. "Just now beginning a life together in God's service."

He looked into my eyes, and the clear peace I saw sunk down inside me.

Perfect submission, perfect delight. Visions of rapture now burst on my sight . . .

The song was so strong in me that I didn't even try to hold it back. I leaned into Frank's arms and let the song float from me with all the joy I felt.

Our guide shrugged his shoulders. "Let me guess. You're ministers."

"Blessed to be his children," Frank replied, leaning to kiss the top of my head.

"Not as stuffy as some I've met," the guide observed. "You reckon the Lord really takes a hand for the people of this world?"

"I know he does," Frank said. "He's had his hand on me all my days. And right now I feel that he's here with us."

318

The old man looked around uncomfortably, though there was nothing to see but the abundance of waters. "I been thinking, you know. Does seem he's out here sometimes. Hard to feel him, though. Hard to know for sure. You think he really cares?"

"So completely he gave his Son for you," I answered. "He loves you so much that he wanted to make a way for you to be with him in heaven. All it takes is trust in him."

The old man looked out over the water, not answering another word. We let him have the silence to think over what was said, and relaxed in each other's arms as the waves gently rolled beneath us.

I can trust you because you are all good, I prayed in my mind. *And I can trust Frank too, because he's given himself into your hand. Thank you, Father, for the promises ahead. For the love and the life you've blessed us with.*

Our ride didn't last much longer, but in a way I knew it would stick with me forever. God of the waters, of the vastness of creation, filled our hearts and gave us each other. And all the days ahead, we would walk with him, side by side wherever the Lord chose to take us. That wasn't scary to me anymore. Instead, I could hardly wait to get home and get started. Our future together held nothing but promise because God would be in our midst, in every joy and every trial.

At the hotel that night, Frank carefully read aloud to me from a favorite psalm. And I drifted into peaceful dreams of our house in Camp Point, decked with flowers, freshly painted, filled with children, and brimming with love.

Thy will be done, Father God. I give you all my praise.

Leisha Kelly is the author of two inspirational fiction series. She and her husband have two children and live in a small Illinois town where Leisha serves on her local library board and is very active in the ministries of their church.

For more information on Leisha and her books, go to www.leishakelly.com.